PRAISE FOR
Shipyard Gals

"Set in the wake of the Port Chicago explosion of 1944, Valerie Stoller's *Shipyard Gals* follows the interconnected stories of three young women from very different backgrounds, all of whom are battling the prejudices of the times to find their purpose and voice. You will fall in love with these strong women, root for them, cry and laugh, and you will learn so much about a little-known, yet essential, piece of our complicated history. I couldn't put it down."

—Anne Raeff, author of *Only the River* and *Winter Kept Us Warm*

"In *Shipyard Gals*, Valerie Stoller brings to life a powerful and rarely told story of women on the home front. Set in a 1944 California shipyard, the novel follows three young women— Latina, Black, and Jewish—as they challenge racism, sexism, and societal expectations. With rich historical detail and emotional depth, Stoller honors the legacy of the real Rosie the Riveter workers who shaped American history with courage and skill. *Shipyard Gals* is both moving and vital. Valerie Stoller has given voice to the working women whose stories still echo today."

—Julia Park Tracey, author of *The Bereaved* and *Silence*

SHIPYARD GALS

A Novel

VALERIE STOLLER

Sibylline Press

Copyright © 2025 by Valerie Stoller
All Rights Reserved.

Published in the United States by Sibylline Press,
an imprint of All Things Book LLC, California.

Sibylline Press is dedicated to publishing the
brilliant work of women authors ages 50 and older.
www.sibyllinepress.com

Sibylline Digital First Edition
eBook ISBN: 9798897409792
Print ISBN: 9798897409808
Library of Congress Control Number: 2025938500

Cover Design: Alicia Feltman
Book Production: Aaron Laughlin

This is a work of historical fiction. Names, characters, places, brands, media, and incidents are either the product of the author's imagination or are used fictitiously with the exception of noted historical figures.

HUMAN AUTHORED: Any use of this publication to train artificial intelligence (AI) technologies to generate text is expressly prohibited.

Sibylline
Press

To Betty Reid Soskin, former Boilermakers' auxiliary union worker and retired National Park Service Ranger, who opened my eyes to the shipyard world with her wisdom and courage.

PART ONE

CHAPTER 1

May 30, 1944

LUISA/ ELENA

Kaiser Shipyard
Richmond, California

Luisa Gonzales worried she needed an alias.
Stepping off the bus in front of the shipyard hiring hall, she stared at the crowd waiting in line despite the rain. She was tempted to ask the bus driver to take her back to the Oakland YMCA, so she could pack her battered suitcase and get on the next train bound for home. But that was impossible. El Salvador had become the most dangerous place for her to live. Getting a job here would change everything.

Luisa got in line behind a young woman with blond wavy hair, so wispy compared to her own lush dark braids. The woman struggled to keep her umbrella from flipping inside out against the wind, clutching her purse as she shifted her weight from one foot to the other, her black patent leather heels spattered with rain. Luisa's own leather oxfords were so worn that rain seeped in along the seams, her socks wet, her toes raw.

"Excuse me," she said to the woman. "Is everyone here wanting a job? Or wanting a house?"

The woman peered at her for a moment, her eyes on Luisa's damp clothing. She lifted her head and laughed, her voice deep and throaty.

"Listen lady," she said, "if you're lucky, you might walk outta here with a job *and* a place to live. Or maybe you'll walk out with nothing. Hell if I know. Here, hold this, okay?" She handed Luisa her umbrella, pulled a pack of cigarettes out of her purse, and lit one with a silver lighter. "Want one? I'm Chrissy, by the way."

When Luisa shook her head, Chrissy frowned and took back the umbrella.

"All I know," Chrissy said, blowing smoke out the side of her mouth, "is that this job at the shipyard pays twice as much as I get taking dictation. I got a kid at home I need to feed. And Uncle Sam's got my guy busy fighting. So here I am." She took a long drag off her cigarette and exhaled.

The line inched forward. Luisa noticed another line had formed, but it looked like they both ended up at the same door. She couldn't risk losing her place. The newspaper she'd read on the train from Mexico City said the California shipyards were desperate for workers, ever since all the young men had left to fight. The ads offered jobs with good salaries for anyone willing to be trained and work hard—Negroes and women included. And anyone needing a fresh start.

"What's your story?" Chrissy said. When Luisa hesitated, she added, "I guess you ain't a talker. No problem." She held the cigarette in her lips as she folded her umbrella. The rain had stopped, leaving a sheen of droplets on Luisa's wool jacket.

"Oh," Luisa said, "I'm sorry, I do not understand. I am . . . Luisa Elena Gonzales Guzmán. I came here from El Salvador for a good job. I can make more money here and send to my family." She took a breath, concentrating. "I want to be . . . a welder? Back home I work in a factory, where we put fruit into cans. But I do good sewing, too, so welding is right for me, I think." She watched the woman's face, hoping her words made sense.

Chrissy raised her eyebrows. "How'd you learn all that English?"

Luisa smiled. "Mi papá," she said. "He does a small newspaper." Her stomach clenched. She was proud of him, but some things were better kept private. "He make me learn so I can read other papers. Citizen of the world, I think you say." She blinked away a tear. Papá had always made these solemn declarations with one hand grasping her shoulder, the other gesturing toward the maps he had tacked to the walls of his office.

"Your daddy sounds like a barrel of fun," Chrissy said, stubbing out her cigarette with the toe of her shoe. She checked her watch. "Well, I'm gonna have to come back tomorrow. I told my boss I had a doctor's appointment today. I need to get back before Mr. Grabby Hands fires me for being late."

Luisa nodded, but was confused by what she'd heard. Barrel of fun? Mr. Grabby Hands?

Chrissy ran a hand through her hair, tucking it behind her ear. "Good luck. I hope you get that job. You look like you could use it." She turned to leave. "Maybe I'll see you around this place one day. You never know."

Luisa watched Chrissy walk through the crowd, her shiny heels sinking into the wet dirt. Her thoughts drifted back to her father. Papá loved those maps. He had used black-headed pins to mark the movements of the Nazis. He'd add white pins to show the Allied troops' advance. The first time the policía paid him a visit, they had questioned him about the maps. That day, the worst they'd done to Papá was to empty the office trashcans onto the printing press, promising to return if he kept publishing articles critical of the government.

"You must understand," he'd told her that night, "the danger of powerful leaders spreading hate. And fear. It's not just our country,

Luisa, where this happens. It's our job, the newspapers and radio stations, to educate people. They must know the truth, even when that knowledge causes them to rise up and risk everything."

He sounded so angry when he'd said this, and the fierce look in his eyes gnawed at her. Papá had just published a story about the new government crackdown on workers who lived outside the city limits of San Salvador. People in the countryside had started to disappear, even women and children, with no warning. Gone. Bodies were left by the side of the road or found in the morning near a stream. Some were never found. Families slept with guns next to their beds.

One week after Papá published that story, the policía returned to arrest him. That was the day Luisa's world exploded. Why she was here, far away and alone.

Finally, Luisa reached the front of the line. She stepped inside the huge hall and saw that the two lines led to different areas, each with a few workers seated behind heavy wooden tables. People bumped up against her, so she pressed her hands against a table to keep her balance when she got to the front, glaring at the older man behind her who stood too close.

"What do you need, miss?" The woman seated before her wore a black wool suit, a pencil stuck behind her ear.

"Yes, I hope to find a job," Luisa said. "A welder's job." She pulled her shoulders back. "I'm a very good sewer."

The woman frowned. "You're in the wrong line. This is for housing."

Ay, the wrong line. Luisa's cheeks felt hot. Across the room, she noticed a group of people crowded around tables under a printed "Job Openings" banner.

The woman tapped her papers. "I can't do anything for you until you're hired. But I just gave an address to those two ladies over there." She pointed with her pencil. "You from Mexico, too?"

"No, I am from El Salvador."

"Well, why don't you talk to them? Maybe there's room for you, too." The woman looked over Luisa's shoulder at the next person waiting.

"Bueno, thank you," she said. "I am sorry to be in the wrong line." If Papá were here, he'd scold her for not paying attention. She had to be more careful.

As she walked over to the two women, she heard them speaking Spanish in quiet voices, their heads bent over a slip of paper with a map drawn in pencil. The shorter woman glanced up at Luisa and stopped talking. Her black hair was pulled back in a single braid. She narrowed her eyes, slipping the paper into her coat pocket.

"Yes?" Her voice was edged with caution.

"Hola," Luisa said, smiling to put the woman at ease. "Me llamo Luisa Elena. Busco un cuarto como ustedes." I'm looking for a room, too.

"Ay, perdon." The woman's shoulders relaxed. "Pensé que hubo un problema. Everything is okay, then? I am Ana, and this is Marisol. My cousin." She took the arm of her companion, who towered over both of them and whose wide eyes darted about the room. "We are a little nerviosas, sí, prima?"

Marisol, the tall skinny one, nodded. "Yes. We should go now, so no one takes the room before us." She said this in Spanish, then tilted her head and switched to a slow, hesitant English. "You come, too, yes? You have good English. I hear you talking. You help us talk to the lady in the house."

Luisa looked at the long line of people waiting at the jobs table. It was tempting to go with these two women. She'd been on her own for so many days, first buses, then trains, and speaking Spanish again felt like a taste of home. Having roommates might be nice. Besides, she'd read that now it was harder to find a place to live than get a job at the shipyard. Richmond hadn't prepared for so many workers needing housing.

"Okay," she said, "I come with you." She'd return tomorrow to apply for a job.

* * *

The map scrawled on the paper led Luisa and the other women to Nevin Avenue, a wide street lined with oak trees and two-story stucco homes set back from the road. An occasional car chugged past, but the block was surprisingly quiet. San Salvador didn't have neighborhoods like this; she'd lived in a tall apartment building surrounded by similar housing. A wooden planter box filled with yellow marigolds stood in the small front yard of a house painted tan with brown shuttered windows. A red-bordered flag with a single blue star hung inside the front window, a flag she'd seen in other houses as they walked.

Ana stopped and looked up at the house. "Número 43." Turning to Luisa, she stuffed the paper back in her pocket. "You should talk," she said in Spanish. "Her name is Mrs. Murphy. And you, Marisol, try to smile. You look like you're at a funeral." She poked her cousin's arm. "Don't scare her off."

"Ay, stop bossing me. I know how to act," Marisol said. "She always tries to push me around," she said to Luisa, "just because she's a year older. But I'm taller. And smarter, too." That made all three of them laugh, which was what they were doing when the door opened.

The woman in the doorway had the reddest hair Luisa had ever seen, fastened back with barrettes, her skin a field of freckles. A small gold cross hung around her neck on a thin chain. Bits of dough flecked the apron tied around her waist, and the scent of cinnamon floated in the air.

"Are you here about the room?" she said. When Luisa nodded, the woman added, "Come in, please. Sit down there in the living room. I have to get the cookies out before they burn. No wasting coupons."

The three of them stepped into the living room and found seats, Ana and Marisol on the brown plaid couch, Luisa in the matching easy chair in front of an oil painting of a brown-hilled countryside. Nothing colorful on the walls. The ivory lace tablecloth on the dining room table looked old.

Luisa had read about the ration coupons, limiting how much people could buy at the grocery store due to the war. Back home, the neighborhood market often ran out of meat and milk. People went hungry. When things got really bad, some stole food to feed their families, or found black-market sellers offering tainted meat or produce past its prime. Papá said the Salvadoran leaders controlled "la gente" by keeping them hungry and afraid. Here, it seemed the government actually wanted to feed the workers so they could do their jobs

The redheaded lady returned, carrying a plate with three cookies that she placed on the dark wood coffee table.

"I'm sorry, I forgot my manners," the woman said. "My name is Audrey Murphy. I teach at Richmond High. My husband, Robert, is working the day shift this week. He's a policeman here in Richmond."

Luisa froze. The house of a policía? "We do not want trouble, señora," she said, her voice shaky. "We need work, make money for our families. No problems with police." What if the policía back home sent a photo of her to these police?

Mrs. Murphy frowned, then relaxed her mouth and laughed. "Oh my dear, don't worry about him. He only goes after criminals. His job is to keep people safe." She pointed to the cookies. "They're best just out of the oven."

Ana and Marisol each took a warm cookie like they were receiving communion. Luisa hesitated, her stomach knotted, but when Mrs. Murphy thrust the plate at her, she picked up the cookie. It dissolved on Luisa's tongue, the flavor brightened by cinnamon and some other spice she didn't recognize. Mamá would love this recipe.

Her mind flashed to an image of her mother bent over the oven, the sewing machine awaiting her return. Their apartment was usually overrun with customers' clothing, pants needing hemming, torn shirts, a dress pattern pinned to folded cloth. The money her mother made from sewing helped feed the family, but she was happiest in the kitchen, baking or cooking up new recipes.

Ana finished her cookie and spoke up. "Thank you. I am Ana and she is Marisol. My cousin." She took Marisol's arm. "And this is Luisa Elena. She speak English very good."

What if she were just Elena? Elena Guzmán. Yes, that would be an easy change, her papers still in order if she needed to show them. And a name she'd still respond to when called.

"Please, call me Elena," she said to the redheaded lady. "And you are a very good baker." Couldn't hurt to compliment her.

"Well, let me show you the bedroom upstairs," Mrs. Murphy said, smiling. She walked down the hall toward the back of the house. "It's Tommy's, my son's room." Her fingers brushed the gold cross on her neck. "He's fighting overseas. We decided one way we could help Uncle Sam was to offer his room to workers at the shipyard. But it's still his room."

They climbed the stairs and reached the doorway to the bedroom. Luisa, now Elena, followed Mrs. Murphy inside, leaving Ana and Marisol looking in from the door. Twin beds, against walls papered with small planes flying through puffy clouds. She wanted to crawl under the quilt and sleep undisturbed on the soft mattress.

A nightstand stood between the beds, with a reading lamp and a copy of the Bible. In the opposite corner of the room, to Elena's delight, was a small wooden desk with its own lamp, perfect for letter writing. On the floor lay a colorful braided rug that would keep her feet warm when she got out of bed. Oh, this could be her home. But with a policía sleeping down the hall? She'd have to stay out of his way.

Marisol leaned in from the doorway. "¿Hay solamente dos camas, sí? No hay espacio para tres." She glanced at Elena, her message clear. After all, the cousins met with the housing lady ahead of her. It was only fair, but still. This room was perfect, minus that wallpaper.

"Only two beds, señora? Ana asked.

"Yes," Mrs. Murphy said. "Some people have made this kind of situation work by signing up for different shifts. That way, you can take turns sleeping here. One works days, another works swing shift 3:00 to 11:00. Maybe one works nights. They call it a 'hot bed' since the sheets may still be warm from the last person sleeping there. I'd charge the same price for all three of you, if you want to stay together."

"How much is rent?" Elena hadn't asked until now. Maybe she couldn't afford it. All she had left from her savings was less than the one hundred dollars she'd exchanged at the border.

"We charge forty-five dollars a month," Mrs. Murphy said. "That includes use of the kitchen and living room, plus the phone for local calls. You'd buy and cook your own food. Unless I end up with extras." She smiled at them. "I'll leave you here to talk about it. I've got to get the last batch of cookies baked before I leave for church. It's bingo night."

The three of them squeezed together in the middle of the bedroom. Elena took a deep breath.

"Fifteen dollars? I can do that," she said. "I really like this room, and you both seem like good people." She pointed to herself. "I can be the one to work night shift so we can make the beds work. And I promise to help you learn more English. What do you think?" She locked eyes with Ana and then Marisol, willing them to agree.

Ana put her hand on Marisol's shoulder. "I think this could work. We would save some money. What do you say?"

Marisol hesitated for a moment. "Okay, I guess we can try it. But if it doesn't work out, Ana and I get to stay. You would have to leave. Agreed?" Marisol was tougher than she'd appeared.

"Yes," Elena said.

They found Mrs. Murphy in the kitchen, busy washing mixing bowls and baking sheets. Cookies lined two cooling racks on the counter. Elena's stomach growled.

"We all stay, please," she said. "Thank you. We come mañana with everything?"

Mrs. Murphy nodded. "Hot beds it is."

CHAPTER 2

June 7, 1944

RUBY MAE

Ruby Mae huddled with her sister and a dozen other young women on a patch of dirt in the shipyard. The wind off the bay made her shiver under her thin sweater. When they'd been told to meet their boss, she hadn't known they'd be working outdoors. Peggy wore the wool jacket she'd bought at the thrift store last week. Although one of the other women was Negro, and the gal next to her looked Mexican, standing close to so many white folks felt strange.

"Hi," she said to the Mexican. "I'm Ruby Mae. This is my sister, Peggy." Peggy frowned, like talking wasn't allowed, and fiddled with a loose button on her jacket.

The woman smiled. "My name is Elena Luisa Gonzalez Guzmán." She looked young like Ruby Mae, with shoulder-length black hair tied under a blue bandana, and she wore a thick wool sweater and canvas pants.

"Well, that's a mouthful," Ruby Mae said. "How about I just call you Elena?"

Elena nodded. "Do you know how long is training? I am excited to work." Her English was good.

"Where you from?" Ruby Mae knew a family back in Baton Rouge who came from a town in Mexico called Chihuahua, like the dog. They had bought a boat and caught shrimp that they sold at the docks.

"I am from El Salvador," Elena said. She tilted her head. "Do you know where that is?"

"No, ma'am," Ruby Mae said, wishing she did. "Is it near Chihuahua? I know some folks from there." On the long train ride out west, she'd been amazed to see all the states and cities they'd passed through, some with familiar names, but mostly not. Before her family had left home, the furthest she'd traveled was to Beaumont, Texas once to visit her aunties.

"Ay, no," Elena said. "El Salvador is very south from Mexico. A different country. People here think we are all mexicanos."

"Oh," Ruby Mae said, "I guess it's like when someone hears me talk and they ask if I'm from Alabama. Or Mississippi. Last week I met some Indians signing up to work. They was from *New* Mexico. That's part of *this* country."

Elena smiled at her. "Yes. Mi papá made me learn all your states."

Ruby Mae stared at the pile of brown leather aprons that lay on the ground in front of them, next to a stack of worn leather gloves, all too big for these women. Black metal helmets with glass visors were lined up in neat rows. She turned to her sister.

"Do you think we'll have to wear all that?" she said.

Peggy shook her head. "I don't know, sis."

Her big sister hated not having the answer. Ever since they'd arrived at the hiring hall last week, Peggy seemed less sure of herself about everything, from where to get groceries to whether to apply for a riveting or a welding job. Ruby Mae had been the one to choose riveting for both of them. She'd convinced Momma to do the same. Momma had got trained last week and was already working nights. Daddy'd been hired to do more of the heavy lifting. Riveting sounded easier, and she knew how to handle a hammer and nail. A rivet gun couldn't be much harder.

She looked down towards the bay, where dozens of workers were already busy, many of them in hard hats high up on stacked scaffolding. Large mechanical cranes screeched as their operators hauled huge pieces of metal siding onto the skeleton of the ship, its hull curved like a giant's ribcage. Several women, outfitted in those black helmets and gloves, bent over their work, sparks flying from their hands over the rails of the scaffolding, like fireworks.

A stocky man dressed head to toe in protective gear approached the group. His face under the upturned visor of his helmet showed a few streaks of dirt smudging his pale skin. He studied the group and spat on the ground.

"Now, you all listen up," he said. "Too many folks signed up for the regular training class at the high school. So I told my boss I'd train you here instead. We need more workers *yesterday*." He sighed. "I'm Mr. Sullivan and I'm gonna teach you how to be damn good welders." He looked at their faces. "Jeez, you all look like you're ready to walk the plank. Go ahead and put your gear on and let's get started." He crossed his arms.

Welders? Oh no. Ruby Mae looked at Peggy and took a deep breath.

"Mister, excuse me," she said, avoiding his gaze, "but me and Peggy are signed up to learn riveting."

Mr. Sullivan stared at her. "Do I look like I'm gonna use a rivet gun? Why would I wear a welding helmet?" He shook his head. "I don't know how you ended up here. You should be over there." He pointed to a group of workers gathered around another older man. "That's Mr. Graham. He's your boss. Now git on over there 'fore you piss me off."

Ruby Mae scowled but Peggy grabbed her arm and pulled her away before Ruby Mae could open her mouth to scold him.

Elena turned to her as she and Peggy left. She said, frowning, "Sorry you don't stay here with me."

"Yeah," Ruby Mae replied. "Maybe I'll see you later." She leaned close to Elena and whispered. "Watch yourself with this guy. He's got a foul mouth. Gonna be trouble." She walked with Peggy to the other group, praying her new boss wouldn't be so rude.

Mr. Graham eyed them as they approached. He wore blue denim coveralls and held a gun-like metal tool in his bare hands. A heavy electrical cord, attached to the bottom, snaked over to an outlet at a nearby shed. The gun's thin barrel ended at a sturdy sharp nail, ready to shoot if he pressed the trigger. The gun looked deadly. Reminded her of the hunting rifle Daddy kept back home.

"Don't worry, ladies," he said, waving the gun in the air as he grinned. "I ain't gonna shoot you." The others hesitated, then laughed like they hoped he was right.

Three of these women were Negro, one looked as old as Momma. The youngest one looked the same age as Ruby Mae, and plump like her, too.

"What's your names, you two?" Mr. Graham asked. "And how'd you end up with them welders?"

Peggy stood up tall next to her. "I'm Peggy Taylor, and this is my sister, Ruby Mae," she said. "We got bad information, mister. Sorry to be late."

"Well, we need all the help we can get," Mr. Graham said. "You from down south by the sound of it." He looked at Ruby Mae, who dropped her gaze. She'd learned early on never to look a white person directly in the eye.

"Baton Rouge is home for us, sir. We here ready to work."

Mr. Graham nodded. "Okay. Everyone follow me." He turned and walked to a table that held three-foot squares of metal sheeting and six-inch steel bars. The plump woman next to Ruby Mae leaned in.

"I'm Marcy," she said. "Nice to have you here, too." She glanced at Ruby Mae's sweater. "Girl, no wonder you look so cold, dressed like that. Wanna wear my jacket? I bet it would fit. I got a sweater underneath. Back in Chicago, this cold wouldn't be nothin'."

"Well, thanks," Ruby Mae said, "but I'm okay for now. I guess I'll need some warmer clothes if we end up working there." She pointed toward the scaffolding against the hull. "I thought we'd be inside some big factory."

Mr. Graham called them over. When the group had gathered around him, he picked up two of the metal sheets.

"Okay, who wants to be my bucker? That's the one who helps fix the rivet in place on the other side. You gotta be strong." He looked at Ruby Mae. "You ready to try, missy?"

He handed her one of the metal bars. "This here's your tool. A bucker bar. All you gotta do is hold it tight against the rivet when I shoot it through. It'll give you a jolt from all that force but not too bad." He put on some safety goggles and handed her a pair. "Put these on. And when you're working, it'll help to wear some gloves. Cushions the vibration."

He thought she was strong enough to do this. She couldn't say no. She slipped the strap of the goggles over her head and adjusted them around her eyes. Her breath fogged the lenses. The gloves she picked up from the pile dwarfed her hands. The bucking bar weighed more than she'd expected. Her heart thudded.

Mr. Graham lined up two metal sheets so they overlapped, with small nail holes matched up along the edge. "Ready? What's your name again?" he said, picking up the rivet gun.

"Uh, I'm Ruby Mae, sir," she said, her voice faint. She coughed a little and took a deep breath. "Ruby Mae Taylor." By now, she expected her heart to pop out of her chest and fly off.

"Okay, Ruby Mae," he said. "Now hold that bar up just behind where I've got the rivet lined up." When she had, he put his finger on the trigger. "Ready? Push hard when I fire."

She tried to hold her hands steady around the bar, leaning her full weight against it. At the instant he fired the rivet, the bar jerked back, shoving her away, but she kept pushing forward. The force of the firing traveled straight up her arms. Her muscles quivered, even after she'd put the bar back.

Mr. Graham put the gun down and turned the two sheets around, inspecting the backside of the rivet. "Well done. Look," he pointed, "see how the rivet's sharp end here—we call it the buck's tail—is nice and flat, smoothed out? That's what you want."

He looked around the group. "When you do this work, it's gotta be in teams. One fires the rivet and the other one bucks it. Except for a few places where you have to work alone, 'cause it's too small or 'cause of what you're attaching. Any questions? Ready?"

She had a million questions, like how could she do something like this all day long? Likely her muscles would give out before lunch. And what if your partner had bad aim and shot the rivet straight at your heart? Those newspaper ads had made it look easy. Just like using a hammer and nail. But now that she'd tried it, this job was a whole different critter, as Daddy liked to say. She didn't feel ready at all.

CHAPTER 3

June 8, 1944

RACHEL

Rachel hurried into the shipyard's clinic. Her first week on the graveyard shift and she was already late. Workers filled every seat in the waiting room, and judging by the impatience etched on their faces, this was going to be a rough night. Before she could even catch her breath, a man with greasy blond hair spotted her nurse's cap and rushed over. The cap worked like a magnet; even on the bus, she'd be asked to check someone's medical concern—this rash, that sore finger.

"You gotta look at this, nurse." He thrust his arm in her face and lifted a blood-soaked bandana off a three-inch gouge in his forearm. His face appeared so pale, damp with sweat. Looked like a fainter. "It ain't that bad, right?" His breath reeked of garlic. "Just slap on some kind of bandage. Stupid saw slipped out of my hand."

The wound didn't appear deep, but she needed a closer look. Something about the guy made her skin crawl. She almost missed the boring routines of her last job on the med-surg ward at the private Merritt Hospital, taking care of well-off patients needing bedpans or back rubs. Even starting IVs for the stuck-up and clumsy interns seemed appealing now. But here, as a sheltered and white Jewish nurse, Rachel had a lot to learn.

"Come with me," she said. "Let's clean this up." She nodded at the clerk, Diana, who bit her lip.

"Sorry, Rachel. It's been one of those nights. We got four bad ones after a piece of scaffolding fell. Two needed to be taken to Merritt. Punctured lung and a broken pelvis."

Rachel shook her head. Everyone at the yard was always rushing. The war demanded more and more ships, right away, like a ravenous beast. Finish one ship, launch it, and hurry to build the next. Pressure like that led to sloppy mistakes and dangerous shortcuts.

"This guy's a little shaky," she said, pulling her unruly hair back into a quick ponytail. "I'm taking him back." She handed her coat to Diana. Her legs itched under the requisite white stockings of her uniform. A loose pair of dark slacks would be more comfortable and infinitely more practical than a starched white dress, on which to spill blood or foul wound drainage. Whose idea was it to stick nurses in white anyway? "Could you put my lunch box away, too? Thanks."

"Hey, nurse, how come he gets to go first?" Another worker stood up, holding gauze against his forehead and frowning. "I got here before him."

"Sorry," she said. "We'll get to you as soon as we can." The man was right, but triaging injuries wasn't easy, and she hadn't yet learned how to manage the chaos of the clinic or the pushy workers. She hated feeling so incompetent.

The treatment room was lit up like a stage against the blackout shades. Each of the exam chairs spread around the room held an injured worker. A nurse she recognized bent over a patient whose hand looked badly burned. The nurse had applied salve and was getting some gauze ready. Across the hall, another nurse hurried out of the eye room. One of the patients inside that room was yelling and moaning, his cries echoing within the clinic. She wondered if a piece of metal had punctured his eye. So many injuries affected workers' eyes when they forgot to use safety goggles.

The chair next to the wall held a large Negro man dressed in stained brown coveralls. His right ankle had swollen, plump as a melon, and his foot hung at an unnatural angle. Tears rolled down the man's cheeks. Dr. Jacobson, an older physician whose skills Rachel respected, held the man's X-ray up to the viewing lamp.

Rachel grabbed a vacant chair, and had her pale patient sit down.

"I'm Rachel," she said to him. "What's your name?"

"Jack," he said. "Hurry up, will ya?" Another rude one.

"I'll be right with you, Jack," she said. "Keep pressure on your arm. And don't get up. I don't want you fainting."

Jack grunted and sat down. "I'm not gonna faint, lady."

He better not. Rachel took a breath and walked over to the cupboards that held the bandage supplies and cleaning solutions. As she passed Dr. Jacobson, she couldn't resist peeking at the X-ray. The large man's shin and anklebones were clearly broken, the small bones in his foot shattered. No wonder he was in tears.

"That looks bad," she said. "I'm sure he'd appreciate some morphine. Can I get that ready?" This patient needed relief *now*, but she couldn't give pain meds without a doctor's order.

The doctor nodded. "They gave him some when they picked him up. But he's a big man, and he's been here a while. Dr. Bishop should be here soon to take over."

Dr. Bishop? Oh, no. Arrogant, short-tempered and condescending. Working with him for eight hours meant extra stress for the nurses, who would need to defuse the tension he stirred up with patients. He'd obviously missed the med school lectures on bedside manner.

Okay, first things first. She grabbed an ampule of liquid morphine out of the medicine cabinet, and drew a full dose into the syringe. Returning to the Negro patient, she noticed Jack scowling.

"Hello, sir," she said, putting her hand on the large man's shoulder. He opened his eyes. "Your leg must be very painful. I have some medication. May I?" He nodded.

She helped him take off one sleeve of his coveralls. After she wiped off his upper arm with alcohol, she injected the morphine into his thick deltoid muscle. "That should help." She washed her hands, and headed back to Jack. He narrowed his eyes.

"What kind of place you running here?" He spoke loud enough for the whole room to hear. "I'm your patient, but instead you're over there tending that . . . that . . ." He sputtered, and then spat out a word Rachel had never heard uttered in polite company. Except once when she was eleven, at the park with her brother, when Charlie Brill had yelled it at a Negro boy on the seesaw. Charlie's mother had grabbed him by the ear and marched him home.

Rachel froze, her fingers clutched around the gauze roll. "Pardon me?" The room went quiet, workers squirming in their chairs. She fought the urge to run away.

"You heard me," Jack said. "It's bad enough I gotta work next to them. Now I have to wait while you fuss over one of 'em. Probably done it to himself to get off work." He sat up straight. "It ain't right."

She made herself take a deep breath. "Sir," she said, her left eye twitching, "what's not right is using that kind of language."

Jack rolled his eyes but said nothing.

Dr. Jacobson appeared at her side. "Nurse Stern, I need your help when you're done." He leaned in close to Jack. "As for you, consider yourself lucky I don't toss you out with the trash."

Jack glared at the doctor but kept his mouth shut. Rachel yanked off the bloody bandana and cleaned his wound with a little too much force. She wanted him gone. The cut wasn't very deep, and she roughly wrapped enough gauze around his arm so he'd be able to finish his shift. Good riddance, she thought, as she watched him leave. It'd serve him right if he did faint and hit his head. She washed her hands and headed to Dr. Jacobson, who had pulled a leg splint out of the cupboard.

"Your patient will need a good surgeon," she said.

The doctor nodded. "These crush injuries are the worst. Merritt might take him. I don't trust the ortho man at Kaiser. I'll call ahead."

She was tempted to phone home and wake her father. He'd know who'd be best. After all, he was one of the general surgeons at Merritt. But Papa wouldn't appreciate being awakened by a late-night call. Especially with her brother Jesse stationed overseas. Midnight calls always meant bad news for families with men in combat.

"Do you know how he got hurt?" She grabbed large gauze rolls to wrap the splint. "I hope his boss got a full report."

They walked back to the patient who appeared to be asleep. The morphine had done its job. Together they carefully lifted the man's mangled leg and applied the splint, listening to his moans and muttering of "Oh, sweet Jesus," as they stabilized him for the ride. The clinic's sole ambulance hadn't returned from the last run, so she asked Diana to call the shipyard's field hospital to transport the worker. Everything took so long.

"Sir?" She perched on the stool next to the patient and touched his shoulder as he opened his eyes. "I need to fill out the transfer form. Can I get some information? I'm Rachel, by the way."

"Yes, ma'am," he said. "Thank you. Ain't you an angel sent to help me. Praise God." Definitely a Southern drawl.

"What's your name, sir? Sounds like you're a long way from home." She knew he'd be dopey by now from the morphine, and hoped he had family close by.

"Yes, ma'am," he said. "My name is Earl. Earl Samuel Taylor. We from outside Baton Rouge. We all got us jobs at the yard. 'Cept the twins. They too young. They going to school now." He tilted his head back. "Praise God, my family gonna help me get through this." He surprised her with his alertness despite the shot. At least he'd stopped crying.

"How'd you get hurt, Earl?" She checked his pulse while glancing around the treatment room. The two other night shift nurses were tending patients. Dr. Bishop stepped out of the eye room. He'd slipped in while she was busy, but thankfully no one was howling anymore.

"Well, ma'am. They called me in early," Earl said. "You know, overtime pay. I was working with a crew of guys I don't know. Maybe that's why it happened. We were hauling a big ol' engine section onto the hull. Somehow the rope got loose outta their hands." He grimaced. "The thing fell and heaved up on my leg so bad I just about passed out. It was a accident, I guess, ma'am." He looked at her, frowning. "Like I said, I don't know those men."

Not the first time an accident sounded like something else. Stories like this happened at night, when hundreds of workers were spread outdoors in the huge shipyard, unsupervised. And the injured worker was usually a Negro or an immigrant, sometimes a new woman just hired.

"Earl, who can I call to let them know you're headed to surgery?" This was the least she could do for him.

"We ain't got a phone back in the trailer," he said, shaking his head. "Still waiting for a real home like they promised. But you can let my girls know. They gonna be working day shift, getting trained as riveters. Peggy and Ruby Mae. I'd be much obliged if you can get word to them. Tell them not to tell their momma yet, not 'til the operation is done. She gonna be real mad 'bout this."

Rachel wrote down their names: *Peggy and Ruby Mae Taylor.* She tucked the paper with his daughters' names into the pocket of her uniform. She'd make sure to leave word before she left in the morning. Their father would face a tough recovery, even with the best surgeon. His leg might never heal properly, and the risk of infection was high. He'd be off work for a long time.

CHAPTER 4

ELENA

June 21, 1944

"Ay, Díos mío, it's so loud." Elena turned to Ana and Marisol, who stood close together in the cold morning air, each carrying a welder's helmet and leather gloves. They'd finished their initial two weeks of training and now waited next to the ship construction site for their first assignments.

The noise down at the docks was unbelievable, between the hammering, rivet guns and welding hisses, the workers shouted to be heard. Large sheets of the hull groaned when moved into position. Trucks rumbled between the pathways, tires humming, next to large "whirley" cranes that lifted pieces into place with a thunderous crash. Most of the workers she saw wore earplugs under their hard hats. No wonder. Her welder's hood might muffle the noise, but she'd ask about earplugs. Eight hours of this would leave her deaf.

"Y mira a los gigantes." Ana leaned in and pointed up to the wooden scaffolding that towered over the dock. Seven stories high, with large wooden planks extended over the arched halves of the hull. Elena stared at a group of workers below that, who labored on what looked like the metal bottom of the ship. Mr. Sullivan had called it the keel, which to her ears had sounded like "kill." Such a funny language. She had been reading the Richmond newspaper every day to improve her English, dictionary in hand. By now, she understood most of what she heard.

"Elena." Marisol nudged her. "What is that word he keeps saying? Dain-jer-is. Very dain-jer-is."

Mr. Sullivan, their leader man—just another name for boss—had grabbed onto a rope ladder that climbed up a section of the hull. Two workers perched on the upper rungs of the ladder, dragging the electrical cord of their arc welding tools behind them like hungry eels.

"Muy peligroso. It's very dangerous," Elena said. "If they fall, they would be badly hurt." Just the thought of climbing that ladder made her queasy. If he asked her to work up there, she'd have to confess she was afraid of heights. She looked down at her feet, her work boots firmly planted on the ground, and waited for her heart to stop pounding.

Once, her family had travelled to the countryside with her cousins for a picnic, near a deep river canyon. She must have been six or seven, and had followed her older cousins along a path that ended at a rocky overlook, the river racing far below. When she'd refused to climb down the rocks to the water, terrified, they'd told her to wait for them, don't move. So she'd sat up top for a long time, trembling, and when she'd needed desperately to pee, she still wouldn't move. She'd soaked right through her panties and blue corduroy pants. Her cousins had teased her on the walk back. Ever since then, that fear of heights had haunted her. She slowed her breathing and focused on her boss.

"Listen up, ladies," Mr. Sullivan said. "You've learned the basics of what you need for this job. I'm gonna pair you with someone who can keep an eye on you." He looked around. "If you can't handle the work, maybe you're in the wrong place." Elena knew enough to keep quiet. "Maybe you should go home, put on a dress, and bake some cookies. Any takers?" No one spoke. "Well, let's get to work."

He assigned her to work with an older white woman whose welding helmet had "Maisie" painted in white across the top. She was at least a head taller than Elena, with fat-knuckled fingers showing several healed scars. Her leather gloves were tucked into the hip pocket of her coveralls, next to the metal cap of what looked like a small flask. Really? Did workers drink on the job here? No wonder they got hurt. Elena had walked past the yard's busy clinic every day and had seen workers limping or wrapped in bandages as they left.

Maisie put down her equipment when Elena introduced herself.

"So, you from Mexico?" Maisie said.

"No. El Salvador," she said, wanting to roll her eyes.

"But you understand English, right? Damn, he always sticks me with the foreigners." Maisie picked up the welding stick. "Well, c'mon. Put on that gear and show me what you can do." She handed Elena the tool, stepped back, and crossed her arms.

Elena needed to impress this lady. If not, it would be too easy for them to kick her out and blame it on her broken English. She had to lay a clean weld. All the years of practice helping Mamá sew had steadied her hands. Welding, she reminded herself, wasn't much harder than sewing a straight seam. Like the recruiting posters had suggested. So why were her hands shaking now? She'd done fine in the training. Breathe, she told herself. You know how to do this.

She settled the helmet's visor over her face and took hold of the welding stinger in her gloved hand, positioning the cord behind her so it wouldn't catch fire. She grabbed the stick of welding flux with her other hand. Breathe. Then she leaned over the two sheets of metal and carefully laid down a fairly straight weld, trying to ignore the blinding sparks that flew off the seam. The metal hissed, glowing red. An acrid stink rose up from the burnt elements and she forced back a cough. Once she'd finished, she put down the stinger and pushed back her visor.

Maisie bent down and examined the weld. "Hmmm . . . not bad for a beginner," she said. "Okay. Work on these pieces I've set out. I'm going on my break. If I don't get more coffee soon, I'll die. And don't let me catch you horsing around with your friends." She walked away, her hands in her pockets.

Elena watched her leave, then turned back to her work, slid the visor down, and picked up the stinger. She doubted that was a compliment, comparing her to horses. Was Maisie going off to drink? She seemed like an accident waiting to happen. Elena continued adding new welds on her own.

When Maisie returned, she helped Elena haul new sheets into position.

"I guess the bosses are desperate," Maisie said. "Bringing in Mexicans and all." She bent down and glanced at Elena before taking a swig from her flask. Didn't try to hide it. Elena stared at her and then looked away. "You just do your job, girl, and keep your mouth shut. We'll get along fine." Maisie put her gloves on and picked up her stinger, turning away.

After three hours of welding, bent over her section of the ship, with Maisie working close by, a shrill whistle announced the shipyard's lunch break. Her nerves had settled, and each weld looked a little better than the last. Elena wiped sweat from her stiff fingers and stretched her back. Ghostly bursts of light, after-images, still flashed in front of her eyes. Blinking didn't help.

"So," Maisie said, "you seeing fireworks yet? You'll get used to it. Time for lunch."

She followed Maisie to the break room, where she had her own locker. The place was packed now with women, some still wearing their hard hats or welding helmets, visors pushed back, while they sat hunched at tables devouring their meal. A few women looked like they'd fallen asleep, slumped in their chairs, their heads resting next to their lunch boxes on the table.

She spotted Ana in the corner next to Marisol. Ana waved and motioned her over. Her arm was around Marisol's shoulders, and when Elena got close, she noticed Marisol's tear-streaked face.

"Qué pasó?" she asked.

Marisol lifted her head and wiped her cheek. Her hand looked red, the palm raw.

"It was awful. I was so afraid," Marisol whispered in Spanish. "I had to go up one of those ladders to reach my work area. When I was halfway up, some men stood at the bottom and yelled up at me." Her shoulders tightened. "I didn't understand what they said, but they sounded mean. I tried to ignore them. They got mad and started shaking the ladder, hard. I yelled down and held tight to the rope, but they wouldn't stop. I almost fell off." Tears fell onto her cheeks. "They were laughing, like I was some funny show. When I finally managed to climb up to the top and step off, they just walked away." She shook her head. "If I fell . . ."

Elena swallowed. If it had been her, she probably would have passed out as soon as the ladder started to shake. If she'd even been able to climb up at all. Why had Marisol been sent up there when she was fresh out of training?

"That sounds terrifying," she said, and put her hand on Marisol's arm. "Did anyone try to help you? Where were the bosses?"

Marisol pursed her lips. "Mr. Sullivan was nearby, but he didn't see it happen. At least I don't think so."

Ana nodded. "I didn't see anything, either. It was so noisy and that visor makes it hard to see." She looked at Marisol. "If I'd seen them, they'd be real sorry now." Ana was even shorter than Elena and her arms were thin, without much muscle.

Marisol almost smiled. "Yeah, I bet. My hero." She squeezed Ana's arm. "And then you'd go to jail and I'd be fired for causing trouble."

"Did you tell him what happened?" Elena didn't know how things worked in the yard. She wasn't about to report Maisie. When she worked at the canning factory back home, newcomers had tricks played on them, like having their time cards hidden. Or men giving them nicknames if they messed up on the assembly line, like Fumble Fingers. But never anything dangerous. No one risked getting fired for doing something stupid.

But the shipyard had its own rules. Women now worked jobs that before the war had belonged only to men; they were not always welcomed by the old hands. She'd read about this in the paper. Some people simply disapproved of women working outside the home, even in wartime.

However, her training hadn't prepared her for this. How could women be expected to do their work if they couldn't trust the men who worked beside them? She and her friends would have to be very careful.

"I didn't tell the boss," Marisol said. "I was too upset. I tried to focus on my work, but I couldn't concentrate. I told my partner I felt sick and rushed back here, waiting for you two." She looked at Elena. "Do you think I should report it? I don't even know who those men were."

Ana shook her head. "Bad idea. We're too new. The last thing you want is to draw more attention."

"Maybe," Elena said. "But we should always have someone we trust watching us. Like if we get assigned to different areas in the yard. Or other shifts." She thought about the rope ladders. "We don't know yet who's on our side. Or who wants us to fail."

CHAPTER 5

RACHEL

June 21, 1944

Rachel hung up the phone and walked into the kitchen where Mama and Papa sat eating lunch. She'd slept for a few hours after her night shift ended, so this felt like breakfast time, even though the kitchen clock read 1:00.

"Guess what, Papa," she said, "that patient I told you about who we sent to Merritt? He got transferred to Kaiser for surgery after all. Once they found out he was injured at the yard, they figured he belonged at Kaiser."

Papa put down his sandwich and wiped his mouth. "Well, I hope they were able to save his leg. It sounded bad. If it severed his femoral artery . . ."

"Stop, please," Mama said, scowling. "I'm still eating here. No shop talk in my kitchen." Her mother enjoyed hearing the two of them talk about their work. Just not at mealtime. When Jesse had studied anatomy at Cal, Rachel and Papa loved to quiz him on the location of bones and organ placement. Once Jesse returned, God willing, he'd join their sometimes grisly chats. She didn't dare imagine him not returning.

"Aren't you going to eat?" Mama said. "I made extra egg salad." That was Papa's favorite, especially the way Mama prepared it with bits of pickles and black olives.

"Thanks, Mama," she said, "but I want to go see him at the hospital. I'll just grab a slice of toast." She ignored Mama's frown and toasted a slice of challah, spreading some homemade strawberry jam on top. She missed buttered toast but rationing required small sacrifices.

"I don't see why you need to visit him," Mama said. "He'll have his own nurses now."

"I know," Rachel said, "but the clinic was crazy and he was in such bad shape. And this other patient was horribly racist. I want to see how he's doing."

Papa nodded. "I get it. Hopefully he's doing better by now." He always followed up with his patients after surgery.

She decided to walk to Kaiser, craving fresh air. Besides, local buses ran less often on weekends. By the time she arrived at the renovated hospital on Macarthur Boulevard, the mile-long walk had left her skin damp. God, she was out of shape, too many daylight hours spent asleep.

Kaiser had bought the five-story former charity hospital after Pearl Harbor. Worn stucco walls painted beige, every story spotted with windows of what had been maternity rooms. This was where the seriously injured shipyard workers ended up now, unless they were able to receive care at one of the private hospitals, but these rarely accepted Negro patients. Kaiser's commitment to caring for its workers was unprecedented, regardless of skin color.

The Orthopedic Ward took up most of the second floor. She found Earl in a quadruple unit, each bed partitioned off by thin curtains. He was lying in bed surrounded by people she guessed were his family: two young women and the twin boys he'd mentioned. No sign of his wife.

"Hello there, Mr. Taylor," she said, smiling at him and the others. "I'm glad to see you're looking more comfortable." His injured leg lay in a toe-to-hip splint, with metal pins and bands poking through the padded gauze dressing. An IV ran fluids into his arm, and she guessed he also had morphine infusions throughout the day.

He frowned at her. "I seen you at the clinic. You work here, too?"

Rachel laughed. "No, I just stopped by to see how you're doing."

"Well," he said, "I been sleeping mostly, but my kids came over. Brought me some of their momma's cornbread. She's at work."

The two young women watched her, looking confused. After all, she was not wearing any uniform or white coat. The taller, thin one was probably the eldest, her mouth pressed shut and her eyes narrowed.

"Hello," Rachel said, extending her hand. "I'm the shipyard nurse, Rachel, who wrote you. You must be Peggy." The tall woman stared at her hand and then haltingly offered her own.

"Oh, nice to meet you, nurse," said the other sister, smoothing her dress over her hips. "I'm Ruby Mae. Our daddy said you were real nice to him at the clinic." She shook Rachel's hand and grabbed her brothers by their collars. "And this here is Aaron and Samuel." The boys were dressed in short-sleeved shirts and denim overalls, staring up at Rachel. "They ain't never been in a hospital before. I told them they better behave like when we're in church." She waved her arm around. "'Course none of us got experience with all this, neither. How long are they gonna keep him here? Momma's wanting him home with us. Says he needs her cooking to heal."

"Hush now, Ruby Mae," Peggy said. "My sister talks a lot when she's nervous." Ruby Mae frowned at her, like this was a familiar dynamic between them.

Rachel watched Earl and his family, thinking about Jesse. If he got injured, he'd have no one there to care for him, bring him his favorite foods. She shuddered.

"You okay, nurse?" Ruby Mae stepped closer.

"Sorry," Rachel said. "I was just thinking how lucky your daddy is to have you all here with him."

"Lucky? Hah," Earl said, placing his hand on the leg splint. "I sure don't feel lucky, ma'am."

"Please, just call me Rachel," she said. "And you're right. How stupid of me." Her cheeks flushed. "My brother is stationed in France. I worry about him all the time. He has no one there . . ." Her throat tightened.

"Well, God bless him, " Peggy said, "and may the good Lord keep him safe." She clasped her hands together.

"Amen," came the chorus from Earl, Ruby Mae, and the boys.

Rachel's eyes watered. "Thank you," she said. "And as for how long your father will be here, Ruby Mae, I'd ask his nurse or the surgeon when he checks on him. I imagine they'll watch for infection and get the pain down first. Once he's home, he'll need a lot of help keeping the incisions clean." She looked at the twins. "You boys ready to help your daddy?"

They both nodded at her, as if she were their teacher giving them homework. This must be so scary for them.

She moved next to the bed. "I'm sorry about that hateful man in the clinic."

Earl looked up at her, his eyelids drooping. "I've heard worse, Miz Rachel. Ain't your fault." He closed his eyes. "I gotta rest now. Bless you for stopping by."

Rachel said goodbye to his family and walked down the hallway, letting the tears she'd held back fall. Earl and his children had touched her, reminding her that family meant everything. She ached for Jesse, and all the young men who had left their families behind. How scared and alone they must be.

CHAPTER 6

RUBY MAE

June 27, 1944

Ruby Mae and Peggy were alone in the trailer, the twins at school, Momma at work and Daddy still in the hospital. Ruby Mae's blue dress stretched over what Daddy called her sturdy frame, the short sleeves pinching around the new muscles she'd grown, working her rivet gun on the ship they were piecing together, like a giant puzzle. Lord, she'd end up looking like a man if she wasn't careful.

"Kind of snug, sis," Peggy said. She ran her hands over her own slim hips. "But you kin wear your red sweater on top tonight." She regarded the one-room trailer the family had found a month ago. No one rented to Negroes in Richmond proper, they'd discovered, even with steady jobs at the shipyard, so they'd ended up in North Richmond. "This place is a real dump, I won't lie. I hate living here."

Ruby Mae agreed. The trailer park sat on a rutted dirt road that melted into mud when it rained. Their kitchen consisted of a chipped porcelain sink, a wobbly table and chairs and a blackened wood stove. They hung out their wash on clotheslines, not far from the outhouse. At night, she shared a mattress with Peggy. Daddy and Momma slept on the larger mattress, the twins pressed between them, the boys a tumble of arms and legs at nearly seven. Momma had enrolled Samuel and Aaron in school now that they had a place to stay. She and Daddy had spent their Louisiana childhoods working the fields, picking whatever crop needed tending. Life here was gonna be different, Momma kept saying. The twins would have choices now.

"Well, they s'posed to be building more housing," Ruby Mae said, taking off her dress. She'd keep it clean 'til after supper. "We gotta be patient a while longer. I hear they got some nice apartments made especially for yard workers. But not us. Not yet." She grabbed her worn slacks and squeezed into them. "And thanks for saying you'll come tonight."

Yesterday at the shipyard, one of her new friends, that funny gal named Marcy, had told her about a nightclub nearby that offered blues bands on weekends. Tappers' Inn. Marcy and her friends were headed there on Friday night, and did Ruby Mae want to come with them?

A live band? She'd heard of such a thing, but she'd never been to any club back home. She'd been too young, and besides, Momma believed that good girls heard all the music they needed in church. Their radio was fixed on the gospel station, except when Daddy listened to a ball game. But at her job in the fancy part of Baton Rouge, when Ruby Mae cleaned house for Miz Simmons, she sometimes heard the radio playing what Miz Simmons called big band music, fast tunes with loud instruments that made her head spin. Ruby Mae would scrub to the beat.

"Make it sparkle, Ruby Mae," Miz Simmons would say, like she'd be serving soup out of that porcelain bowl. Cleanest toilet in all of Baton Rouge.

"Oh, yes ma'am." She'd kept her head down, making faces no one saw. Her knuckles bled when she washed off the bleach solution, that smell clinging to her clothes and hair. Moving out here had been like coming to the Promised Land.

Now she couldn't wait to discover what else she'd been missing. She'd told Momma she was going to a Bible study meeting at church that night, and she'd invited Peggy along to make it look convincing. Besides, having her big sister there would feel less scary, in case the Devil really was gonna show up.

By the time she and Peggy walked out of the trailer that night, Holy Bibles tucked under their arms, the sun had set. Fog crawled in from the bay, upping the night's adventure. Peggy had almost ruined things at dinner, talking about the great night they planned.

"This study group is gonna be fun," she'd said, pushing the rice around on her plate with her fork. Ruby Mae had pinched her under the table.

"Yeah, that pastor sure knows how to tell a good story," Ruby Mae had said, watching Momma sideways. "We's lucky the good Lord's looking out for us. Once he finds us a new home, we be all set. Right, Momma?"

"Momma looked at me like she smelled a rat," Ruby Mae said now. She laughed. "You need more practice telling a good lie, if we're ever gonna have any real fun." She tugged on the arm of Peggy's long coat.

"Well, you're so easy," Peggy said. "Like back home when you'd walk inside after being out with Lester. I knew you'd been kissing and all that, pretending to Momma that you'd been helping *his* momma with that baby of hers. I can always tell when you lying." Peggy grinned. "I know my baby sister."

Lester was the boy she'd dated back home. He had two sisters and a baby brother. Ruby Mae sometimes ate dinner over there, and she did like to hold that sweet baby, little Frankie, who smelled like sour milk and had a full head of soft black curls. He'd focus his big eyes on Ruby Mae's face and smile up at her. Lester's momma and his sisters answered all her questions about everything, from sex to how to put on lipstick. Then later, she'd be outside on his porch, kissing Lester in the dark, smelling the jasmine, and remembering how she felt holding Frankie. She carried all of that home, her heart full, wishing she'd been born into that family.

But the Holy Scripture ruled her own house, with no room for a curious girl like her. Asking *why* something happened in a Bible story just came natural to her, much as it irritated Momma. When she got an answer she didn't like, well, then she'd push harder. Daddy said she was stubborn as a mule. Nothing wrong with that. Mules usually got their way. Anyway, Lester got so mad when she told him they were moving, he quit talking to her and got himself a new girlfriend two days later. Fine with her. She'd find someone better out here.

"Now listen, Ruby Mae," Peggy said, using the big-sister tone she favored. They walked down the dirt road away from the trailer park. "I don't know how you talked me into this. I admit I'm kind of curious about the club. But remember that we are two Southern gals brought up to be good Christian ladies."

"Yes, Momma Peggy," Ruby Mae said, rolling her eyes. "Thank you for being my other momma, even though you barely got two years on me. Turning twenty-one didn't make you my boss."

Peggy made a face and followed her down the dark street in the direction of the club. Marcy had said to meet them at nine, and the club was almost a mile away. The bus back into town didn't run often at night, except during the shipyard's shift changes. They'd told Momma that their Bible study meeting served tea and cake afterwards, and leaving before that would be rude. So they'd be home by eleven. Hopefully Momma wouldn't ask too many questions.

Tappers' Inn came into view when they turned onto Chesley Street. The squat building took up the entire block, with laughter and music spilling out the wooden double doors cracked open into the night. Ruby Mae grabbed her sister's hand and walked into the large lobby.

Despite the late hour, they found a bustling scene, like downtown Richmond at lunchtime. On one side of the lobby, there was a full barbershop, where several men were getting their hair trimmed and beards groomed. Next to that was a beauty parlor, women lined up in hair rollers or getting their fingernails painted. Across the way, she spotted a busy restaurant, with groups of folks gathered at white-clothed tables. Everywhere she looked, the faces she saw were shades of brown, from the barbers to those devouring the food. Like some fancy family reunion.

"Will you look at this place, Peggy," she said.

"Uh-huh," Peggy said, squeezing her sister's hand and looking a bit overwhelmed. "Is this whole thing all Tappers'?" Ruby Mae, too, had expected a small and cozy nightclub, not this giant cluster.

Just then Ruby Mae heard her name.

"Hey girl, you made it!" Marcy rushed up and hugged her. "Ain't this something?"

She introduced her other friends from work, Lucinda and Dorothy. From down the hall, Ruby Mae heard music, a woman's voice singing as loud as what she heard at Sunday morning services, but this lady sounded like she'd met the Devil and made friends.

"Let's go listen." She pulled Peggy by the hand and walked towards the wailing notes. Marcy and her friends followed them down the hall towards the nightclub.

"Ruby Mae," Peggy said, "I think Momma and Daddy would whoop us if they knew we was here listening to this."

Ruby Mae stopped at the entrance to the nightclub, where the smoky darkness was lit only by flickering candles in glass jars. Men and women leaned close together over the small tables, clinking glasses and laughing. Most of the women were dressed as pretty as for church, with broad-brimmed hats studded with feathers and ribbon. A few wore furs wrapped around their shoulders. The men wore dark suits and ties, except for several sailors looking handsome in their navy uniforms. A sea of brown faces, some familiar from the shipyard. No wonder folks flocked here after work.

She wished her own dress was fancier, and that she had borrowed a nice hat from Marcy, who was dressed all in red, with a jaunty black beret. Lucinda and Dorothy both wore pencil skirts and satiny fitted tops, their faces made up the same, with bright red lipstick and heavy eye shadow, like they'd copied the same picture in *Glamour* magazine. Each of them had a crocheted snood pinned to their hair.

Peggy turned to her. "Ruby Mae, we surely got ourselves to the Devil's house."

Ruby Mae looked at her and laughed. Peggy needed to learn how to have a good time. Momma's grip on her was too strong. "Well, as long as we're here, we might as well find out what he's got to say. No way I'm leaving. C'mon, girl."

The five of them found two empty tables in the back and pushed them together. Ruby Mae sat between Peggy and Marcy and unbuttoned her coat. She checked her watch. They had at least an hour before they'd need to leave, plus time to buy Momma a piece of cake on the way out. They ordered drinks, Peggy insisting Ruby Mae stick to soda.

"It's almost time for the live band, Ruby Mae." Marcy smiled at her and leaned in. "They say this here is part of the Chitlin' Circuit 'cause so many blues bands from all over come through to play. And wait 'til you hear the sax player. Oh my Lord, that man can play." She grabbed Ruby Mae's arm. "I'm glad you gals came. Time to have some fun after working so hard, right?"

Ruby Mae nodded. "Who's this singing?" The recorded music streamed from speakers mounted on the walls. The woman's voice, singing about her man and raining all the time. Like she'd been through a lot.

"Don't you know Lena Horne, girl?" Marcy said. "You got a lot to learn. Lucky you got me as a friend." Marcy laughed. "It's called 'Stormy Weather.' Yeah, it gets me, too."

Ruby Mae sipped her ginger ale from a thick glass, relieved that the club served soft drinks in addition to cocktails. The one time she drank whiskey back home with Lester, she'd sicked up her whole dinner. Peggy sat close to her now, drinking black coffee, acting like she did this kind of thing every day, except her leg bounced up and down, a dead giveaway of her nerves.

The band members walked onto the stage and started setting up equipment. She counted five men, all dressed in suits and ties, who looked as old as Daddy—a drummer, a piano player, a guitarist, a shiny-brass saxophone guy, and one man who carried out a large stringed instrument, like a violin's overgrown cousin. Their church back in Baton Rouge had a choir who performed during the service, but only with the church organ or a guitar to accompany the hymns.

Peggy leaned over. "I don't think this is gonna be like church," she said, reading her sister's mind. "What is that thing anyway?" She pointed to the stringed instrument.

Dorothy heard this and clapped her hands. "You two gals crack me up. Ain't you ever seen a bass fiddle?"

Ruby Mae shook her head. "We ain't got none of this back home. I feel like we in some kind of dream."

"Yeah," said Peggy, "but if we get home late, Momma ain't gonna let us out at night ever. Bible study or not." She pressed her hand on the Bible she'd set down on the table.

Ruby Mae sighed. "I know. But let's just pretend we belong here. Okay?" She put her hand on top of Peggy's.

"Fine," Peggy said. She picked up her coffee cup with her other hand and sipped.

The musicians warmed up, tuning the guitar, squeaking out a few notes on the saxophone, tapping the drums, and smiling at the audience. The piano man played a chord and then a wave of melody rose into the room. The heavy drumming and deep bass notes vibrated right through Ruby Mae's skin.

Some of the people seated close to the stage got up and started dancing, mostly couples, but Ruby Mae saw that a few women grabbed their friends and got up, too. No reason to miss out, just because they didn't have a date.

"C'mon, girls, let's go dance." Marcy stood up and looked over at Peggy. "You, too. I know you're feeling it." Peggy frowned.

Lucinda tucked some stray hairs into her snood and giggled as she got up. "Yeah, let's dance," she said. "I got my eye on one of those sailors." Dorothy checked her lipstick in a small mirror from her purse, then followed her friends onto the dance floor.

"You gals coming?" she said as she turned back.

Ruby Mae grinned. "Well, why not?" she said to Peggy. "If we're gonna be sinners, might as well go all the way." She got up and snapped her fingers to the beat.

Peggy shook her head. "No. I'm fine right here." She kept her hand on the Bible.

"Okay, fine, be a stick-in-the-mud."

Ruby Mae turned and followed the others up front. Her heart raced. No one on the dance floor tried to talk over the music, they just surrendered to it, and moved their bodies any way that felt right. Marcy swayed her hips and clapped with the beat. Ruby Mae watched her and Lucinda and Dorothy dancing. She wished she could be like that, just let go and dance how she wanted, no matter who was watching. Besides, no one knew her here. No one to squeal to Momma.

So when the piano player announced the next song, their version of "Don't Cry Baby," she closed her eyes and let herself really feel the music, felt it touch something buried deep. Her body moved in response, her head bobbing, her arms lifting at times when the saxophone's high notes cried out. A feeling like the Holy Spirit possessed her, took her outside herself, not holy but very alive.

Someone tapped her shoulder. Startled, she opened her eyes and found herself staring into the face of a young man dressed in the dark uniform of a sailor. His white sailor's cap sat squarely on his close-cropped hair, and when he smiled at her, she thought he was the handsomest man she'd ever met, with such kind eyes.

"Excuse me, miss." He leaned in close. "I hope you don't mind, but I saw you dancing over here all by yourself. And I thought, Freddy Parker, you must not allow that pretty girl to dance alone. So here I am, at your service, Miss . . .?"

She had to laugh. "I'm Ruby Mae, and that is some talking. Freddy Parker, huh?" A shiver rippled down her spine. She touched her hair and hoped her dress still looked fresh.

"Ruby Mae, a name as pretty as the girl herself. I would be honored if you'd let me buy you a cold drink. But first, will you dance with me?"

The band switched to a slow bluesy ballad. She nodded and he took her hand in his and pulled her closer. They moved to the beat, her heart pounding so hard she thought she might faint. His hand on her back felt warm and solid. When she looked up at his face, he smiled and she felt giddy in his arms. The song ended and Freddy spoke close to her ear.

"Before we go deaf, let's find a place where we can talk." He placed his fingers under her elbow and led her to the other corner of the room, away from the band, who now were playing a song she recognized. She waited while Freddy got them each a cold soda.

"I've got you under my skin," she said, smiling, when he returned. Out of the corner of her eye, she caught the heat of Peggy's fixed stare. Her sister sat alone at the table.

"Say, what?" Freddy frowned.

"Oh, this song. I used to hear this on the radio where I worked." She surprised herself, chatting with this stranger like they were old friends.

"Yeah? Where you from, Miz Ruby Mae?" Freddy said. "I swear I hear some kind of Southern charm when you talk. Me, I was born and raised in Chicago, but my daddy's family's from Georgia. I spent some summers sweating and swatting mosquitos down south. Am I right? You a Southern gal?"

Maybe he was nervous, too, his words all rushed together, like he was in some kind of hurry, or maybe he was afraid she'd walk away if he stopped talking.

She nodded. "Outside Baton Rouge. My whole life. 'Til we moved out here. Now I'm working at the shipyards." He didn't need to know she'd been a cleaning lady back home. "One of the best riveters you'll ever meet. Better than my big sister Peggy, who's over there making sure I behave myself." Lord, she couldn't stop talking, either. "But it's dangerous work, you know. People get hurt all the time, burns and cuts and even some broken legs if they fall off their ladder or Lord knows what else." Her mouth was flapping overtime, as loose as his. She thought about her daddy and how badly he got hurt.

Freddy put down his glass. "If you think that's dangerous, try coming to work for the Navy. Not that they'd let girls in," he added. "Up at Port Chicago, where I'm stationed, they got us loading these heavy shells off of train cars onto the ships. Ammo. And bombs, too."

"Wait, where's Port Chicago? Near here?" She knew Chicago wasn't close by.

"Yeah," Freddy said. "It's just outside Concord. Less than an hour if you drive fast."

"Well, sounds like scary work," she said. "What if one of them goes off?"

"Yeah, that's what worries me." He took a deep breath and exhaled slowly. "But let's not ruin the night talking 'bout this." The band had stopped playing and recorded music came back over the speakers.

She looked over to check on Peggy, who had stood up at the table, tapping her watch with one hand and jerking her head toward the exit.

Ruby Mae had lost track of time. She turned back and faced Freddy. Just a few more minutes with him couldn't hurt.

"You're right," she said. She could talk to him all night.

But Peggy appeared at her side, her coat buttoned all the way up. She barely nodded at Freddy, like he was some annoying salesman pestering them.

"I'm Peggy, her sister," she said, giving Ruby Mae the evil eye. "We have to go. It's late. Momma's gonna be fit to be tied."

Freddy put out his hand. "Nice to meet you, Miz Peggy. I'm Freddy Parker. Your momma must be proud of you two gals. Doing your part for our country." He turned back toward Ruby Mae. "I sure hope we get to continue our conversation sometime. Can I call you?"

"We don't got a phone at home," she said. "How 'bout we meet up here next week? Friday, say 8:00?" Like she was used to making dates with strangers. Peggy stared at her.

"Yes, ma'am," Freddy said. "Friday sounds good. As long as I don't have to work. And Miz Peggy, I hope you'll come, too. I could invite my buddies to join us, make it a party. Sound good?"

Ruby Mae nodded and before she could say anything else, Peggy pulled her towards the back door. She waved goodbye to Marcy, who was dancing with another sailor. She'd lost track of Lucinda and Dorothy. Freddy stood there watching them leave and when she turned around, he touched his cap and smiled.

Peggy steered her to the restaurant. "You better get that look off your face before we get home. Momma's gonna take one look at you and tie you to the trailer door. Let's buy her that piece of cake fast, and get home before she sees how late it is. Here, hold these Bibles while I get the cake."

Ruby Mae stood outside the entrance to the restaurant, her arms wrapped around the Bibles. The band had started playing again, and the music drifted out to the lobby. She closed her eyes and swayed back and forth.

* * *

By the time they'd walked home to their trailer, almost an hour late, the two of them had gotten their story down. Bible study ran late, and then they forgot and had to run back to church for an extra piece of cake for Momma. A small shaft of light shone out the side of the blackout curtains. Momma was still up. Peggy nodded at Ruby Mae and quietly opened the metal door, wincing as it squeaked against the linoleum floor. Momma sat, unmoving, in the old rocking chair, and the twins slept side by side in the back. The small table lamp cast shadows into the corners.

"Momma, we're home," Ruby Mae said, keeping her voice low as she stepped inside and walked closer to her mother. "We got you some of the lemon cake they served after Bible study. Not as good as yours, but we wanted you to have some, too."

"Huh? Mmm . . . sounds nice."

Momma had been asleep, Ruby Mae realized, sitting up so straight in that chair, like a judge waiting to pass sentence, but she must have dozed off. This was going to be easier than they'd imagined. She hoped Momma couldn't smell the cigarette smoke on their clothes.

Peggy took off her coat and started to get undressed right away.

Momma stretched her arms up over her head and yawned. The twins didn't stir. She eyed the slice of cake wrapped in a napkin. "I guess I better eat that now, 'cause if those boys wake up and see it, I'll have to fight 'em off." She smiled at her daughters. "That's real considerate, bringing your momma some cake. I'm proud of you two."

Ruby Mae felt a twinge of guilt over how easy it was to fool Momma. Especially if cake was involved. She hung up her dress and changed into her nightgown. Peggy had already crawled under the covers and Ruby Mae slipped in next to her.

"Goodnight, Momma. I love you." Ruby pinched her sister's arm. "Don't you dare tell her," she whispered in Peggy's ear.

"Night, Momma," Peggy said. She pinched Ruby Mae back. "Hope you like that cake."

Momma switched off the table lamp but stayed in the rocker.

Ruby Mae lay on her back, eyes closed, listening to Momma eat her cake in the dark. The fight she'd expected didn't happen. No bad ending to this day. Freddy Parker's face floated into her mind, just a sweet memory of a special night. Tappers' Inn might be her lucky star.

CHAPTER 7

RACHEL

June 30, 1944

Rachel waited in the dark at the bus stop on Grand Avenue; the 10:00 p.m. shipyard bus was late. As the newest nurse, she was stuck working nights, heading off to work when almost everyone else in the entire world was home, cozy in bed with a good book, and if they were lucky, another warm body. She shivered against the cold wind that gusted under her coat.

When the bus finally arrived, she climbed up the steps and looked for an empty seat next to a woman. Most of the night-shift workers were men in their forties or older, too old to fight but not too old to be annoying to women. The bus was already pretty full. Some of the passengers had nodded off, others were smoking and talking with their neighbors.

She sat down next to a young woman in denim coveralls, who held an open thermos that smelled of strong coffee. Perched on the woman's head was a bulky welder's helmet, its thick visor pushed back.

"Don't they let you keep that at work?" Rachel pointed to the helmet and smiled at the woman.

"Yeah, I could," the woman said, "but one of the gals had hers stolen, and this one fits me just right. I've made it personal, too. See?" She turned her head. Painted on the other side of the helmet was a large red rose. The woman tilted her head forward and pulled down the visor. Behind it, she'd written "CHRISSY" in white paint on the front of the helmet.

"Wow, look at that," Rachel said. "No one would dare take it now. Good idea."

"Yes, siree," Chrissy said. "Now my friends can pick me out, 'cause once we all have our leathers and gear on, you can't tell the gals from the men, let alone who's who." She laughed and Rachel joined her.

"I don't have to worry about that," Rachel said. "I'm easy to pick out." She pointed to her white uniform and stockings that screamed nurse.

This was what she liked about her job: talking to people, whether it was her patients or the other clinic staff. Making that connection satisfied her curiosity, understanding how people felt about their own lives. Sometimes people told her things, even shocking things they had never told anyone. She would listen intently and offer support. Her best friend, Bertie, said she always felt better after talking things out with Rachel. Even Jesse, just before he left for basic training, had confided that he was terrified of dying alone, or being caught by the Germans and tortured. He'd made her promise not to tell their parents. She had wedged his confession inside her heart, next to her love for him.

The bus had picked up more workers in Berkeley and headed north towards the shipyard. One of the men in the back must have told a joke, laughter spilling down the center aisle. They were all in this together, men and women, everyone doing their part to help win the war. Rachel felt humbled to have this job.

"I'm just hoping I can keep working at the yard a while longer," Chrissy said. "The money's real good compared with my last job. I was the secretary for a guy who made me wear short skirts and heels that killed my feet," she said, pointing to her work boots, "not like these shit kickers, pardon my French. And I hated how fresh he got." She shrugged. "At least at the yard we have plenty of gals working together. It feels safer. I saw a man try to grab a gal, and her friend turned her welding stick on him real quick." She laughed. "Earned her the nickname of 'Stinger'. He's not gonna try that again."

Rachel understood. A few of the doctors at her last job at the hospital acted like the young nurses were ripe fruit. Of course, some of the nurses loved the attention, hoping to snag one of the single men left. She found most of the doctors either patronizing or downright pathetic when they flirted with her. Someday she'd find a man who treated her like she had a brain.

"Well, for me, this war can't end fast enough," Rachel said. "My brother's stationed overseas. I worry about him all the time. We need to defeat the Nazis and bring our boys home."

"Yeah, I guess so," Chrissy said, pulling out a cigarette lighter and rubbing it between her fingers. "But is it really worth it, just to protect those people? Dirty Jews." She flicked the lighter open and lit a cigarette. "Maybe we should let the Germans finish what they started, if you catch my drift." She looked up at Rachel, her eyes narrowed.

"What?" Rachel's breath caught in her throat. God, how did this happen? She'd let her guard down, and been blindsided by this stupid prejudiced woman. Her pulse pounded in her ears.

She wanted to grab Chrissy by the throat and throttle her. Or confront her for her antisemitic slur. Or she could get up and move to another seat. Rachel's brain felt like it would explode, flipping through her choices. But her body had gone numb, her tongue paralyzed. She said nothing and looked down at her lap, barely breathing. What was wrong with her?

"Well, never mind," Chrissy said after a minute, stowing her thermos in her carry-all bag. She stood up, Rachel watching her. "Don't matter. The war's gonna be over soon, anyways."

The smile on her lips felt like a kick in the ribs. Rachel stayed frozen in her seat while Chrissy walked up to the front of the bus as it entered the gates of the shipyard. Only after the woman had climbed down the steps did Rachel take a deep breath.

She waited until the other passengers exited, her mind still racing. She should have done something. Instead she'd sat there, while her Jewishness had been attacked and she'd gone mute. It wasn't the first time she'd heard an antisemitic comment and let it slide. She was pathetic. People were being murdered for being Jewish, and she'd let this woman spit out her hatred, uncontested. She shook her head. Shame on me.

Here in this country, people might assume she was a Christian. Her appearance gave away nothing, unlike the Japanese families forced to abandon their homes and farms. Unlike the Negro shipyard workers forced to live in shacks or flimsy trailers, while they sweated over the bones of warships. Here she wore no yellow star sewn onto her coat. But she should have spoken up. She needed to find some courage.

CHAPTER 8

ELENA

July 3, 1944

Elena put down the welding stinger and pushed up the visor on her helmet. She desperately needed some water. Her hands, damp with sweat, slipped out of the too-big leather gloves. In spite of the cold night air, her body was overheating inside the thick protective leathers.

She'd just snagged her left glove on a jagged piece of the hull. Now she stared at the one-inch hole. No, this will not do, she thought. I need a new pair. One that fits, not leftovers from someone else. But she was scared to ask Mr. Sullivan. He had a bad temper, and the last thing she needed was to make him angry.

Yesterday he'd yelled at another welder when the man had complained that his visor was so scarred by sparks, he couldn't see his hands while he worked. All the equipment needed to be replaced. Everyone knew that. But the military had seized needed supplies, repurposed them, and sent them to the men fighting on the frontlines. The bosses promised new gloves and visors. Eventually. Meanwhile, they were told, make do with what you've got.

Elena picked up her thermos and gulped some water. Her first few days, she had brought fresh coffee with her, but she'd kept needing to rush off to the bathroom, and Mr. Sullivan had scolded her for wasting time. She'd vowed from then on to "stay under the radar," a new expression she'd learned from Ana, who had gotten that advice from another worker. That was how the newly-hired women working at the yard kept their jobs. No demands. No mistakes. No special favors.

She stashed her thermos in her lunch box, put on her gloves, and picked up her stinger. Grabbing a fresh stick of flux, she pushed it into place, flipping her visor down. Everything went dark for a moment until she pulled the trigger. Sparks flew up at her face and chest as she applied more pressure with the tip of the stinger's electrode. The heated flux melted cleanly onto the seam, forming an even line.

She kept her left glove tilted away from the sparks, the work area illuminated by their flashes of light. So far so good. Tomorrow she'd rig up something to cover the hole, or borrow a glove from someone on a different shift. Now that she had some money, she could try to find a pair downtown, but that was unlikely. Most stores' empty shelves displayed "out of stock" notices due to the war.

"*Ay!* No!" she yelled as a jolt of pain shot through her left hand. She dropped the stinger and struggled to lift her visor, blinded in the darkness. She yanked off the glove. A glob of molten flux, glowing orange, had stuck to the back of her hand. She brushed it off, tears burning her eyes. "Me quemé!"

The burned skin had already turned from ash-white to red. A translucent blister bubbled over the surface and she smelled a bitter mix of burnt flesh and hot flux. Her hand throbbed in time with her pulse.

"Elena!" Somehow Ana was at her side, staring down at the burned skin. "What happened?"

Elena grimaced and held her injured hand close to her chest. "That," she said, nodding at the singed glove, the hole's edges now blackened.

"Ay, diós mío," Ana said. She put her arm around Elena's shoulders. "You need to go to the clinic. It looks bad."

She looked at Ana, taking a deep breath. "I know. It hurts so much, but I'm scared to tell Mr. Sullivan. What if he fires me?"

"If they fired everyone who's been hurt here, this place would be empty," Ana said.

The whistle signaling the end of the shift sounded. Elena looked around at the other workers packing up their tools. She felt queasy when she looked at the wound. The pain was intense.

"Okay," she said. "I'll go to the clinic. See what they can do. Get something for this pain, so I can work tomorrow."

Ana looked at her sideways. "I doubt you'll be cleared to work for a while. How would you even get a glove on?"

She was right. Even the cool air on her skin made it worse. "Wait, what are you even doing here, Ana? I thought you worked day shift this week."

"I did," Ana said. "And then I did a double. But it doesn't matter now. Let's get you to the clinic. Are you okay to walk there by yourself?" Elena nodded. "I'll get your things from the locker room and meet you there."

Elena picked up the damaged glove and stuffed it in her pocket. Walking towards the clinic, she spotted Mr. Sullivan near the administration building. Maybe she'd tell him now, get it over with.

He was talking to a worker wearing a hard hat, hands on his hips and frowning at the man. She hesitated then stepped over to the two men, holding her injured hand by the wrist. Ay, the pain made it hard to think straight.

The guy in the hard hat looked her over, shook his head, and left, muttering to himself.

"What do you want?" Mr. Sullivan practically barked at her. She was tempted to run away. Tell him tomorrow. But the pain kept her there.

"I . . . uh . . . well, I'm sorry, Mr. Sullivan," she sputtered. "I had an accident." She shifted her left arm and extended it in front of her, the blister shiny in the reflected light.

"God damn it, Guzmán." Mr. Sullivan grabbed her by the elbow and pulled her closer. His fingers gripped her arm as he examined her hand. This was a mistake, telling him now. She felt like crying.

"What did you do?" he said, shaking his head. "Why weren't you wearing your gloves?"

"I was!" She pulled the damaged glove out and waved it at him. "I'm not stupid!"

Mr. Sullivan sighed. "Well, go to the clinic. Damn, you better be able to work soon." He let go of her arm and walked away.

Great. Now on top of this pain shooting through her hand, she had made her boss angry. Flew way over the radar. She wanted to shove that glove in his face. But what was the point? All he cared about was getting the job done.

The shipyard's clinic, housed in a low wooden building, was a few minutes' walk away. A large red cross was painted over the entrance, like *La Cruz Roja* back home. Elena hurried down the dirt path, holding her burned hand like an injured pet. Seeing the line of workers waiting to be seen, she decided she would send Ana home. Her friend would be desperate for sleep.

A cement ramp led up to the front door, where another worker hobbled out, leaning on crutches, his right ankle and foot wrapped in a bulky bandage. He nodded at Elena and shook his head when he saw her hand.

A young woman sat at the desk in the waiting room. On the wall were several posters, one a *We Can Do It!* image of a woman dressed in coveralls flexing her biceps. Another poster showed illustrations of burns on sketched hands and faces. A blister like hers covered some of the burns. Others were worse, with blackened bits of dead skin. Her stomach lurched.

She hoped Ana was wrong. She needed to get back to work right away. Missing shifts meant less money in her pocket, and less sent home to her family. They were counting on her. But how could she possibly wear a glove when the pain in her hand already made her cry?

CHAPTER 9

RUBY MAE

July 3, 1944

"You're working up there tonight." Mr. Graham pointed to the two-story scaffolding next to the ship's hull. Overhead lights cast harsh shadows onto the skeleton of the victory ship. The cold night air smelled smoky from recent welds.

Ruby Mae stared up at the narrow wooden ledge twenty feet above her head. She'd always been afraid of heights, ever since Momma had dragged her, barely seven years old, up the wooden stairs to the balcony of Mount Zion Baptist Church back in Baton Rouge. "Closer to God," Mama had insisted, but all Ruby Mae had felt when she looked down at the pews was a rush of dizziness and the urge to sick up, which she did, onto her church dress and Mary Janes. Momma had been so mad.

"Please . . . sir," she stammered now, her throat constricted. Be polite, don't yell, and for God's sake, don't cry. "Couldn't someone else do it? I'm not used to climbin' up that high. We ain't got no mountains back home."

"If you can't do as you're told, you might as well go home." He frowned. "You hear me?" His ears, sticking out under his hard hat had turned bright pink.

"Yes, sir," she muttered, turning away before she said something she'd regret. The knot in her stomach tightened. There were already three other workers, all men, perched up on the scaffold landing she needed to reach. They had stopped to watch her. If she walked away now, she might as well keep going and turn in her gear.

Forcing her shoulders back, she picked up her equipment, put on her gloves and hung the long air hose attached to the rivet gun around her neck. She needed both hands free to climb. Her legs trembled as she placed her right work boot on the bottom rung.

"Please, Lord, give me strength to do this," she said quietly. Then she reached up and grabbed hold of the sides of the rope ladder and pulled herself up. It swayed under her.

"It's gonna break," she moaned. But it held. One step at a time, she inched her way up, not daring to look down. Seventh step. Keep going. The creaking from the ladder sounded like a cry for mercy.

By the time she reached the landing, sweat soaked her bandana and the sick in her throat reached her mouth. Don't look down. Someone close to her on the scaffolding laughed. She swallowed hard. Almost crawling, she hefted her body over the edge and sat back against the hull, her breath coming in short bursts.

One of the men on the landing stood up, hands on his hips. He was built thick as a tree stump, with straggly blond hair over his balding scalp. "Well, lookie here, boys. We got us a fresh one. Dark meat." He laughed and nudged the man next to him.

Ruby Mae flinched, and looked down at her lap. Don't speak, you'll make it worse.

"Shut up, Jack. We don't need no trouble up here." This came from one of the other workers, a light brown-skinned man, who stepped closer to where Ruby Mae sat. "You here to work or not?" His accent sounded like Elena's.

He reached out his leather glove toward her. "C'mon, let's go." As he pulled her up, he leaned in. "Ignore them. Just do your job. You can work here on this section." He pointed to an area away from the other men. "It ain't too close to the edge."

She locked eyes with the man. "Bless you. I'm Ruby Mae." Her breathing had slowed.

"They call me Ralph. Just do your work, okay? They'll leave you alone."

Ruby Mae nodded. She adjusted her goggles and pulled her rivet gun into position, then bent down over her section of the hull, facing away from the edge. Her earplugs helped muffle the noise in the cavernous shipyard, but they also left her isolated. She didn't like the feeling so she pocketed the earplugs; hearing all the racket was better than the quiet. Out of the corner of her eye, she noticed Jack watching her, his lips pulled back in a leering grin. She shuddered and looked away.

Taking a deep breath, she got to work, driving each rivet into place. Her nerves and nausea quieted. You can do this, girl. Prove them wrong. That's what Momma and Daddy would say if they saw her up on this ledge. They'd be proud of me. 'Course Daddy would have grabbed Jack by the neck. No one better talk to his daughters like that. She smiled. Even Peggy would want to see that action. Not that Daddy could do much now, still crippled.

For the rest of her time up on that ledge, she focused on those rivets and not on how the scaffold practically dangled midair. Finally the whistle blew for their break at 3:00 a.m. There was still one small section she needed to attach. She watched the others climb down the ladder ahead of her, Jack going first. Maybe he'd fall and split his head open. Ralph went last and paused on the top rung.

"You okay, Ruby Mae? Want some help getting back down?" he asked, his goggles loose around his neck.

"No, I'll be fine, thanks. Gotta finish my section," she said. She should have brought her lunch pail up at the start and stayed put, except she'd need to use the bathroom eventually.

"My advice?" he said. "Face the ship when you climb down. Don't look at your feet, just feel for the next rung." Then she watched him disappear over the ledge.

She put her goggles back on and picked up her gun, liking the power she held in her hands. One rivet after another, straight through each perforated hole in the steel. Her arms strong as Daddy's. No more climbing up ladders today. She'd beg Mr. Graham to put her somewhere else.

"Hey you!" It was Jack's voice, much too close to her.

She lurched and lost control of the gun, which slipped out of her hands onto the ledge, shooting out a rivet when it hit the wood. The rivet ricocheted off the hull and fell to the ground below.

Jack had climbed back up the ladder, only his head visible above the ledge. He peered up at her, his eyes slitted, like some gruesome carved pumpkin. Down below, the rumbling tractors on the ground hauled clanging sheets of steel.

"Serves you right, clumsy bitch," he hissed. "Working through lunch. Trying to make the rest of us look bad." He looked like he wanted to spit on her, then he climbed back down the ladder and left her there.

Ruby Mae sat down, trembling. Tears streamed onto her cheeks. She was a mess. No way could she climb down that ladder now. She'd just sit there and wait. Maybe Peggy would come look for her. As long as Jack stayed away. But the men would be back soon to finish their work.

"Are you hurt? What happened?" Mr. Graham's head appeared at the top of the ladder. "I saw you up here bawling like a stuck pig." His cheeks were pink and his breathing labored;

he smelled like raw onions. He stared at the rivet gun lying a few feet away.

She pulled her bandana off and wiped her cheeks. "I'll be okay," she said. "I . . . uh . . . well . . . the gun slipped. But I'm scared to climb down."

"God almighty, Ruby Mae," he said, frowning. "Let's go. Drop your gear and follow me down the ladder. I'll help."

She did as instructed, clinging to the ladder, Mr. Graham's hand under her elbow below her as she stepped down. It felt strange to be so close to this white man, him touching her arm. She forced herself to keep breathing and look straight ahead. *Don't you faint, girl.* One more rung, finally, and they were at the bottom.

"Look, I won't make you go back up there," Mr. Graham said. "Finish your lunch and I'll put you over in another section. Get Ralph to bring you your things."

As she walked toward the locker room, she spotted Jack and some other men lounging against a stack of wooden crates. Jack watched her as she walked past. She avoided his gaze. He was probably worried that she'd tell on him. Good, let him worry. What if she did tell Mr. Graham? Would he even believe her? Her word against a white man's. Not likely. Better just stay out of his way. That guy was nothing but trouble.

CHAPTER 10

RACHEL

July 3, 1944

Rachel glanced at the clock on the clinic wall and yawned. 10:00 p.m. She'd switched shifts with another nurse who wanted to attend her friend's wedding party. Now she'd need another shot of caffeine to get through the last hour. By the time she got home, she'd be as jittery as Sadie, Aunt Pearl's yappy Chihuahua. After she drained the lukewarm coffee from her thermos, she told Diana she was ready for the next patient.

"Elena Guzmán," Diana called out to the full waiting room. She handed the chart to Rachel. "Bad burn."

A young woman with thick black hair in a braid got up and walked over, holding her left hand against her body. Her coveralls looked too large for her petite frame, and her eyes telegraphed pain.

"Hello. Come with me," Rachel said. She ignored the frustrated expressions on the others waiting their turn. One man shook his head, stood up and walked outside, lighting a cigarette.

"Buenas noches." Elena grimaced. "I burn my hand. My boss says to come here." She looked at Rachel's uniform. "You are enfermera, sí?"

Her English sounded heavily accented but clear. Rachel had only studied French in high school, which she never needed after she'd graduated. Spanish would have been more useful, especially now with so many immigrant workers at the shipyard. A week after starting this job, she'd bought a Spanish dictionary that she kept at the clinic.

She led Elena back to an available station in the treatment room. This spot had decent lighting, and she'd made it her own by setting up supplies in metal trays labeled with her name. One tray for bandages. One for cleaning wounds. One for ointments. The other nurses had teased her but she liked to have what she needed close by. Her father had suggested this approach as a way to organize her thinking. Surgeons, Papa had said, needed clear minds when they held a scalpel poised over a patient's flesh, knowing exactly where the liver or the spleen or the heart lay beneath opaque layers of skin and dense muscle. A good nurse, he said, also knew how to organize her tasks.

She pointed to the exam table. "Have a seat and I'll take a look. I can see that it hurts."

Elena nodded. "Yes, okay, *Señora.*" She sat down on the table and gingerly released her left wrist.

"Please, just call me Rachel. And I'm not a señora." She gave a small laugh. "Not yet, though Mama is ever hopeful." She glanced at Elena's fingers. "Still a señorita like me?"

Elena winced. "No tengo marido." No husband.

Rachel washed her hands and sat down on a stool next to Elena, then reached for a small bottle of sterile saline and poured it over the burned skin. The wound extended almost three inches across the back of Elena's hand. A large blister had bubbled up on the swollen red surface. Second degree.

Elena bit her lip. "It's bad, yes? My boss he is very angry with me."

Rachel looked up at her. "Why? How did this happen? Weren't you wearing gloves?" The woman had to be a welder, seeing the size of the burn. Why would she work barehanded?

Elena looked back at her with tears in her dark eyes.

Great job, Rachel, she thought. Make your injured patient feel worse. Not what she'd learned in school, but this job drove her nuts. So many of the injuries could have been avoided with proper training and safety equipment.

Elena thrust out her chin. "They promise me new gloves last week. These," she pulled a pair of worn gloves out of her pocket, "do not fit. And look." She poked her right index finger through a singed hole in the back of the left glove. "I *do* wear them, señorita." She glared at Rachel, her lips pressed tight. "La chispa saltó."

"What does that mean?" Rachel said. Sounded like swear words.

"The spark . . . it jumps in the hole."

Rachel put down the bottle of saline. "I'm so sorry." She put her hand on Elena's other arm. "I didn't mean to blame you. It's been a long day. Too many patients and too much caffeine." She sighed. "Look, let me clean your hand and put a proper dressing on it."

Elena looked at the burn. "And my job? I can work tomorrow?"

"What?" Rachel stared at her. "No. How could you possibly work with this?" She held up Elena's left hand.

"But, my boss . . ."

Rachel shook her head. "He'll have to make do without you. For at least two weeks. I'm sorry. But if you try to work before it's healed, it'll get infected. That's serious. You could even lose your hand. Do you understand?"

Elena wiped tears from her eyes. "Two weeks? I lose my job. Por favor, is there anything you can do?"

Rachel didn't blame her for crying. No one got paid if they couldn't work. But she wasn't a miracle worker. Another nurse walked past them and shot Rachel a sympathetic look. They heard this request from patients all the time.

"Do you have family here to help you?" Rachel asked. "You'll need to change the dressing every day. And keep it completely dry."

Elena looked down at her lap. "No, mi familia is back home. El Salvador. I live in a family's house here, with two roommates."

"El Salvador? You really came a long way." Rachel tried to imagine making that journey alone. "Why did you come?"

"Why do you want to know?" Elena squirmed on the table.

"Talking will help distract you," Rachel said. "This is going to hurt. How about I give you something for the pain first?"

"No," Elena said, her mouth set. "I don't want medicine. And I don't want to tell you my story." She pinched her lips. "I am here to work. That is my job. Your job is help me back to work."

Rachel was caught by surprise. On one hand, she admired this fierce young woman who had left home and found skilled work here in a foreign country at war. On the other, she found Elena stubborn as all get out, pushing back and refusing Rachel's attempts to offer comfort. This was her last patient for the day, and what she really wanted was to go home and crawl into bed.

She took a deep breath, let it out slowly and placed the necessary supplies on the table. "I'd like to put some of this sulfa cream onto the burned skin. It will keep the gauze from sticking and protect against infection," she said. She handed Elena a wrapped ace bandage. "Here, hold onto this with your other hand. Are you ready?"

Elena nodded. "If it helps me to work soon." She looked like she had more to say, but kept her mouth closed and gripped the ace wrap with her right hand.

Rachel applied the pungent sulfa cream using a wooden tongue blade, like icing a very delicate cake. Elena moaned and grunted while Rachel wrapped a thick padding of gauze around Elena's hand and used plenty of tape to hold it in place. Elena's cheeks had turned red and her forehead was damp.

"Here's more of the sulfa," Rachel said, handing a small jar to Elena. "And some gauze and tape. Have someone apply the cream every day with fresh gauze over it."

Elena raised her eyebrows.

"You have to do this, Elena. If not, infection is very likely. Come see me here in clinic if that's easier for you. I'm glad to help." She did feel sorry for this stubborn woman.

Elena nodded. "Grácias . . . I will come see you." She stood up. "Tomorrow I go ask my boss to please keep my job." She walked away, small and defeated in her coveralls.

Rachel was relieved to see her leave. She cleaned up her workstation and washed her hands for the hundredth time, thinking about this last patient, wondering if she'd really come back.

CHAPTER 11

ELENA

July 6, 1944

Elena had just finished the night shift and was walking home with Ana and Marisol. She had returned to work as soon as she could put a glove back on without crying. Only missed two days. Finally got a new pair of gloves, too, that fit.

Somehow the three of them had been assigned to the same shift that day, which meant the two cousins would share a bed. They seemed fine with that. Now all Elena wanted was to get home, pull off her work boots, close the blackout curtains, and sleep for as long as possible.

But she'd promised to meet Gabi, a new worker, downtown at the Richmond branch of the union office. Gabi needed a union card, and Elena had offered to help, knowing it was hit or miss that a Spanish-speaking staffer would be available. Gabi was originally from Zamora in Mexico, and she'd fled Houston with her daughter when her husband became abusive.

Elena had explained that getting a union card would give Gabi some job protection and good benefits, like childcare for her daughter and healthcare for them both. After three months on the job, Elena felt like an expert on the union.

"Listen, Gabi," Elena had told her, "the Boilermakers' union practically runs the shipyard. All the workers are required to pay union dues, including the Negro workers who aren't even allowed to join the union." She paused. "Who knows why they let us Spanish speakers join. Maybe they see us as less dangerous."

"Really?" Gabi said. "The Negroes have no union but still have to pay?"

"Yeah, it's not right," Elena said, shaking her head. "They have a separate auxiliary union." Ruby Mae had told her about it. Not the same benefits, but it was better than nothing.

Elena couldn't fix the whole unfair system, but at least she could help translate. Papá had always reminded her that one small step led to the next one.

Ana and Marisol walked in front, arm in arm, as they arrived at the house. She envied the two cousins, lucky to have each other. Her own little sister and brother were growing up without Elena. Her heart ached, missing them so. Their occasional letters only magnified their absence.

Marisol led them inside. The house smelled like fresh lemons, and there was a plate of iced cookies on the coffee table. Elena picked up a note next to the plate, written in Mrs. Murphy's careful cursive.

Hola señoritas,

Estoy en la escuela hasta las tres de la tarde. How's my Spanish so far? You have been good teachers. Please leave me your ration cards. I will go shopping at the market and make you a nice dinner tonight. Mr. Murphy has his bowling game, so I welcome your company.

Hasta luego,

Mrs. M.

Elena showed the note to her roommates and they all laughed.

"She is very kind to us," Marisol said. "Just not the best cook."

Mrs. Murphy liked to put them to work chopping vegetables, while she helped Ana and Marisol with their English, coaxing them to practice with her, even after a full day teaching at the high school. It usually went like this:

Mrs. Murphy: "Repeat after me. I am hungry for dinner. I hope we will have chicken and baked potatoes."

Ana: "Yes, and I hope we have cake and ice cream también." Then she'd giggle and Mrs. Murphy would make a face, like she'd found one of her students reading a comic book during class.

Marisol: "And I hope we have alcohol. *Mucho* alcohol." She and Ana would crack up while Mrs. Murphy shook her head, pretending she was upset, but she had a smile on her lips. Elena figured she must be lonely for adult conversation, since Mr. Murphy's job as a policeman kept him working long, unpredictable hours. Elena rarely saw him, which was a relief. He basically ignored her and the cousins.

Their landlady was a good baker, but her dinners were too bland. Elena had offered to teach her how to use the spices she loved from home. Not just garlic but ancho and guajillo chiles, achiote, and roasted pumpkin seeds. She'd been so excited when she'd found a Mexican market down in Oakland that sold them. Shopping there on her day off had become a weekly habit, pulling up memories of meals she helped Mamá cook, scenting the kitchen as the flavors blended on the stove, the achiote paste staining their fingers a dark orange as they worked it into the masa for tamales or filled the meat pupusas.

"Save me some cookies, amiguitas," Elena said now. "I promised Gabi I'd help get her union card. It's too late for me to shower and change. I better hurry. Last time I went down there, we had to wait two hours, until someone told us we needed paperwork from the shipyard before they'd issue the card. Qué feo, no?"

Marisol picked up a cookie and handed it to her. "Here. Take one now, just in case we eat them all." She laughed and squeezed Elena's shoulder. "You are an angel, helping people like this." She grabbed two more cookies and headed for the stairs. "Vamos, Ana. Time for bed."

"Ay, cállate." Ana glanced at Elena and followed her cousin up the stairs.

By the time Elena got to the union office, it was past 9:00. Gabi paced back and forth on the sidewalk, and kept looking around, frowning.

"Elena," she said, rushing up to her and continuing in Spanish. "I'm so sorry, but I just got called in to work early." She twisted a red bandana in her hands. "They left me a message with my auntie. Something about needing to be screened for disease. I'm scared they will find a reason to send me back to Texas. Or even deport me."

"Oh, no," Elena said. "Well, it's probably nothing serious." She took Gabi's hand. "I think they're worried about tuberculosis coming into the shipyard. Look, I've been to the clinic there and the nurses are pretty nice. You can talk to the lady at the front desk. Diana. She often works the day shift. She's half Mexican."

"I'm sorry you came here for nothing," Gabi said, "but I didn't know how to reach you." Her eyes teared. "My aunt is tired of watching the baby so much. I need to find a better option."

"Don't worry," Elena said. "We can do this later. Maybe something will open up at the childcare center. I'll see you at work and we can figure out another time to meet."

She pulled a pen out of her purse. "Wait, here's the phone number at the house where I live." She wrote down the number and handed it to Gabi. "Call if you need my help." She patted the young mother's arm. "Your little one is lucky to have you. She will learn how to be strong from you."

Gabi nodded and hugged her before she hurried down the street toward the shipyard. Elena watched her leave and wrapped her arms around her chest. So many workers she'd met had uprooted their lives and made the difficult journey here, based only on the promise of a job. No guarantees. No fall back plan.

She checked her watch. Waiting for the bus would be worse than putting one foot in front of the other to cover the half mile home. She stopped at the office of the *Richmond Independent* newspaper to pick up a copy. She'd read it over a cup of tea and breakfast, fry up one of the fresh eggs Mrs. Murphy bought from a local farmer. Then she'd nap on the couch until Ana or Marisol woke up and left one of the beds empty. Two beds for the three of them worked best when their shifts at the yard were staggered. At least the couch was pretty comfortable and neither of the Murphys would be home until later in the afternoon.

When she got home, she slipped off her work boots near the front door and realized she'd sleep better out of her dirty coveralls. The house was quiet. The cousins were already asleep. Her pajamas hung on a peg in their bedroom. Maybe she could just tiptoe up and grab them without waking her friends. Maybe even take a shower, use the oatmeal soap that smelled like roses. Breakfast could wait until she'd cleaned off the grime.

The door to the bedroom was closed, and she heard something on the other side, like someone moaning in their sleep. She opened the door as quietly as she could, and heard a gasp from inside. Light from the hallway illuminated two naked female bodies wrapped around each other on top of the quilt. The other bed stood empty. The cousins. Together? Lovers? She stared at them for a moment, mute, then stepped back and closed the door behind her and ran down the stairs.

Ay, Diós mío. Thoughts raced through her mind. What just happened? Maybe it was something else. What to do? Make a cup of tea, she thought. Manzanilla, what Mamá advised when she was upset, good for the stomach and the nerves. Or maybe a shot of the whiskey Mr. Murphy kept in the cupboard. The floorboards creaked over her head. Definitely time for some whiskey.

* * *

She stood at the kitchen table, her hands clutching the tin of manzanilla, the teakettle behind her shooting steam into the air. The burned skin on her left hand throbbed. Mr. Murphy's bottle of whiskey sat on the counter. Just a small shot. He'd never miss it. She poured a bit of the amber liquid into a glass and chugged it, her throat burning. Outside the window, the fog had rolled in from the bay, dense and uninviting. She considered slipping out the back door before the cousins came downstairs.

Footsteps approached and Ana entered the kitchen, alone.

"Elena, por favor," she said. She'd put on her bathrobe, tied tight. "Please, can we sit down? Let me make the tea." She saw the whiskey bottle and sighed.

"Where's Marisol?" Elena looked towards the hallway.

"She's too upset," Ana said. "She sent me."

Elena sat down, fingers gripping the empty whiskey glass, her neck muscles clenched. "She's upset? What about me?" Whatever was going on, tea wouldn't make things right. "Hand me that bottle." She had so many questions. The image of the two naked cousins together kept scrolling in her head. Incest? Two women? Homosexuals?

Ana hesitated then got herself a glass, poured some whiskey for both of them and sat down at the table. When she put her hand on Elena's, Elena pulled her hand back.

"It's not what you think, Elena." Ana drained her glass.

"Pues, entonces, what is it exactly?" Elena stared out the window at the fog. She couldn't look Ana in the eye. Her body pulsated with the whiskey's heat. She wished she could go back in time to an hour ago and pretend this had never happened.

Ana got up, poured the boiling water into the teapot, and brought two teacups to the table. Manzanilla, made from chamomile flowers, with its familiar woodsy smell, would fix whatever ailed you. But some things weren't easily fixed.

Elena poured herself the first cup, before the steeping flowers grew bitter. She waited, her fingers wrapped around the cup. What was Marisol doing upstairs now? Would she come barging in and make things worse?

"I'm sorry you had to find us like that," Ana said. "We should have told you before now."

"Told me what?" Elena asked. She drank some tea, but the liquid was too hot and burned her tongue. "What kind of family raises cousins like this?"

Ana shook her head. "No, no. Let me start from the beginning. First of all, we're not cousins." She poured her tea and sipped it.

Elena's eyes widened. She put down her teacup. "Well then, what are you exactly?"

Ana's face softened. "We are enamoradas. We're in love," she said, blushing a deep pink. "We wanted to tell you, but we were afraid." She leaned closer. "You've been such a good friend to both of us. We were scared we'd lose you."

Elena's thoughts raced. Oh, so not cousins at all. But two women, in love with each other? Good Catholic girls. Back home that would never be allowed. The church would condemn them.

"What do your families think?" she blurted, imagining her own family's reaction. Mamá would clutch the gold cross that hung around her neck and sob. Papá would shake his head and then give her one of his stern lectures, about the dangers of committing a mortal sin in a country where a corrupt government would use any excuse to "disappear" a citizen.

Ana sighed. "Our families? They don't *think* at all. They only judge us. They go to church and pray for our souls." She shook her head. "One of my brothers threatened Marisol. And me. We had to leave."

Elena remembered the two old men who had shared an apartment in her neighborhood. They'd seemed like a couple, though they never held hands or kissed. She would see one or the other man at the mercado or sitting together on a bench in the zócalo, reading the newspaper her father published. They would smile when she passed by, but never engaged in conversation with her beyond "Buenos días." The boys on her block used to make jokes about the men. Called them names, cruel epithets. Maricón. Culero. One day one of the men disappeared. There were rumors of course, involving la policía, but no one ever knew what happened to him. The other man had moved away soon afterwards.

She shook her head and looked at Ana. "You should go to church and confess. Marisol, too. It's not too late. God will absolve you, and then you can start over." She drank some tea, her tongue raw. "I don't think I can be your friend until then." Ana and Marisol were the closest thing she had to family here. Tears welled up and rolled onto her cheeks.

"Ay, Elena. Please." Ana stood up and walked over to the window. The fog had started to burn off, patches of the sky a brilliant blue. "We're still the same people we were yesterday." She turned back from the window. "We've done nothing wrong. We just love each other."

"For how long?" Elena thought about those old men.

Ana smiled. "For a year now. We met through friends. That's all we were at first. Good friends. And then we fell in love. It just happened."

Elena sat back in her chair. Her tongue pressed against her front teeth, stinging where the tea had burned her. She knew what the church taught, could hear Father Jorge back home urging them to resist temptations of the flesh. Women were meant to be with men. To honor God by creating children. Period.

She stood up. "I feel like you tricked me. Like I don't really know you." She wiped her damp cheeks. "I don't know if I can trust you again."

Ana walked over to her and gingerly put her hand on Elena's shoulder.

"We all have secrets," Ana said. "Things we won't speak out loud."

"What are you talking about?" Elena stepped back and her hand brushed against the teacup on the table, tipping it over. A thin puddle of pale green tea dribbled out. She dabbed at it with a napkin. She had never spoken to anyone about what happened to her the night Papá was arrested. No one knew except those who were there, and they were far away. And one of them might be dead.

She walked unsteadily toward the living room. "I just need to lie down and sleep. But now, where am I supposed to do that? I can't sleep in that room." Her tongue felt thick in her mouth. "Do whatever you want. Just leave me alone."

She wished she could slip into her flannel nightgown and bury herself under the quilt upstairs. But instead she climbed onto the couch and pulled the crocheted coverlet around her. Her coveralls rubbed against her skin, and the couch's pillow was hard and too small. Nothing felt right. Now she'd have to move. Make new friends. When she heard footsteps moving up the stairs, she covered her ears and closed her eyes.

"Elena?" Marisol's voice was close. Oh God, now she had to deal with her, too.

Elena opened her eyes. "What?" She sat up on the couch, holding onto the coverlet. She did not want this conversation.

Marisol stood in the doorway a few feet away, her arms crossed. "So, are you going to tell Mrs. Murphy?"

Elena stared at her. "Am I what?" It hadn't occurred to her to do that. She was still dealing with her own confused feelings.

"Look," Marisol said, taking one step forward. Elena couldn't tell if she was just scared or angry. Probably both, judging by her strained expression. "Don't tell her. Ana and I will find a new place. Give us a little time, okay?"

Oh. Maybe she wouldn't have to move out. They could leave.

She nodded, feeling a wave of sadness wash over her. "Okay. And I wasn't about to tell her." She tugged the coverlet tighter.

Marisol looked at her. "I told Ana you wouldn't be able to accept the truth about us. I was right." She turned and walked up the stairs.

Elena stared at the doorway, then lay back down. This wasn't her fault. She hadn't caused this mess. But now her whole world had been upended again.

CHAPTER 12

July 7, 1944

Ruby Mae checked her reflection in the mirror of the ladies' room at Tappers' Inn.

"Lookin' good, girl," she said out loud, thankful to be alone. She applied a fresh coat of the deep red Heart's Delight lipstick she'd bought at Woolworth's. Momma would not approve, but then Momma would not approve of anything about this night.

The dress she'd borrowed from Marcy, with its fitted waistline and bright red flowers set on a black background, complemented her curves. Her friend had promised the dress would fit. The green wool skirt and white blouse she'd dressed in back at the trailer now lay folded in a brown paper shopping bag at her feet. She would change back into those clothes before she left the club. Momma would never know.

The restroom was softly lit, a small vase of daisies nested on the counter next to the sinks. Daddy had promised to get them out of their trailer soon, into a place with running water and a toilet, but meanwhile they made do with a washtub for bathing, the water heated on the wood stove. They used an outhouse for their business. This room felt luxurious.

She blotted her lips and patted her hair into place. She'd scanned the dining room for Freddy when she'd arrived but hadn't seen him. He was late and she hoped he'd only missed the bus, not changed his mind. Tonight was their first time out by themselves, and she'd promised Peggy to be back to the church in time to walk home together. Home by 10:00, they'd told Momma. Poor Peggy stuck in Bible study. Freddy had offered to bring a friend for Peggy tonight, but Peggy had said no. She was fine on her own. Later, Peggy had confided to her that she didn't want to get involved with a sailor, or any man who might be killed in the war. Besides, the men she'd met out here were not as polite as the Louisiana gentlemen back home. Ruby Mae didn't buy it. Peggy was plain scared of men.

Music and clouds of cigarette smoke surrounded her as she walked towards the dining room of the inn. Freddy stood inside the entrance, wearing his dark blue uniform and fidgeting with his sailor's cap. His face brightened when he spotted her and he hurried over.

"There you are," he said. "I was worried you gave up on me." His eyes lingered on her dress. "Sorry I'm late. There was some trouble at the base. And then the bus took forever." He touched her elbow and smiled. "And you, Miss Ruby Mae Taylor, look good enough to eat, as my daddy likes to say."

"Well, I don't know about that," Ruby Mae said. Now that she was finally alone with him, her old worries reared up. Don't talk too much. Don't make a fool of yourself. What if he wasn't as sweet as he seemed? She had a bad habit of trusting the wrong men. "What kind of trouble?"

Freddy took her elbow. "I'll tell you after we get us a table. I'm starved. I been smelling all kinds of goodness from the kitchen. Onions frying, maybe in bacon fat and some kind of meat roasting. Mm . . ."

They walked into the spacious dining room, where the hostess led them to a table, past couples and groups gathered around tables loaded with tempting dishes. Each table held a tea candle and a small vase with a single rose. Definitely a step up from the barbecue joints she knew back home. The waitress, an older woman whose graying hair framed her tired face, brought menus and recited the daily special, pot roast and a baked potato.

Ruby Mae studied the menu, surprised that the prices were reasonable. Having that first fat paycheck of her own made her feel like a queen. She ordered roasted chicken and mashed potatoes with greens and a Coke. Freddy chose the special, with green beans and a pot of coffee.

"I swear, Ruby Mae," he said, "I got coffee running in my veins now. Never drank it back home in Chicago, but we get it 24/7 at the base. I'm hooked." He laughed. "That's how they keep us working hard, pouring coffee down our throats."

"So what happened today?" She hoped she looked less nervous than she felt. At least he couldn't see her heart jumping under her ribs.

Freddy took a sip of water. "We got these officers pushing us to work faster. Today one of the big ammo shells slipped out of a guy's hands when he was loading it onto the ship."

"Oh Lord," she said. "Did it explode?"

He shook his head. "We were lucky. It bounced off the dock and fell into the water. But he got yelled at for being careless." He fiddled with his fork. "We all know the work we doin' ain't safe. An accident waiting to happen."

"Well, I'm sure glad you didn't get hurt." She glanced around the room. "And I'm glad we get to eat at places like this, and . . ." She looked at her lap. "And I'm happy to be here."

Once their plates arrived, they dug in and let the piped-in music and nearby conversations fill the space while they ate. She needed a break from trying so hard to impress him, as long as she didn't spill gravy on Marcy's dress. Freddy paused, knife and fork in hand, and watched her.

"I swear, I do like to see a gal enjoy her food," he said.

Her cheeks flushed. Was he making fun of her? Peggy once said she ate like a pregnant sow. She put down her fork and wiped her mouth with the cloth napkin.

"I guess I'm done now." There was still a drumstick on her plate and a small hill of potatoes. She'd devoured the greens first. Leaving food on her plate would kill her. Momma had taught them to always finish every bite. The Lord had provided his bounty and only He knew when their next meal might come. "Yeah, I'm pretty full," she lied.

"Really?" he said. "You looked like you could keep going. Do you mind if I finish that drumstick? Don't want to waste it." He hunched his shoulders. "In our family, we always had to clean our plates. Sometimes my brother and me would slip a carrot or soggy squash under the table to Scruffy, our dog. He'd eat anything."

That earned him points, a member of the clean plate club. She gave him her plate and watched him eat the drumstick with his hands. When he was done, he dabbed some water from his glass with a napkin and wiped his fingers.

"Tell me more about you, Ruby Mae. What are you working on at the shipyard?"

At least that was something she could brag about. He listened and nodded while she told him about the details of riveting, how much she enjoyed doing her job. "Helping our men fight this war, building the ships to keep them safe. I never did work that mattered before. Lord knows I'm lucky to have this job."

"Yeah, I know what you mean," he said. "But I should be out there on one of those ships. That's why I signed up for the Navy. Not to do this grunt work. All that training I got in boot camp is wasted." He frowned. "Tell you the truth, Ruby Mae, every morning I wake up in my bunk, and wish I'd never enlisted. I don't want to die loading ammo onto a ship they won't let me sail on." He looked down. "Sorry to lay this on you, but that's how I feel."

She reached across the table and took his hand.

"Listen, Freddy Parker," she said, "you can tell me anything. In fact I'm glad you did. I don't blame you for being frustrated. And scared."

The waitress came over then and cleared their plates.

"How 'bout some dessert for you two lovebirds?" She smiled, and Ruby Mae realized she still held Freddy's hand in hers. She inched her hand away, but he held on and squeezed her fingers.

"If you have a slice of pie, I think we'd like that," he said, looking at Ruby Mae.

"We sure do," the waitress said. "Apple or peach?"

"Peach," Ruby Mae and Freddy said at the same time, and laughed. Nothing better than peach pie. She'd have to remember to take dainty bites.

After the waitress walked away, Freddy let go of Ruby Mae's hand.

"Here's the last thing I'll tell you about my job," he said. "Cause I want to enjoy our time. The truth is, all of us men loading ammo 24/7 know how dangerous it is. The officers don't care if something happens to one of us. We're just the dumb Negro sailors."

He shook his head. "Last week, one of the boxes being loaded off the freight train fell from the hoist. The box caught fire, bullets exploding and scaring us to death." He drank some coffee. "We were lucky they got the fire out fast, but two guys got burned. Another got hit in his leg by a bullet. They blamed the men doing the unloading!"

"Could you switch jobs?"

"I wish," he said. "But look at me. The only place where a Negro man gets treated with respect, where he feels like a real man, is in a place like this." He raised his arm, sweeping his hand around the dining room. "With his brothers and sisters. Out there at the Navy depot or the shipyard, they see us like some kind of work animal. No better than a mule, too stupid to do more than follow basic orders."

Ruby Mae's eyes burned. His words rang true. Most of the bosses at the shipyard weren't much better. She was lucky to have Mr. Graham.

The waitress arrived with a large slice of pie and two forks. A big scoop of vanilla ice cream sat on top.

"I figured you wanted it à la mode," she told them.

Ruby Mae stared at the plate. The waitress had somehow shaped the ice cream into a smooth glistening heart. The pie and its sculpted heart were about the most romantic thing she'd ever seen.

"Oh my Lord." Freddy burst out laughing. He had such a nice deep voice and his laughter reminded Ruby Mae of her daddy, who laughed with his whole body. "Ain't that somethin'?" He handed her a fork and winked. "You too full to help me eat this pie, Ruby Mae?"

"Well," she said, "I s'pose I got room for a few bites." She waited, figured she'd only take a bite after Freddy had taken two. Two for him, one for her pretend-full self. And don't drip ice cream on the dress. She looked up at the clock on the wall. 7:45.

"You know, Ruby Mae, with you sitting here, looking so pretty, and after all that good food, I'm feeling mighty lucky," Freddy said. "I hope I didn't talk too much about work."

Either he was a real good con man, or he was talking with his heart wide open. She wished she had a Bible handy. She'd slap his hand on top and make him swear he was telling her the truth, so help him God.

"Listen, Freddy," she said, "I'm gonna need to leave by 8:30. Peggy'll be waiting for me at church. Bible study. Momma don't know 'bout this."

He nodded and cut into the pie and forked some of the ice cream heart on top.

"Here, you take the first bite," he said, reaching across the table. "Tell me how it is."

She opened her mouth and tasted the fresh peaches and the cold vanilla creaminess and cinnamon and the flaky piecrust. A small moan escaped her lips as she chewed. "So good, it'd be a sin not to eat it all."

When they were done, Freddy paid the bill and insisted on escorting her back to meet up with Peggy. The church was a fifteen-minute walk away, and she was glad for the extra time with him. Outside the club, the sunset lingered, the sky traced with bits of pale orange and lavender clouds. She'd planned on changing her clothes at the inn, but now with Freddy next to her, she carried the paper bag of clothing on one side, and let him drape his arm around her shoulders. Night blooming jasmine scented the air. It was all a little too much.

"You crying, Ruby Mae? What's wrong?"

She wiped her cheek. "I'm sorry. I ain't usually much of a crier," she said. "I feel like I got split open tonight. Like my heart hurts and feels good at the same time."

He faced her, lifted her chin, and gently kissed her lips. Her eyes closed.

"There. I been wanting to do that all night," he said, his voice husky. "Hope that was okay."

She opened her eyes and looked up at him. "Yeah. Do it again." This time she kissed him back. Warmth flooded her body. A perfect ending. Nothing could ruin this night. As soon as they reached the church, she'd slip inside real quick, change back into her skirt and grab Peggy for the walk home. Momma would never know.

CHAPTER 13

RACHEL

July 7, 1944

By the time Rachel got off the bus and walked up the steep hill of Mandana Boulevard to her family's house, the summer sun had risen over the treetops. Nearly 8:00 a.m., the beginning of a new day, but for her, almost bedtime. Working nights still felt surreal, like swimming upstream against the normal current of everyday life. Luckily, one of the evening shift nurses had asked Rachel to switch shifts starting in two weeks.

She wanted to talk to Mama or Papa about Chrissy, that horrible woman on the bus yesterday, but her parents would be busy getting ready to start their days. As she opened the front door, she smelled onions frying. Mama was already cooking, getting food ready for Shabbat dinner that night. Their talk would have to wait.

"Hi, I'm home," she called, and dropped her bag and jacket on the leather couch in the living room. Bending over to unlace her clunky nursing shoes, she felt a twinge in her lower back. When the clinic got busy, she helped patients onto exam tables without thinking how to protect herself from injury. *"Use your legs, ladies, when you lift something heavy, not your back."* Her old nursing instructor's frequent caution. A bad habit she needed to break, along with skipping her mid-shift meal. Low blood sugar led to careless mistakes.

"Come sit down, honey." Her mother's voice from the kitchen made her smile. "I'll fix you some breakfast before you climb into bed." Mama was happiest when she had an apron tied around her waist, fussing over the seasoning of her pot roast or nibbling the batter of a new cookie recipe. Her latest idea was to put together a cookbook for housewives like herself, one with recipes using very little of rationed ingredients like butter or sugar. Mama hoped to donate the cookbook's proceeds to the Red Cross.

"Smells great in here." Rachel stepped close to Mama and gave her a gentle hug. Her faded floral apron had belonged to Rachel's grandma. Mama's gray-streaked black hair had been pulled off her neck into a loose bun. "What enormous meal are you planning?" She picked a caramelized onion out of the spoon in Mama's hand. "Who's coming, besides The Regulars?"

Mama pushed her hand away. "There's coffee, still warm. I was able to get some with my coupons yesterday. A little sugar, too. I had to wait in line for almost an hour."

She looked at Rachel. "No, I forgot. You're headed to bed, so coffee's out. I don't know how you manage these hours. Your father used to fall asleep at the table when he was in training. And we'll be six tonight, if your father's able to get out of surgery on time. Uncle Max and Aunt Pearl and your favorite cousin."

They both laughed. She only had one cousin living close by, Gordon, and he was one of the most irritating young men she'd ever met. He'd been kept out of the draft due to severe asthma, and now worked for the Santa Fe Railroad coordinating freight deliveries to military bases all over the Bay Area. But by the way he boasted, you'd think he manned the front lines of combat.

"Well then, Mama, your chopped liver better be pretty darn good, so my mouth is full when he starts driving me crazy." And if she really wanted to shut him up, she knew how to rattle him. Gordon hated being teased.

"Oh, here's my girl." Papa swept into the room, already wearing his white doctor's coat over a blue collared shirt and striped tie. "How'd your shift go?" He poured coffee into his thermos.

Papa enjoyed hearing about her clinic work at the shipyard, and would sometimes suggest other ways to treat a certain condition. Lately he had started quizzing her about cases that he'd seen at the hospital, even illustrating on scratch paper the medical oddities that required a surgical repair. Like the large and ominous-looking tumor growing on the side of a young woman's neck that turned out to be a benign calcified cyst, not cancer after all.

"It wasn't too bad last night." She sat down at the kitchen table and yawned. "There was one gruesome case I'll tell you about later, when Mama's not listening." The house rules. Eating and explicit bloody details of the operating room did not mix. But for Rachel, these discussions with her father were a treat, a chance to prove herself.

Before Jesse had enlisted, he had been the one to sit with Papa and talk about the fascinating cases at the hospital. Jesse's summer job as an orderly had been Papa's idea, a first glimpse of the world ahead of him once he graduated from Cal and started med school. The war had put everything on hold for him, and she'd taken his place as Papa's eager student.

"But honestly, Papa," she said, "I'm tired of seeing injuries that could have been prevented. There's so much pressure to finish building the ships quickly. I know we're all trying to give our boys what they need as soon as possible, but these workers are suffering terribly."

She sighed and picked up the small loaf of challah that sat on the table next to a larger loaf, both sprinkled with poppy seeds and shiny from an egg wash. Always the extra small loaf for nibbling. Mama must have gotten up before dawn to bake, or stayed up really late to prep the dough. Insomnia had stalked the family since Jesse had gone overseas with his unit. Mama's solution was to keep busy in the kitchen, no matter the hour. Papa and Rachel never objected to her efforts.

The bread was still warm and fragrant. "Okay if I take a little piece?"

Mama put a plate with a scrambled egg and sliced tomatoes in front of her. "You'd bite my hand if I tried to stop you. No butter to be had, though. And you'll have to share that with your father."

"Not today," Papa said, kissing Mama on the cheek and squeezing Rachel's shoulder. "I've got an early case and need to get on the road. But I hope to be back in time to see you light the candles tonight." He inhaled. "Mm, maybe just a bite." He leaned over and grabbed the small challah from Rachel and tore off a piece. He winked at her and left out the back door.

While she ate breakfast, she watched Mama work at the counter, chopping up the hardboiled egg and fried chicken liver and onions. What looked like an apple strudel sat cooling near the kitchen window. No one cooked liked Mama. On Shabbat they ate like kings, and then the rest of the week Mama found a way to make what she found in the market taste interesting despite the rationing.

"Any news from Jesse?" She studied her mother's back and watched it stiffen. The challah and egg tasted divine.

"No," Mama answered. "We listened to the morning news and they talked about the Allies advancing through France. I wish we knew where he was exactly. I hate thinking of him out there, too close to the front."

She didn't turn around, just continued chopping the liver, onions, and eggs into a chunky paste, adding salt and pepper, tasting until she was satisfied. "There." After she scooped it into a bright orange Fiesta ware bowl and into the refrigerator, she turned to Rachel. A tear trickled down her cheek, and she brushed it off, as if annoyed by a fly. "Go up to bed, sweetheart. What time do you want me to wake you?"

Rachel got up and put her plate in the sink. Out the back window she spotted a red-winged blackbird perched on a branch of the oak tree in the backyard. His trilled call sounded mournful.

"I'll use my alarm clock, Mama. Maybe you can take a nap, too, before they arrive. I'll set the table and do whatever you need once I'm up." She planted a kiss on Mama's cheek.

The phone rang in the hallway as she passed by, and she answered, hoping it wasn't for her. But it was Bertie, her best friend, confirming their shopping date on Sunday. Now that Macy's had expanded their hours, accommodating the needs of evening and night shift workers, you could visit the department store any time, day or night. The two of them planned to shop in San Francisco for dresses to wear to their friend's wedding.

It was rare for Rachel to have a long weekend off, and she needed to pack in some fun before returning to the clinic on Monday night. Not that she liked shopping for clothes, but at least Bertie would help her find something suitable. Bertie would have a definite opinion, too, on how to respond to the incident on the bus. She knew all about speaking up.

When she was nine, Bertie had contracted polio, and had worn a leg brace since then. Some of the children at school had been cruel. Rachel admired the way her friend had handled the taunts with either a sharp retort or a clever diverting joke. By now Bertie just rolled her eyes and didn't bother responding to insults. But what Rachel had faced on the bus was different; this kind of ignorance and hatred felt evil and needed to be confronted, like some toxic ooze of tar seeping through the ground. Adults spouting prejudice were far more dangerous than insensitive children.

* * *

Gordon and his parents arrived just before 6:00, their arms filled with glass bowls of side salads and jars of pickled cucumbers and carrots Aunt Pearl had offered to bring. She couldn't compete with Mama's cooking, but had mastered the art of pickling the vegetables she grew in her victory garden. Together, the two sisters fed their families well, and Mama usually sent leftovers home with her grateful brother-in-law.

"Boy oh boy, smells great in here, Auntie." Gordon walked into the kitchen and put down his load and kissed Mama, then turned to Rachel. He was over six feet, and tended to stand too close, his breath stale over her head. She took a step back.

"Hey there, cousin," he said, bending towards her. She let him hug her for a moment and moved away before he tried to kiss her, too. No thanks.

"Hi Gordy," she said, smiling to herself. He disliked the childhood nickname.

"Gordon. Remember? I don't call you Ray-Ray anymore, do I?"

Ignoring him, she greeted her aunt and uncle, offering them some wine. She opened a bottle and poured each a healthy glassful. When Gordon held out his glass she gave him half as much. He frowned but said nothing. Gordon drunk was twice as obnoxious.

"Let's go sit in the living room," she said. "Mama's still got a few things to finish up in here."

Mama smiled, looking grateful to get them out of her kitchen. She'd already taken the chicken out of the oven, letting it rest before carving. They were lucky to have their backyard garden and lemon tree to grow what they needed, including garlic and rosemary that added lots of flavor.

"So, tell us more about your job at the shipyard," Uncle Max said, settling onto the couch. He owned a floorcovering store downtown, and thought that caring for sick or injured people was noble but unpleasant work he'd never want his son to pursue. Owning a business meant a solid future, and there was always a need for new carpeting or linoleum. Gordon would take over in due time, after the war had been won.

"Well, it's like its own world out there," Rachel said. "So big. Every shift has several thousand workers, all focused on getting the next ship built as fast as possible. Accidents happen all the time. The clinic stays very busy." She avoided the gory details, not with this group.

Once, when they were kids, their families had picnicked out at Neptune Beach in Alameda before the amusement park had closed. She and Jesse and Gordon had walked down the beach together looking for shells and buried treasure. They'd stumbled onto an injured seagull, its wing bent at an unnatural angle as it lay on its side, its thick white feathers stained crimson.

She and Jesse had bent down to examine the bird, while Gordon had recoiled and rushed back to the picnickers. Her father, summoned to the site, had been the one to pronounce the seagull dead and then disposed of the body. Gordon, distraught and wheezing, had retreated to his mother's lap. Then, after using his inhaler, he had thrown up on the picnic blanket, close to the food they were about to eat.

Gordon leaned forward on the couch and put down his glass. "Our boys need those ships, Ray-Ray. I'm sure the workers want to help." He shook his head. "I know that my freight orders with all the munitions headed to the Port Chicago base get top priority on the rail schedules. They depend on me to get the job done. And I do a damn good job."

He was such a pain in the neck, acting like the boss of the US Navy. Admiral Gordon T. Blowhard. She took a big swallow of wine and excused herself to help Mama get dinner on the table. Papa had called on his way out of the hospital and would be home soon.

Rachel placed the vegetables on the dining room table next to the unlit Sabbath candles and covered challah. For most Shabbat dinners she and Gordon sat across from each other. Tonight she'd see if she could swap seats with Aunt Pearl.

By the time Papa got home, Rachel had cooled down and promised herself she'd hold her tongue at the table. When they all were seated, Mama stood close to the two candles, lit them, and held her hands in front of her closed eyes and said the blessing. After the prayer over the bread, Mama passed around the loaf of challah and everyone tore off pieces as Papa carved the chicken with quick, precise strokes.

"Careful, Uncle Paul, I think that chicken only needed his liver removed," Gordon said, laughing hard while the others rolled their eyes. He was so predictable. If Jesse had been there, she'd have kicked her brother under the table. He'd have been more patient with his cousin, maybe even forced a little laugh. Not me, Rachel thought. I am not in the mood for his foolishness. But Gordon kept talking and refilled his wine glass. The platter of chicken and the bowls of vegetables were passed around and everyone began to eat.

"You should see those boys," Gordon said, "loading ammo on the pier at Port Chicago, Uncle Paul. I drove out there to see for myself. They haul it off the freight cars, box after box of bombs and shells, and stack them onto those victory ships day and night. The sailors—Negro boys—are so grateful to have the job." He drank some wine and wiped his mouth. "The officers, *of course*, are white. I saw them betting on whose team could load the fastest. It's dangerous work, but the boys don't mind. Better than picking cotton back home."

Rachel couldn't take anymore. She gulped some wine.

"Well, speaking of ignorance," she said, pointing her fork at her cousin, "I had something awful happen on my way to work." What was she doing? Mama and Papa both stared at her. "It was very upsetting. Maybe one of you can help." God, she'd lost her mind, asking her family for advice. She just wanted Gordon to shut up.

Everyone put down their forks and looked at her. Shabbat dinner usually was a time for good will and pleasant conversation, not upsetting stories. She took another swallow of wine and described her conversation with Chrissy, the welder on the bus, and then her shock when Chrissy referred to "those dirty Jews", that she hadn't known how to respond.

Gordon leaned forward. "You know, Ray-Ray, it's best to ignore those kinds of comments. Pretend you didn't hear what she'd said. Nobody needs to know you're Jewish. Just try to blend in. That's what I do." He sat back and sipped his wine.

She noticed Uncle Max and Aunt Pearl nodding. Mama looked uncomfortable but said nothing. Papa stood up.

"I can't believe you, Gordon," he said, frowning. "I'm proud of being Jewish. I don't hide it. There were only a few Jewish men in my med school class. We faced some cruel comments from classmates and from hospital staff, even from patients." He looked at Rachel. "It's our responsibility to stand up to prejudice. Look at Europe to see what happens when you don't."

He shook his head and sat down. Rachel was about to respond when Mama suddenly smacked the table with her palm, jostling the wine glasses.

"Here's what I think." Mama's sharp tone surprised Rachel. "That shipyard has so many workers who've arrived from all over the country. Some of them will be ignorant or racist or antisemitic. That's how it is. Rachel, honey, you're there to do your job, like everyone else. Just focus on that. Don't stir up more trouble for yourself." Mama got up and started to clear the plates, but Rachel put her hand on her mother's arm.

"Mama, stop. We're not done eating." She looked around the table at her family. "I think Papa's right. I do need to do something. I'm not sure what, but if I do nothing about what that welder said, it feels like I'm condoning her prejudice. It reminds me of Rabbi Hillel when he said, 'If I am not for myself, who will be for me? If I am not for others, what am I? If not now, when?'"

Her heart pounded. The wine had made her lightheaded. How many other workers at the shipyard felt like Chrissy? What would happen if she confronted Chrissy at work, if she could even find her? Or was there something bigger she could do to make more of an impact?

She looked again at her family. "Now, let's finish eating so we can have some of Mama's dessert." And Gordon and his weak-kneed parents would finally go home.

CHAPTER 14

ELENA

July 7, 1944

Elena woke up in the living room hearing the front door open and the *click-click* of Mrs. Murphy's heels on the hardwood floor. She must have finally slept after tossing and squirming to get comfortable on the couch. Grabbing a copy of *Life* off the coffee table, she pulled her tangled hair off her face. The pain from her burn felt worse.

"Oh, you're down here," Mrs. Murphy said, walking into the room, her arms wrapped around a cloth grocery bag. The light blue shirtwaist dress complimented her blue-green eyes and pale skin. Teacher attire, but her narrow-heeled navy shoes were fancier than any teacher's back home. Salvadoran teachers barely earned enough to put food on the table, and their one pair of shoes was usually black and thick-soled.

"Buenas tardes, Señora. It must be afternoon if you're home already." Elena stood up and stretched. "I must have fallen asleep here reading." She had no intention of talking to her landlady about what had happened. Not until she figured out what to do about it.

"Yes, buenas tardes to you. It's almost 4:00. I stopped by the market on my way home and picked up some half-decent fixings for dinner. I'm hoping you girls plan on joining me." She put the bag of groceries down and pulled out a bunch of fat leeks.

"I'm in the mood to make my grandma's soup recipe. May she rest in peace back in her beloved Ireland." She made the sign of the cross. "Potato and leek, though I wasn't able to get any butter. I'll add extra onions and seasoning to keep it flavorful. Have you ever eaten a leek?"

"No, but it looks like a *gigante* onion," Elena said, laughing. Chatting with Mrs. Murphy almost made her feel like things were normal in the house. She listened for signs of life upstairs, but it was quiet. Just as well, since she wasn't ready to face her friends.

They still *were* her friends, weren't they? After a few months living in the same house, walking or riding the bus to work together, even sharing lunches with Ana and Marisol, they had become a big part of her life here. Could she accept their relationship and still be friends?

"Are you okay, my dear?" Mrs. Murphy frowned. "You've got this tortured look on your face. Is it your hand?"

"Oh, lo siento. I just remembered a bad dream I had. Must be from sleeping on the couch," she lied.

No matter how upset she felt, the part of her that remained a loyal friend did not want to jeopardize the other girls' living situation. Mrs. Murphy and her husband, the policeman, would insist they move out if they learned the two were lovers. Devout Catholics, their landlords would evict the not-cousins without any regret. Elena was sure of this.

But there was another option. What if *she* decided to move out and find another room? Now that she had saved a good bit of money from her months at the shipyard, she might find a room of her own, something she'd longed for since she was a child. Such a thing would have been impossible in San Salvador, her family crammed into their small apartment, she and her sister, Lupe, in one bed, her parents in the other, her brother Guillermo, restless on the child-size mattress he'd outgrown.

"Well, I need a shower," she said. "I have to go down to the union hall on an errand, but I should be back in time for supper, by 6:30 at the latest." She hesitated. "I don't know about the others."

"Oh, I hope they'll be hungry, too," Mrs. Murphy said. "I splurged and got a few small sausages to have along with the soup. I'll bake some rolls. Mr. Murphy has to work late tonight and I do hate to eat alone. It's been a treat to have you girls here. Estoy muy contenta," she added, smiling. "See how much Spanish I've learned?" She picked up her grocery bag and walked into the kitchen. Bueno, not so *contenta* if she found out the truth about her tenants.

Once Elena had climbed the stairs, she held her breath and knocked on the door to their shared bedroom, not her usual practice. When there was no response, she opened the door to discover that the room was empty, both beds neatly made, no sign of the girls. They must have gone out while she slept. She exhaled and got out of her dirty coveralls and into the shower. It would be easier if she could leave the house before they returned.

Elena hadn't lied about going down to the union hall, she had simply left out the reason: to check out housing options. Whether she moved out of the Murphys' house or the other two left, something had to change. If she found an available room now, she could see it in the morning and, if she liked the place, announce her leaving tomorrow night. This plan helped her feel less desperate, although she had to admit her mood alternated between feeling angry then resentful then sad that any of them had to move. She had felt so comfortable.

According to the local newspaper, new housing was being built as fast as possible to accommodate the huge number of shipyard workers arriving in Richmond. But many of the new units were reserved for families with young children. Well, maybe someday that would be her, but for now, she'd settle for some place clean and quiet, with no surprises.

* * *

When she arrived at the Boilermakers' Union Hall downtown, it was hopping. In the back of the central meeting room, she spotted several workers from the yard, gathered in folding chairs, having a heated conversation. Curious, her reporter instincts kicked in and she wandered over to the group. Papá had trained her how to sniff out a story.

All in the group were women, and from the sound of it, they were not discussing favorite recipes or movie star gossip. They were talking about their jobs. She stepped closer.

"Okay if I join you?" She pulled an empty chair into the circle and sat down, making it hard for them to say no.

"Yeah, sure. The more the merrier, right, gals?" The speaker was an older welder she recognized named Shirley, with graying curly hair. "We're trying to figure out how to deal with all the crap at work, pardon my French. Things are getting worse, if you ask me. You know, the men act like they can get away with anything. The grabbing, the sexual jokes, rubbing against us when we're working." Elena thought about Marisol's upsetting encounter. Not an isolated incident.

"It's a game for them," Shirley continued, "but we didn't sign up for that. We just want to do our jobs and be left alone." She looked around at the others. "So, ladies, anyone got some good ideas on what we can do?"

"Yeah, I do," said a short, stocky woman dressed in blue jeans and a faded work shirt. "Kick 'em in the balls. Always works for me. Shuts 'em right up." She sat back and laughed.

Elena caught her breath, but the rest of the group laughed, too, nodding.

"I wish," said another woman, sighing. "You know we'd be out on our ear the minute we tried to fight back. Last hired, first fired. There are plenty of other workers looking for jobs, ready to jump over our sorry selves. We need to find a way that protects us and keep our jobs, too."

"Here's what I think." Shirley stood up and began to pace. A few other women had wandered over and stood close, listening. "We need to stick together. Get a buddy whenever you need to move around the yard. Someone who'll be your witness. Makes it easier to speak up if there are two of you." Elena agreed, but that wasn't enough.

"And keep notes on every incident, so there'll be a record of the date and time and what happened," added someone else.

"What about the union?" Elena asked. The women looked at her. "Isn't that why we pay them our dues, so they can protect us at work?"

Back home she'd seen how the labor unions had helped workers win better conditions in the canning factory. The crew in her area had been all women, so she hadn't experienced troubles like this. Not at the factory itself, anyway. Out on the streets of her city, she'd learned to ignore the catcalls and whistles from men who enjoyed making girls and women uncomfortable with their taunts. But this was different, not feeling safe at the yard while doing dangerous work could be disastrous.

"Well, we need a new union rep," Shirley said, "since the last guy we had just moved back to Fresno to help his parents on their farm. They were shorthanded. Anyone interested in the job?" She looked at Elena. "How about it? It's high time we had a woman representing our interests."

"What? No, thank you," Elena said. "You don't want me. My English is not so good," she added, her heart racing. Taking on that position would make her even more of a target for any boss who resented what the union did.

"Well, one of us should step up, and I'm too old to do it." Shirley said. "But I'm tired of being hassled on the job. Things won't change until we do something about it." She sat down and nodded when the other women clapped and raised their fists.

Elena looked at the group and clenched her fist, too. Maybe she could use her reporting skills to document the harassment, by gathering stories like Marisol's. Power in numbers. An article in the shipyard newsletter. But how could she fight to protect the women at work and yet judge her friends so harshly? They needed her support, too. It couldn't be easy for them to hide the truth.

She glanced at her watch. 6:15 already and Mrs. Murphy expected her home soon. She prayed that Ana and Marisol had made other plans. As for finding a new place to live, that would have to wait until tomorrow. But leaving Mrs. Murphy's home would break her heart.

CHAPTER 15

RUBY MAE

July 7, 1944

Ruby Mae walked with Freddy toward the church, a little breathless, his arm still tucked around her as the summer evening's fog inched closer. Down the block, the Missionary Baptist Church, her family's spiritual home since they'd arrived from Louisiana, held its doors ajar, a narrow shaft of light spilling onto the front steps. Bible study must have ended, Peggy'd be inside tapping her foot. They were late.

A small group huddled outside the church in the dark. Blackout curtains blocked light from the stained-glass windows, so she couldn't make out their faces. Then she froze. A voice rose over the others, angry and all too familiar.

"Oh my God. That's Momma," she whispered, stepping behind a telephone pole. "Well, it's been nice knowing you, Freddy, 'cause you ain't ever gonna see me again. She's gonna kill me."

Freddy laughed. "C'mon, Ruby Mae, she can't be that bad," he said, and took her hand. "I want to meet her. You ain't embarrassed to be seen with me, are you?"

"No, 'course not. That ain't it at all." She glanced at the group, praying Momma hadn't already sensed her presence, like an old bloodhound. Some folks had peeled off, hurrying down the street. Now only two familiar figures remained outside, silhouetted against the fog. Oh no. What had Peggy told Momma? Had she lied to cover for her baby sister? Or had she folded under Momma's questioning, her Bible pressed against her chest, squeezing the truth out of her.

"She ain't gonna leave till I show up," Ruby Mae said. "No use trying to slip away now." She looked up at Freddy. The magic of their evening had dissolved, and tears filled her eyes. "I'm sorry for what you about to hear. In fact, let's say goodbye right here. I would if I was you."

Freddy kissed her cheek. "Let's go meet your scary momma," he said, pulling her towards the church. When they got close, he took his arm off her shoulders and called out, "What a wonderful surprise. You must be Miz Taylor. Ruby Mae never told me she had such a pretty momma." Like he'd practiced his lines. Peggy shot her a look, mouthing, *Sorry.*

He stepped forward, and reached for Momma's hand, brought it to his lips, and grazed it with a soft kiss. "So nice to meet you. I'm Frederick Parker, United States Navy." He pulled off his cap. "I'm stationed at Port Chicago. I've had the great pleasure of meeting both your lovely daughters." He nodded at Peggy, who said nothing, wide-eyed.

"Ruby Mae kept me company for dinner this evening, at my insistence," he continued. Momma stood with her arms crossed, her eyes shooting daggers at Ruby Mae. In one hand Momma held a paper cup full of fragrant popcorn.

Before Momma opened her mouth, Freddy turned to Ruby Mae and winked. Then he turned back. "Today's my birthday, Miz Taylor, and I hated celebrating alone. My family's all back in Chicago. You're lucky to have your whole family out here with you." He bent his arm and offered Momma his elbow. "Would you do me the honor of letting me walk you lovely ladies home?"

Momma stood there, momentarily speechless. Ruby Mae watched her face go through an emotional tug-of-war. Those pinched eyes and clenched jaw fought against the tiniest curve of her lips. Freddy knew his way around women, and Momma looked like she couldn't refuse him. Not that she'd forget how angry she was with Ruby Mae. No, she'd just bottle that up until Freddy was gone. Then she'd explode, like that bottle got all shook up.

"Well, fine," Momma said, frowning. "We headed home right now, so I s'pose you can walk us back." How long would it take for her to pop her top? And what was she doing out there anyway? How late were they?

Freddy linked arms with Momma and coaxed her down the street, leaving Ruby Mae next to Peggy, whose eyes remained wide as dollar pancakes. His charm had dazzled them all.

"I'm sorry, Ruby Mae," Peggy whispered, gripping her sister's arm. "I walked out of our Bible group, and there she was, sipping juice in the hallway. I had to think fast. Told her you were in the restroom. I even got her some popcorn. But after five minutes, she just stormed in there, looking in every toilet stall, calling your name, like you was a kid lost at Woolworth's."

"Now, wait just a minute," Momma called out, her tone harsh. Yes, Ruby Mae thought, the magic of Freddy's words had already faded. "You, young man," Momma added, turning around to face Freddy, "are one smooth talker, that's for sure. But listen, I ain't no country fool, and I don't want you sweet-talking my baby girl. If her daddy was here, I can't say what he'd do, catching you out like this. Now go on home." She glared at Freddy, who nodded and put on his cap.

Momma turned around and walked back to her daughters, leaving him standing alone in the street. He glanced at Ruby Mae, like he didn't know whether to slip away or stay and try again. The night had grown chilly, the fog thick now, its mist wetting their coats and hair.

"I'll just say goodnight to Freddy," Ruby Mae said. "He needs to get back to the base anyway."

"You stay right here," Momma said, grabbing her and handing the popcorn to Peggy.

"You take care, Ruby Mae," he said. "You, too, Peggy. And I'm glad I got to meet you, Miz Taylor." He turned and walked off down the block. The three women stood watching him for a moment until the pastor stepped out of the church and locked the wooden doors behind him. He saw the three of them and hurried over.

"Everything okay, ladies?" he said, looking first at Momma, then at Ruby Mae. "I see you found your daughter." He wagged his finger at her. "Your Momma was mighty worried 'bout you, Ruby Mae. Praise the Lord you ain't hurt."

"Thank you, Pastor," Ruby Mae said, her chest tight. "Momma, I'm sorry. I know you mad." She was really only sorry she'd been caught.

"Amen, Pastor," Momma said. "But no telling what happens when we get home and I tell her daddy what she's been up to. Courtin' the Devil hisself." She held onto Ruby Mae's arm hard enough to make her wince. "Let's get home, girls. We ain't gonna burden the Pastor with our troubles."

Clutching Peggy with her other hand, she marched them down the street in the direction of their trailer. Ruby Mae turned back and peered into the dark night, and sure enough, she made out the lone figure of a sailor with his cap on, standing still and watching them, the fog almost obscuring him.

Momma pulled both girls forward by their arms. "Now move, you two. Your daddy's gonna be worried with me gone so long."

"Here, Momma," Peggy said, her voice falsely cheerful. "You forgot your popcorn." She offered the cup.

Momma reached out and knocked the cup out of Peggy's hand, scattering popcorn onto the ground. "Don't you dare pretend things is fine. You in as much trouble as your sister for lying to me." She shook her head but kept walking. "I don't know what I done wrong. Raised you girls 'cording to the Bible. Now I catch you sneaking around and lying to my face. I s'pose it was bringing us out here from Baton Rouge, letting you girls be tempted by the Devil and his kin. Maybe it's time we packed up and went home."

"But, Momma . . ." Ruby Mae said.

"Don't you say another word, Ruby Mae Taylor," Momma said. "I wish you was little again. I'd put you on my knee and whip your behind."

The muscles in Ruby Mae's backside twitched at the memory of that wooden spoon. The twins still got their lickings that way, not that it kept them down for long. Momma always begged Daddy to use his belt, but he'd only done that once. Told Momma he wasn't cut out for it. Ruby Mae had been barely six. She'd come home from an overnight at her auntie's place, and told Momma that Uncle Melvin was mean and smelled like rotten eggs and she hoped that he got bit by a snake. Momma scolded her, said to take it back.

Momma had made Daddy unclasp the belt from his pants. He only hit Ruby Mae with it once, and when she'd cried out, the leather cutting into her bare thigh, he pushed her off his knee and stood up and walked out, saying, *No, not doing that ever again.* After that, she avoided Uncle Melvin when she could.

* * *

When they got back to the trailer, Momma entered first. Daddy had fallen asleep at the kitchen table, his head down, resting his arms on the checked oilcloth, his lips puffed open with soft snores. Ruby Mae looked into the darkened rear of the trailer where her brothers slept side by side.

Momma pulled her close. "You lucky, girl, that your daddy's sleeping," Momma spoke into her ear. "In the morning, once I get the boys off to school, you and me and Daddy are gonna sit down. You hear me?"

She yanked Ruby Mae's hair back and forced her to look straight at her. "I ain't about to let one of my girls end up pregnant by some sweet-talking sailor boy." She tugged on the handful of hair in her fist. "I mean it. I will pack your bag and send you back to Baton Rouge. Is that what you want? Go back to work cleaning house for that white lady?"

Ruby Mae's eyes watered. "No, Momma." She felt Momma loosen her grip.

"Now get to bed," Momma said, giving her a push toward the mattress. "And no sneaking out of here in the morning, you hear me? And that goes for you, too, Peggy. You part of this."

Peggy nodded and changed into her nightgown, slipping into bed. Ruby Mae struggled out of Marcy's pretty dress and folded it before tucking it into the shopping bag. Her head pounded. She put on pajamas and crawled under the covers next to Peggy. The events of the night raced through her mind like a favorite movie reel gone bad, starting with meeting Freddy at Tappers' Inn, the delicious dinner they'd shared. That ice cream like a heart. Their kisses. Walking back to church in the dark. And then Momma shattering the mood, like a surprise enemy attack.

She wouldn't let Momma's anger ruin everything. The best thing she could do in the morning was let Momma talk, get it out of her system. She promised herself not to talk back, keep her head down. But one thing was very clear: she refused to move back home. Momma couldn't force her. After all, she wasn't a kid anymore, not at nineteen. She'd left her old life behind.

The next morning, Ruby Mae and Peggy sat at the table in the trailer, waiting for Momma. Their shifts at the yard wouldn't start until 3:00. Daddy had hobbled over to a neighbor's trailer to help fix a leak. Not that he could do much with his leg still so bad.

"Listen," Ruby Mae said, "let's let Momma speak her mind. No use trying to reason with her when she's like this." She watched Peggy. "It'll only make things worse."

Peggy picked up a fork, raking the tines across the table. "I didn't do nothin' wrong, sis. 'Cept lie for you. You the one in big trouble."

"Yeah, you right," Ruby Mae said. "But who had more fun last night, huh?" She grinned. "You in your Bible group, bored and fidgety? Or me, being kissed by Freddy and eating peach pie with ice cream in a heart?" She pointed to her chest. "Me. I win. No matter what Momma's got to say."

Peggy's eyebrows shot up. She stabbed the fork in the air toward her sister. "We'll see 'bout that, Miz Peach Pie."

Momma huffed inside, pulling off her jacket, her lips pressed tight.

"So, you girls decided to listen to your momma," she said. "Ain't that something?" She grabbed a chair, pulling it closer to the wood-burning stove. "You eat yet? I don't see no food on the table. You too scared to eat?"

"No, Momma," Peggy said, tightening her grip on the fork. "We been waitin' for you. Want me to cook up some eggs and grits?" Miz Innocent reminding Momma who was the real naughty daughter. Ruby Mae rolled her eyes.

"I done ate with the boys," Momma said, "while you two slept in." She leaned forward. "And when I'm done talking, maybe you won't feel like eating. Here's what I got to say. I been praying about you girls half the night. You ain't kids no more, I know. But sometimes you can lose your way, like in the Bible story, in Luke. The little sheep gets lost and that shepherd has got to go find him. My job, as your momma, is to protect you from danger, like getting hit by a car or being sweet-talked by a handsome sailor boy. Lord knows if I could keep you safe at the shipyard, or anywhere else, I would."

She heaved a big sigh that lifted her chest up and exhaled slowly. "But I can't. So I got to trust you girls to do the right thing. Be careful. Know right from wrong. Stay away from the Devil."

By then, Ruby Mae had to speak up, before Momma got out the Bible and made them read it out loud, starting with that snake in the garden. This was worse than her yelling at Ruby Mae. Peggy squirmed in her chair, like she wanted to crawl out the door.

"Momma, I know you been worrying about us," Ruby Mae said. "Working at the yard on our own, doing some late shifts. We got a whole new life out here, all of us do." She put her hand on Momma's arm, half expecting her to knock it off. Momma looked up at her. "And it *is* dangerous sometimes. But you gotta trust us. Trust me." Her eyes grew wet. "Freddy ain't no Devil. He's a good man, and I'm lucky to find him. I don't like sneaking around, lying to you and Daddy. But things are different now."

Peggy reached out and put her hand on top of Ruby Mae's. Momma held still.

"She's right, Momma," Peggy said. Ruby Mae stared at Peggy. She hadn't expected her sister's support. "Me and Ruby Mae don't want to lie about what we do. You ain't always gonna like it, but don't turn your back on us. You and Daddy raised us just fine." She squeezed her sister's hand. "We'll take care of each other, right, sis?"

Momma hadn't expected this either, judging by the surprise on her face. Momma had confessed how scared she felt for her daughters. Peggy had defended her sister. Ruby Mae felt the unexpected shift in her family the way she imagined an earthquake would feel, kind of unsettling but still standing, and with an unexpected ally at her side.

CHAPTER 16

July 10, 1944

They had finished breakfast, and Mama stood at the sink full of dirty dishes, her apron slipping down one arm, her bangs wispy from the hot water.

"I want you to come to temple with me," Mama said, pointing her soapy finger at Rachel.

"Today?" Rachel felt the muscles in her shoulders stiffen. She leaned her elbows on the kitchen table, nursing her second cup of coffee. The kitchen radio played Benny Goodman's band, the music Mama liked to hear while she cleaned.

Before the war, Mama had only gone to services for the High Holy Days and other special occasions. But she was a practical Jew. Ever since Jesse had been sent overseas, she showed up at temple every Saturday morning, dressed in her pearls and heels and navy linen suit, ready to soak up the Hebrew prayers and Torah reading. In exchange, she expected God to do His part. Keep her son safe.

"When was the last time you set foot in temple anyway?" Mama shook her head. "Maybe for Yom Kippur, last year. That's too long, sweetheart. We all need to pray for our troops. And remind God especially to watch over Jesse." Mama excused Papa's absence from temple; after all, he was busy saving lives every day.

"But Mama," Rachel said, "I promised Papa I'd clean out the garage. The hospital is holding a war drive. They need scrap metal and rubber. And any clothing and blankets we can donate."

She stood up and edged her way toward the back door. Gathering worn tools and broken fixtures that could be melted down into ammunition felt more important than sitting in a hard wooden pew at Temple Sinai, gazing up at the stained glass.

When she'd reached puberty, no one had offered her the chance to be blessed with a bat mitzvah ceremony and party. Only Jewish boys, when they turned thirteen, got to study with the rabbi and read from the Torah in front of the entire congregation. Missing out on that had soured her on religion. If God didn't think she, or any other girl, was worth that effort and celebration, fine. She had quit Hebrew school then, to focus on her music and studies. By the time Jesse stood up on the bema for his bar mitzvah five years later, chanting his Torah portion, the small seed of bitterness in her heart had grown into a sturdy sapling. Going to services during the Holy Days of Rosh Hashanah and Yom Kippur every year felt like a chore done to appease her mother, not a spiritual immersion. The only saving grace was the beautiful music.

"I know how you feel about services," Mama said, hands on her hips. "I don't expect you to suddenly become a devout Jew, though that would be welcome." She gave a short laugh. "Come with me because I want you by my side when I pray. I feel like Jesse will know you're there with me, asking God for His protection. It's the least you can do for your brother. He's risking his life for our country."

Rachel sighed. There was the trump card. No use pointing out that her job at the shipyard helped the country, too. "Fine, Mama, you win. I'll go shower. But I'm not sticking around for the schmoozing afterwards. I've got things to do."

When she was in her first year of nursing school, she'd tried to explain her hurt feelings to Mama. She had done well on her exams and rushed home to tell her parents. The conversation hadn't gone well. Mama had been on the phone, bragging to Aunt Pearl how Jesse, barely thirteen, had vowed to become a doctor like Papa. He'd go to Cal, then a great medical school. His parents' dream would come true. Rachel waited until Mama hung up.

"I know you and Papa don't mean to," she'd complained, her hands clenched together, "but ever since he began studying for his bar mitzvah, Jesse gets all the attention. It's not fair. Because he's a boy he got to have a bar mitzvah. I never had the chance. All I hear is *Jesse this and Jesse that*. What about me? Don't I count?"

Then she'd burst into tears, which she never did, certainly not in front of Mama. She'd covered her face with her hands, wishing she'd never said anything. Maybe the stress of nursing school had pushed her over the edge.

"Don't be silly," Mama had said. "Papa and I are just very proud of your brother. He studied so hard for his bar mitzvah. You should be proud of him, too. I can't believe you're jealous. Jesse looks up to you. He adores you." She patted Rachel's arm. "Now stop crying. You're too sensitive. Honestly, I don't understand you sometimes."

Well, that was still true. But something had shifted inside her that day, a hardening against having intense feelings, or worse, to share them with someone and then have those feelings discounted. Best to keep them under wraps.

* * *

Mama usually rode the streetcar to temple, but Rachel insisted they walk, since the sun was out, and the exercise, she said, would do Mama good.

"Ha, I get plenty of exercise keeping the house clean," Mama said, putting on the thick-soled shoes she wore out in the garden. "And these stompers do not go with my pearls. But this way I won't ruin my heels if there's mud near the lake."

She paused, looking at Rachel's outfit, a maroon shirtdress and black flats, her hair pulled back in a ponytail, just a touch of lipstick, and a black cardigan around her shoulders.

"I wish you cared more about how you look," Mama said. "Maybe you'd find yourself a decent fellow." She placed her good heels in a canvas shopping bag. "Let's go. And we're taking the streetcar home."

"Fine, Mama." Even now, at twenty-four, she often felt like she'd regressed, a defiant six-year-old with her mother, despite her best efforts to act like an adult. Living at home didn't help either. She and Bertie needed to find an apartment and move out. Between the two of them, they'd figure out things like cooking and cleaning. They could visit the thrift store and find some not-too-worn used furniture, fix the place up how they wanted. Someday.

She walked with Mama down Grand Avenue towards Broadway, past shuttered shops, nothing open except the local market. When they reached tidal Lake Merritt, Mama stopped and pulled a paper bag from her purse. The lake shimmered in the sunlight, and the air smelled of low tide. Several cormorants bobbed near the shoreline.

"Just a minute," Mama said. She stuck her hand deep into the bag and withdrew some hard crusts of bread and a few stale crackers. "Here you go, duckies." She tossed the bits of bread onto the muddy shore of the lake, where several mud hens and mallards scrambled to get their share, quacking and wings flapping as they bumped against each other. "There, that's my mitzvah, to feed the hungry. Okay, let's go."

Rachel smiled. "Never waste good food, right?"

"Of course," Mama said. "Especially now, when what we have feels so precious."

By the time they reached Temple Sinai, Rachel had taken off her sweater and used her handkerchief to wipe a film of sweat from her face. Mama insisted on changing into her heels before she entered the sanctuary, leaning on one of the stone columns at the entrance.

"Rachel? Hey, what's buzzin', cousin? I can't believe you're here for services. Mama must have bribed you."

She turned toward the voice. "Hello, Gordy."

Of course her cousin would be there, along with Aunt Pearl and Uncle Max. Maybe there was a way she could slip out, she thought. Mama embraced her sister and brother-in-law, hooked arms with Gordon, and they all walked inside. Rachel slowed behind them and waited until they found an open row, hoping she'd get an aisle seat. She'd ease out the front door and find a cup of coffee. Read the newspaper and come back in time to pick up Mama. But then she'd have to deal with Mama's anger.

"I'm running to the ladies' room," she told Mama, leaning over the wooden pew where her family was seated. "Be right back." She hurried to the hallway, debating her escape, and ran right into a man holding a paper cup. Water splashed onto his shirt and tie, leaving damp patches.

"Hey, what the . . ." he said, frowning at his wet clothing.

"Oh, I'm so sorry," she said and looked up at him. "I didn't see you." Oh no, not *him*. "I know you. You're Noah. Noah Pearlman." She fidgeted with the sweater in her hands. "We were in geometry class together." Would he remember her? "That fuddy-duddy teacher with the bowtie?"

Noah smiled, and her cheeks grew warm. She'd always liked his lopsided grin, a small dimple only on one side. He was taller than she remembered, and his hazel-green eyes reminded her of

Rascal, the tuxedo cat she'd had years ago. Not that she'd say that out loud.

"Hello, Rachel," he said, brushing his fingers over the damp spot on his tie. "Of course I remember him. Mr. Bolbach. I'm amazed I made it through his class."

"I don't think I've seen you since we graduated," she said. "It's been what, six years?"

It was always tricky asking men her age what they were doing, since most able-bodied men in their twenties had enlisted soon after Pearl Harbor. The guys still home usually had medical problems that made them unfit for service. Noah definitely looked healthy.

"Yeah, I think you're right," he said. "I've been buried in law books. Just started my internship with the NAACP." He looked away as the sound of the organ spilled out of the sanctuary. "Well, I better go." He smiled again. "Say, I think you owe me a cup of coffee for soaking me. Okay if I call you?"

"Sorry, I'm such a klutz," she said. "And sure, let's have coffee. It'd be nice to catch up. I promise not to get you wet." Did she really say that? She looked down at her feet, her heart pounding.

He laughed, and when she looked up at him, his hazel eyes gazed back. "Well," he said, "at least I'll have something to look forward to." He walked away towards the sanctuary.

Rachel stayed in the hallway, waiting for her pulse to slow. The urge to flee had vanished. Maybe sitting in temple wouldn't be so bad. She decided to use the bathroom after all, and when she walked back into the sanctuary, she was relieved to see Noah seated closer to where the rabbi and cantor stood on the bema. The candles had been lit and the pews were filled, mostly with older couples. Several women were seated alone.

When she sat down next to Mama, she could see the back of Noah's head, his brown curly hair reaching the top of his shirt collar.

"What took you so long?" Mama whispered, studying her face. "Are you okay? You look flushed."

"I'm fine, Mama," she said quietly. "I'm just fine." She sat back and closed her eyes, as the low thrumming of the organ's notes vibrated. In spite of the solemn setting, the hushed congregation, her relatives packed so close, her mind wandered, to Noah's cat-like eyes, that lone dimple. Her thoughts were anything but holy.

* * *

The next morning Rachel had just finished sweeping the floors when she heard the familiar knock on her front door. Bertie always rapped out the rhythmic tune of Chick Webb's "*I can't dance, I got ants in my pants.*" It had become their favorite phrase.

"Well, look at you," she said, opening the door. Bertie wore a two-piece outfit, black pencil skirt topped with a fitted polka-dot jacket. Her left leg brace extended down to her customized patent leather pump. "From the pages of *Vogue*. And here I am; I've worn this so often you must be embarrassed to be seen with me."

Her indigo blue dress was cut as plainly as her nurse's uniform, with thin shoulder pads and a slight flare to the skirt. She felt completely comfortable in it—the goal for her entire wardrobe. High fashion had never seemed worth the effort or the expense, especially now with the war limiting supplies of just about everything. But they both needed a dress, one suitable for a wedding.

"Yeah, you're right," Bertie said. "I'll have to pretend I don't know you. Or," she spread her arms wide, "we could be examples of how to dress smartly—me—and," she pointed at Rachel, "I guess you'd call it *dumbly*. Honestly, I don't know how you expect to find Mr. Right." She ran one hand through her own black hair, cut short in a bob with stylish bangs brushing her eyebrows. "At least you could do something with this mop of hair." She tugged on Rachel's ponytail.

"Well, Roberta Lynne," Rachel said, stepping onto the front porch, "maybe I don't care about clothes enough, but . . ." She leaned in. "I've got a lot to tell you. Good and bad. Wait till you hear who I ran into yesterday."

Bertie's eyes widened. "Who? C'mon, tell me!"

"Ha, not yet," Rachel said. "You'll have to wait. Let's get going or we'll miss the train."

"Wait, where are your folks? I want to say hello."

"Sorry, they're not home," Rachel said. "Papa drove Mama to her favorite market across town. That's their idea of a romantic outing." She pulled on her black blazer and locked the front door behind her. "Mama needed a distraction anyway. We haven't heard from Jesse for a while."

Bertie grabbed her hand. "I know how hard this must be. I pray for him when I'm at church. To keep him safe." She squeezed Rachel's hand. "Remember that time we dressed him up for Halloween to look like a hobo, then we all made popcorn balls and he got the caramel stuck in his hair?" She laughed. "He looked more like a scary monster, his hair sticking straight up."

"Yeah." Rachel's heart ached. Of course she remembered. Images of Jesse flickered through her mind off and on all day. Lately she'd been waking up early, startled by terrible dreams about battles and wounded men.

They walked towards the Key Train stop on Grand. She automatically slowed down to match Bertie, whose brace caused a lopsided gait. The Sunday morning traffic was light, one bus, an occasional delivery truck, a few cars with families headed to church.

"Okay, now spill the beans," Bertie said, linking arms with her. "Who did you see?"

"Mama dragged me to temple yesterday," Rachel said. "When we got there, I pretended to need the bathroom, thinking how

I'd escape for a while. Then, right there in the back hallway, I literally ran into Noah Pearlman, knocking his cup of water onto his shirt. Remember him?"

"Of course," Bertie said. She poked her index finger into her cheek. "You always liked that dimple. Why is he still around?"

"I didn't ask, nosy. He's in law school and working at the NAACP office." She hoped she sounded casual. "He said he might call me."

"Really?" Bertie grinned. "Then we'll have to buy you something nice to wear on your first date."

The electric Key Train arrived and Bertie stepped up onto the stairs with a small hop to swing her left leg aboard. They walked down the center aisle to an open seat. The young boy sitting across from them couldn't take his eyes off Bertie's leg. He tugged on his mother's sleeve and pointed.

"What's wrong with that lady's leg, Mama?" he said, loud enough for those sitting nearby to hear. Uh oh, here we go, thought Rachel. The train car felt warm, its electric motor humming below their seats.

His mother frowned and pushed his hand down onto his lap. "Hush now. Don't point, it's rude."

Rachel's usual reaction when this kind of thing happened was to distract Bertie, pretend she hadn't heard. But Bertie never missed a chance to enlighten curious children. What was it about riding on public transit that made people speak their mind so freely?

"I'm glad you asked, young man," Bertie said, leaning forward. "When I was younger than you, I'm guessing, I got very sick with something called polio. Like our President. Have you ever heard of that?"

The boy shook his head. Rachel noticed the look of pity in his mother's eyes. Bertie pressed on.

"Well, it made my leg muscles so weak, I couldn't walk for a long time," she said. "And now," she rapped her knuckles on the brace and smiled at the boy, "thanks to this brace, I can."

"Does it hurt?" he asked.

"Not much," Bertie said, "I just can't run like I used to."

He looked at the brace again, then up at her and nodded. Then he turned to his mother. "How much longer, Mama? Will Papa be waiting for us?"

The train car itself seemed to exhale as the other passengers resumed their routines. Rachel put her hand on Bertie's shoulder. "You, my friend, are amazing," she said. "I need you to teach me how to do that."

"What?" Bertie said. "No big deal. Kids just want to understand. Stick with me, kiddo, you'll learn."

Once the train had rumbled over the Bay Bridge into San Francisco, they stayed on until Market Street, and got off in front of the arched stone entrance to The Emporium. The dress department was up on the fourth floor, and Bertie pulled Rachel towards the elevator.

"C'mon, Rach," she said. "I promise this won't be painful. We need something not too fussy for the wedding. Then we'll stop by the shoe department. My shoe guy can work wonders, as long as the leather is soft." Bertie needed specially fitted shoes with wedges and orthotics. "We'll look so gorgeous, we'll have to fight off the men with a stick." She tossed her head like Hedy Lamarr and they laughed.

Ninety minutes later they left the store, arms full of packages, exhausted and hungry. Rachel had even found a red wool jacket that Bertie said made her look positively darling. Mama would be delighted.

The basement of the City of Paris store had been transformed to resemble a quaint cobblestone street in a French village. Normandy Lane enticed shoppers down its stone steps with aromas from roasted meats and hearty soup. The perfect spot to grab a bite. They ordered at the counter and sat down, chatting with their heads bent together over glasses of Chablis.

The waitress brought their croque monsieur sandwich and two cups of onion soup. Rachel took a bite of her half of the sandwich, chewing slowly, and swallowed.

"I need your advice about this upsetting thing," she said. "I already got too many opinions from my family. But I trust yours."

Bertie sipped her wine. "What happened?"

"I was riding the bus to work, and I sat down next to this young woman, carrying her welder's hood. We were having this friendly talk and she must have decided to confide in me." Rachel swallowed some wine and looked around the cafe, half expecting some trouble. The radio broadcast horrible stories of the Nazis' occupation of France. "Out of nowhere, she announced that she just couldn't understand why we were trying so hard to stop the Nazis from killing those dirty Jews."

Bertie's eyebrows shot up. "What??"

Rachel frowned. "I didn't handle it well. I was so shocked. And angry. I couldn't get any words out. I guess I was scared, too. She could tell that she'd upset me, and so she shut up. It was really awkward." She sighed. "And I just sat there, fuming and mute. When the bus finally got to the shipyard, I practically ran down the steps." Her tears surprised her now, splashing down into her wine glass.

"Oh, Rach, that sounds awful," Bertie said. "No wonder you got upset. She needed to wear a sign, like 'Bigots Only Section.'" She sat back and looked at Rachel's wet cheeks. "Here, dry your tears," she said, handing her a napkin. "What do you want to do about it?"

Rachel wiped her face. "I don't know. I hate knowing that she works in the shipyard. She probably spreads that toxic garbage to other workers."

"Is there something you can do?"

"Maybe I can write something for the newsletter. They encourage workers to submit articles. Most of them are fluff, but I could make it a general caution about being respectful towards your fellow workers." She leaned back and drank some wine. "It's not only the Jews. Look what happened to the Japanese Americans, how badly they've been treated. Not to mention the racial prejudice towards the Negroes. There's so much mistrust and hatred."

Bertie nodded. "Sounds like it's worth getting that article written. I'll look it over if you want." She pressed her lips tight. "What do you wish you'd said to her?"

Rachel stared back. What exactly did she imagine, if she could re-do that moment on the bus? Her first impulse, really, was to put her hands around the woman's neck and squeeze. Shake some sense into her. Not even try talking.

"Well," she said, picking up her spoon and tasting the lukewarm soup, "once I let go of my revenge fantasy, I'd tell her how offended I am. That I'm a proud Jewish woman. And how she's no better than Hitler." She hesitated. "Then I'd probably slap her. Or maybe I'd do that first." She took another bite of the sandwich and swallowed. Talking it out with Bertie had helped. "Anyway, thanks for listening."

"You know, Rach," Bertie said, "next time you might find the right words. Trust your gut. It took me a long time to figure out how to respond to tough situations in a way that felt honest."

* * *

Later that week, Rachel stayed late at the clinic one night to finish some paperwork, and missed a ride home with another nurse. It was past midnight and the bus she caught was almost empty; the quiet ride gave her a chance to review the day and decompress. Outside, Oakland's streets were dark due to the blackout. A few cars drove past with shadowy passengers, shuttling the next shift of workers or late-night partiers. She had begun a mental list of safety measures the shipyard ought to implement, things like sturdier protective gear for welders, and hands-on training for specialized tasks. She'd write up her recommendations and visit the union hall that week, maybe invite some of the workers to join her. Hopefully the union bosses would be open to her ideas.

She got off the bus and walked the few blocks to Mandana under a moonless sky. A few of her neighbors walked their dogs on the sidewalk, likely just off a swing shift, too. After she'd huffed up the hill, she stopped outside the wooden gate to her childhood home. The front porch was empty, except for four pairs of rubber boots lined up under the redwood bench. Mama had insisted on keeping Jesse's boots out there along with the rest. An American flag hung in the front window, the blue-star banner pinned to the curtain a reminder that a member of that family was fighting in the war.

As she climbed the steps, she pressed her hand against the window, and murmured a quiet prayer to a god whose existence she doubted. In his last letter, Jesse had sounded exhausted, ready to come home. The light in the living room shone through the curtain. Someone was still up, or maybe Papa had fallen asleep reading on the couch. But as soon as she opened the door, the sound of Mama sobbing hit her like a blow, and Papa's deep voice shook as he called out.

"Sweetheart, I'm glad you're home," he said. "We're in the living room."

She didn't bother taking off her coat, just followed his voice down the hall, her legs suddenly leaden. When she reached the living room, the first thing she saw was Mama, crumpled on the couch, her face contorted, one hand grabbing a swatch of her hair.

Papa had both his arms around her, holding her as if she might slide off the couch onto the rug. His cheeks were wet.

Then she spotted the telegram lying open on the coffee table. It practically shrieked of death. Why else would this be happening? Oh dear God, not Jesse. Please, let this be news of someone else. Uncle Martin back in Chicago, whom she barely knew. Or Cousin Gertrude. Anyone but Jesse. Her throat tightened and she struggled to take a breath.

"Who?" she managed to squeeze out, starting to pant. She grabbed the back of the easy chair.

"Come here, Rachel, next to me," Papa said, unfolding one arm from around Mama, who slumped against his shoulder. He waited until she sat down and then he put his arm around her and pulled her close. "I'm afraid it's Jesse, sweetheart. Our dear Jesse," he said. He burst into tears, his body rocking back and forth. "It's Jesse." He and Mama clung to each other. Rachel leaned forward from his grasp and picked up the telegram with her fingertips, as if it might scorch her skin.

The Secretary of War expresses his deep regret to inform you that your son, Sargent Jesse Michael Stern was killed in action on 10th June 1944 in France in defense of his country.

Letter will follow.

Signed, Adjutant General Morrison

Oh, dear God. Today was June 15th. He'd been dead for five days and no one knew. That made it so much worse. She and Mama and Papa had just been going about their usual days, while he lay dead somewhere. Alone. Her chest tightened and a shrill wail came up from her throat, almost choking her.

"No, no, no, dear God, no, please. Not Jesse," she sobbed, leaning back into Papa's embrace. The telegram fluttered to the floor. "We should have known. All this time and we didn't know he was gone." Her pulse pounded in her ears and she couldn't catch her breath. She felt like she was dying, too.

Papa helped her lean forward on the couch and gently pressed her head down between her knees. "Take a deep breath, sweetheart. Go on, breathe." He held her there, his arm around her back, his voice tender. "Now another slow breath. Good."

Mama seemed to focus on Rachel for the first time.

"Oh, thank God you're home," she said between sobs. "I wanted to call you, but Papa said to wait until you got here." She hiccupped. "He was right to wait." Then her face collapsed again. "My beautiful boy is gone. My precious Jesse."

They sat together on the couch for a long time, crying and hugging, sometimes lost in their own thoughts. Rachel remembered once when they'd gone swimming at the beach in Santa Cruz. Jesse must have been about five, she'd been the one, barely eleven, to pull him back to shore when a rogue wave knocked him over as he carried a bucket of water to fill the moat of his sandcastle. She had always been her brother's protector. When he'd enlisted, that first time she'd seen him in his Army uniform, she'd been shocked to discover not only was he several inches taller than her, but that he had grown into a man. And now he was gone. He was barely twenty. She'd failed to keep him safe.

After what felt like hours, Mama eventually pushed herself up off the couch, brushing her hair off her face. "I need some tea," she said. "I've got some spearmint I picked this afternoon." A sob escaped from her chest and she let the tears fall onto her dress. "Then we should think about what we need to do. Call our family. Call the temple."

She took a deep breath, and looked down at Papa and Rachel.

"Either that or I'll sit back down and cry myself inside out. There'll be nothing left." She wiped her cheeks with the back of her hand and shuffled toward the kitchen.

Rachel stayed on the couch next to Papa, who leaned his head back against the padded cushion and closed his eyes. After a few minutes, she watched his eyelids flutter and wondered if he was dreaming of his son. Of what would never be.

Later that night, when Rachel found she couldn't sleep, she went into Jesse's room and curled up in his bed under the quilt Mama had stitched for him. Teddy Threadbare, his old brown stuffed bear with black button eyes that he'd refused to give away, sat on the pillow close to her head until she took the bear in her arms and finally fell asleep. She woke up several times, her heart racing. Through the walls of his room she heard her mother crying in the darkness.

CHAPTER 17

ELENA

July 10, 1944

When Elena arrived for her shift, she found Mr. Sullivan waiting while she punched her time card. He smoothed back his gray hair with one hand, staring at the welder's helmet she'd tucked under one arm.

"What the hell is that?"

"It's a flag," she said, tilting the painted side upright. "El Salvador's flag. *My* flag." Mrs. Murphy had shared the paint and brushes from her classroom. "The top blue stripe shows the sky," she pointed, "the bottom blue is the ocean."

Mr. Sullivan squinted. "What about the gold mountains?"

At least he was curious. Most of the other women welders had only painted their first name across the front of their helmet or a colorful flower. Some of them would make fun of her, but painting the flag had re-ignited the love for her homeland. "Those are the five volcanoes in my country. And they rest against a white stripe for peace." Not that peace existed back home, but she longed for the day when good people would run things and the killings stopped. When she might feel safe enough to return.

"Did I ever tell you, missy," he said, "about my time in the foxhole, the bullets flying over my head?" He puffed out his chest. "The Great War."

Not again. "Sí," she said. "Very brave."

She started to walk past him, but he grabbed her arm. Now what? Her thoughts still tumbled over the situation with Ana and Marisol. She needed a new home. Maybe she'd post a note in the locker room that she was looking for housing. Whatever her boss had to tell her, she was not in the mood to listen. Besides, she needed to go see Nurse Rachel. Her burn looked worse.

"Well, now you can do something for our country." Mr. Sullivan focused his pale blue eyes on her.

He was making less sense than usual. She had heard his war stories. He sometimes drifted off into memories of the battles themselves, and forgot to make his point. Someone had told her he got this job because his son had been working right there at the Ford motor plant until he enlisted. He had died at Pearl Harbor. Mr. Sullivan, a widower, had shown up at the union hall soon after, in full uniform, the story went, and demanded to be hired at the shipyard. He'd insisted his previous work in the repair shop for Southern Pacific Railroad qualified him. Otherwise, he'd said, he would end up inside a whiskey bottle or facing the barrel of his gun. The union had hired him onto nights, giving him a new purpose.

"We all must do our part," he said now, squeezing her elbow with his tobacco-stained fingers. He glanced at her bandaged hand. "Even the wounded."

"What are you saying, Mr. Sullivan?" How could someone talk so much and yet say nothing?

"They need someone to switch to evenings," he said, "someone without a husband or kids. I chose you. An eager beaver."

Move to the evening shift? She'd expected an awful assignment, like welding down under the escape hatch in a cramped corner, kneeling on the ship's bottom, sparks flying at her face. And what exactly was an eager beaver?

"Okay, if that's what you need," she said, "I can do evenings."

"Good job, soldier," he said, and let go of her elbow. "You'll start next week." He walked away, his arms straight at his side, mission accomplished.

* * *

After her shift ended the next morning, she caught up with Ana and Marisol as they were walking home. They'd been assigned to work at the other end of the ship, welding on the bow section, so she hadn't seen them during the night.

"Buenos días," she said, her heart racing.

Ana clutched her lunch box in front of her. Marisol stopped and took a step back.

"What do you want?" Ana said, her eyes narrowed. "Are you going to scold us again?" she added, reverting to Spanish.

"No," Elena said, "I have good news." She looked at them. "I'm going to start working evenings next week. I think that will solve our problem. At least one part."

"Oh," Marisol said. "This is because of us . . . ?"

"No," Elena said, "not really. Mr. Sullivan is transferring me. I pretended I wasn't too happy but I think it's a good change. Now none of us has to move out."

When she stopped talking, neither Ana nor Marisol moved a muscle, their expressions unreadable. Something was wrong.

"Are you done?" Ana asked, arms crossed.

"Yes," Elena said, the skin on her arms tingling. This was not going as she'd hoped.

"Good, now it's your turn to listen," Ana said. She put her hand on Marisol's shoulder. "You've made it very clear how you feel about us. We've been here before. You want to make us feel bad for who we are. When you look at me, I no longer see a friend who cares about me."

Elena's eyes burned. She started to speak, but Ana cut her off.

"We don't want to live in a house where we're not wanted, where we don't feel safe. We're going to find a better place to live." Her eyes had a fierce look Elena hadn't seen before. Hearing Ana's words touched a nerve. A tear fell onto her cheek. They wanted to get away from her.

Marisol stepped closer and put her hand on Elena's arm. "We are not a problem that needs to be fixed. But our leaving will be better for everyone."

Elena watched her two friends walk away as tears wet her face. Instead of getting a big thank-you for fixing things, she stood alone in the morning fog. She shivered and pulled her coat tighter, the wound on her hand starting to throb. She longed to be back in San Salvador, her mother's arms wrapped around her, Papá safely home from jail and time turned back by some magical spell. She had no one here to comfort her, not anymore, she thought, as Ana and Marisol's silhouettes disappeared into the fog.

* * *

A few days later, when Elena came home from work, she walked upstairs to their shared bedroom, exhausted. Her friends were gone, their drawers emptied, sheets folded on the twin mattress. No note, no phone number, no address. She sank onto the other bed, curled up, and cried.

CHAPTER 18

July 17, 1944

Ruby Mae stared at the ornate chandelier hanging above the lobby. Outside the Fox Theater, a quarter moon and a sprinkling of stars had lit the night sky, but nothing like the sparkling light that ricocheted from the crystal teardrops over the crowd. The line of customers at the candy counter snaked around a wide marble column. People mingled in small groups, laughing and smoking, sipping soda from straws, like they'd all been invited to a fancy party. The movie, *Stormy Weather*, promised a night of drama and music, an escape from the dark cloud of war.

"Will you look at this, Peggy," Ruby Mae said, eyeing the crowd. "White folks next to Negroes next to Mexicans."

Peggy nodded. "Momma and Daddy are gonna think we're making it up." Momma had agreed to her daughters seeing an evening show, as long as they kept an eye on each other. Freddy had to work that night, so it was just the two of them.

Ruby Mae squeezed her sister's arm. "Let's get some popcorn and a soda pop. I wanna get good seats near the front."

"What?" Peggy said, hands on her hips. "You looking for trouble? There must be a section up in the balcony for us, like back home."

Ruby Mae glanced at the carpeted staircase and crimson flocked wallpaper. "I don't see no signs."

"Well, look who's here!" A familiar voice called out from across the lobby.

Ruby Mae turned to see Marcy hurrying toward them with the two girls she had met at Tappers' Inn. Lucinda and Dorothy worked at the shipyard, too.

"Hi, ya'll." Ruby Mae waved.

"Wait," Peggy said. "I thought it was gonna be me and you." She pulled her purse close. "Marcy's gonna talk through the whole movie."

"Peggy, stop," Ruby Mae whispered. "Look, you don't have to sit next to her, okay?"

"Fine." Peggy jutted her chin. "I'm getting popcorn." She stepped to the line.

When Marcy and her friends arrived, Ruby Mae pulled Marcy aside.

"So where exactly are we s'posed to sit in this fancy theater? I don't see signs pointing me to the Negro section."

Marcy laughed. "Girl, you ain't in Baton Rouge. Sit anywhere you want, long as you don't go up to some handsome white boy in uniform and plant a big kiss on his skinny lips." She threw back her head and laughed again.

"Marcy, you crazy, girl," Ruby Mae said. She looked around her but no one seemed to overhear her friend.

"Just kidding," Marcy said. "I know you sweet on Freddy. Your sister just gave me the evil eye. What's her problem?"

"She ain't used to this whole scene," Ruby Mae said. "Everyone all cozy with each other. Me neither. Was it like this in Chicago?"

"Only in a few places. Mostly we had our own section upstairs."

Marcy grabbed Ruby Mae's arm and walked past the line at the candy counter, where Peggy stood with her arms crossed. Maybe Peggy would decide to sit by herself. That'd be fine with Ruby Mae. She just wanted to disappear into the movie and live in that world for a while. According to Marcy, the singer, Lena Horne, was a big movie star. Marcy had already seen the movie three times. Ruby Mae had never seen any movie more than once. Tickets cost thirty-five cents, but now that she got her own paycheck, she felt as rich as the silk robe that hung in Miz Simmons's bathroom back home.

She followed Marcy inside, past rows of plush chairs in front of the towering red velvet curtains hiding the screen. The chandelier here was even bigger than the one in the lobby. Marcy had told her that over a thousand people could fit in the theater, but from the look of things, maybe only half of the seats would be full today. Ruby Mae noticed several people, mostly men, scattered in seats off by themselves, slumped down and asleep.

"Why would you come to see a movie and then go to sleep?" she said and shook her head. "I don't want to miss a minute of this."

"Yeah, well sometimes sleeping here is all they got 'stead of a bed," Marcy said, looking around and rubbing her neck. "Like say you get off the bus after traveling here alone from Chicago, 'cause you heard about these good jobs at the shipyard. There ain't no housing set up for you. All you want is to put your head down and close your eyes and hope nobody's gonna steal your last dollar. You see this grand theater with soft seats inside." Her eyes grew wide. "So you slip into one of these seats like you just got to heaven. You close your eyes and thank the Lord." She sighed. "And they don't make you leave after the movie ends. You can stay and watch it again."

Ruby Mae stared at Marcy. "Ain't you something." What else didn't she know about her friend?

Marcy gave her a quick smile. "Yeah, I guess so. Now c'mon, it's almost time." She walked down the aisle to an empty row and sat down smack in the middle seat.

Ruby Mae, Lucinda, and Dorothy followed her, and Ruby Mae set her coat down on the empty seat beside her, in case Peggy wanted to keep an eye on her little sister. Not that she was exactly little anymore. In fact, lately she'd worried about this size she'd eaten her way into. Doughnuts and cookies at the shipyard cafeteria. Hush puppies dipped in honey at Tappers' Inn. At least Freddy seemed to like how she looked.

Peggy slipped into their row as the lights dimmed. She leaned down.

"Here." She handed Ruby Mae a cup of Coke. "This seat better be for me." She pulled Ruby Mae's coat off the seat and settled back in the chair. Didn't offer any popcorn.

The heavy curtains pulled back and the huge screen filled with the image of GI's fighting in Europe, tanks rolling off huge ships onto beaches, gunshots blasting overhead. The newsreel's announcer described the Allies' progress with the invasion in Normandy, and how American troops were taking back cities from the Nazis. Everyone applauded and cheered. Ruby Mae thought about Freddy, and how much he wanted to be part of that fight.

The next short film starred two funny characters both dressed in dark suits and bowler hats, one guy real skinny, wearing a bowtie. The other man had a thin mustache and a blimp of a body. They teased each other and made silly jokes, and Ruby Mae felt her sister relax into her seat. She glanced at Peggy and hovered her hand over the bag of popcorn.

Peggy rolled her eyes but shifted the bag so it sat between them. Ruby Mae helped herself to a big handful.

Then the featured film began. Lena Horne and Bill Robinson's love affair radiated off the screen. He danced graceful as a cat and she responded with singing sweet as honey. Like how Ruby Mae felt with Freddy—filled up, like after a good meal, but even better 'cause this feeling wouldn't make her bust out of her dress.

She turned to Peggy and whispered, "Ain't you glad I made you come?"

"Shhh. Yeah, I guess so." Peggy's mouth turned up in a half smile, but she kept her eyes on the screen. Ruby Mae soaked up the singing and dancing in between the movie's romantic scenes.

The movie was almost over when Marcy leaned in and said, "Here comes your favorite song, Miz Love-struck Ruby Mae."

Lena Horne stood against the backdrop of an open window. Her black long-sleeved satin dress clung to her body, the bodice low-cut and jeweled, her hair slicked back into a long bob. Behind her, the rain had started and a strong wind blew open the raincoats of passersby, knocked hats off men's heads, and snapped umbrellas inside out. Ruby Mae trembled as the soulful melody washed over her.

Suddenly the screen went blank. The lights in the crystal chandelier flickered and went dark. The entire theater shook, violently, for what felt like forever to Ruby Mae.

"Help!" Peggy shrieked. She grabbed Ruby Mae by the arm and squeezed hard. There was a very loud rumbling groan, followed by a boom and then rougher shaking that lasted even longer.

"Hold on to me," Ruby Mae said, her voice sounding more confident than she felt. "We'll be okay." Were they being attacked?

"Earthquake!" someone shouted in the dark. Ruby Mae heard the crystals in the chandelier swaying overhead. They clattered against each other. Some fell down onto the people in the audience. One man yelled like he'd been hit. Other people screamed, but it was too dark to see what was happening. Her heart raced. She squeezed Peggy's hand. They'd heard about these California earthquakes, some so strong entire buildings collapsed. At least the ceiling hadn't fallen on their heads. Not yet.

Finally the lights came back on. Everyone around her was still seated, with dazed or frightened expressions. Her friends looked unhurt but terrified. Lucinda and Dorothy stared up at the chandelier, holding onto each other. One man nearby had a cut on his forehead, oozing blood onto the handkerchief he held against his head.

"Oh, good Lord," Ruby Mae said. "That was the scariest thing I ever felt. You okay, Peggy?" Her own palms were damp.

"No." Peggy ran her hand over her hair, looking up at the lopsided crystals still swaying.

"Lucky we didn't get seats right under that light. We coulda been killed."

A man's calm voice spoke out of the overhead speakers. "Ladies and gentlemen. Thank you for your attention. Please stay seated. We'll have an announcement shortly. The movie should resume in about five minutes. This theater is very sturdy. You'll be safe here inside." He paused. "And we'll bring out free popcorn for everyone."

Not very safe if you'd chosen the wrong seat, Ruby Mae thought. She glanced up at the ceiling. The light fixture could still come crashing down on their heads.

"Momma and Daddy and the twins must be scared to death," she said to Peggy. "They'll be wondering if we're okay. Momma's likely got her Bible out. Our first earthquake."

"Hopefully the last, too," Peggy said. "My nerves can't handle this." She wiped her palms on her skirt. "At least when there's gonna be a hurricane, they warn you on the radio."

Marcy nodded. "I been through a few of these since I been here. They still scare the heck out of me."

The man's voice came back on the speaker, and Ruby Mae jumped.

"Attention, please. We have been asked to announce that all sailors stationed at Port Chicago report back to your post. All Port Chicago men, please report to the base immediately." Several Negro sailors stood and hurried up the aisles.

Ruby Mae jumped up. "Did the earthquake hurt Port Chicago?" She hadn't known Freddy for long, but he already felt like The One. She couldn't lose him. "I have to go." She picked up her purse. "Maybe I can catch a ride with one of those sailors."

"Ruby Mae, hold on," Peggy said. She stood up next to her sister. "Momma will throw a fit if I come home without you. Besides, we need to make sure they're okay. You can go to the base in the morning."

Marcy got up and wrapped her arm around Ruby Mae. "Peggy's right."

Marcy was backing up Peggy? Peggy looked as surprised as Ruby Mae felt. "He's probably fine," Marcy continued. "Besides, they ain't gonna let you onto the base in the middle of the night."

Ruby Mae shook her head. They were making sense. But this wasn't about being sensible. She needed to lay eyes on him. "I gotta try."

CHAPTER 19

July 17, 1944

Rachel's shifts at the clinic passed in a blur. Images of Jesse haunted her sleep and she'd wake up in tears. He couldn't possibly be gone from her life forever. His death had drained all the joy from her family, each of them lost in mourning. At work, she forced herself to focus on taking care of her patients, something she could control.

Elena, that stubborn welder, didn't return to the clinic for two weeks. She finally showed up at 10:00 p.m. asking to see Nurse Rachel for her dressing change. Had her roommates been doing the daily bandaging or had she ignored Rachel's instructions?

Elena's face looked flushed, her eyes inflamed. Rachel sat her on the exam table and pressed her fingers against Elena's forehead. Too hot.

"You've got a fever."

The bulky dressing on Elena's left hand was soiled, and Rachel got a whiff of what she'd come to recognize as infected tissue. A sickly sweet odor. "I need to check your temperature." The glass thermometer registered 101.2 degrees. Not good. "Let's see how it looks."

She gave Elena a dose of aspirin for the fever, washed her hands, and unwrapped the dirty bandage. Then she poured saline to remove the last layer of the dressing, where dried pus had attached to the gauze. Elena cried out. The burn looked awful, swollen and bright red, oozing greenish-yellow discharge. The blister had broken, allowing bacteria to enter. Rachel touched the intact skin surrounding the burn; it felt hot. Two red streaks ran up Elena's arm.

"Your hand is badly infected," she said. "Didn't anyone help you keep it clean?" She frowned. "You'll need to start some medicine. Antibiotics. And a strict routine for dressing changes." She looked Elena in the eye. "Have you been working?"

Elena nodded. "After the ampolla opened, I put my glove back on. I only miss two days. After that, he would fire me." She held Rachel's gaze. "I need money for my family."

Rachel sighed. "I understand, but look at your hand. It's much worse now." She felt bad for this patient, but annoyed that she had ignored Rachel's advice.

"I know," Elena said. "That's why I come see you."

"I'll need to debride it first," Rachel said. She hoped Elena would trust her this time. "Get rid of the dead skin that makes it harder to heal." She paused. "It can hurt a lot, so I want to give you something for the pain. Okay?"

When Elena nodded, Rachel went to the medication cabinet and signed out pills for a week's worth of morphine plus a ten-day supply of penicillin.

"Take your first dose of both medicines now," she said, handing Elena the pills. "The morphine takes a while to work, so wait here while I see my next patient." An injection of morphine would be better, but that was in short supply due to the war. The clinic often had to make do with oral pain meds. Soldiers got the good stuff.

Elena swallowed the pills and sat back on the table and closed her eyes. A single tear slid down her cheek. Rachel reached for the woman's shoulder.

Boom!

The floor underneath Rachel's feet shook. She grabbed onto the table to keep from falling. The shaking continued for several seconds. Then another thundering boom. The lights dimmed, fluttered, and came back on. Glass bottles of saline and medication skidded off shelves and shattered onto the floor. Elena jumped up, eyes wide, looking around the room. Everyone else in the treatment room stood, too: doctors, nurses, patients, their faces frozen. The rumbling and shaking finally quieted. A few patients stumbled toward the exit.

"Whoa. Earthquake. A big one," Rachel said, her voice shaking. "Must have been nearby. Everyone okay?" She looked at the broken glass littering the ground, liquid seeping around the jagged edges. The astringent smell of rubbing alcohol drifted up. All that precious supply wasted.

"Please, everyone, don't walk around in here until we've had a chance to clean up this mess," she said. "Let's not make it worse with new lacerations." She checked that Elena was okay, while the other doctors and nurses tended to their patients. Then she walked carefully up to the front desk.

"Diana, all okay here?" she said. Everyone in the waiting room looked unhurt, just shaken. "Can you find Joe and ask him to help clean up the mess back there? I'll get the broom and get that glass off the floor." She thought about calling home to check on Mama and Papa, but that would have to wait.

When she returned to the treatment room, the nurses had thrown down towels to sop up the spilled liquids. A few minutes later the janitor, Joe, appeared, looking pale below his graying crew cut, his Yankees cap pushed back on his head.

"You okay, Joe?" she said, wondering if she could catch him if he fainted. She stepped closer to him. He raised his eyebrows at the mess.

"Yeah, I guess," he said. "Never got used to these damn earthquakes." He looked at her and shook his head. "Shoulda stayed in the Bronx. Only thing we got there is a hurricane once in a while. Or a blizzard." He laughed, his smoker's raspy cough coming right after. He bent over his mop and started to clean the floor.

"Rachel, there's a phone call for you," Diana called out, the front desk's receiver in her hand. "He said he was Dr. Stern. I thought you were single."

"Oh, that's my dad," she said, and hurried over. Was someone hurt at home? For all she knew, the earthquake might have hit Oakland harder than Richmond. Her family was still reeling from Jesse's death. She couldn't bear more bad news.

"Hello Papa." Her heartbeat bounded in her chest. "Are you and Mama okay?"

"Yes, we're both fine," Papa said. He sounded subdued. "Just a few broken dishes that we hadn't secured in the cupboard."

"That was a strong quake," she said. "We've got a big mess here, but no one was hurt. I haven't heard from the yard itself." The riveting guns and welding tools and tall ladders were hazards even without the ground shaking.

"Sweetheart, that wasn't an earthquake," Papa said. "It was an explosion! At Port Chicago, the Naval base near Concord. Remember what Gordy described? They load ammunition 24/7. It was a disaster waiting to happen." He was quiet for a moment. "They think the casualties are in the hundreds. But it's hard to get accurate information yet. They've called for all available medical professionals to help out."

"Are you going, Papa?" Of course he would go. She couldn't imagine the scene, horrific injuries from exploding shells and ammunition. Thoughts of Jesse burrowed up and she pushed them away.

"Yes. I just got dressed," he said. "Mama made some coffee. I have enough gas in the car, so I'm headed up there." She heard the question before he asked. "Do you want to come? I understand if it's too much for you. But I'm sure they could use your triage skills."

The compliment coming from her father made the decision easier, despite the fatigue and worry she felt. Worry whether she had the stomach for what lay ahead. Papa would be disappointed if she said no. Glancing into the treatment room, she saw Elena leaning back on the exam table, her burned hand limp in her lap.

"Yes, Papa. I'll go with you," she told him. "I'll be ready by the time you get here. And I'll tell the other staff. Some of them may want to come, too."

She hung up the phone and walked back to the treatment room. Adrenaline coursed through her body.

"Listen up, everyone," she said. "It's worse than we thought. That was an explosion at Port Chicago. Not an earthquake." Her coworkers' expressions were grim. "Many serious injuries. Those docks were loaded with ammo." She looked around the room. "They really need our help. My father's on his way here. We can take a few of you with us. I'm hoping more of you can follow if you have a car. It's close to Concord, less than an hour's drive."

The doctors and nurses hurried to finish with their patients. Diana came in and said that several waiting patients had left to return home, worried about their families, especially those without telephones.

By the time Rachel returned to Elena to debride her burn, the treatment room had almost emptied. It would take Papa at least a half hour to get there.

"Okay, I'm back," she said, and sat down next to Elena, whose constricted pupils showed the effects of the morphine.

Rachel picked up the scalpel and began to gently remove dead skin from the burned flesh.

"How did it happen?" Elena said. "Was it an attack? How many hurt? Did anyone die?"

Rachel lifted the scalpel. "So many questions."

Elena stared back. "I was a reporter back home. My papá ran a small newspaper."

"Really?" This woman was full of surprises. Rachel hurried to finish up. Papa would be there soon and she still had to clean up her area. She put down the scissors and scalpel and applied a layer of sulfa cream over the burn, then wrapped Elena's hand in a fresh gauze dressing.

"You'll need to come in every day now. Get a new dressing. Keep your arm up at home, like on a pillow. I want to make sure the infection doesn't spread. And take the antibiotic. Don't skip doses. And no work until I say so. Will you promise me you'll do that?" She studied Elena's face, those dark eyes staring back.

"Sí, I promise. But I need to ask you un favor," Elena said.

A favor? What could she offer this woman? Would she beg Rachel to allow her to return to work tomorrow? That was out of the question.

"What is it?" She held her breath, ready to explain again how dangerous the infection was. She could lose her arm, or die from sepsis, the infection ravaging her body.

"Take me with you tonight. Por favor," Elena said.

"What? Are you serious?" Rachel said.

Elena leaned closer. "I need to see what happened. I know how to cover a big story like this. Maybe sell my article to a newspaper." She held up her bandaged hand. "It feels much better now. And," she managed a smile, "I'm right-handed. I can still use a pencil. No hay problema."

"No!" Rachel told her. "Absolutely not." God, this woman was stubborn and maybe delusional from the morphine. "That's the last place you should be now. Go home."

Elena didn't move. Rachel gathered the dirty bandages, separating out the metal instruments she'd used and dropping them into a tray of disinfectant. The scalpel slipped out of her hand and fell to the floor. A sloppy mistake. Whatever bacteria had found a home in Elena's burn could easily spread to other patients. She shook her head and carefully picked up the scalpel and placed it in the tray.

"I can't even imagine what I'll find when we get there," she said, "but I don't want to worry about you being there, too." She placed the contaminated gauze and skin debris into a separate bag for disposal. "Besides, you've got morphine working now. It's not safe for you."

"I'll be careful," Elena said. This from someone who had already risked her health to keep her job.

Rachel sighed. "Look, as far as I know, I'll be back here tomorrow, on swing shift now. I can fill you in then. I doubt they're even allowing civilians access. If the newspaper and radio reporters have been cleared, I'll let you know. Go home and rest now. That's important for your healing."

Elena reached into the pocket of her coveralls and pulled out her wallet. She carefully slid out the slightly tattered card with "*PRENSA*" stamped across the front, next to her photo and *La Voz de La Gente,* printed in a newspaper font at the top.

"I've held on to this," she said, running her finger over the lettering. "Mi papá's newspaper." She looked up at Rachel, eyes moist. "I don't know if it is still there. Y mi papá . . ."

Her voice caught. "Lo siento." She took a deep breath and let it out slowly, looking down at her lap.

Rachel stood up. She didn't have time for whatever sad story Elena had to tell. "My shift tomorrow starts at 3:00. Come see me and I'll let you know what the situation is at Port Chicago. Okay?"

Elena got up slowly and nodded, tucking her press card and wallet back inside her pocket. "Grácias por tu ayuda, Rachel," she said, and walked away towards the entrance.

Rachel glanced around the treatment room. A few patients were still being examined. She gathered up some bandage supplies, hoping the Navy had their own. Once the shipyard's night shift started, a new crowd of injured workers would show up here, one after the other all night long. But nothing compared to what she'd see at the Naval base. She shivered as she put on her coat and headed outside to meet Papa.

* * *

Rachel hurried toward her father's black sedan. Scores of workers lined up to catch the bus home to Berkeley, Oakland, and beyond. They stood in small groups, smoking and talking like any other night. As she walked past the line, she heard someone comment on the earthquake, worried about coming home to broken dishes. Then it hit her: they didn't know about the explosion. Like when Jesse died, and her family didn't find out for days. She wanted to shout out that a tragedy had occurred. Instead, she climbed into Papa's car and hugged him hard.

"Papa, this is awful. Look, everyone's acting so normal. They don't know." She sobbed, her father's arms around her such comfort, crying for her brother and for all the sailors, too.

"I know." He kissed her forehead and started the engine. "Let them have this moment. They'll find out soon enough. But we need to get there quickly. See how we can help."

Somehow, he had shifted from Papa mode to Doctor mode. But she knew his heart ached for Jesse, too. The car smelled of Papa's pipe, the cherry-scented tobacco. He only smoked when he was alone in the car. Mama didn't permit it at home. His pipe sat in the open ashtray, a bit of tobacco smoldering in the bowl.

He drove northeast, his headlights glaring against the asphalt, the engine growling as he pressed the gas pedal. She noticed a lot of other cars, and a few empty Greyhound buses, their destination signs shut off, headed in the same direction. Word must have spread.

"Did you find out any more details?" she asked. Her nurse's brain wanted to know, but at the same time she wanted to cover her ears and drown out the facts.

Papa nodded. "My colleague knows an officer there. He told me the explosions came from two ships docked at the pier. Sailors were loading cases of live ammo on board from the dock. At first, they thought the Japanese had attacked. Or maybe sabotage."

He took a deep breath and exhaled slowly. "That looks doubtful now. All we know for sure is that a lot of sailors were working on the pier when hell broke loose." He glanced at her. "It's going to be very bad, Rach. Things you won't forget. But our job is to help those sailors who can be saved. Do you understand, sweetheart?"

"Yes, Papa."

They rode in silence the rest of the way. If Papa hadn't been with her, she might have backed out. It wasn't the blood and gore itself that frightened her; she was used to that. But how many dead bodies lay there? She didn't need reminders of Jesse. And what if Japanese Navy ships were hiding offshore?

A sailor in a bloodstained uniform stopped them at the Naval depot gates. He had a gash on his cheek and a small towel wrapped around his hand. She rolled down her window, and when he bent down and leaned unsteadily into her side of the car, Rachel worried he might fall right through the open window.

"Do you need help, sir?" she asked, her hand on the door handle. He couldn't be the actual security guard.

"No, ma'am," the sailor said. "I look worse than I feel. Just got hit by some broken glass in my barracks. I was asleep when it happened." He looked at her white nurse's uniform and her father's white coat. "Thank God you're here to help." He shone his flashlight off to his right. "Head down to the dining hall, they're doing triage there. Well, where the dining hall used to be. Ain't much left of it now." He pointed again. "Look for the ambulances. That's the spot."

Several Army Jeeps had parked in a large semicircle, engines running, their lights illuminating the way down to the makeshift triage area, past flattened buildings and downed electrical wires. Pockets of flames shot sparks into the night sky.

Papa drove slowly, and Rachel caught her breath as the headlights revealed what looked like a battleground. Men lay wounded on the ground, with improvised bandages, a towel or sheet wrapped around their chest. Others wandered past, bleeding, their faces contorted in pain. One sailor clutched his arm, bent at an odd angle. The men still standing looked wide-eyed and numb. In the distance, she made out more bodies, with blankets thrown over their faces. A foul stench of burning wood and rubber and what might have been human flesh filled the air.

"Oh my God. No wonder they thought it was an attack." She gripped Papa's arm. "And we're not even close to the waterfront yet. It must be even worse down there."

"I'm sorry I brought you, honey," Papa said. He frowned. "I made a mistake. Maybe you should take the car and go home." He squeezed her hand. "I wouldn't blame you. And Mama will be glad to have you there. I had to talk her into bringing you with me."

She understood. Papa must have felt torn when he asked her to come help. She wasn't just another nurse to him. She was now his only living child.

"I'm staying." She straightened her spine against the car seat. "There's no way I can go home now. Let's go." Better to act brave despite her fear.

They parked and got out of the car next to an ambulance being loaded with three injured men, all Negro sailors. One of them thrashed about on his gurney, grabbing his leg, which didn't seem to have a foot attached, the stump wrapped in blood-soaked gauze.

Other doctors and nurses bent over the wounded, under spotlights from diesel generators. The air was thick with smoke. Men cried out in pain, their voices echoing in the dark. Dante's Inferno made real. Rachel shuddered.

Papa grabbed his medical bag and turned to her.

"Focus on one patient at a time. Help those you can. If it's too much, come sit in the car. I'll find you later." She watched him walk over to one of the doctors and get to work. The ambulance next to her drove off, sirens wailing. The nurse who had helped load the patients caught Rachel's eye, her face familiar.

"Hello," Rachel said. "I've seen you at the clinic. Tessie, right? I'm Rachel. Can you put me to work?" Her stomach knotted into a ball.

"Yeah, I thought that was you. Glad you're here," Tessie said, brushing blond bangs off her forehead. Her white uniform was spattered with blood. She picked up some Army blankets from the ground and folded them against her chest. "Follow me. We're still trying to find the worst injuries and get them transported. The closer to the dock you get, the worse it is. The stuff of nightmares. I'll never complain about the clinic again."

"Where are they taking them?"

Tessie bit her lip. "Probably Camp Stoneman. The Army hospital. It's in Pittsburgh, so pretty close. And the Navy hospital in Vallejo. They're gonna need a lot of beds."

She led Rachel to a raggedy line of men, standing or seated on folding chairs, bloody towels pressed against their wounds. "Let's start here. Greyhound sent buses to transport the less severely injured." Oh God, busloads of the wounded.

The two of them got to work, bringing the injured, one by one, to a stretcher or chair near one of the bright lights. Rachel wished she had soap and hot water to use between patients. The last thing these men needed was to get an infection. She found a bottle of rubbing alcohol and some cotton wads. Those men who only needed a few stitches or wound cleaning were walked over to the doctors, who had been set up with suture equipment and instruments for wound care.

She spotted Papa wearing surgical gloves, probing a large open wound on a sailor's leg, the jagged edge of his shin bone protruding like a freakish appendage. An IV hanging on a coat rack ran fluids into his arm.

"Some of these wounds aren't any worse than what we see in clinic," Rachel said to Tessie. "Why can't we take care of the simple ones ourselves?"

"I know," Tessie said, grabbing a gauze roll and wrapping it around a sailor's head, his scalp oozing blood. "It's hard to only triage them and send them on. But we can't take the time. We need to find the serious wounds quickly. Get them moved. Some of the men are in shock from blood loss. They might die waiting to be seen."

Tessie was right, but Rachel hated doing this patchwork kind of care. She moved on to the next man, a young sailor with bleeding cuts over his face and arms. She had him sit on a folding chair. His hand covered his left eye, and he cried out when she moved his hand.

"I'm sorry, sir. I need to examine you," she said. "What's your name, sailor?"

Tears and blood oozed down his face as he grimaced. "Freddy," he said. "Freddy Parker, ma'am. My whole barracks collapsed. That window over my bunk rained down on me like a river of nails."

He looked so young. She wiped away the blood around his eye, and shined a flashlight on his face while she gently pulled his eyelid up. He jerked his head back and squinted while she examined him, his tears falling.

"I'm afraid there's still a piece of glass or wood in your eye, Freddy. I'm going to patch it shut. Until one of the doctors can see you." Injuries like his were common at the shipyard. She knew the pain was excruciating. He hid it well.

Rachel cleaned and inspected his other lacerations. One on his neck looked pretty deep. It required suturing, and she worried whether the glass might have nicked his jugular vein. He needed the wound probed for any foreign bodies before applying a dressing, otherwise a bandage could kill him if a shard of glass remained inside.

She walked Freddy over to where her father had stepped back from his patient, who was carried off to a waiting ambulance. Another stretcher held an unmoving body under a pile of bloody towels, his face covered. She tried not to think about Jesse.

Papa was speaking to another doctor, leaning against the long table that had been set up as a makeshift surgery center. She waited for Papa to finish, her arm around Freddy's shoulders as she sat him down. Fires still burned down on the beach, smoke billowing as the fire crews doused the burning dock and buildings at the water's edge. Men shouted instructions as more bodies were loaded onto stretchers. The wind shifted and she smelled burned flesh. Her stomach churned and she felt faint.

"Rachel." Papa motioned her over, his eyes narrowed. "Have you got a patient for me?" He took Freddy's arm. "Hello, young man," he said to Freddy, guiding him to the exam table. "Sit down, please." He turned to Rachel. "I'm desperate for some water. Would you mind getting me some? Maybe a little for you, too." He must have sensed her distress, that Papa/Doctor instinct.

She nodded and walked over to a table with water pitchers labeled "US Army." Paper cups were stacked in neat rows. Closing her eyes, she took a few slow breaths, shutting out the sounds and smells as best she could. When she opened her eyes, nothing had changed. Her stomach still felt queasy. She poured water for herself and Papa and turned around, bumping into someone. Someone with a freshly bandaged hand and a press pass hanging around her neck.

CHAPTER 20

July 18, 1944

"What are *you* doing here?" Rachel frowned at her.

Elena flinched. She hadn't expected a warm welcome, but at least Rachel could give her credit for getting to the Port Chicago base on her own in the middle of the night.

"I had to come," she said, crossing her arms. Her burned hand ached. "It's important, what happened here."

The nightmarish scene around them looked worse than Elena had imagined. But even in the darkness, with smoke from the burning buildings and cries from the injured men assaulting her senses, she didn't regret her decision. She'd needed to see this with her own eyes. Papá had taught her that a good reporter never turned away from the truth, no matter how ugly. If only she had a camera.

"Well, stay out of the way." Rachel shook her head. "I don't know how you expect to get your story. Everyone is too busy helping the wounded. I can't believe they let you in."

"I'll be fine," Elena said. "And don't worry, I'll keep this clean." She waved her left hand with its bulky dressing, her fingers wrapped around a notepad. "I'm just going to write."

Rachel didn't need to know that no one had cleared Elena to cover this story. She'd slipped onto the Naval base with a carload of nurses from the shipyard. *Act like you belong and people will leave you alone.* Papá's lessons worked in this country, too.

She nodded to Rachel and walked away from the generator lights where doctors worked on their patients. Folding tables had been set up for examination, with adjacent trays of metal instruments in some disinfecting solution. The nurse was right. Everyone rushed about, carrying injured sailors to the triage area, or dragging hoses to put out the fires still burning. She didn't want to get in their way, so she wandered down a cement path, over to a spot on the edge of the darkness, with barely enough light to jot down notes. Her watch read 2:15. Even though the explosions happened hours ago, the chaos continued.

A plaintive voice came out of the darkness. "Ma'am, can you help me?"

Elena whirled around and there, several yards in front of her, she made out the silhouette of a man sitting on the ground. When she hurried over, she saw that he was holding his leg, his knee bent, the leg of his uniform torn. He was young, swaying slightly. Next to him lay a knapsack with rolled bandages spilling out. He moaned when she got close.

"Are you okay? What happened?" she asked.

"I'll be alright," he said. "I was bringing supplies to the doctors. I guess I tripped. And now it hurts to walk." He grimaced. "Could you bring these bandages to triage?"

She bent down next to him. She looked for other injuries, bleeding wounds, but it was too dark to see much. He seemed to be in a lot of pain.

"Are you hurt anywhere else?" she asked. "I think I need to get one of the nurses to check you."

"I was lucky," he said. "I was headed into the dining hall. On my break." He took a deep breath and winced. "Then all hell broke loose. The windows shattered. The whole damn building collapsed." His voice had grown weak. He slumped forward. "I got some wood or glass stuck in me. But I'll be okay." His head inched down onto his bent knee as he sat, sagging. Definitely not okay.

"You need help. I'll be right back," she said. She jumped up and grabbed the knapsack of bandages. Her heart pounding, she rushed back toward where she'd left Rachel. She stumbled in the dark. No sign of the nurse. She pivoted, searching for her, and finally spotted Rachel working on a patient.

"Hey." She ran over. "I need your help."

Rachel stood up and faced her. "I told you, I'm busy. Can't you see that?"

Elena nodded. She wasn't going to take this personally, not when that sailor was waiting.

"I know," she said. "But there's a very bad sailor . . . I mean, not bad, but hurt. Please come. He says it's just his leg, but I think it's worse. He was near the dining hall when it fell down." She held up the knapsack. "He was carrying this."

"Fine," Rachel said. "I'll come as soon as I finish this dressing. Wait over there." She pointed to a stack of folded blankets on a table.

"Please hurry," Elena said. Her chest tightened. "I am very scared for him. I don't know what's wrong, but . . ." She walked a few steps away and dropped the bag of bandages on an empty chair, watching Rachel carefully wrap gauze around her patient's arm.

This was taking too long. But if she tried to find some other nurse, one who didn't know her, that would take even more time. No, she'd stay right there and insist this nurse come. Right away. The muscles in her shoulders tightened. She was about to grab Rachel by the arm and drag her over to the sailor when Rachel straightened up and picked up a medical bag.

"Okay," she told Elena. "Show me where he is. If it's just a twisted ankle, he'll have to wait. That's low priority. Doesn't he understand that?"

Elena kept walking, trying to remember exactly where she'd left the sailor, but the darkness played tricks on her eyes, shadows jutting out of nowhere. Then she heard a moan. She rushed over.

"He's here," she yelled.

The sailor had toppled over, lying on his side. Maybe he'd fallen asleep. But when she got close to him, she heard him sobbing quietly.

"I brought help." She put her hand on his shoulder and he flinched. She held her breath.

Rachel knelt down next to him. "Hello, sir. I'm a nurse. I need to examine you."

Elena stood up and stepped back. She let out her breath and felt a rush of blood to her brain. She could leave now. Rachel would take care of him. Elena could find others to talk to. But something made her stay.

"Elena." Rachel's voice broke into her thoughts. "I need you to get back to the triage area fast. Grab one of the nurses. Tell her to bring a stretcher. Walk her back here right away."

"What is it? What's wrong with him?"

"I think he's losing blood. But it's too dark here to figure out where. Now go."

Elena dropped her notepad and pencil, and turned around, running toward the lighted triage area, like a kid in a foot race. That sailor's life depended on her. She sprinted up to a nurse whom she recognized from the shipyard.

"Please, you come with me," she said to the startled nurse. She was panting and must have looked a little crazy. "I'm with Rachel, the nurse from the clinic. She needs you to help. Bring a stretcher. I show you where." She pulled on the nurse's arm. "Hurry."

To her surprise, the nurse didn't argue. "There's a stretcher over by that ambulance. Follow me." The nurse jogged over to the waiting ambulance, and picked up a canvas stretcher. "Let's go."

Elena grabbed the front of the stretcher with her uninjured hand and led the nurse over the uneven ground toward the dock, hoping she recalled the sailor's location. Finally she spotted Rachel's white uniform against the night sky. The sailor's body hadn't changed position.

"Rachel, we're here," Elena called and rushed over, the nurse next to her. They placed the stretcher on the dirt. She looked at Rachel, who shook her head.

"You're too late," Rachel said.

"What? No, it can't be," Elena said. "It was just his leg." Then she noticed Rachel's hands, both turned palms up, stained with blood. "Ay, Diós mío." She could barely breathe.

Rachel bent down and picked up one of the forgotten bandages and wiped the blood off her hands.

"I know," she said. "I'm sorry, Elena. You tried your best. But you were right. He must have been badly hurt. All the flying glass and wood when the dining hall collapsed. He was in shock. He'd already lost a lot of blood by the time you found him."

Something bitter rose up in Elena's throat and she stepped back. Her eyes burned. She should have been able to save him. Tears spilled down her face.

Rachel moved closer and put her arm around her, but Elena shook her off.

"Don't," she said, and looked at the two nurses. "Go do your jobs." She took a deep breath. "Wait." She bent down close to the sailor's lifeless body. His eyes were closed, and he looked like he was sleeping. Rachel must have done that for him. "Que Diós te bendiga, señor. May God bless you."

She crossed herself, then picked up the notepad and walked away. She didn't want to be comforted. Adrenaline still pumped inside her. If only she'd found him sooner, he might have lived. She felt as helpless as when they came to arrest Papá.

* * *

She got a ride home to Richmond and slept for a few hours. Gruesome images haunted her dreams. By the time she returned to the base later that morning, a crowd of reporters had gathered outside the entry gate. A truck stenciled with the US Army logo rolled past, an anti-tank gun mounted in the back. Had rumors of a Japanese attack been confirmed? Drizzle from heavy fog added to the gloom. She'd tried to talk to some of the other sailors last night, but no one had time for her, too busy helping the injured men and still reeling from the shock of the explosion.

A Navy officer at the gate addressed the reporters, his khaki uniform streaked with dirt, dark circles under his eyes. "Okay folks, we're going to allow you inside," he announced. "Let you see some of what's happened. But you can't go down to the waterfront."

"Why not?" one of the reporters asked. He had a camera slung around his neck. His pass said he was from the *Oakland Tribune.* "What are you hiding?"

"Trust me, you don't want to see that area," the officer said. "We're still cleaning up. We'll have a brief press conference in thirty minutes. 0900 sharp. At the dining hall, or what's left of it."

Elena lined up at the gate with the others, each of them showing the officer their press pass. There was only one other woman in the group. She was tall and dressed in Army fatigues, her red hair pulled tight in a bun. Did the Army put out a newspaper? In El Salvador, that would never happen. There the soldiers operated more like a secret gang, using their power to intimidate citizens, especially those who spoke out.

When the officer got to Elena, he held her pass in his hands and squinted.

"What paper do you work for, miss?" he said. He looked like he hadn't slept; probably no one on the base had. And he must have known many of the men who'd been injured or killed. He wouldn't have heard of Papá's small progressive paper, but she'd come up with her story on the bus ride, how she'd present herself if anyone questioned her credentials.

"Well, sir," she said, "I'm a welder at Shipyard #3 in Richmond. I belong to the Boilermakers' union. I'm going to write this up for the union newsletter." That sounded better than saying she hoped to sell her story to *La Voz de México*, the local Spanish language newspaper. Grácias a Papá for teaching her how to worm her way in anywhere.

The officer nodded. "Go on, then," he told her, and turned to the next reporter. Relieved, she followed the group past the gate and took out her notebook. She peered at the redheaded woman who nodded and studied Elena's press pass.

"*La Voz de la Gente*. Never heard of it," the woman said, stumbling over the Spanish. Her own pass said "US Army," and underneath that, "WAC." The other reporters had moved ahead, taking photos and scribbling in their notebooks. Things were much quieter than last night, no one shouting orders or screaming in pain, just a few generators thrumming. Bodies had been removed.

"My pass is a little old," Elena said. "I worked in El Salvador for my father's paper. Now I work at the shipyard. I'm writing this for the union newsletter." Saying it again made it real. Of course the union would want to cover this. She'd go down to the union hall tomorrow after she'd written the article. Maybe they'd even pay her.

"Sure, I get it," the woman said. "Like me. I'm writing an article for the weekly report we do at Camp Stoneman. I'm Betty, by the way."

"I'm Elena. What's WAC? Are you a soldier?"

"Stands for Women's Army Corps. So yeah, I'm a soldier, but they don't send us into combat. I work at the Army base." Betty looked around. "We better catch up. Don't want to miss the press conference."

The first barracks they passed had nothing but shards of glass in its windows, the shades flapping, a piece of the roof torn off. The remains of another building that must have caught fire were now only a pile of rubble, with water-soaked ashes and the sharp smell of burnt wood.

Chunks of metal were strewn across the grounds, and a bloodied bandage had been left behind. The area where the doctors and nurses had cared for the wounded sailors stood empty, just a few tables left, with stretchers lying about. They must have worked all night to get the rest of the men triaged and transported to the hospital. Or the morgue. She shuddered, imagining all those bodies.

* * *

At 9:00 she walked to the dining hall. Half of it had been torn off from the blast, and inside she saw splintered tables, chairs scattered upside down, some piled high like a giant's hand had tossed them. A few sailors stood around, holding plates of food someone must have delivered. None of them were eating. One man had his arm around another sailor who was bent over, crying. All of the men she saw were Negro. Were there no white enlisted men on this base?

Another officer stepped forward and faced the reporters.

"Hello. I'm Captain Nelson Goss," he said. "These are the facts of what happened on our base last night. There were two ships docked down at the pier, the *Quinault Victory* and the *E.A. Bryan*. Both of them were completely destroyed. Everyone on those ships died instantly." He paused, looking down. "The total number of men who were killed is 320."

Elena gasped and covered her mouth. So many, worse than she'd imagined.

Captain Goss continued, grimacing. "Out of that, 202 were our sailors. The explosion injured another 390, mostly men in their barracks. The injured have been transported to Camp Stoneman's hospital in Pittsburg for further care."

"Do you know yet what caused the explosion?" a reporter asked.

"We don't know," Captain Goss said. "There are no survivors to give evidence of what happened." Elena found it hard to understand him. What was he saying?

"Do you think it was an enemy attack?" Betty asked. Several of the reporters turned to look at her. Women writing serious articles for newspapers was unusual, even here. And Betty was in uniform, even more rare.

"At this point, we don't know," Captain Goss said. "There is some suspicion of sabotage. We will conduct a full investigation as to the cause of the explosions."

"I have a question, sir." A reporter from the *San Francisco Chronicle* spoke up, tipping his cap back. "Those ships were being loaded with all kinds of ammo, right? Bombs and bullets and God knows what else." He pointed with his pencil toward the damaged dining hall. "So how dangerous was the work your men were doing? Did you have safety measures in place?"

Captain Goss glared at the reporter. "Of course. Our sailors had plenty of training. They died in service to our country." He rubbed his hand over the back of his neck. "That's all for now. We'll provide further information as it becomes available."

"What about getting us a list of the names?" Betty said. "The sailors who died."

Elena was impressed. This redheaded reporter was persistent, not intimidated by anyone. Elena used to be more like that, even when pushing for the truth could land you in a Salvadoran jail cell on some trumped-up charge. Somehow she'd lost that nerve, like a muscle gone weak from lack of use. Ever since they'd arrested Papá.

The captain shook his head. "No list yet. Not until we've notified the families." He started to walk away.

Elena took a deep breath, her mouth suddenly dry.

"Uh, one more question, sir." She stepped forward. "All these sailors, the ones who died, and the injured men. How many of them were Negroes?" No one had said anything about the race of those who had died. That mattered.

Captain Goss cleared his throat. "Our entire crew here, all the enlisted men, are Negroes."

He folded his arms. "Except for the officers. That's all for now." He glanced at Elena and turned, striding away from the group.

The other reporters stood still, writing notes, a few shaking their heads. She wasn't the only one who realized how important this story had become. It was no longer just a horrible tragedy. Now it was also about race. Why were those Negro sailors the only ones assigned to load ammunition? Had they really received proper training? There was certainly more to the story, and she intended to uncover the rest.

PART TWO

CHAPTER 21

July 18, 1944

Ruby Mae paced outside the corner market on MacDonald Avenue, waiting for the morning newspaper delivery, Peggy fretting close by.

"I'm real worried about Freddy," Ruby Mae said, shivering in the cold air. "He might be hurt from that earthquake." Last night when she'd tried to catch a ride up to Port Chicago, the sailors had warned her to go home; no one would let her inside the gates. So she'd gone home with Peggy, and slept poorly, imagining the worst. Momma and Daddy and the twins had waited up for them. Momma had announced that it was time for the family to go back to Baton Rouge; she believed the earthquake was a sign from God.

On the street in front of them a truck pulled up and delivered a thick stack of newspapers. The shopkeeper piled them onto the display racks. Peggy saw it first. "Oh my God, look!"

The front-page headline stopped Ruby Mae's heart.

"300 Die in Bay Arms Ship Blast!"

The second headline read, *"Port Chicago Razed by Two-Ship Explosion!"*

"Oh, sweet Jesus, no," she said, grabbing a newspaper off the rack, almost dropping the groceries in her hands before Peggy snatched the bag. Tears filled her eyes. The article described a gruesome scene. So many sailors dead. Others seriously wounded. Burned or injured by flying debris. Her lungs fought for air.

"I knew it," she said. "I have to go look for him." The names of the dead and injured men were not listed. Her hands shook as she clutched the newspaper against her chest.

Even if Freddy was okay, he had no way to reach her. No phone in the trailer. She had to get to the base, and she needed Peggy's help. Momma would never allow her to go. Not after she'd been caught sneaking back to church. Chasing after a boy like this. Momma had called her a khaki wacky, something she'd heard at church, warning parents to keep a close eye on their daughters, with all those soldiers and sailors out on leave.

"If you want me to go by myself, that's fine," Ruby Mae said. "But Momma'd be mad at you for making me do this alone." Not that she planned to tell Momma.

She hoped Peggy would take the bait. When they were little, way before the twins came along, Peggy liked to dress Ruby Mae up and strut about, pushing the baby carriage, her heels bouncing out of Momma's church shoes as she clomped through their small house.

"Now, Ruby Mae, you be a good girl," Peggy'd say in a fake-adult voice, "and Momma's gonna buy you some candy. Too bad you ain't as pretty as your big sister." Ruby Mae had loved being fussed over and ignored the sisterly insults.

But now Peggy pushed back. "They prob'ly won't let you see him anyway. It's not like you're married. You don't even know if he got hurt, or where he is."

Ruby Mae wiped her eyes. "Please."

"Look," Peggy said, pointing, "they got a pay phone here. You got his number, right? Call him. I'll go pay for the paper."

Ruby Mae stepped into the phone booth, pulling loose change and the slip of paper with Freddy's number from her purse. But once she'd dialed, she only heard a busy signal. Over and over and over. Peggy came out of the market.

"I can't get through," Ruby Mae said. "You gotta help me."

Peggy looked at her and sighed. "All right. Lord help me, I don't know why I let you talk me into these things. You got a bit of the Devil in you."

"Maybe I do."

When they got back to the trailer, Daddy was up, making himself some breakfast. He leaned on his cane as he bent over the electric hot plate, stirring some grits in the fry pan. He'd been off work since his leg injury. Two weeks in the hospital after his surgery, and now he'd hobbled around the trailer for weeks, miserable and ornery over every little thing. The earthquake had been the final straw.

"There you are," he said. He eyed the grocery bag. "What'd you bring your old man?"

"We got you some eggs and bread, Daddy," Peggy said, and kissed his stubbled cheek, putting the bag on the kitchen table. The smell of heated lard overwhelmed the small space. Ruby Mae cracked the door open.

"If you want, I'll scramble you an egg to go with those grits," she said. "Then me and Peggy got some shopping to do. We need new coveralls." She looked around the trailer. "Where'd Momma go?"

Daddy shook his head. "I can cook my own damn egg." He reached into the bag and pulled out the carton. "I ain't no cripple. Your momma's gone with some ladies from church. Working on a quilt or some other damn thing. I don't know." He sighed. "Sorry for the foul language. Lord help me, I ain't cut out to be idle like this. You girls go do your shopping. I ain't fit for company right now." He leaned his cane on the table, took an egg, and cracked it open onto the grits and watched it cook.

Ruby Mae stepped close to him and hugged his broad back, her short arms not reaching around his belly. Being off work for so long had broken his spirit. He needed something to do until he could go back to work. Otherwise he and Momma would start packing up.

By the time the bus dropped her and Peggy off at the Port Chicago gate, it was nearly noon. Everyone on the bus had talked about the explosion, worried about what they'd find at the base. A crowd of reporters had gathered in front of the sailors guarding the entrance. Two green Army Jeeps exited the base; the drivers Ruby Mae saw through the windshields looked like they'd been through hell. An ambulance drove slowly out of the gate, its siren silent.

"I don't think they're letting people inside," Peggy said, walking toward the gate. "Looks like some families came looking for their kin. They probably don't got phones at home neither." She linked arms with her sister.

"C'mon, let's go talk to that guard," Ruby Mae said.

When they approached the sailor, he was talking to one of the women with young kids who'd been on the bus. The boy and girl looked about the same age as the twins. The sailor held a stack of papers on a clipboard, and thumbed through the pile.

"Here he is, ma'am," he told the woman. "Looks like he's been sent to Camp Stoneman. They got a hospital there."

"Oh my God. What happened to him?" The woman pulled her children close.

"Sorry, ma'am, that's all I can tell you," the sailor said, frowning. "The hospital will help you. Take the bus to Pittsburg. Tell the driver where you're headed."

The woman stood for a minute, wild-eyed. She grabbed her children's hands and led them back towards the bus stop. The little girl dragged a worn teddy bear by one arm behind her.

The sailor wiped his forehead and looked at Ruby Mae and Peggy. "Can I help you ladies?"

Peggy squeezed her arm. "Ask him."

"Yes, sir, I . . . uh," Ruby Mae practically whispered, afraid to jinx things. "I'm looking for Freddy Parker."

He narrowed his eyes. "You ain't his wife. 'Cause he ain't got one."

Peggy pursed her lips. "Naw, but she's sweet on him."

"You hush, Peggy," Ruby Mae said under her breath. Please let him be okay.

"Look, I'm sorry," the sailor said. "It's been a rough morning, giving out so much bad news. My brain is soft as mush." He smiled. "You must be Ruby Mae."

She caught her breath. "You know Freddy?"

"Sure," he said. "We in the same barracks. I was lucky, bunk at the other end, away from the windows. I got thrown out the bunk and banged up, but thank God that's all." He touched a spot on his forehead where a knot had formed. "He told me about you." He looked at his list. "Well, you ain't family, but I reckon I can tell you, since he ain't got no family out here."

"What happened to him?" she asked, still barely breathing. Her head felt like it might spin off, like a loose balloon.

"Freddy's tough," the sailor said. "I swear that guy should be dead by now. But he's gonna make it. They sent him over to the Navy hospital in Vallejo. For surgery."

She braced her weight against Peggy, suddenly lightheaded. "Just tell me what happened," she said, pulling some air into her lungs.

"Well, he sleeps right next to the window," he said, "so when things blew up, he got hit. It was glass and wood that cut him up. One piece got him bad in the neck; the other one got his eye." Ruby Mae's stomach lurched. "He was one bloody mess. They gonna have to fix him up at the hospital. He'll be good as new, least I hope so. That's what the doc here said 'fore they took him away."

He looked at Ruby Mae. "He told me to get word to his family and you, but I ain't had time to find you. You okay?"

She shook off Peggy's arm and took a deep breath. "Not really," she said, "you just surprised me with all that. Sounds bad."

"Is there a bus to that hospital?" Peggy said.

He nodded. "Yes, far as I know. The hospital's at Mare Island. I'd take you if I could, but they need us on base. Orders from the top."

"Thanks," Ruby Mae said. "What's your name?"

"I'm Charlie. Tell Freddy I sent you." She walked towards the bus stop, her fingers pressed into her sister's woolen coat, her mind already at the hospital, searching for Freddy's wounded face.

* * *

When the bus finally dropped them off at Mare Island, they were exhausted. Ruby Mae stared at the hospital that loomed in front of them, like some kind of royal palace, all columns and carved stone designs at the entrance. Not the look of a place that cared for wounded sailors. It was nearly 2:00 and they hadn't eaten since breakfast.

"I don't know 'bout you," Peggy said, "but if I don't eat something soon, I swear I'm gonna sit down and cry."

"Maybe we can grab something quick," Ruby Mae said. "But we have to go find Freddy." They found a snack bar and Peggy bought them each a molasses cookie.

"Better than nothing," she said.

Ruby Mae wolfed hers down as they headed to the information desk in the marble-walled lobby. The gray-haired woman seated at the desk asked the name of the patient they wanted to visit.

"Freddy Parker," Ruby Mae said. "He's a sailor. I'm . . . uh . . . I'm his sister." Peggy raised her eyebrows. "Yeah, and this is his other sister." She hoped Peggy would keep her mouth shut.

"I see," the woman said, looking like she indeed did see and didn't care. She studied the papers on the desk. "We've been very busy here since that terrible explosion. Let's see, Parker, Frederick. It looks like he had surgery early this morning. He should be up on 3-West by now. Third floor. Check with the nurses there."

The nurses' station on 3-West was chaotic. Staff scurried in different directions, calling down the hall. The doctors' white coats, worn over their Navy uniforms, flapped as they rushed about; a few wore only green scrubs. Not that different from Kaiser where Daddy had been.

She and Peggy watched the turmoil until one of the nurses directed them to room 307. She told them Freddy might still be groggy from the anesthesia, and his nurse would stop in to talk to them as soon as possible.

Ruby Mae led Peggy down the hall, suddenly worried she should have called first. What if he wasn't ready to see her yet? The molasses cookie sat like lead in her stomach.

She paused at the doorway and looked into his room. The air smelled of antiseptic and the sulfa that Daddy used on his leg wound. The room held four beds, separated by thin curtains. A brown-skinned man lay in each bed. Two had bandages covering most of their faces. One of them had an eye not covered in gauze, and that eye was open and staring right at her. An eye she knew. Relief flooded her body.

"Hey there, Freddy," she said, trying to sound normal.

"Ruby Mae?" Freddy said. "I must be dreaming." He lifted his head off the pillow, but then he groaned and laid his head back down. "Whoa. Too fast." He shut his eye. "Come closer." His mouth formed a droopy smile, and now he looked more like himself. When she stepped next to him, he opened his eye and said, "Closer." He patted the blanket next to him.

"Okay, you two," Peggy said. She put her hand on Freddy's arm. "I'm glad you made it. I couldn't handle my baby sis if you'd been blown to pieces."

Freddy started to laugh but then he winced. "Don't make me laugh, Miz Peggy. I'll bust my stitches open."

Ruby Mae pulled a chair closer to him and sat down. Seeing him there, breathing and talking, lifted her heart. He was not going to die.

"We met your friend Charlie at the base," she said. "He told me you got hit worse than him on account of your bunk being by the window." She put her hand on top of his, kind of shyly, with Peggy right there.

"I was in my bunk, almost asleep," he said. "Pitch black outside. All of a sudden there was a loud boom. The whole barracks shook." He squeezed her hand. "We thought it was an earthquake. A second boom. The windows exploded. Part of the roof flew off." He closed his eye. "Glass and wood flew down. Fires busted out everywhere, ammo boxes shooting off. Men were screaming and running, yelling for help."

"Oh, Freddy," she said. Her stomach tightened, a sick feeling edging up her throat.

He touched the bandage over his eye. "I started walking down to the dock. One of the ships we'd loaded was burning. Bodies lying on the ground. Some just in pieces. Everyone stumbled around trying to help the guys who got wounded. I didn't know how bad I got hurt 'til Charlie found me. He made me see a nurse right away."

She stared at his face. "What about your eye?"

"Piece of wood stabbed my eye. It'll be okay. But I got cut real bad on my neck." He took a deep breath and yawned. "A sliver of glass sliced an artery, they told me. Once they pulled it out, they had to sew it all back up again," he said. "I could have died. All that blood . . ."

She felt the nausea moving up and swallowed hard. "Uh-oh. I'm gonna be sick." Covering her mouth with her hand, she jumped up. "Where's the restroom?"

Peggy grabbed her arm. "Let's go. We passed one in the hall." They barely made it there in time. Ruby Mae retched into the toilet. Peggy cleaned her up afterwards with some wet paper towels. Ruby Mae rinsed out her mouth and drank some water from the tap.

"Thanks," she told Peggy. "I ain't cut out for this." When she checked her reflection in the mirror, she saw a speck of vomit on the collar of her dress, and wiped it off. "Good Lord, I am a sight."

"Quit asking him those fool questions," Peggy said. "He needs to rest, and we need to get home. It's gonna take a while on the bus." She smoothed her skirt in the mirror. "Let's buy a few cookies for Momma and Daddy and the boys. They're cheap downstairs. It'll distract Momma since we ain't got no shopping bags in our hands."

Ruby Mae stared at her sister. "Well, look at you, gettin' so good at lying to Momma. Okay, I'll go say goodbye first." A sour burp bubbled up. No cookies for her.

They walked back to Freddy's room. He'd fallen asleep and was snoring. She went to him and kissed him gently on his cheek, hoping her mouth didn't smell like sick. He kept snoring, so she walked out and headed down to the snack bar with Peggy. Maybe he'd wake up thinking it really had been a dream. Better than the nightmare he'd just lived through.

CHAPTER 22

RACHEL

August 5, 1944

Rachel ran a dust rag over the piano keys in their living room. Sheet music sat on the stand, a nocturne by Chopin. No one had played the instrument in weeks, not since they got the news that Jesse was dead. Mama couldn't bear to hear her play. Papa avoided the piano like an open wound he couldn't suture. He had always played beautifully, his long slender fingers perfect for reaching chords as much as gripping a scalpel.

She and Jesse had taken lessons when they were younger, but Jesse had quit once he was old enough to play sports.

"Gotta save my strength for the pitcher's mound," he'd teased Mama when she urged him to keep up with his lessons. "I still like to play, but it's gonna be up to my big sister to make it to Carnegie Hall. Right, Rach?" Typical Jesse, knowing how to frame things so his parents couldn't stay mad at him. But it had put more pressure on her. Occasionally Jesse had surprised her, plopping down next to her on the piano bench, and playing something from memory, a Mozart etude or some other classical piece.

The last time they'd played together, right before he left for boot camp, it had been with an improvised version of "Heart and Soul," Hoagy Carmichael's sweet melody, even singing along, much to their parents' delight.

Heart and soul, I fell in love with you
Heart and soul, the way a fool would do, madly . . .

Her tears fell onto the keys and that was how Mama found her.

"Oh, honey." Mama tried to wipe her cheek.

Rachel turned her head away and dried her eyes on her sleeve. "I was just thinking about him." She got up. "I keep waiting for him to walk through the door and throw his things down, all jazzed about some class at Cal, or bragging about his team's win. Remember?"

Mama squeezed Rachel's shoulder, her eyes wet. "Of course I remember. Every detail."

She turned and walked toward the kitchen. They were hosting the family's Shabbat dinner in a few hours, and Mama had several dishes cooking on the stove, challah already in the oven. The aroma felt like an old friend.

This would be the first time Mama had offered to host Shabbat since the telegram. Uncle Max and Aunt Pearl had been very attentive to Mama and Papa since then, and tonight they were bringing Gordon. Rachel groaned. She had considered inviting Noah, but realized it would be too much for her, with Gordon pumping Noah for details about his life. It felt too soon.

She was still figuring out her relationship with Noah, this tender early stage. It had occurred to her that she might be using him as a way to heal the aching absence of Jesse. When she was with Noah, holding his hand or deep in conversation, she sometimes felt like a down quilt had wrapped around her shoulders. He seemed glad to offer her the comfort she needed.

That night, seated at the table, she regretted not having Noah next to her. Gordon decided that it was his job to tell stories to distract them from their grief. At first, Mama and Papa looked relieved they didn't have to keep the conversation going. Rachel poured herself a second glass of wine and poked at her food.

"So then I headed to Mare Island," Gordon said, brandishing his fork loaded with Mama's pot roast, "to check on the trains carrying ammo. When I got there, I found out the Navy had transferred those sailors who'd survived Port Chicago." He stuffed food into his mouth, chewed a moment, then added, "And then those same sailors decided to mutiny! Tried to take over the base." He kept chewing and looked at Rachel.

She took the bait. "It wasn't a mutiny, Gordie." Her heartbeat quickened. "I've been reading about it. Those men were terrified to return to their old jobs. Not after what they'd been through." She wished he'd shut up and go home.

"Yeah, well, that's what happens in wartime, Rachel," he said. "Men get hurt. And some die." Everyone stopped eating. Gordon put down his fork and glanced at her parents. He bowed his head. "Oh God, I'm sorry."

Papa got to his feet and wiped his mouth. His hands were shaking.

"It's not the same thing, Gordon," he said, his voice low, as if he were afraid he might lose control. "Jesse died fighting the enemy. He understood the risk. Those sailors died because they were never trained properly." He gripped the napkin in his fingers. "No one ever taught them how to load live ammunition."

He looked down at his nephew. "Shame on you. Don't you dare talk about those men like that. I was there. So was Rachel. We saw so many badly injured men. Dead bodies strewn on the beach. But you, you're safe in your office job, yammering on about things you know nothing about." He threw his napkin on the table and stalked out of the room.

"Bravo, Papa," Rachel said. She didn't care if the rest of the family were shocked by his words. He'd said what *she* wanted to say, though she might have thrown something at her stupid, big-mouthed cousin, too. Gordon, for once, was quiet, his cheeks reddened. She couldn't tell if he was angry at being chastised by Papa, or embarrassed by his ignorance.

Aunt Pearl and Mama got up and cleared the dishes off the table. Dinner was definitely over. Rachel joined them in the kitchen as they packed up the leftovers. None of them said much, the air thick with their shared grief. Aunt Pearl apologized for her son's outburst before they left.

Rachel offered to clean up, and Mama went to find Papa upstairs. Rachel filled the sink with very hot water and too much dish soap, plunging her arms in until her skin turned red. She slowly washed each plate and glass until the drain board was full. Drying them and putting the good china back on its shelf in the sideboard helped soothe her. She let her thoughts drift back to Jesse. She missed him so. He'd be rolling his eyes at Gordie, and mouthing some sarcastic comment only she would see.

* * *

The next day Rachel sat at the desk in her bedroom. Gordon's rant at dinner had gnawed at her. Bertie lounged in the wingback chair by the window nearest the gingko tree. The Royal typewriter sat ready.

"Is this going to be a long-winded piece about safety violations at the shipyard, Rach?" Bertie played with the window shade's cord.

"Ha ha, very funny," Rachel said. "No. Something different. I want to write about what happened to me on that bus ride."

She fanned her face with the newspaper. The upstairs got so hot in summer once the fog burned off. Thankfully a slight drop in temperature now meant the fog had again crept back across the bay, like an annoying neighbor who keeps poking his head over the fence.

Bertie sat up and let go of the cord. "Really? You're going to tackle antisemitism? Who's going to publish it? Your temple newsletter?"

Rachel shook her head. "No, silly. I want it published in the *Fore 'n Aft*, the shipyard's bulletin." She took a deep breath. "I want everyone at the yard to read it. I keep thinking about that woman on the bus. She's not the only one who's prejudiced. I mean, just read the newspapers. It's everywhere."

She stood up and paced. "Charles Lindbergh. Henry Ford. Even FDR. It took him until this January to set up the War Refugee Board. And that happened only after Eleanor pressured him. A lot of Jews could have been saved if he'd acted sooner." Her eyes filled. "I can't fix all of it, but I can write about my experience." She looked at Bertie. "Do you think I'm nuts?"

Bertie let out a low whistle. "No. I think you're becoming brave." She leaned forward. "Do you think they'll print it?"

Rachel nodded. "If I write it as a letter to the editor. They're always asking for input from the workers. People write in about all kinds of things, like a favorite casserole made with rationed ingredients, or getting a singing group together after work. This would be different. Maybe they'd print it just to get people stirred up. I don't know." She fiddled with the typewriter roller, clicking it back and forth.

"Well, I say go for it," Bertie said. "You never know who might read it and think twice about their own beliefs. Remember in high school when those guys teased me about my brace? That field trip to the art museum."

"Of course," Rachel said. She had urged Bertie to ignore the cruel comments.

"And Miss Fox?" Bertie's eyes seemed to replay the scene. "She walked right up to those boys and said, 'Gentlemen. What if this lovely young woman was your sister? What if your sister had polio? How would you feel if someone spoke to her like that?

Think about *that* the next time you open your mouths.' Their faces, oh boy. She shut them right up."

"Yeah, she surprised all of us, right?" Rachel said. "She was always so focused on Shakespeare. But that day, wow. After that she was my hero."

"Well, now you get to be your own hero. Or heroine," Bertie said, wiggling her back against the chair's cushions. "Your own Eleanor Roosevelt. Just tell your story. Be as honest as you can. How you felt when you were chatting with that woman, all friendly, then how she shocked you with her hateful words."

Bertie was right. This was her story to tell. She didn't need to write a dry essay on antisemitism. She would describe her experience, with enough detail to make the reader feel her emotions. What she wished she'd been able to say but was too afraid. How her silence had haunted her ever since. She turned back to the typewriter and began to write, the keys *clacking* under her fingers.

Letter to the editor from Rachel Stern, RN at the shipyard clinic.

Bertie would be the first to read it. Then, she thought, I'll share it with Elena. I want her opinion, too.

Rachel began to type. *Prejudice can show up anywhere. Even when you least expect it. Riding the shipyard bus.*

CHAPTER 23

ELENA

August 6, 1944

When Elena next returned to the clinic, she saw Rachel talking to an older worker whose foot and lower leg were wrapped in a bulky bandage. He stood against the doorjamb, leaning on crutches, his face creased with pain. Seeing him reminded Elena again of Port Chicago, her nerves still raw.

"I know you don't want to miss work, Laurence," she heard Rachel tell the man. "Maybe your boss can find you a desk job."

The man shook his head. "I ain't got no office skills, ma'am," he said and hobbled out of the clinic. Elena sensed the defeat rolling off his stooped shoulders. Not working was worse than even the lousiest job.

Rachel noticed Elena and came over. "Hi. Sorry but you'll have to wait your turn. Sign in at the desk."

She signed in and sat down, glancing at the other patients. She'd never had a job where so many workers got hurt every day. And no wonder. Each update from the war pushed the shipyard bosses to build ships faster.

"I went back to the base," she said when it was finally her turn, watching Rachel unwrap the dressing on her hand. The burned skin still hurt like el diablo when anything brushed against it. She winced. "Did you know almost all the sailors who died were Negroes? The white officers didn't do any of the loading. They only supervised."

"Yes," Rachel said. "I've been reading the paper. The Navy makes it seem like the men were careless. I mean, come on."

"It makes me so angry." Elena tried to sit still while Rachel removed the last bit of gauze. "Now the sailors refused to do that work again. Who could blame them?"

"I know," Rachel said, examining the burn. Elena felt like she was back in school being graded on a paper. She'd tried to protect her wound on the job, but it wasn't easy. "The infection is improving, but you still need to be careful."

"I am," Elena said, surprised at the tears that blurred her vision. She sniffled. "I don't cry for me. Not after what I saw. Those men."

She hadn't slept well since then, some nights waking up gasping for air. Images of bloodied limbs and corpses chased her. The only thing that helped was writing in the journal she'd started when she couldn't sleep, watching as the sun rose outside her window. Getting it onto the page helped. But it couldn't undo what had happened.

*　*　*

A few days later, on a hot afternoon, Elena was walking to the shipyard to start her shift when someone called her name. At least she thought so, but she was so tired from not sleeping, she might have imagined it. She turned around, shielding her eyes from the bright sun, and bumped into Ruby Mae, the riveter she knew from their early days of training.

"Look at this! I can't believe it," Ruby Mae said, panting. She shoved a newspaper at Elena. Sweat beaded on her face. She must have been running to catch up.

The headline read "*SAILORS CHARGED WITH MUTINY.*"

Elena read the article while Ruby Mae fanned herself. Fifty sailors from Port Chicago had been moved to the base at Mare Island where they had refused to load ammunition. She knew all this. But now the Navy had reacted. They had charged the men with mutiny. The country was at war. Orders had to be obeyed. There was going to be a trial. If convicted, the men would face prison.

"This is awful," she said to Ruby Mae, who nodded, wiping her face with a bandana. "I went to the base that night. I saw it all." They started walking together toward the yard.

Ruby Mae raised her eyebrows. "Why did you go? Did you know someone there?" Rings of sweat had stained her denim shirt.

"No, I had to see it for myself," Elena said. "I worked as a reporter back home." She hadn't told many people besides Rachel about this. Reporters were viewed with suspicion in San Salvador, accused of being spies for the government, or anarchists trying to take down those in power. Papá was neither, but he never shied away from reporting the truth.

They arrived at the entrance to the shipyard. "Thanks for showing me the story," she said to Ruby Mae, who glanced at her watch and sighed.

"I better get going," Ruby Mae said. "You know, I have a . . . uh, a friend, one of the sailors who got hurt that day. He's still off work 'cause of his injuries. Maybe you can talk to him 'bout what happened. He was there for all of it, 'til they sent him to the hospital."

"Oh, I'm so sorry. How's he doing now?" Elena asked. Her dressing change could wait. Her ears were on high alert.

"I don't know for sure," Ruby Mae said. "They still got his eye bandaged shut. They can't say yet how good he'll see once it heals." She stuffed the newspaper into her purse. "You should hear his side of it."

"Yes, I'd like that very much," Elena said. Talking to a survivor, getting a scoop like that would be great. Maybe she could sell the story. Her own byline.

CHAPTER 24

RUBY MAE

August 20, 1944

Ruby Mae hunched down, leaning her weight against the hull. She'd had to climb down a narrow walkway to reach this corner section deep inside the ship. The air was thick with eye-watering fumes from hot welds and machine grease, making it hard to breathe.

A three-day job, tops, Mr. Graham had promised. No climbing ladders. She wished she had Peggy's skinny scarecrow of a body. Peggy wouldn't have a problem folding herself like a pretzel to fit here, but Ruby Mae was fighting the walls that closed in on her. The belly of the ship, they called it, and her stuck here like Jonah inside that whale. Three days of this and she'd be begging for the whale to throw her back up onto the top deck.

"Hey, Taylor, you sleeping down there?" Her boss's voice echoed down the stairs.

"No sir, I ain't sleeping," she called.

Her goggles had steamed up, sweat coating her face. She pushed the goggles up, and pulled out her bandana. At least she was working on her own, trusted to get the job done. Back home, those rich ladies had watched her like a hawk while she cleaned.

Miz Simmons claimed she had a bad attitude. Maybe so, but she'd been fed up with being treated badly. For the most part, things were better here. A good paycheck, more than she'd ever earned back home, an okay boss and even some new friends.

"I don't hear those rivets going in," Mr. Graham called. "Don't make me come down there." Lord have mercy. Now that man was acting like Momma. Ever since she'd busted Ruby Mae for sneaking off to be with Freddy, Momma was on her like flies on a dog turd. No more nights out. Even now, with Freddy out of the hospital and back at Mare Island, she'd only seen him once. They'd met up for a matinee movie, but it was kind of a double date, since Peggy and Freddy's friend Charlie had joined them. They'd watched *Crash Dive* starring Tyrone Power, about two submarine officers who fell in love with the same woman. Kind of a dumb story, but all Ruby Mae had cared about was holding hands with Freddy and stealing a few kisses in the dark. Peggy had told her afterwards that Charlie was a real gentleman, and he made her laugh.

The clang of heavy work boots stomping down the walkway snapped Ruby Mae out of her daydream. Great. Her boss was coming to check on her. She pulled the safety goggles back on and grabbed the rivet gun. *Strit. Strit. Strit.* The rivets went in smooth as satin. She grabbed another handful of rivets in her left hand. *Strit. Strit. Ping.* One of the rivets fell from her fingers and clinked to the floor. She took off her glove and leaned over, stretching her fingers out to grab the rivet, her behind stuck up in the air. The rivet rolled away from her reach, under the sharp edge of steel plating.

Smack. She felt the slap on her behind at the same time that she heard a man's voice.

"Now, that's as tempting as a Georgia peach."

Ruby Mae froze. That wasn't Mr. Graham. No, but she knew who she'd see when she turned around. Jack, who had hassled her that day up on the scaffolding. She'd avoided him, but felt his eyes on her when she walked past. How had he found her?

Ruby Mae loaded another rivet into place and stood up. She turned around and aimed the rivet gun straight at Jack's crotch. Every muscle in her body vibrated. She took a deep breath to steady her hands. His eyes widened. He took a step back, banging his head on the low-hanging metal stairs. He grimaced but instead of grabbing his head, he crossed his hands in front of his crotch.

"Now, look here, you piece of trash," she said, her voice a low growl. "If you ever try anything like that again, I swear on the Bible I will drive this rivet right into you. God help me, I'll do it." She locked eyes with him. "Don't think I won't." She made herself stare at his face. People got lynched for doing that back home.

"Whoa there," he said. His face twisted into a leering smile. "Put that thing down. I was just having some fun with you, all bent over like that. I couldn't help it."

What kind of pathetic excuse was that?

She jerked the gun forward a few inches, and he jumped back, his head slamming into the stairs again. His pupils dilated. Good, he should be afraid. She was scared, too, scared she might not be able to stop herself. This anger welling up inside her had some wild force of its own. Like some rabies-infected dog.

"Say you're sorry," she said. Her breath came in short bursts.

"What?" He stared at her.

"You heard me. Say you're sorry."

She raised the gun and pointed it at his face. "Say you're sorry and you'll never do anything to me again." Some part of her mind had jumped outside her head and was shocked, watching her as she stood there, pointing her gun at this scared white man. Don't do anything stupid, Ruby Mae. They'll get you for this. But the rest of her pulsated with the power of holding that gun. Felt so good. "Say it. Tell me you're sorry. Or I swear to God, I'll do it."

"You crazy bitch," he said. He took a breath and shook his head. "Okay. I'm sorry." A bead of sweat trickled down his forehead.

"No," she said. "Say it like you mean it." She shoved the gun closer. Her ears were ringing, every sound was magnified, every breath more like a shout.

"I'm sorry, dammit," he said. "Okay?" He raised his arms in surrender. "There, I said what you wanted. Can I go now?" He wiped off the sweat that had dribbled down to his eyes. In that moment he looked pathetic, and something shifted inside her.

"Go on, git out of here," she said, pointing to the walkway with her gun.

He turned and walked back up the stairs, his footsteps thudding. She watched him leave, the muscles in her shoulders loosening. Her ragged breathing quieted. She put down the rivet gun and collapsed on the ground. Tears fell in her lap.

He was right. She'd gone crazy. But it sure had felt good, despite Momma's voice in her head. *Girl, you in trouble now. That man's gonna report you. They gonna fire you for sure. You almost murdered that man. Lord have mercy.*

She sat there for a long time, quiet, the wild energy fading. Her heartbeat slowed. Then she stood and picked up the gun. It felt light in her hands. For the rest of her shift she waited for Mr. Graham to show up. She feared they'd drag her upstairs and haul her to jail. Or worse, force her outside to some forsaken corner of the shipyard, rig up some scaffolding, and tie a rope from the top.

She'd never seen a lynching, but Daddy had once told her and Peggy that two men had been found hanging from a tall oak a couple of years ago near Baton Rouge. The men had been accused of stealing eggs from a farmer's chicken coop.

* * *

When her shift ended, Ruby Mae climbed up the walkway and found Peggy waiting for her. Peggy looked at her with raised eyebrows.

"What's wrong with you, girl? You don't look right. You sick or something?"

Ruby Mae looked around. No sign of Mr. Graham or Jack. "Yeah, well . . . I don't feel like myself," she said and took a deep breath. "Let's get out of here."

Peggy took her by the arm and led her outside to the shipyard entrance. The sun had come up, and the fresh air smelled good, the wind off the bay salty and damp. Ruby Mae stretched her legs and reached her arms up high, stiff from all those hours in the cramped space.

"Let's walk home, okay?" she said. "I'll tell you what happened."

When she got to the part about aiming that rivet gun, Peggy stopped short and grabbed her by the shoulders.

"What were you thinking, sis?" Peggy's eyes bore into hers.

"That's just it. I wasn't thinking. I was remembering how mad I get when people treat me bad. It all came out of me like a wild animal. You know, I came real close to doing it, too."

"I'm scared for you, Ruby Mae," Peggy said. "He's gonna report you for sure. And then what?" She shook her head. "You better warn Momma and Daddy."

"No. No way I'm telling them. They'll kill me. You can't tell them neither, okay? Promise me." She squeezed her sister's arm.

"Okay, fine. I promise," Peggy said. "But ain't you scared about what's gonna happen?"

She thought for a minute. "You know what? I been scared, waiting to get in trouble. But right now, telling you about it, I feel all right about what I did. That's kind of funny, huh?" She looked up at Peggy. "I bet he ain't gonna bother me no more. I scared him good. You should have seen him." She laughed when she saw Peggy's face. "I know. You think I'm crazy. Maybe so. But I'm not sorry. Not one bit."

CHAPTER 25

RACHEL

September 3, 1944

"I swear you're swooning over this guy," Bertie said. She lounged on the living room couch, her braced leg propped up on a pillow.

"Am not," Rachel said. She lay on the Oriental rug, sunlight streaming through the window onto her back. These surprise visits from Bertie were a welcome change. The house felt more like a funeral home these days. Missing Jesse led to moments of despair.

Bertie had complained of a shooting pain down her leg when she'd arrived. She blamed it on her job at Oakland's YMCA, a "girl Friday" position. The "Y" had recently converted some of its guest rooms into housing for returning soldiers. Bertie was tasked with arranging the services the men required, such as transportation and job search support. Rachel knew how much this new job meant to Bertie, her contribution to the war effort.

"You hardly know him," Bertie said, bringing Rachel's focus back to her love life. "For all you know, Noah could be a psycho, leading you like a lamb to the slaughter." She sliced her finger across her neck.

Rachel smiled, listening to Mama rattling pans in the kitchen. Lately, Rachel would find Mama sitting alone on the couch, sobbing, a photo album next to her, or back in the kitchen furiously baking at odd hours of the night. She had quit going to temple, too. What was the point?

Papa had gone in early to the hospital to follow up on his patients. Sunday morning no different to him. He needed to keep busy, and seemed lost around Mama's grief. Rachel was more like Papa, doing a few extra shifts at the clinic, but some days she'd join Mama on the couch, sharing Jesse stories.

Six weeks had passed since the explosion at Port Chicago. By now the injured sailors had received the necessary surgeries. A few men were still hospitalized with severe burns and penetrating wounds from the shrapnel-like debris. Her shifts at the clinic had returned to normal, though the nurses and doctors who had volunteered at the base still talked about the horrors they'd seen.

Noah was a welcome distraction. They had gotten together a few times since their awkward encounter at temple, gone to a couple of movies and once to hear a string quartet. He was easy to talk to, asked her opinion on all kinds of subjects, then sometimes challenged her ideas in a way that made her pause and think hard about how she saw things. Not only that, but he was also a very good kisser, kind of shy but eager, his lips soft on hers.

"I think you're jealous, Bertie," she said, tracing the intricate design of the rug, its deep reds and blues. "He's no psycho."

"Why isn't he off fighting?" Bertie said, loosening the brace and rubbing her leg. "Too busy studying?"

"Don't be a nitwit," Rachel said. "He tried twice to enlist, but they rejected him because of his heart murmur. They don't want men who might collapse in combat." Glancing at her watch, she groaned and stood up. "Shoot, I'm gonna be late, and it's your fault. I'm meeting him for lunch before I start my shift. I need to kick you out, unless you want to stay and help Mama in the kitchen."

Bertie fastened her leg brace and pushed herself up off the couch, wincing as she put weight on her leg. "No thanks. The last time I tried that, she yelled at me for eating too many cookies." She pointed at Rachel. "I don't know how you manage to keep your figure. I'd be fat as a pig if I lived here."

Rachel laughed. "I'm too busy to eat at the clinic. I'm lucky if I remember to drink any water. Thank God for my coffee thermos. That's my secret fuel." She nodded toward the kitchen. "Of course when I get home, Mama makes up for all that, feeding me like I've been lost in the desert for forty days."

Bertie walked over and hugged her. "Have a nice lunch with your beau. Tell him if he's got a smart and rich friend for me, I'm game. Ha ha. As long as he's a sharp dresser. I'm not interested in some schlub like your cousin." They both laughed as she walked Bertie to the door. Rachel had taught her a few choice words in Yiddish. Bertie hugged her. "Later, alligator."

"In a while, crocodile," Rachel said, closing the door. Since Jesse's death, Bertie had become her personal comforter, offering hugs or tissues or goofy distractions. Between Bertie and Noah, Rachel felt well cared for.

* * *

Noah picked her up in his parents' maroon Chevy. He wore tan chinos and a navy sweater over a collared shirt. She was glad she'd decided to wear street clothes, gray slacks and a pink sweater that Bertie had insisted she buy on their last shopping trip. Once she got to the clinic, she'd change into her uniform. If she'd worn that stiff dress now, she'd feel like she needed to document the rest of his medical history, or at least check his pulse.

She suggested they drive over to the Berkeley marina for a picnic. The sun had stayed out all morning, and she longed to walk by the water. They had three hours before she needed to be at the shipyard, and he'd promised to drive her to work.

"I hope you're hungry," she said, holding up a wicker basket. Mama had packed egg salad sandwiches, pickles, and enough snicker doodles to induce a diabetic coma. Mama's idea of how to win a man's heart was to dazzle him with delicious home-cooked meals, and avoid difficult conversations about politics or racial injustice, at least until he'd presented the ring. That's how Mama had snared Papa, or so she insisted. Rachel considered this a half-truth; Papa would not have been so easily swayed.

"Looks like your mother's been busy," Noah said, grinning. "And I'm always hungry."

He drove toward the bay. The windows were rolled down and the air carried the musty scent of the sea.

"What's happening at work?" she asked. Noah had a summer intern job at the NAACP office in Oakland during his break from law school classes.

"I wanted to talk to you about that," he said, running his hand through his hair. "There's a lot of anger about how the Navy is handling what happened at the base."

"Yeah, I get it," she said. "Accusing those sailors of mutiny is outrageous. After what I saw that night, it's no wonder they refused to load ammo again."

"Agreed," he said. "Now they'll have to stand trial, on top of what they've already been through." He turned onto the frontage road. The bay sparkled before them, shifting from gray to green to blue as the current changed.

"Look at this," she said, gesturing toward the water. "It's beautiful. We're so lucky to be here. But I keep thinking about the unfairness of everything. Men go off to war, men die on the job here at home, and the war keeps going. Men in power make bad decisions and more men die. So many unnecessary deaths." She caught her breath and stared out the window, thinking of Jesse. How had he died? Fighting or in some careless accident? "Sorry for ranting."

"Don't apologize, please," he said, putting his hand on hers. "I love that you aren't afraid to speak your mind." He parked the car close to the shoreline. Seagulls squawked and dive-bombed around the water's edge. "Let's walk before we eat, okay? I need to stretch my legs. I've been studying all morning, reading about Naval law. The sailors need to know their rights."

They walked along the path close to the water. The wind had picked up, pressing against them like an invisible hand. She leaned in close to Noah, and he put his arm around her shoulder.

"I talked to one of the lawyers yesterday," he said, his voice muffled by the wind. "He's really worried the sailors won't get a fair trial." He tightened his fingers around her. "I don't trust the Navy brass to do the right thing. They pretend this whole disaster wasn't their fault. The men say they kept telling their officers the work was too dangerous. No one listened." He stopped walking. A seagull squawked overhead and flew down onto a rock at the water's edge, a mussel shell clasped in its beak.

"What can the agency do?" she asked.

The gull banged the mussel on the rock, picked it up, and banged it again. Then pried it open, holding the shell with its foot, its beak reaching inside to pluck out the mussel. The bird flapped its wings and flew a few feet away. Once it landed, the gull dropped its prize on the ground and ate it. "Those men are defenseless." She shuddered and turned away from the gull. "I'm getting cold. Let's go back. If we can't find a sheltered spot, we can picnic in the car. Okay?"

"Sounds good to me," he said, grabbing her hand. "Let's go."

They found a spot behind a large outcrop of rocks and spread the blanket Noah kept in his trunk. Rachel unpacked the basket and laid out the food.

"Good lord, there's enough here to feed an army," he said, laughing. "If I didn't know better, I'd say your mother is trying to win my heart." He looked at her. "Tell her it's working."

"Wait, you're falling for Mama? What about me?" She bit into the egg salad sandwich, tasting the dill Mama used. Her cheeks felt warm. She looked down at her lap, and then peeked up at him.

"You? Well, let's put it this way," he said, picking up a snicker doodle. "If I had to choose between you and this cookie . . ." He took a big bite, chewing it slowly and locking eyes with her as he swallowed. "I'd have a hard time." He leaned over and kissed her. "But I'd choose you. Every time."

PART THREE

CHAPTER 26

ELENA

September 14, 1944

Treasure Island

Elena showed her press pass to the sailor stationed outside the makeshift courtroom and stepped inside. First day of the Port Chicago sailors' trial. Now she had two passes, one from Papá's paper back home, and this new one she'd gotten from the union. They weren't going to pay her, but the article for their newsletter would get her a byline, and a sample of her writing she'd use later. It was a good start.

The Navy had commandeered an empty barracks on Treasure Island for the trial. The location seemed so inappropriate. The barracks faced the blue-green bay that glistened under a bright blue sky, the San Francisco skyline a dramatic backdrop. They wanted to keep the trial low-key, but this island, halfway between the city and Oakland, reminded Elena of a Hollywood movie, not a somber setting for a military trial.

She took a seat in the chairs set aside for reporters. Her evening shift at the yard would keep her on her feet for another eight hours. What if she were able to find a job as a real reporter?

How much money could she make? Probably a lot less than what she earned now.

The man she'd sat down next to turned and stared at her press pass. He rolled his eyes. "Damn, the union's hiring women? Who are you?"

"My name is Elena Guzmán," she said, looking him in the eye. "And yes, they do hire women." He didn't need to know she wasn't getting paid. "Who do you work for?"

He pulled his pass out and thrust it towards her. "I'm with the *Oakland Tribune*, see?" He grinned. "A real newspaper. You're not from around here. Mexican?"

Why did everyone with an accent have to be from Mexico? "No," she said, the muscles in her shoulders tightening, "I'm from El Salvador. A proud union member. I work in Shipyard #3 as a welder. I build the ships your Navy needs to win this war." She pointed to her scarred hand. "That's how I got hurt." Her heart was pounding by the time she was done. The man's eyes widened. He shook his head and turned away. Another idiota.

She got out her notepad and wrote down what she observed. The small barracks, cleared of metal bunks, pressed everyone close together. Steam pipes hung from the ceiling, and American flags were pinned along the walls. The air felt thick with tension and the smell of sour sweat.

She couldn't tell who exactly was in charge, but several important-looking officers sat at a large curved table shuffling papers. They wore service ribbons pinned to their dark uniforms. In front of them were two smaller tables, each with several other officers seated. One table must be for the prosecution and one for the defense lawyers. There was no group that looked like a jury. And every officer was white.

"Attention."

The officers stood. The fifty Negro sailors on trial, in their dress blues, were marched in. They sat close to the back wall, like school kids dragged into a classroom for detention. Elena studied their faces. Most of them couldn't be more than twenty. They looked terrified.

Someone poked her shoulder. It was Betty, the redheaded reporter she'd met at Port Chicago. She took the last open seat behind Elena.

"Hi," Elena said, relieved to know someone else there. They were the only female reporters. "I wondered if you'd be here."

"Are you kidding? I needed to be here," Betty said, tucking some stray hairs into her bun. "I feel so bad for those boys. They're screwed."

Elena narrowed her eyes. "What do you mean?"

"Well, look around." Betty leaned in. "What chance do you think they have? The defense lawyers are all Naval officers. It's not exactly a fair trial, not when they're accused of mutiny. Besides, refusing an order in wartime . . . everyone knows what happens."

"But I don't understand. Where is the jury?"

Betty pressed her lips together. "There is no jury in a court-martial trial. Those officers you see at the big table? The seven of them make up what's called the court. They're the judge *and* jury. That one in the middle is Admiral Osterhaus. He's in charge."

Elena had been reading about the case ever since the work stoppage a month ago, followed by the arrest of the sailors. The defense lawyers would need to prove that the men had simply refused one specific order, to load ammunition. They were not intending to mutiny or take over command. If the men had been civilians, they'd only be guilty of going on strike.

But the Navy rules made their refusal a serious offense, especially during wartime. If this had happened back home, she thought, the men would have already been taken out to the countryside at night and shot, their bodies left as a warning. No trial. At least here they had a chance to plead their case.

Looking around the room, she caught sight of Ruby Mae, sitting off to the side, next to a sailor with an eyepatch. Had to be Freddy. How had Ruby Mae gotten admitted? She locked eyes with Ruby Mae and mouthed hello.

Ruby Mae nodded. She looked like she wished she were someplace else. These were Freddy's friends on trial, and the deck was stacked against them. Elena had heard that expression, and knew the truth of it. These sailors faced a powerful deck of cards, dressed in officers' uniforms, determined to teach the enlisted men a lesson: here's what happens when you stand up for yourself.

Admiral Osterhaus stood. "Court will come to order." He addressed each of the accused sailors, one by one, and asked how they pleaded to the charge of mutiny.

"Not guilty, sir," answered the first sailor. And the next. And the next. Fifty times.

The admiral sat and the prosecuting officer, Lt. Commander Coakley, presented the basics of his case. He claimed the accused men had conspired to commit mutiny. They had planned to refuse the work assigned to them. Several of them had made threats against their commanding officers. Elena wrote down the details as best she could, hoping Betty could explain some of the words she didn't understand.

Lt. Coakley called his first witness, who stepped forward and was sworn in.

Elena leaned back and whispered to Betty. "Who is that?"

"That's Commander Tobin," Betty explained in a quiet voice. She frowned at the reporter next to her when he put his finger to his lips. "He's in charge of the Mare Island base."

"Commander Tobin," Coakley said, "please describe the events of August ninth."

"Yes, sir. I issued orders for the three divisions from Port Chicago to load the *USS San Gay*. When I ordered "Column left," many of the men stopped in the middle of the road. Their attitude was they would obey any order, except to handle ammunition," he said. "I explained that the choice of duty does not rest with any individual."

"What happened next, Commander?"

The room had grown quiet. His account was critical for the rest of the trial. The newspapers had explained that the intention of the accused made all the difference to their case. "Conspiracy" was the word often used. If the men had planned or conspired to refuse the order to load the ship, that qualified as mutiny.

Commander Tobin leaned forward and looked at the Admiral's table of judges.

"Well, sir," he began. "There were 258 men who initially refused to load the ammunition. They were then confined to a barge for several days. We kept them there until Admiral Wright arrived. Even after he warned them they would be charged with mutiny, these fifty accused still would not load the ship."

Lt. Commander Coakley approached his witness. Elena figured he and Commander Tobin had already discussed what he would say. They were on the same side. The only hope for the fifty men would be if the defense team actually believed the sailors were innocent. And were willing to fight for them. The other 208 men, who'd initially refused to load, had backed down when threatened with the charge of mutiny and execution. They had already been tried and convicted in their own court martial cases. Their sentences had not yet been determined.

"So, Commander," Coakley said, puffing out his chest, "even after hearing they would be charged with mutiny, the accused men would not follow orders?"

"Yes, sir." Commander Tobin nodded and looked at the judges. "They knew what that meant."

"Thank you." Coakley sat down. One of the defense team's lawyers stood up to cross- examine Commander Tobin. He looked much younger than Lt. Coakley, with his blond hair slicked back.

"That's Lt. Veltmann," Betty said to Elena, her voice low. "He was a lawyer in Texas before he enlisted. I hope he knows what he's doing. This sure ain't Texas."

Lt. Veltmann smoothed his uniform and faced the witness. "Commander Tobin, I believe you said the men told you they would obey any order except loading ammunition. Is that correct?"

"The attitude of the men was that they would obey what they chose to obey," Tobin said.

Lt. Veltmann looked at his notes. "That wasn't your statement a while ago, was it, Commander?"

"That is the statement of fact, regardless of what I said earlier." Tobin sat back in his chair and crossed his legs.

"Did any of these men tell you that they were willing to obey *any* order except loading ammunition?" Lt. Veltmann persisted, and Elena understood the point he was making.

"Yes, a number did," Tobin replied.

"In other words," Lt. Veltmann said, "there wasn't a complete disrespect of your authority?"

Lt. Coakley jumped to his feet, his chair squealing. The whole room snapped to attention. Elena noticed that one of the judges, who had nodded off, opened his eyes, startled. How much of the testimony had he slept through?

"I object," Coakley said, his voice harsh, "on the grounds this is too broad and indefinite. Calls for the conclusion of this witness."

Lt. Veltmann turned toward the judges. "I withdraw the question." But he had made his point. Not a bad start for the defense. She felt encouraged.

After another hour of testimony, Elena urgently needed a bathroom. *Ay, diós mío,* don't think about your full bladder. But she couldn't concentrate. She stood up and tiptoed over to the exit, ignoring the frowns from reporters whose shoes she stepped over.

The air outside felt wonderful, cool and briny. She breathed it in and looked around the unfamiliar base. The sailor guarding the barracks' entrance watched her. He had blue eyes and a friendly face.

"I expect what you're looking for, miss, is over there," he said, pointing to a windowless wooden building. "That's the head."

"What?" The head? Maybe he thought she wanted to talk to the officer in charge.

"I'm sorry, miss." His pale cheeks turned pink. "The head, you know, the bathroom."

"Oh, thank you," she said. "So many words I still don't know."

He smiled. "Come talk to me when you're done, okay?" Was he flirting with her?

She nodded and hurried to the building with a painted "Women Only" sign nailed over the entrance. When she stepped inside, she found a long row of urinals on one side with a few stalls on the other. Men had clearly used the place until recently. It reeked of stale urine. Holding her breath, she used the toilet as quickly as she could, then washed her hands in the cold water at the sink.

Once outside, she saw people milling about. The lawyers must have requested a break. Several reporters and spectators had gathered in small clusters. The armed sailor stood by the barracks' door, talking with other sailors, but he glanced at her. Just as well he was busy. She was not looking for any romance. Her life was already too hectic.

She spotted Ruby Mae and Freddy and walked over.

"Hi Elena." Ruby Mae put her hand on Freddy's shoulder. "This here is Freddy. I told you about him. Elena works at the yard, too. She does welding."

"Nice to meet you, Miz Elena," Freddy said, offering his hand. His black eyepatch and the bandage on his neck reminded her of that night. "Don't worry," he said, "I ain't gonna run off on some pirate ship. I just need this eye to heal, so I can get back to work."

"I understand," Elena said, shaking his hand. His grip was firm, his skin callused. "Takes a long time."

The wind had picked up, and fog drifted into view over the city. Freddy looked over at the officers and lowered his voice.

"Yeah, it's been rough," he said, "but nothing compared to my buddies. Officers trying to make it look like they're being fair, with all their fancy lawyer talk. I bet every one of them already made up their minds." He adjusted his eyepatch.

Ruby Mae pulled her sweater around her. "Freddy says his friends want to trust their lawyers, but they pretty scared of what's coming."

Elena looked at Freddy. No harm in asking. "Would you be willing to talk to me sometime? I'd like to hear your side." She held up her notepad. "I want to be sure people learn the whole story."

"Who you writing this for?" Freddy asked. He stepped back and glanced at the officers near the barracks, heads bent in conversation.

"Well, so far, just the union's newsletter," she said. "But I'd like to get it published with a bigger paper. Maybe the *Tribune* or the *Examiner*. They've been reporting on Port Chicago since the explosion."

Freddy raised his eyebrows. "Whoa, girl," he said. "That's the big time. I don't think so. I can't say much without getting my behind in trouble with the brass." He chewed his lip. "They don't want us talking 'bout how dangerous our job was. How none of us was surprised when that ship blew up." He touched the small bandage on his neck.

That was exactly what she wanted to hear about. But she didn't blame him for being scared to talk. He was still in the Navy. Ruby Mae had said he'd been assigned to a desk job until he could return to the docks. She wondered if he would have been one of the men on trial if he hadn't been injured.

"Okay," she said. "I understand, but please think about it. Maybe one way we could do the interview is if I kept you anónimo? No names." People opened up once they knew their names wouldn't be used in the story. She wrote down the phone number at the Murphys' house and handed him the slip of paper. "Call me if you change your mind. I think people should hear your story."

Freddy hesitated, then shook his head. Ruby Mae took the paper instead and stuck it in her purse, snapping it shut.

Elena checked her watch. People had started walking back into the barracks, but she needed to leave for work. Busses didn't run very often out to Treasure Island, and she wanted to grab some lunch before she had to report to the shipyard.

"I've got to go," she said to Ruby Mae. "I'll try to be here tomorrow. Are you coming again?"

"Yeah, maybe," Ruby Mae said. She looked at Freddy. "We can give you a ride. Freddy's got a car they let him use."

That would be perfect. He'd be more relaxed in the car.

"Uh, I can't make it tomorrow, Ruby Mae," Freddy said. He turned his head and looked back at the officers. "I got to work day shift." He frowned. "And I can't talk to you, Miz Elena. Not about what happened. Not now. Them officers be watching all of us real close." He shrugged. "I'm sorry 'bout that."

* * *

Later that week Elena returned to the courtroom just as the first witness of the afternoon took the stand. Betty had saved her a seat. The prosecution had called several witnesses over the past few days. Lt. Coakley seemed determined to get them to say what he wanted to hear, that in fact the accused men had conspired to refuse orders. He had not succeeded, and now clutched his papers, like he intended to wring the truth out of them.

Seaman Ollie Green took the stand, one of several witnesses wounded in the explosion. He described how he was injured by flying glass and had been hospitalized. Once he returned to work days later, he unfortunately broke his wrist, so he was not present on August ninth when the sailors' work refusal occurred. But he had plenty to say, admitting he would have also refused to load ammunition, because he was scared.

Admiral Osterhaus asked him if he had more to add.

"I got a couple things to say, sir," Green said. The judges looked surprised, and Elena felt a jolt of energy. None of the witnesses had offered more than short answers.

"The reason I was afraid to go load ammunition," Green said, "is them officers were *racing* each division to see who put on the most tonnage. I knowed the way they was handling ammunition, it was liable to go off again."

Green paused and looked around the room. He took a deep breath. Even the defense lawyers were wide-eyed. "If we didn't work fast, they wanted to put us in the brig. When the top brass came down on the docks, they wanted us to slow up. That's why I was afraid."

When Green had finished, Admiral Osterhaus immediately excused him from the witness stand, before anyone had a chance to question him further. The courtroom buzzed. He was the first sailor to describe the dangerous working conditions at Port Chicago. Green had simply told the truth, in front of all the reporters and the top Navy officials. Until then, the trial had focused only on the actions of the accused sailors, three weeks after the deadly explosion.

Elena watched Green step down. She remembered that night, the gruesome scene at the base. These sailors on trial had been there, too. Each of them had seen what happened when a small spark buried in a crate of ammunition touched off one fuse. Then another and another, sinking the packed ship, ripping apart those sailors unloading the docks. She bit her cheek to keep from crying.

Betty leaned over. "Finally, someone willing to tell the truth. The judges are squirming."

Elena wiped her eyes. "Too bad they didn't keep him on the stand."

"Yeah, well, he'd said his piece," Betty said. "Now it's up to us to make sure that all of his testimony is reported. Let people read it in their newspapers tomorrow. Get angry. That's how change happens."

Betty was right. Elena needed to get her story written and published. Did the Navy care about what the public thought? In El Salvador, the government did whatever the generals demanded, regardless of the public's outrage. Maybe it was different here, but she doubted one newspaper article held that much power. Nevertheless, she could hear Papá in her head. Not just one article, but a whole series that exposed the Navy's unfair treatment of its Negro sailors.

* * *

The following morning was day eleven of the trial. Elena found her seat. Lt. Veltmann, the lead defense lawyer, finally had his chance to prove there had been no conspiracy, no secret vote to mutiny.

"This courtroom will come to order. The defense will present their case."

Veltmann called up his first witness, a twenty-three year old sailor named Joe Small, the supposed ringleader of the men. Elena had seen Small on the stand earlier. She admired the way he'd stayed calm when Coakley confronted him with accusations of defying orders. But Small's eyes had revealed his bottled anger when answering Coakley.

"Tell us about the night of the explosion," Veltmann said. He wanted to set the stage for how the men reacted that night, how terrified they were.

"I was thrown out of my bed. Got a few cuts," Small said. "All the men were running wild. The barracks was collapsing. I got myself together and turned to help the men who were injured."

"What happened later that night?" Veltmann asked. "Who had to deal with the dead men on the beach and floating in the water?" Several of the sailors closed their eyes. Elena's stomach clenched.

Small looked down. "That was part of our job, those of us who weren't hurt too bad. It was worse than you can imagine." The courtroom hushed.

"What was the mood of the men in the days after the explosion?" Veltmann stepped closer to the witness stand.

Small described how tense and scared the men were. "One night," he said, "one of the guys jammed his bed sheet into the fan. He laughed when everyone in the barracks panicked at the awful noise."

"What else happened, Small?"

"Well," Small said, looking at the judges' table, "another night, that same guy dragged his metal bunk across the floor, made a terrible sound. The men started running . . . there was cursing and swearing. I quieted them down and got them back to bed."

"Why did they run, Small?"

"Just a minute," Coakley spoke up. "Objection, calling for his conclusion."

"Objection sustained."

"Why did *you* run, Small?" Veltmann said.

"Objected to as irrelevant and immaterial," Coakley said.

"Overruled."

Admiral Osterhaus glared at Coakley and leaned forward in his chair.

Small looked at the admiral. "Because the first thing I thought of was an explosion."

"What happened to that sailor?" Veltmann asked.

"They got him out of there and took him to sick bay," Small said, his lips pressed tight.

Elena wasn't sure exactly what that meant, but it sounded like the man needed help. She understood how traumatized he must have been. Like her, still haunted by it.

"So, from your observation, would you say that the men were afraid?" Veltmann said.

"Yes, sir," Small said, and nodded his head. "Terrified." He looked over at his fellow sailors.

Lt. Coakley's face had reddened. He must be frustrated, she thought, that he couldn't stop Small from speaking up. Fear, not a whispered conspiracy, was the real motivation for why the sailors had refused their instructions to turn "column left." Small had made his point.

When the trial adjourned for the day, Elena noticed a well-dressed, tall Negro man who approached the accused men just as they were led out. She'd seen him in the courtroom the previous day as well.

"Who is that?" she asked Betty as they gathered up their belongings. "He can't be Navy, not in that suit and tie." He stood out from everyone else, stiff-backed, a serious expression on his face.

"That's Mr. Marshall," Betty said. "Thurgood Marshall. What kind of name is that, *Thurgood*?" She chuckled. "But he's here representing the NAACP. He's their lawyer."

"Oh," Elena said. "And what is NAACP?" She wished she understood more of these things, but thankfully Betty didn't get annoyed by her questions. Once the trial was over, she'd have to buy Betty some kind of thank you gift. Something for that red hair, a tortoise shell comb or some pretty ribbons.

"It's short for the National Association for the Advancement of Colored People," Betty said. "They get involved in cases where Negroes have been treated unfairly. The local branch contacted headquarters in Washington about the trial. Mr. Marshall flew out here to see for himself."

So the story wasn't just local now. Elena needed to talk to this lawyer, get a good quotation for her story. Her heart racing, she followed him out the door of the barracks and tried to keep up with him as he walked toward the parked cars and bus stop. A few other reporters were also trying to get his attention.

"Excuse me, sir. Mr. Marshall?" Elena was practically shouting, but she might not have another chance to talk to him. He stopped and turned around. Elena stood with the other reporters trailing around her. She stepped forward and brushed her hair off her face. "Thank you, sir. I would like your opinion of how the accused men acted," she said, ignoring the scowls on the faces of the male reporters.

Thurgood Marshall looked first at Elena, then at the rest of the reporters. "There is not sufficient evidence of mutiny or conspiracy," he said. "These men are being tried for mutiny solely because of their race." The reporters wrote down his words verbatim.

"What can your group do?" another reporter asked, his tie flapping in the breeze.

Marshall crossed his arms. "The NAACP is going to make this its job. Expose the whole rotten Navy setup that led to the Port Chicago explosion, and in turn the so-called 'mutiny' trial of fifty Negro sailors. This is not an individual case. This is not fifty men on trial for mutiny. This is the Navy on trial for its vicious policy toward Negroes."

He shook his head. More people had gathered. That seemed to inspire him to elaborate, his voice raised so no one missed a word, despite the wind kicking up the pungent scent of low tide.

"Negroes are not afraid of anything, any more than anyone else," Marshall continued. "Negroes in the Navy don't mind loading ammunition. They just want to know why they were the only ones doing the loading! They want to know why they are segregated, why they don't get promoted."

Elena felt someone nudge her from behind. She turned around and there was Ruby Mae, clutching her sweater, her eyes wide.

"Who is that?" Ruby Mae spoke in Elena's ear.

Thurgood Marshall had finished speaking. He thanked the reporters for their attention, urging them to get the whole story out there. He turned and walked away, leaving the group to scribble their notes.

"That was Thurgood Marshall," Elena said, pleased to have the answer. "He works for the NAACP. Do you know about that? And where's Freddy?"

Ruby Mae shook her head. "He had to stay behind and help out with something. What's it stand for?"

Elena looked at her notes. "National Association for the Advancement of Colored People," she read out loud. "He's a lawyer and he goes around the country to help when Negroes get in trouble with the law."

"What?" Ruby Mae shook her head. "Never heard of such a thing. He's here to help those sailors?"

"Yes," Elena said, buttoning her coat. She needed to head to the bus stop. She took Ruby Mae's arm and guided her away from the crowd. "Did you hear him talk? He sounds so confident."

"I ain't never heard anyone talk like him," Ruby Mae said. "Like he was the boss and you better listen to what he's saying." She stopped walking. "Maybe he can help me."

Elena frowned. "Help you with what?"

Ruby Mae looked around as if to make sure no one listened. She described what had happened to her at work, how Jack had touched her and how she'd reacted.

Elena's mouth fell open. "Oh, Ruby Mae," she said. "I'm so sorry. That sounds awful." She understood Ruby Mae's reaction. Holding that rivet gun must have made her feel brave, even powerful. But she'd pay a price for what she'd done.

"I know he's gonna tell on me," Ruby Mae said. "And Mr. Graham is gonna fire me. But it was *his* fault. I was only trying to protect myself." She looked like a young girl explaining to her mother why she'd hit her brother with the rolling pin.

The public bus lumbered into the parking lot and they hurried over and got in line.

Elena put her arm around Ruby Mae. "Maybe Mr. Graham will understand."

"Do you think Mr. Marshall could help me?" Ruby Mae said. "Peggy thinks I should talk to the folks at the auxiliary union. I don't know what they can do."

"I don't know either," Elena said. "But maybe Jack won't tell anyone. Maybe nothing will happen."

She thought about her own experience. When people with power over your life decide to punish you, your only choices are to fight back or run away as far as you can. Those who stay and fight back risk everything, including their lives. And sometimes the lives of those they love. Those who run, she knew, always look over their shoulder, waiting for their luck to run out.

CHAPTER 27

October 24, 1944

Treasure Island

Rachel drove onto the Naval base at Treasure Island and found the barracks where the Port Chicago trial was ending. Noah had urged her to attend the lawyers' closing statements. He and Elena had given her frequent updates during the six weeks of testimony, and they both would be there today. Despite Noah's prediction, she believed the judges would have to find the men innocent. The facts of the case mattered.

A sailor guarding the courtroom door stood checking ID's. He nodded at her white uniform and didn't bother inspecting her name tag. The Navy had made the trial public. They claimed they had nothing to hide.

She spotted Elena and grabbed the seat next to her.

"Glad you made it," Elena said. "This row's for the press, but it's probably fine." She had already written notes on her pad and had that intent reporter look on her face.

Rachel stared at the uniformed men filling the courtroom. They reminded her of Jesse, except that all the accused men were

Negro sailors. In the photo on her nightstand, taken just after boot camp at Fort Riley, Jesse beamed at the camera in his Army fatigues. He'd written funny letters about the Kansas cornfields and how much he missed Mama's cooking. A month later he'd shipped out overseas. After that, the letters arrived censored and somber. Then nothing at all, for weeks, until the telegram that shattered her family arrived.

She spotted Ruby Mae in the back, next to a sailor who had to be Freddy. Rachel knew him, recognized the scar on his neck and the patch over his eye. She shuddered, remembering the bloody trail of injured men. The defense lawyers needed to convey that horror to the judges. The prosecutors couldn't deny the truth of what led to the work stoppage: the accused men had been assigned dangerous work, again, that no white sailor was ever ordered to do.

Admiral Osterhaus stood, glancing around the room as he banged his gavel. "Court will come to order. Lieutenant Coakley, your summary argument, please."

"He's the main lawyer for the Navy," Elena whispered.

Rachel nodded. Out of the corner of her eye, she saw Noah slip in the back door of the barracks. There were no available seats, so he stood against the wall. His presence was somehow comforting.

Coakley stood and faced his fellow officers. He appeared at ease despite the tension in the room. Rachel had read that he'd been an assistant DA before the war, no stranger to a trial. He described how the accused men talked of mutiny once they were transferred to Camp Shoemaker after the explosion. Then, once they were reassigned to Mare Island, he claimed these same sailors had intimidated the men who didn't support the work stoppage.

"Mutiny means insubordination. Disobedience of lawful orders of a superior officer," he said. "There's a war on. Ammunition ships needed to be loaded. Fear is no excuse."

Rachel squirmed, listening to this pompous man drone on. No one challenged him. She looked back at Noah who shook his head in disgust. The defense lawyers needed to push back.

Coakley paced in front of the judges and then stopped short.

"A man who says he's afraid is capable of giving false testimony. What kind of morale would we have if men in the United States Navy could refuse an order and then get off on the grounds of fear?" He looked towards the accused sailors and shook his head. He turned back to the judges. "Thank you."

The judges nodded. He was preaching to the choir. A knot tightened in her stomach. How could they not see that fear in battle was different than the fear of dying just for doing your job?

Lt. Veltmann, the defense lawyer, was called up next for his closing argument. He, too, looked confident, his uniform snug and his hair freshly trimmed. He had to convey how traumatized the sailors were by the night of the explosion. Only one month had passed before they'd been asked to load ammunition again. Surely the Navy had a duty to protect its sailors. Rachel's heart ached. How dare the Navy try to punish them to cover up its own negligence?

Veltmann faced the accused sailors. "Remember, these men had handled all types of explosives in their daily work," he said. "They were subjected to the danger and uncertainty of that job. No opportunity to fight back, if danger should rear its head and strike without warning, and strike it did on the seventeenth of July."

Elena whispered. "I don't know what else he'll say, but it doesn't really matter, does it? The judges made up their mind before the trial even started."

Rachel hoped Elena was wrong.

Veltmann glanced at the judges. His cheeks flushed. Rachel got the impression he knew he was in over his head, like David hoping to slay Goliath with only a slingshot. But David had surprised everyone. Veltmann took a sip of water and continued.

"The terror and the shock were new experiences for these men. When the explosion has wiped out the lives of your fellow workers, when you see them picked up in baskets—an arm, a leg, or just a head and shoulder—or you help pick up the remnants, genuine fear can be engendered. Fear that controls your actions and influences your reasoning."

Rachel tensed. So many of the sailors she'd treated had been in shock, numbed by what they'd seen. Like the soldiers who'd returned from the Great War. Some of those men never fully recovered. But in this case, danger hid in plain sight, loaded into crate after crate. Why hadn't the defense called doctors who could explain psychological trauma? Or safety experts to review the risks inherent in loading live munitions?

Veltmann turned again to the judges. His face looked damp. He put down his papers. "The prosecution has presented no evidence of a plot, or any attempt to seize authority from officers. Without proof of these elements, the case of the prosecution most certainly has not been proven."

He took a deep breath and straightened his spine. "We submit that these fifty men," pointing at the accused, "are not guilty of the offense of mutiny. Thank you." He sat down at the defense table, his palms flattened.

No one spoke for a moment. Veltmann tugged at his collar. The defense lawyers had never directly addressed the reality of a segregated Navy. What chance did the sailors have now when their fate was in these white officers' hands?

Admiral Osterhaus stood up. "Thank you, Lt. Veltmann. The courtroom will now be cleared for lunch."

He and the rest of the judges hurried out of the barracks, like they hoped to avoid the reporters. Elena hurried toward the accused men, notepad ready. Rachel joined everyone else exiting the barracks. Noah was waiting for her by the door.

"I'm glad you got to hear the closing arguments," he said, watching as the accused men left through a side door under guard, their expressions grim. "But I think they're screwed."

Outside the barracks, Rachel stood next to Noah and watched the crowd disperse. Elena came over, tapping a pencil on her notepad.

"This is Noah," Rachel said. "He's an intern at the NAACP. I've told him about your reporting."

"Nice to meet you," Elena said. "What did you think of Veltmann's closing statement?"

Noah raised his eyebrows. "He tried. But to be honest, I wanted him to be more inspired, more angry. I don't think he changed anyone's mind."

"And he didn't address the elephant in the room," Rachel said.

"Un elefante?" Elena frowned. "Explain, please."

"It's an expression," Rachel said. "It means the obvious thing everyone sees but no one talks about. They didn't highlight that all the accused sailors are Negro. They were the only ones doing the dangerous work. The white officers mostly stayed out of harm's way."

"That's what the Navy wants to play down," Noah said. "Veltmann included." He kicked some dirt with the toe of his shoe. "It looks bad in the newspapers. Thurgood says change won't happen unless there's a spotlight on the racial discrimination in the military."

Rachel watched Elena take notes. She wondered what the judges were discussing in their lunch meeting. They were probably glad to be almost done with the trial.

"Elena and I need to head up to the shipyard," she said, squeezing Noah's hand. "Call me later at the clinic with any update."

* * *

"It's over." Noah's voice on the clinic's phone sounded flat.

"What?" Rachel checked her watch. It had only been an hour and a half since the trial had adjourned for lunch. They couldn't have reviewed six weeks of witness testimony already.

"All fifty men found guilty of mutiny." Noah sighed. "I guess we shouldn't be surprised. But it's so blatant. They didn't even pretend to review the case. Thurgood was right."

Rachel stared at the room full of clinic patients waiting to be seen. A woman clutching a gash in her arm. An older man limping. She thought about the risks they took every day when they came to work. They strained their bodies and put up with nasty bosses or co-workers who objected to their skin color or accent, or that they were women doing a man's job. But the workers here had a union to fight for them when problems occurred. Even the Negro workers had their auxiliary union. Those sailors had nothing. They'd put their trust in the US Navy and it failed them. They were being punished for trying to stay alive.

"It gets worse," Noah said.

"Their sentence?" She held her breath.

He groaned. "Fifteen years in prison. Hard labor. Dishonorable discharge."

"Oh my God," she said, exhaling hard. She clenched her fists. This was so wrong.

"Thurgood's already drafting a letter to the Secretary of the Navy. He says the battle is over but the war is on."

CHAPTER 28

ELENA

October 24, 1944

Elena spotted Ruby Mae in the shipyard cafeteria and hurried over. The crowd had thinned and empty plates clattered as staff cleared the tables.

"Have you heard the verdict?" she said.

"Verdict?" Ruby Mae frowned. "I thought they had to go over all the evidence first."

"The Navy does what it wants," Elena said. She put her hand on Ruby Mae's shoulder. "Guilty. They got fifteen years in prison."

Ruby Mae gasped. "Oh, dear Lord, no." Her face crumbled. "This will kill Freddy. His friends . . ." Tears dribbled down her cheeks.

"I know." Elena understood Ruby Mae's grief, but anger outweighed her own sadness. The injustice of it. As bad as back home. "Thurgood Marshall is writing a complaint to the Navy bosses. I don't know what good it will do, but at least it's something."

"Fifteen years?" Ruby Mae said, drying her eyes. She stood up and grabbed her purse. "I need to call Freddy. But listen, I promised Marcy I'd meet her at Tappers' Inn tomorrow night.

Why don't you come, too? Hear some good music and maybe we can figure out how we can help the sailors."

* * *

She met up with Ruby Mae and Marcy at the bus stop outside Tappers' Inn. Inside, it was as big and welcoming as promised.

"This is wonderful," she said, happy to be out with friends.

"Yeah," Marcy said. "Our people always make do when kicked to the gutter. We take care of our own." She grabbed Ruby Mae's arm. "I wish I'd been there to see that cracker's face when you pointed that gun at him. Too late now to do much, except hope he ain't mad enough to tell on you."

They walked from the lobby toward the nightclub, removing their coats. Elena, in her burgundy shirtdress was underdressed. Ruby Mae and Marcy, like the other women she saw, wore two-piece outfits with sparkly tops and snug skirts. When she'd fled El Salvador, the one suitcase she'd hurriedly packed, listening for the police at the door, held only basic work clothes, underwear, and a few of her favorite books.

"I'll get us a pitcher of beer," Marcy said. "You two find a table."

Elena followed Ruby Mae to a booth in the back that hadn't been cleared. She watched Ruby Mae load a tray with the dirty glasses, then grab a napkin to wipe the table. The waitress came over and picked up the tray, frowning.

"I can't help myself." Ruby Mae laughed. "I been cleaning up after folks my whole life." She looked at Elena. "That's what I did back home. Clean other folks' homes."

"Yes? I worked at a canning factory," Elena said. "Besides helping Papi with the newspaper." She sat down next to Ruby Mae on the soft leather cushion. "I never made good money before this."

"Me neither." Ruby Mae crossed her arms. "I'm praying that man keeps his mouth shut. He knows he shouldn't a slapped my butt. It was his fault I turned my gun on him. Besides, I never touched him." She clenched her jaw. "He ain't hurt. Just his pride, being scared by a colored gal."

"But no one else saw what happened, right?" Elena said. "It's your word against his."

Ruby Mae nodded. "Who you think they gonna believe?"

Marcy returned with a full pitcher, and the three of them sipped their beer and listened to the recorded blues music. Several men dressed in suits set up instruments on stage. Elena wondered whether she'd know any of their music. Her body already swayed to the bluesy beat.

"How y'all doing?"

Elena looked up. The woman asking the question, at least forty years old, was dressed in a plain black two-piece outfit, a strand of pearls her only adornment. She held a lit cigarette in her left hand, and exhaled a smoke ring over their heads.

Marcy wiped her mouth. "Hey, Margaret. This here is Ruby Mae, she's from Louisiana. And this pretty thing is Elena, all the way from El Salvador, wherever that is," she said, smiling at Elena. "Ladies, this is Margaret Starks. She manages this place. And now she's putting out a Negro newspaper, too. She has meetings here to talk about the problems folks is having."

"What kind of problems?" Elena asked. She put down her glass.

Margaret pulled her shoulders back and stared at Elena. "Girl, how come you don't know 'bout all the problems going on? Where you been?"

"No, I didn't mean it like that," Elena said. Blood rushed to her face. "I'm interested in the newspaper. That's what I did back home, I helped Papá run a small paper. And now I'm covering the Port Chicago trial. For the union newsletter."

Margaret's face softened, and she sat down next to Marcy. "The paper's called the *Richmond Guide*. We cover the rest of what the *Tribune* and the *Examiner* leave out. And we published the Navy's press briefings about the trial." She paused. "Not that they told the whole story." She sighed. "Thank goodness for the NAACP."

Elena looked at Ruby Mae.

"I guess everybody knows about them, huh?" Ruby Mae said. "Me and Elena heard Mr. Thurgood Marshall. He came to the trial."

Margaret cocked her head. "Girl, we got a branch of the NAACP right here in North Richmond. In fact, the meetings are here at Tappers'." Ruby Mae's jaw fell open. Margaret laughed. "Thurgood met with us when he was out here from Washington. He's got his hands full now that they convicted those sailors."

"What?" Ruby Mae said. "He came here?" She turned to Elena. "See, I told you that maybe he could help me." She covered her face with her hands. "He came to Tappers' and I missed him."

Elena put her hand on Ruby Mae's arm. "I think they only take big cases."

Margaret leaned forward. "What kind of trouble you in, Ruby Mae?"

Elena listened as Ruby Mae described the incident with Jack. Hearing the details again made her stomach turn. Women at the yard were always having to look over their shoulder. She thought about her own assault. She understood Ruby Mae's rage. Whatever it took to make him stop.

Margaret sat back and shook her head. "I'm sorry 'bout what happened, Ruby Mae," she said. "But you didn't actually nail him with that gun, right?"

"I wish I had," Ruby Mae said, picking up her glass. "If I'm gonna get fired, I want something to show for it. All I got is remembering that scared look on his face. Wish I had a photo of that. He knew how close I was to shooting off his pecker. I guess that's something, huh?"

Elena laughed and so did the others. They all understood what Ruby Mae meant. Were there women anywhere who didn't have a story to tell?

By then the band had finished setting up. A woman walked onto the stage and stood in front of the microphone. Her teal satin dress was floor-length, one-shouldered, with a satin rose perched on that shoulder. She'd swept her dark hair up on one side, with soft curls on the other. The effect was elegant.

"Who's that?" Elena asked Marcy, who shook her head.

"That's Mabel Scott," Margaret said. "She used to have an all-girl gospel group. Now she's on her own, singing different music."

Elena wondered what it would feel like to look glamorous and perform for an audience. Not that anyone would want to hear her sing. Mami once told her she sang with passion but not an ounce of pitch.

Mabel Scott's voice broke into Elena's thoughts, full-throated and with attitude. She pleaded for a man, any man, to join her, even if he snored or had bad breath. She just needed a man.

Elena laughed at the song. The lyrics were ridiculous, but she understood the feeling behind the words. There were days when loneliness gnawed at her. Not that she'd ever had a serious boyfriend. Always too busy. That had been her excuse. But maybe one day. For now, having new friends helped, especially since losing Ana and Marisol. She'd keep busy with work and writing. Boyfriends would have to wait.

CHAPTER 29

RUBY MAE

October 28, 1944

Ruby Mae stood at her locker next to Peggy, dressing for their shift, when a woman she didn't know walked up and handed her a folded slip of paper.

"This is for you." The woman turned and left.

Ruby Mae opened the note, her heart thudding.

Come see me in my office right away. Mr. Graham.

"Oh, no. No, no, no, no." Ruby Mae sat down hard on the wooden bench. It had been two months since her run-in with Jack. She'd avoided him when she could, and so far nothing had come of it. "Oh, Peggy!" Her throat tightened. "He finally told." Why now? She felt sick.

"I knew it!" Peggy said. "That man is the Devil, and he's coming for you." She pulled Ruby Mae up by the shoulders into an embrace. "Dear Lord, don't forsake us now in our time of need."

Ruby Mae leaned against Peggy. Around them other women came and went, changing into coveralls, putting on gloves and goggles, fastening welding hoods. Some glanced at the two sisters but left them alone. It wasn't the first time for drama in the locker room.

"Maybe I should go with you," Peggy said, stepping back. "You know, in case you lose it."

Ruby Mae took a deep breath. A tempting offer. "Thanks, but you better get to work so we both don't end up in trouble." She locked up her belongings and hurried to the drinking fountain, gulping the lukewarm water before she left.

Outside, the afternoon sun beat down, no sign of fog. The sounds of whirley cranes and tools clanging grew louder as she reached the brown stucco admin building. Beyond that loomed the huge skeleton of the victory ship being assembled.

She knocked on the door of Mr. Graham's office. Her heart felt ready to explode.

He opened the door. "Come in, Ruby Mae."

She stepped inside and Mr. Graham shut the door. And then she saw him. Jack, slouched on a chair in the corner of the small office. Oh no. She hadn't expected him.

"I need to sit down," she said, grabbing the oak chair near the door. There was no air in the room. She closed her eyes and tried to steady her breathing. Why was *he* here? Maybe this was only an awful dream and he would be gone when she opened her eyes. But no, there he was, his eyes on her.

"Look, Ruby Mae. I don't like this anymore than you do," Mr. Graham said. "You've been a hard worker. Never had any problems with you." He wiped his forehead. "But Jack here showed up in my office today. Told me this crazy story. I needed to hear your side of it."

Her side? What had Jack said? Did he tell the whole story, or just the part where she picked up her rivet gun and scared the daylights out of him? She doubted he said how he touched her. That he started it.

She took a deep breath and blew it out slowly. She would not let Jack scare her off. Mr. Graham was a reasonable guy.

"So, Ruby Mae, why don't you tell me your version of what happened." Mr. Graham sat down at his desk and pulled out a notepad.

"Does he have to be here?" She jerked her chin toward Jack.

Jack leaned forward. "I'm here for justice. You," he pointed his thick finger at Ruby Mae, "crossed the line."

Justice? The word hit Ruby Mae like a smack on the head. What did this man know about justice? Justice would have been the housing her family was promised months ago, instead of the tiny trailer they rented. Justice would be working a job where the workers didn't hate her for doing a white man's job. Not with men who tried to punish her with their racist cracks and crude insults. Her face grew hot.

"You want to know what happened?" she said. "Fine. I was working down below deck. A small space." Her eyes darted to her boss. "Where you sent me." She took a shaky breath. "And Jack here snuck up on me. Looking for trouble. He had no business being there. Then he slapped my behind. Made a rude comment." She glared at Jack, who scowled. "Said it was like a Georgia peach."

Mr. Graham grimaced and looked up from his notes. "He told me he bumped into you by accident. That you went crazy over nothing." He looked at Jack. "Did you do what she said?"

"No, it wasn't like that, Mr. Graham," Jack said. He crossed his arms. "I was just passing by. She's so fat there wasn't room for me to get by without brushing against her. That's all it was."

"You lying now," said Ruby Mae. She was so angry she forgot to be scared. "You been hassling me ever since I started here. You can say anything you want and he's gonna believe you. 'Cause you is a white man."

She stood up, breathing hard. The room felt stifling. "I need some air, okay?" She opened the door and fanned herself. The fresh air from the hallway felt good. She fought back the urge to run out of the building, all the way to their trailer. Pack up and join her family on the next train to Baton Rouge.

"Okay, Ruby Mae," Mr. Graham said. "Let's finish this." He picked up his pen. "What happened next?" His shirt had damp stains under his arms.

She left the door open and sat down. "Well, after he did that, surprised me and all, I turned around. Told him to apologize. He laughed. Said he couldn't help himself. I got really mad. I had my gun in my hands and I waved it at him. Told him again to say he was sorry." Her hands got hot remembering.

She glanced at Jack and for a second saw the fear she'd seen before. "Then he finally apologized and left. That's it, Mr. Graham. If he's telling you something different, he's lying."

Jack jumped up. "You lying bitch! You threatened to cut off my balls with that gun." His cheeks reddened and his eyes looked like they'd pop out of his head.

Mr. Graham had stopped writing. His eyes flew from Jack to her. "Now, just a minute," he said.

Ruby Mae stared at Jack. "I never said that."

"Well, you sure as hell looked like you wanted to," Jack said. He put his hands on his hips, still on his feet. "Mr. Graham, I'm a member of the union," he said, "and this woman threatened me with her gun. The union protects us from that kind of dangerous behavior." He ran his hand through his greasy hair. "I expect you to do the right thing. You have to let her go."

Mr. Graham put down his pen. "Ruby Mae," he said, "did you threaten to hurt Jack?"

"I never said that," she said. "I just wanted him to apologize." Her heart raced. If he hadn't said he was sorry, she might have done it. Deep in her bones, she knew that.

"Okay. I've heard enough." Mr. Graham stood up. "Jack, you head on out now. I'd like to talk to Ruby Mae."

Jack glared at her on the way out, pushing past her chair. He slammed the door as he left.

Ruby Mae leaned forward. "Mr. Graham, you know as well as me that Jack is nothin' but trouble. All the gals know to stay away from him. It's not fair to punish me."

Mr. Graham rubbed his cheek. "I'm afraid this isn't about fairness. Once you waved your gun at him, everything changed. I don't really have a choice, Ruby Mae. I'm gonna have to fire you. Otherwise, if he goes to the union, I'll be in big trouble."

Ruby Mae listened, his words dropping like stones inside her. Why would she expect anything else? Jack had told his story and she had told hers. His counted and hers did not.

She looked at her boss. He could barely meet her eyes.

"I'm real sorry," he said.

"Well, I sure liked working here," she said. She stood up. "This was the best job I ever had." Her eyes burned. "I don't know what I'm gonna do now." She turned and walked out of the office. Justice and fairness? Not words meant for her.

CHAPTER 30

RACHEL

October 30, 1944

Rachel wiped her hands on her apron, stained pink with beet juice from years of Mama's pickling. The kitchen smelled of honey and yeast. "Now we knead the dough," she said.

Elena looked confused. "We need it? For what?"

Rachel smiled. "Not need like that. Knead, with a "K" in front." She demonstrated, pressing her fingers into the dough.

"Oh," Elena said, "Amasar." She copied Rachel. "Like this?"

Rachel nodded. Making challah was the only time Mama allowed her to help in the kitchen. A good Jewish girl should know how to bake a perfect loaf for Shabbat.

Jesse's one kitchen job had been to take out the garbage. Period. Rachel knew early on that his real job, the only goal that mattered, was to become as good a doctor as Papa. He'd come into the kitchen to grab some challah or leftovers, never to help. She used to resent the ease of his role in the family. None of it mattered now.

"The dough needs to rest," she said when they'd finished kneading. She tucked the bowl into a corner where the morning sun added a few degrees of heat. "Let's see that story you asked me to proof."

She sat with Elena at the dining room table. Mama had gone over to Aunt Pearl's for the day. Thank God for Aunt Pearl, who insisted Mama get out of the house, distracting her with some cooking project or shopping. Otherwise, Mama might never leave the house, her grief like an anchor.

Rachel grabbed a pencil and read Elena's article. It described the Port Chicago trial summations by the prosecution and defense lawyers, the swift verdict that same afternoon. No deliberation. The sentencing that followed. Still unbelievable. Elena had captured it well on the page, including people's shock at the outcome.

"It's very good," Rachel said. "Just needs one tense change that I marked. I want to help you get this published. People need to understand what happened." She clenched her fingers around the pencil. "But that's not enough. The whole system is unfair."

Elena put down her pen. "In El Salvador, people go out in the streets when they're angry. They protest. But it's dangerous. The military runs the country. The Army shows up with their guns out. Have you ever done that, joined a protest?"

"No, I never felt this outraged," she said. It was one thing to get angry, and quite another to join a protest. "I don't think writing to the admirals or the President himself is enough. It won't make a difference." Her heart beat faster. "I'm ready to do more."

Elena stood up. "I can find out if anything is planned. I'll go see Margaret Starks at Tappers' tomorrow." She glanced at her watch. "Do you have time for un favor? I hope to visit the *Tribune* office, since I'm here in Oakland. See if they will publish my article."

"Boy," Rachel said, grinning, "you're going for broke, huh?" She laughed when Elena frowned. "Sorry, another funny expression. It means to take a big risk. Anyway, let me check the recipe timing. Making bread always feels like you're babysitting the dough."

"We're fine," she said when she came back from the kitchen. "Let's take a walk. I'll show you the *Tribune* office. We can catch the bus back here."

"What about the bread?"

"Don't worry. I'll be back in time to bake it."

The day was warm, and Rachel was glad to be outdoors. When they reached Lake Merritt, Elena stopped and stared at the tall oak and bay trees surrounding the lake. A few ducks paddled on the water, their heads iridescent green in the sun.

"This is beautiful," Elena said, "right here in the middle of the city. You're lucky to have this in your neighborhood."

Rachel looked at the lake. "You're right. I take it for granted. Before the war, a necklace of light posts lit up the lake in the evening. It was so pretty. The blackouts forced them to shut it down."

They walked down Broadway past small mom-and-pop shops squeezed in next to Capwell's department store and I Magnin, with its tiled façade down to 13th Street. The *Tribune* tower rose overhead, its copper roof and clock face much taller than the other buildings.

"It's very elegante," Elena said, her eyes wide. "Looks more like a church than a newspaper office."

"Wait until you see their reporters," Rachel said. "Most of them look like they just stepped out of the corner bar."

Elena entered the building first, as if she knew what she was doing. She walked right up to the front desk in the spacious lobby. Rachel held back, letting her take the lead. Elena certainly had more experience dealing with newspaper people than she did.

"Hello," Elena said.

The older man at the desk, in a security guard uniform, looked up and frowned.

"Yes?"

"We're here to speak to the editor." Elena sounded confident, her accent noticeable but not a bit difficult to understand. Her command of English had blossomed since Rachel had first met her.

"Look," the man said, "unless you have an appointment with him, forget it, lady." He eyed the two of them. "He's a busy man. Whatever you got, he ain't buying. Get lost."

So rude. Rachel wanted to grab him by the collar, tell him to stop treating Elena like garbage. But Elena wasn't done.

"You have no right to talk to me like that," she said, and turned toward Rachel. "Let's go." She tugged Rachel's sleeve and pulled her towards the elevator. "I'm going to find him myself." The sign posted on the marble wall said the newsroom was on the second floor. They rode up before the man at the desk had time to stop them.

"I can't believe you just did that," Rachel said. Mama would say Elena showed a lot of chutzpah, more than Rachel ever had.

Once they got to the newsroom, they were greeted with a noisy bunch of reporters on their desk phones or hunched over their typewriters. In a windowed office in the far corner, several men sat around a table, engaged in a heated conversation. Elena spotted that group and headed toward them.

Rachel followed her through the maze of desks, convinced they would be arrested for trespassing and hauled off to jail. Mama would be furious that Rachel had ruined their Shabbat.

Elena stopped at the open door of the meeting room and knocked on the wooden frame. The men inside stopped talking and stared at her. One of them, who looked like the boss, with his black glasses and gray goatee, a striped shirt and tie, glared up at her.

"What the hell?" he said. "We're on deadline." He stared at Elena. "And who are you? You don't work here."

"No, sir, I don't," Elena said. "My name is Elena Guzmán. I am a reporter. I've written a story I think you will want to publish."

The other men at the table rolled their eyes, some chuckled.

"This is about the Port Chicago trial and verdict," she said. "I'd like to do a follow-up piece on one of the sailors who survived the explosion. He's got a good story."

"Look, miss, I don't give a rat's ass about his story right now," the goateed man said. He stood up and tried to usher Elena out of the room. Rachel stepped back.

"Okay, sir," Elena said. "I know about deadlines. I used to run a paper with my Papá back home. I made a copy of my story to leave with you. I've put my phone number at the top. Please call me." She handed the pages to him, which he accepted with a scowl. He went back into the meeting room and shut the door.

Elena turned and marched out of the newsroom. Rachel followed, her mouth hanging open. When the elevator opened, the security guard stood inside, hands on his hips. "I told you to get lost," he said.

"Don't worry. We're leaving," Elena said.

The guard rode down with them, and made sure they left the building. When they reached the sidewalk, Elena turned and looked at Rachel. "That," she said, grinning, "felt really good."

"You were amazing," Rachel said. "I would have left when the guard warned us."

"I'm tired of being told 'no.'" Elena glanced up at the *Tribune* office. "When we were in the newsroom, I remembered how much I believe in newspapers. I want to be part of that again."

Rachel put her arm around Elena's shoulders. "I have faith in you, my friend." She thought about her own failed efforts to speak out. Finding that kind of courage took practice.

CHAPTER 31

ELENA

November 2, 1944

A few days later, Elena met up with Rachel again before work. She sipped the shipyard cafeteria's bitter coffee and wrinkled her nose. Workers on their lunch break streamed past them carrying trays from the long food lines.

"What's the matter?" Rachel said, watching her with those nurse eyes that didn't miss anything.

"This," she said, holding up the thick ceramic cup, "this burned liquid would never pass for café in my country. Coffee is worshipped there. El Salvador's coffee families ran the country for years." She put down the cup. "Until the generals decided it was their turn."

"I don't really know much about your country," Rachel said. "But I agree about this coffee. I always bring my own." She glanced at her watch. "I'd like to hear more about your life there sometime."

The only person Elena talked about home with, since Ana and Marisol had left, was Mrs. Murphy, her landlord, who prided herself on knowing a little bit about every country in the Americas. But Mrs. Murphy only taught the big countries, like Brazil and Argentina. Elena had made it her mission to fill in those gaps, in exchange for Mrs. Murphy's help with reading the local newspaper.

"I like your idea," Elena said, "to see if *Fore 'n' Aft* will publish my story. Especially now that the NAACP is involved."

She'd missed the thrill of covering significant stories. Writing was in her blood, Papá had said, when she'd shown him the first article she ever wrote. Walking home from sixth grade with her girlfriends, the sun beating down, the air rippling with heat. They'd stopped for a polo, the icy crystals sweet on their tongues. Sitting together in the shade on a splintered bench, the girls had licked the melted juice off their lips.

Three campesinos, farmers who hauled their produce in wheeled carts, one with a cage of live chickens balanced on top of his carrots, had been selling their vegetables just off the street in an alley. The men froze when a policía van pulled up. The policía had jumped out and pinned the men against the brick wall, shouting in their faces. They dragged the farmers into the van and drove off in a swirl of dust, the abandoned chickens squawking in their cage. Everyone else on the street had hurried home. Shaken, she'd told Papá about the incident over dinner that night. Mamá had tears in her eyes.

Papá had put down his fork.

"Elena, what you witnessed is a terrible thing," he'd said. "An example of the government's attacks on innocent people. Farmers accused of siding with the communists. Hunted everywhere." He put his hand on hers. "I'm sorry you had to see it. But it's a good lesson. Now you must write down exactly what you saw, so you won't forget."

That night she'd captured the incident on the page, her pencil dull from pressing so hard. She sat close to Papá on the couch while he read her words.

"Yes, mija, yes," he said. "You've brought me there. I can taste the dust, the fear in those men. The caged chickens, like a metaphor for all of it." He hugged her close and looked at his wife. "I think she'll soon come help me with the paper, mi amor." Mamá had stared at him, her mouth pulled tight.

"Well, maybe not quite yet, mija," Papá had added, "but when the time is right."

"Elena?" Rachel's voice brought her back. "You okay?"

"I'm sorry," she said, shaking her head. "I was remembering my papi. He was arrested for what he wrote in his newspaper." She shuddered and looked up at Rachel. "I was there that night when they came for him." Her stomach knotted.

"You were?" Rachel's eyes held hers.

"Yes," Elena said. Heat rushed to her face. She took a deep breath. Telling her friend would make it real, not just an awful nightmare. "I was working with Papá when the policía showed up. They took him away in handcuffs." She heard the metallic *clink* in her mind. "He didn't resist. Just looked at me, his eyes calm. Told me to take care of mami and the little ones. After they'd left, one of the men stayed behind. He was young, with wild eyes. I thought he wanted to destroy the presses. Teach us a lesson." The horror movie in her mind kept going. "But no. The only thing he wanted was me." She looked down.

"Oh, Elena," Rachel said. "I'm so sorry." She reached across the table and put her hand on Elena's arm.

"I had to make him stop." Her breaths quickened. "I was so upset about Papá." She felt the cool metal of the letter opener in her palm. "He pinned me against the desk, pushed his leg between mine, telling me what he intended. Then he ripped my blouse and grabbed my breast. I had to make him stop. So I stabbed him."

Rachel's eyes sparked. "Oh my God. You had a knife?"

"No. An ordinary letter opener," she said, a laugh escaping. It struck her now how lucky that she'd had one right there on the desk. Because he had a gun holstered on his hip. "I hit him in his chest, as shocked as he was when it went through his uniform. I dropped it and he fell back. Then I ran. I ran and ran and ran."

Rachel came and sat down next to her. "I can't imagine how terrified you were." She put her arm around Elena.

A sob burst from Elena's chest and she leaned into Rachel's embrace. Telling had released the tight coil around her heart. She sat and cried a long time.

When her tears stopped, Rachel handed her a napkin and held her by her shoulders. "What happened to him, Elena?" she said, her voice almost a whisper.

Elena shook her head. She took a deep breath and let it out slowly. "I tried to find out, after I left. Maybe it was only a shallow wound. I don't know. There was never any mention in the newspapers." She looked at Rachel. "Sometimes I feel like I imagined the whole thing."

"No, you didn't make this up," Rachel said. "You've carried this for months."

Elena's breathing quieted. Rachel believed her and didn't seem horrified by what she'd done. Relief flooded her body.

"Thank you, Rachel," she said. "It's why I don't think I can go back home. Ever. The policía will be waiting. Mamá keeps writing letters begging me to return. But she knows I can't. All I can do is send them money and tell them how much I miss them."

"Are they in danger, too?" Rachel asked.

"Yes," she said, her voice low. "I made them leave home that night. They went to my tía's house on the other side of the city." Elena pictured them all crowded together, her young cousins playing with her little sister and brother. Mami and Tía, the fierce defenders of home, one ear cocked for an unexpected knock or the howl of a siren. Mami had written about her secret search for news of Papá. She had even paid someone to nose around the jails. The money Elena sent gave Mami hope she'd locate him and bribe his way out. Unless he was already dead.

"Where did you go that night?" Rachel said.

Elena sipped her coffee, now cold and metallic on her tongue. "I knew I had to leave," she said, wiping a stray tear. "Leave the country, too. Go somewhere I could earn good money and not be noticed. Papá and I had talked about the risks of our reporting. He'd shown me the ads in the American newspapers. Workers desperately needed in the shipyards. I took a bus early the next morning."

She paused, recalling the terror she'd felt on that bus ride. "It wasn't until we got to Mexico City that I felt I could breathe. From there, I caught the train. Two days later I got off in Oakland. I found a Catholic church and fell asleep on a wooden pew. The priest discovered me. He fed me and told me about the shipyard's hiring hall." She sighed. "And here I am. It took a long time to stop looking over my shoulder."

"Thank you for telling me," Rachel said, leaning back and wiping her eyes. "I wondered how you ended up here."

They sat quietly then Rachel checked her watch. "Do you still want to visit the *Fore 'n' Aft* office?" she said. "I've got time, but we could go another day."

Elena stood up. "No, let's go now." Better to focus on something else, something that gave her purpose.

* * *

She and Rachel walked over to the yard's admin building. Elena expected to find a small printing press inside the newsletter office, but the room held only two desks where a couple of middle-aged men sat at typewriters. They looked bored. An ashtray on one desk overflowed with cigarette butts.

One of the men looked up when she and Rachel walked in. He frowned.

"Yeah?" he said, coughing as he put down his cigarette.

Rachel looked like she wanted to lecture him about smoking. But instead she said, "Hello. How do we submit articles? Are there guidelines about subject matter or length?"

"You a nurse?" the man said, staring at Rachel's snug uniform, his gaze lingering on her breasts. He looked at Elena as if he couldn't figure out exactly what she was. Her colorful street clothes—teal blouse and black-striped pants—didn't define her.

"How'd you guess?" Rachel said, smiling in a way Elena recognized. She'd been around Rachel often enough at the clinic to know that I'll-be-nice-to-you-even-if-you-are-an-idiot look. It was how she handled patients who came in ready to pick a fight or harass the nurses.

"Look, lady, I'm just saying we could use a nurse," he said, scowling. He pointed to a stack of the newsletters on his desk. "Might help get the message across. How to keep safe on the job. Management's on our backs to do more of that. You know, prevent injuries by wearing goggles. That kind of thing. You interested?"

"Yes, she is," Elena said. Rachel stared at her. "What will you pay her?" It couldn't hurt to ask. If it did pay, and she helped Rachel, she might earn a little extra.

The man laughed. "You think there's money in it, missy?" He picked up his cigarette, which had burned down, tapped off the long ash and inhaled. "Nope, sorry." He exhaled a cloud of smoke. "Not a penny. Just the thrill of seeing your name in print. Read by hundreds of workers. Or used to wrap potato peels at home."

"Fine, I'll write up something," Rachel said, stepping back from the smoke. "I have other ideas, too. Is anything off-limits?"

"Not as far as I'm concerned," the man said. He winked and stubbed out his cigarette. "Get me the article by noon on Wednesday."

"I don't see any printing press," Elena said. "Where is the newsletter printed?"

"Aren't you the curious one?" The man leaned back and stretched his arms up, folding them behind his head. "We don't print it here. We send it to a print shop downtown."

"Fine," Elena said. "You'll have something from her. And something else from me. Let's go." She took Rachel's arm and led her out the door. Outside, she rolled her eyes. "He was un cochino, a pig."

"I know," Rachel said. "I wanted to say something, but he's the type who'd probably lose my article. God, I'm tired of men like that. Makes me appreciate Noah."

"Yeah. You're lucky," Elena said. She hooked elbows with Rachel like she did back home with her old friends and walked off.

CHAPTER 32

November 12, 1944

Ruby Mae sat down at one of the open tables in Tappers' restaurant. Peggy and Marcy were late. She'd invited them to lunch, mostly for support. The lunch crowd buzzed with news: the Allies were preparing for another German offensive. More ships were urgently needed.

Not her problem anymore. Twenty-four hours ago she had a job. Now she didn't. She dreaded looking for work. Her only skills were house cleaning and riveting. If people found out why she'd been fired, no one would hire her. What would Freddy think when she told him?

So far Peggy had agreed to keep her secret, but word would get out at the yard. Jack would brag about it. Heat rose from her body. That man had ruined everything. All he'd gotten from their boss was barely a scolding.

"Hey girl," Marcy said, rushing in and throwing her arms around Ruby Mae in a bear hug. "How you doin'?" She took off her coat and stood with her hands on her hips. Her fitted dress was royal blue. "I hope you ain't feeling sorry for yourself. 'Cause it ain't your fault. All you was trying to do was protect yourself from that . . . that cracker." She sat down and squeezed Ruby Mae's hand.

Marcy's concern washed over her, rinsing off some of the self-pity. Thank goodness for friends. "I'm going a little crazy. One minute I feel like crying, then I get so mad it scares me." She took a deep breath and let it out. "I got to find a new job."

Soon Peggy showed up dressed for work, a long-sleeved denim shirt tucked inside her coveralls. A red bandana covered her hair, and her mouth was set in a hard line.

"Why, look at you, Peggy," Marcy said. "Got all fancy for us, huh?" She laughed, the big belly laugh Ruby Mae loved. But Peggy and Marcy didn't share the same sense of humor. More like two magnets that kept pushing off each other.

Peggy sat down. "Look Marcy, this ain't exactly a birthday party. My sister just got fired. I'm having to cover for her at home. If she don't find another job soon, the two of us is headed back to Baton Rouge." She looked at Ruby Mae. "And neither of us wants that."

"Don't you think I know that?" Marcy said. "I'm only trying to lighten things up."

"I know you both are worried 'bout me," Ruby Mae said. "Let's order us some food first. Then you can listen to my idea." She looked at the menu posted on the chalkboard. Daily specials were listed below the regular items. One of them, sausage gumbo, was crossed out.

"Well, I ain't sorry they ran out of gumbo," she said. "I won't miss picking that slimy okra out of my bowl. I'm gonna try that pot roast. Looks so good."

"You know," Peggy said, "if you got a job here, they'd prob'ly teach you how to cook, too."

Ruby Mae stared at her. "You reading my mind, girl? I already been thinking of talking to Miz Starks." Not that she had any restaurant experience.

The waitress walked over, her graying hair pulled back in a soft bun, her slender frame covered by a black shirtdress and white half-apron.

"Hello, ladies," she said. "What can I get ya'll today?" Ruby Mae heard the drawl.

They placed their orders and before the waitress left, Ruby Mae put her hand on the woman's arm. "How you like working here, if you don't mind me asking?"

The waitress shrugged. "It's all right. Better than a lot of jobs I done before. I still go home bone tired. But you can't beat the free food." She winked at Ruby Mae and headed off to the kitchen.

"You ever waitress before?" Marcy asked.

Ruby Mae shook her head.

"Back in Chicago," Marcy said, "I applied for a waitress job in this restaurant downtown. They took one look at me and told me I was too fat and too dark. Made me feel like dirt." She pursed her lips. "So I got a job with the janitor service. They didn't care how I looked. We cleaned all them fancy offices down near the lake."

"Well, I know about cleaning up after folks," Ruby Mae said. "Being a waitress looks a whole lot easier than scrubbing down bathrooms on my knees."

She looked up when the waitress appeared, her arms loaded with plates of food. So fast? They must cook up the meat dishes ahead of time, she thought, knowing how long it took Momma to prepare. "Besides, it sure would feel different to work some place where they don't hate the skin you was born with."

Once the plate of pot roast, mashed potatoes, and collard greens was placed in front of her, a smile spread across her face. "I believe if I could get a job here, I'm gonna need a extra large uniform."

Peggy shook her head and Marcy laughed out loud. Ruby Mae dug into her food, trying not to get grease stains on her clothes. She watched the waitress hurry back and forth to the kitchen, shuttling plates and drinks as she pushed through the swinging doors. The job wouldn't be easy, but she could handle it, as long as no one yelled at her or tried to grab her. No telling what she might do if someone tried that again. The three of them ate until their plates were clean.

"Lord, I am full as a tick," Peggy said. She dipped the corner of her napkin in water, wiping her fingers clean. "Marcy, maybe you can help me and Ruby Mae." Ruby Mae had no idea what Peggy was up to. "We are gonna need a place to live if Momma and Daddy decide they're moving home for sure. I figured you might know of a place that's gonna open up. Seems like you got your ear on all the news coming out of the yard." Peggy put down her napkin and folded her hands on the table.

Marcy tilted her head. "What you up to, Miz Peggy? You never asked me for advice before." She glanced at Ruby Mae, who kept quiet. If Peggy could be nice to Marcy, anything was possible. Ruby Mae would get a new job. Freddy would declare his love. Thurgood Marshall would free the jailed sailors.

Peggy tucked stray hairs under her bandana and sat back. "I figure you and me should quit snapping at each other. Ruby Mae needs us both. We on the same team. Okay?"

"Well, fine by me," Marcy said. "Maybe you ain't a lost cause, Miz Peggy," she added. "All you need is to get out from under Momma's thumb. No telling what you might do, girl."

Ruby Mae wiped her mouth and grinned at Peggy, who looked a little embarrassed.

"Anyway, I'll see what I can find out," Marcy said. "Folks is always moving once they get a little money, find themselves a better place."

"Okay. Thanks. And I'm paying for our lunch," Peggy said. "No arguments."

Marcy looked at Ruby Mae.

Ruby Mae patted her sister's hand. "We accept. Thank you." Across the room she spotted Margaret Starks speaking with a couple of men. "As long as I'm here, I think I'll go ask Miz Starks if she has any openings."

Marcy looked over. "Better wait 'til they're done. It don't look friendly."

Ruby Mae said goodbye to Marcy and Peggy, and edged towards Margaret's group in the doorway, arguing now in loud voices. She hurried past them to the ladies' room, where she spent several minutes fixing her hair just so, and putting on some fresh lipstick, smoothing out the wrinkles in her church dress.

Smiling at her reflection in the large mirror, she thought about Freddy. He didn't seem to mind the extra pounds. She sucked in her belly and turned sideways, but the view was about the same. He'd asked her to meet him on Sunday. Said he had some news. Well, she had her own news. He'd be upset to hear about losing her job, but he sure would like hearing that she and Peggy were planning to stay and get their own place. She could have him over for dinner soon . . . well, maybe once she'd learned to cook something besides scrambled eggs and grits. Momma would have to teach her all the family recipes before she left.

Her throat constricted and tears burned her eyes, out of nowhere. A piece of her heart broke loose. Momma and Daddy and the twins were leaving. She'd never lived away from them, not even for a day. It would just be her and Peggy. The hugeness of the loss hit her hard, and she collapsed onto a cushioned chair. Sobs shook her body and she leaned forward, elbows on the vanity counter, gasping, just as Margaret Starks stepped into the restroom. Oh Lord, not now. Not like this.

Margaret took one look at Ruby Mae, walked over and put her arms around her shoulders. She pulled another chair close and held on. "It's okay, honey," Margaret said. "You just let it all out now." She tightened her grip. "Whatever it is, I've been there."

They sat together for a few minutes, Margaret patting her back until Ruby Mae was able to catch her breath. She wiped the tears and snot off her face. This was not exactly how she planned on presenting herself for a job. But she'd needed a good cry, holding so much in since being fired. Maybe she'd been brave for Peggy and Marcy's sake.

"Sorry about this," she said, glancing at the mirror. Her eyes were puffy and she'd smeared her lipstick. "I look like something the cat dragged in."

"Now, don't you fuss," Margaret said. "Why don't you come to my office and tell me what's bothering you. I'll make us some good strong coffee. You wash up and meet me there. Down the hall on the right." She stood up and smiled at Ruby Mae. "Ain't much that a cup of coffee and a slice of apple pie can't fix."

By the time Ruby Mae had finished the pie and coffee in Margaret's office, her mood was much improved. She raised the coffee cup and inhaled. "You got some chicory in here, right?"

Margaret nodded. "Reminds me of home. Arkansas. Most folks 'round here who ain't from the South don't recognize the flavor. They just like how it tastes." She watched Ruby Mae. "Now talk to me, girl."

So Ruby Mae told her everything, about getting fired, her family moving back home, needing a place to live. And a new job. She looked down at her lap. "I was hopin' you might have some work for me here. I ain't fussy. I just need a steady paycheck. I never done waitressing or cooking much, but I'd like to learn."

"Well, ain't you something," Margaret said. "No wonder you was crying hard." She sat still for a minute, chewing her lip, then reached for a clipboard hanging on the wall. "How soon can you start?"

Ruby Mae leaned in. "Really? How 'bout tomorrow? I got my good dress on today and my nice shoes, otherwise I could start right now."

Margaret sat back and laughed. "Don't you want to know what the job is? Girl, you sure are eager." She put her hand on Ruby Mae's. "Look, one of our cooks has been out sick, so we been short in the kitchen. They could use help getting things chopped and ready for the lunch and dinner rush. Later on, when it quiets down, you can learn about the waitress work. How does that sound?"

"Sounds like you answered my prayers," Ruby Mae said, a little lightheaded, "'fore I got a chance to pray." She stood up and hugged Margaret. "Oh, wait. What should I wear? What time do you want me here?" She hesitated. "I'm gonna get paid, right?"

Margaret laughed. "Be at the kitchen at 8:00. Wear pants and a shirt you don't mind getting dirty. As for the pay, I can't match the shipyard, but I promise you and Peggy will make rent. Plus your meals during work hours are free."

"Thank you," Ruby Mae said. "You won't be sorry."

She walked out of the office, her body trembling. A new job. At a place that already meant so much to her.

* * *

When she got home, Momma and Daddy were sitting at the kitchen table with the twins having supper.

"What you doin' home so early?" Daddy said, his forehead creased.

"Hi Daddy, Momma. Hey boys." Ruby Mae pulled a chair up and sat down between the twins. "I got news." Everyone stopped eating.

Because her brothers were listening, she left out the ugly details of her firing. "But guess what? I already got me a new job. In the kitchen at Tappers'. I start tomorrow. I'm helping the cooks for now. Maybe I'll waitress later on." The boys went back to eating.

Momma stared at her. "Girl, you done all right." She reached across the table and squeezed Ruby Mae's shoulder. No lecture, no fussing. Ruby Mae might even tell her about Jack later.

"Sounds like a good place to work," Daddy said. "No one hating on you 'cause of your skin." He glanced down at his injured leg.

"Yeah. I think so, Daddy," she said. "The money won't be as good, but still. I'm ready for something new." No Jack or anyone like him causing her more grief. Margaret would never put up with any of that, not at Tappers'. Getting fired started to feel like a blessing.

CHAPTER 33

ELENA

November 13, 1944

When the bus arrived at Tapper's Inn, Elena hurried off and almost ran into a couple leaving the club. They reeked of stale cigarettes and liquor. The man tipped his hat as they stumbled down the sidewalk, the woman on his arm unsteady in heels. Really? At 11:00 in the morning? She'd never understood why people squandered their lives, not when there was so much work to be done. She had no time for fools.

Elena had written up her idea for an article, one she couldn't pull off alone. She needed Margaret Starks's newspaper, the *Richmond Guide,* to get the word out fast.

Margaret was waiting for her in the club's back room, a space obviously used for meetings during the day. Chairs sprawled here and there, a battered blackboard with chalked notes leaned against one wall. An ashtray on the wooden table overflowed.

"Hi, come sit," Margaret said, stylish in her black turtleneck and tan slacks. What was her story? Where was she from? What struggles had she overcome to run this busy nightclub and restaurant? As a Negro woman, she must have had plenty of challenges.

"Now, how can I help?" Margaret picked up a pack of Lucky Strikes and lit up.

Elena sat, coughed, and waved the smoke out of her face. "I'm sure you've heard about the verdict."

Margaret nodded. "It's outrageous." She stood and paced. "Not that anyone was surprised. Our chapter has been meeting about it."

"Chapter?"

"Yes," Margaret said, exhaling. "The NAACP here in Richmond."

Elena's pulse quickened. She wasn't the only one compelled to do something. Lying in bed the night before, she remembered the times back home when she'd covered strikes and protests after the military government clamped down.

"Here. Can you take a look at something I wrote?" She thrust the typed papers towards Margaret.

"Oh, sure, why not," Margaret said, letting out a bark of a laugh. She inhaled again and sat down, putting on a pair of tortoise-shell eyeglasses. Elena watched her read, making a note here and there with the stub of a pencil. When she'd finished, she took off her glasses and looked at Elena. "This is really good," she said.

Elena's cheeks grew warm. "Back home I wrote stories for my papi's paper."

"Is your daddy still doing that?" Margaret finished her cigarette and snuffed it out. The smoke burned Elena's eyes.

"No," she said. "He was arrested for what he wrote." Tears leaked onto her cheeks. "I'm sorry. We don't know where he is. Five months with no answers."

"No need to apologize, hon," Margaret said. She looked away. "We all got our sorrows."

"Where did you grow up?" Elena dried her cheeks with the handkerchief she kept in her purse. Mamá had sewn her initials onto one corner of the thin blue cotton cloth, along with a tiny bouquet of yellow daisies.

"Arkansas. Pine Bluff, 'til the war started," Margaret said, closing her eyes for a moment. "Me and my husband came out west on the train. Got jobs in the shipyard for a while. Then I got out. Of everything." She grimaced. "This," she gestured to the expanse of the club, "suits me better. That riveting 'bout broke me."

"Yes," Elena said. "Most days after welding, my hands feel numb and my eyes ache from all those sparks flying. This burn," she held up her scarred hand, "has taken forever to heal." She put her elbows on the table. "Those sailors worked hard for their country, too."

Margaret sighed. "What do you have in mind?"

Elena took a deep breath. She didn't want Margaret to think she was foolish or too naïve to take this on. She exhaled slowly.

"The Navy hopes they can lock those sailors away and act like it's no big deal." She hit the table with her fist. "We can't let that happen."

Margaret smiled. "Girl, you're preaching to the choir. Mr. Marshall wants a formal investigation by the government of what led to the work stoppage. He wants to know why Negro seamen were restricted to shore labor when they'd trained for sea duty."

She shook another cigarette loose from the pack and lit up. "They say those sailors received no proper training on how to load ammunition. Even when local dockworkers offered to instruct them, the Navy declined. He laid it all out in a letter to Admiral Forrester and the White House."

Elena jumped up. "We need to get people out in the streets. Otherwise the Navy will just cover it up." She thought about Freddy, wondered if he'd be willing to speak out, or would the Navy punish him, too.

"So you want to get folks mad enough to take to the streets?" Margaret leaned back in her chair, exhaling a cloud of smoke. "Girl, I like your spunk. But around here, Negroes protesting in the streets, well, it don't usually end well. We get our heads bashed in. The big papers report we was rioting. That the police had no choice but to step in."

Elena stood. "If we do nothing, the Navy will figure they can get away with anything. They need to hear from us. If everyone who feels like we do walked into the streets and shouted, 'No, this is wrong!' over and over, day after day, they couldn't be ignored."

Margaret tapped off ash into the too-full ashtray. "How do you want to do this?"

"You'll help me, then?" said Elena. "I was afraid you'd send me away."

Margaret got up. "Well, first of all, let's get this piece of yours out in our next issue," she said, picking up the pages. "That's set for Monday. And then we need a flyer written. Call for a public protest. We can get it out to our NAACP branches in the whole Bay Area, plus the local churches and union halls. Everywhere." She inhaled and coughed. "Gotta quit these things." She stubbed out the butt. "I want you to write it. You got a way with words."

"I'll get it to you tomorrow," Elena said. Her mind was already racing, how to lay out the flyer, get people inspired to show up. The familiar rush of doing this work swept through her. Papi, wherever he was now, spoke in her ear, urging her on.

CHAPTER 34

November 14, 1944

Ruby Mae slipped an apron over her head and tied it around her waist. The morning sunlight slanted through Tappers' kitchen window. Only her third day there, but so far this job felt right. Why waitress after all? Not after she'd watched the women running back and forth to their tables, trays balanced on their aching arms, smiles pasted on their faces. No way, not in her nature. She'd likely be fired on day one for mouthing off.

This steamy kitchen suited her, like a muggy summer day in Louisiana. Instead of cousins and nieces surrounding her, she'd joined a staff of men and women who joked and told stories while their hands chopped and stirred and readied the day's specials. Most of them had journeyed up from the South, too.

"Here, Ruby Mae, I need these peppers chopped up." This from Chickie, a tall skinny guy, graying at the temple, whose real name was Clarence. He'd earned his nickname as the guy in charge of frying up all that chicken. He also helped prep the daily special, which that day was gumbo. Ruby Mae had been assigned to him.

"I hope you ain't putting okra in your gumbo," she told him, eyeing a mound of it on the counter. "'Cause if you do, I ain't gonna have none."

Chickie laughed. He leaned across the cutting board and pointed his butcher's knife at her.

"Girl, you ain't the only one that don't care for okra. I always make a small batch without it. Just for fools like you." He shook his head. "Gotta have okra for it to be real gumbo."

She picked up a clean knife and sliced into the first bell pepper, its skin smooth and deep green, its scent grassy and familiar. The day before, Chickie showed her the proper way to hold the knife, how to chop without nicking her fingers. She worked carefully now, her knuckles bent, focused on each stroke of the blade.

One pepper done, pretty good work. She looked up and watched Chickie eyeball two whole chickens on the table, de-feathered and decapitated. He carved them up, tossing the giblets and neck into a stockpot destined for soup. Nothing went to waste.

Ruby Mae had decided that she'd taste every dish they served at least once, except anything with okra. If she liked the dish, she'd learn how to cook it. So far, she'd discovered that pastrami was delicious, especially with some spicy mustard, and that rhubarb pie made her mouth pucker in a good way.

She didn't miss working at the shipyard, plus she enjoyed the added bonus of free meals now. Working with a group of Negroes, no white boss meddling or barking out orders, this was a first. No Jack lurking around the corner. Even though the work was hard, standing on her feet and chopping for hours, this was heaven compared to the shipyard's noise and nasty smells, the toll on her body after hours of riveting. She'd make do with the smaller paycheck.

"Excuse me, I'm looking for Margaret Starks."

Ruby Mae stared at the young white man in the doorway to the dining room, his blue collared shirt ironed smooth, brown curly hair framing a face she recognized. The kitchen crew had come to a standstill, knives poised midair.

"Hey there," she said, putting down her knife and wiping her hands on her apron. "You're Noah, right? I met you at the trial." She walked over. The others went back to their food prep, but glanced over at the newcomer.

"Yeah," Noah said. "Nice to see you, Ruby Mae. You working here now?" He looked behind him. "Rachel's here with me, too, dropping off something to Margaret."

Ruby Mae hadn't seen Rachel since she'd been fired. Did she already know? Probably everyone knew. Just yesterday she'd run into a gal from the yard eating at Tappers'. That conversation had been awkward.

She turned and called to Chickie. "Okay if I take a minute and show him where she's at?"

Noah followed her down the hallway into the meeting room. Rachel stood next to Margaret, who held a sheet of paper in her hand, her glasses set low on her nose as she read.

Margaret looked up at Ruby Mae and Noah, and waved the paper at them.

"Did you write this?" she asked Noah, pulling her cigarette from her lips and exhaling. Rachel took a step back, looking confused, and Ruby Mae couldn't help grinning. This was gonna be rich, watching Margaret take him down. Margaret wasn't scared of any one, not even this handsome law student.

"What, you don't like it?" Noah said. "What's wrong with it?"

Ruby Mae leaned over to read the title typed on the page.

UNFAIR VERDICT! JOIN THE PROTEST!

She couldn't read the rest without grabbing it from Margaret's hand.

Margaret took another drag off her cigarette and flattened the stub. "Ain't nothing wrong with this, young man," she said. "This is a damn good piece of writing. Tells the truth 'bout those sailors." She nodded at him. "You gonna be a fine lawyer. 'Cause you give a damn." Ruby Mae cringed at her language. Good thing Peggy wasn't there.

Noah grinned. "Truth is, I didn't write it. Elena did. She said you're going to print them up."

"Well, no wonder," Margaret said. "That girl has the gift." She turned to Ruby Mae. "And you s'posed to be helping Chickie get ready for lunch."

"Wait." Rachel stared at her. "What's going on, Ruby Mae?"

"It's a long story, but I better get back to work," Ruby Mae said, "before Chickie hunts me down." Grateful not to tell that story again. "But listen," she said to Rachel, "if you two ain't never been here before, you oughta stay and eat something. Best food in town."

Margaret snorted. "Go on back now. This here's your first week. Don't make me regret hiring you." Ruby Mae hurried back towards the kitchen. Those peppers weren't gonna chop themselves. After that, Chickie had promised to teach her how to spice the gumbo so good it made folks cry for their momma.

* * *

The next day she was set to meet Freddy on the bay side of Shipyard #3. He'd planned a surprise. But standing outside the shipyard now, watching the crowds of workers stream in and out, she wished they'd met in town. She did miss one thing about working there: how valuable she'd felt doing her part for the war effort. Each rivet she'd driven, each tight seal of metal on metal, mattered. She straightened her shoulders and stared at the water. Crews of sailors out there in the Pacific were fighting onboard ships she'd helped build with her own two hands.

"Hey there, Miz Ruby Mae." Freddy appeared at her side and bent to give her a quick kiss. He wore his Navy uniform with his cap perched at an angle. His eyepatch was gone. The raised scar on his neck still looked angry.

"Hi Freddy," she said. "Looking good." So handsome.

"So do you," he said, smiling. "Now that I can see you better. I hope you're ready to get out in the water."

"What?" She grabbed his arm. "What are you up to? We going for a swim? Looks mighty cold, and I ain't got my bathing suit."

She'd learned to swim back home in sandy inlets where the Mississippi slowed. Daddy fished while Momma watched her and Peggy splash about. Long before the twins were born. Her cousin Floyd had taught her how to sweep the water with cupped hands to stay afloat, how taking long arm strokes and kicking her legs slipped her through the water like a minnow.

Freddy put his arm around her shoulders. "Don't worry, we ain't swimming to San Francisco. C'mon, or we'll miss the ferry."

"The ferry? Sounds nice, Freddy," she said. He knew she'd never seen the city. I sure am lucky, she thought. She'd found herself a new job and she had Freddy, who treated her real nice. She had her new friends and her family. A good life. It was almost too much.

They walked to the ferry dock, and Freddy paid her ten-cent fare. Some of her coworkers from the shipyard used the ferry every day to commute to Richmond. They'd filled her head with stories of what San Francisco offered: fresh crab and fish, caught right in the bay, like back home except different kinds, petrale sole and halibut instead of catfish.

Freddy found two seats in the back of the top deck, packed with workers whose shift had just ended. Ruby Mae smelled the machine grease and burnt flux on their coveralls. She closed her eyes and braced herself.

"Freddy, I need to tell you something," she said, turning to face him. He nodded, concern flooding his face. "Remember that man Jack I told you about, what happened between us?"

His eyes widened. "Did he try something again? I swear, Ruby Mae, I'm gonna kill him." A vein in his neck, near his healed scar, bulged.

"No, nothing like that. But last week I got called into Mr. Graham's office." Her heart started to pound. "Jack was in there, too. He made it sound like he didn't do nothin', like it was all my fault. That I aimed my gun at him for no reason."

The whole scene lit up in her mind. Her eyes teared. "When I told what really happened, Mr. Graham looked like maybe he believed me. But it didn't matter. He had to fire me, he said, 'cause I admitted I aimed my gun at him." Tears dribbled down her cheeks, and Freddy wiped them off with his fingers.

"I'm real sorry," he said. "I figured it wasn't gonna end well." He hugged her close and she heard the ferry's horn blast across the water. The gray towers of the Bay Bridge grew closer.

"The good news is that I already got a new job," she said, smiling at the look on his face. "Guess where I'm working?"

"I give up." He bit his lip. "Just tell me. Then I got something to tell you." Some kind of worry passed across his face.

"Well, remember Margaret Starks at Tappers'? I talked to her, and she decided to take me on, have me learn all the kitchen skills. I been there a few days already. Getting pretty good with the knife. My boss, Chickie, he's in charge of the fried chicken. I'm liking it there a lot." She took his hand and squeezed. "So that's all my news. Now what about you?"

The skyline of San Francisco stood out against the bright sky, the elegant Ferry Building soaring ahead. It was even prettier close up. A wave splashed up close to the boat, spraying them. Seagulls squawked overhead.

"Well," Freddy said, "the good thing is that the doctors finally cleared me to return to active duty. I start next week." He looked down at his lap and squeezed her hand.

There was something bad coming, she could feel it.

"And now the Navy," he said quietly, "'cause of what came out at the trial, decided to order some of us sailors to ship out. Ruby Mae, I'm going out to sea."

Oh no. Please, Lord, don't take him away from me. This felt like some cruel joke played on her. Payback for sneaking around behind Momma's back. Find yourself a good and honorable man, then watch him get snatched away. She looked at him, saw the excitement in his eyes. She couldn't blame him for that. He'd get to do what he'd dreamed of. But what if he got killed?

She forced her mouth into a smile. "Congratulations, Freddy. You've waited a long time for this."

"I know you ain't happy to hear this," he said. "The timing is bad for sure. But it's all I ever wanted. I finally get the chance." He put his arm around her. "This war ain't gonna last forever. When I come home, we can pick up again." He squeezed her shoulder. "Please. Tell me you'll wait for me."

The ferry slowed as it approached the harbor. On the dock, waiting for the next run, stood groups of workers, smoking and chatting like always. But today was different for her. This might be the last day that she ever spent with Freddy. He might never come home. He'd be dead and all she'd have left would be some sweet memories of the sailor she'd loved during the war. She looked up at him.

"Yeah, I'll wait for you," she said, her heart thudding, "of course I will. But Freddy, you better not get yourself killed. You hear me?"

She put her palm on his cheek, leaned in, and kissed him hard on the lips. If this was going to be their last day together, she didn't care who saw them or what they'd tell Momma. All Ruby Mae wanted was to hold on to every minute with Freddy, etch his handsome face into her memory one fine feature at a time.

CHAPTER 35

RACHEL

November 16, 1944

Rachel spoke into the phone, her voice low. "Come with me, Bertie." She sat on the couch, twisting the phone cord with her fingers. "It's my first demonstration. I'll feel better if you're there."

Mama was busy in the kitchen out of hearing range. Not that she wouldn't support the purpose of the protest, but Rachel didn't want to worry her. Ever since Jesse died, Mama hovered over Rachel, as if the extra attention would somehow keep her daughter safe.

"Do I have to march?" Bertie's loud sigh echoed through the receiver. "I'd rather meet you for the speeches. I know this is important, but I doubt the Navy will pay much attention to a few upset civilians."

"I agree," Rachel said. "They might ignore us. But we have to show up. Meet me after work at Franklin and 10th, down the block from the *Tribune*."

The NAACP organizers had chosen the protest site because of its proximity to the newspaper. There'd be no excuse for not giving the story full coverage. This wasn't the first demonstration since the sailors' verdict, but this time they expected such a big crowd that Washington had to pay attention, especially Admiral Forrestal, the Secretary of the Navy. The only officer with the power to overturn the verdict.

When it was time to leave, Rachel stuck her head in the kitchen. Mama was seated at the kitchen table, her eyes closed, a colander of green beans in front of her. Something bubbled in the stockpot on the stove, scenting the room with garlic. Rachel thought about leaving a note and sneaking out, but Mama would hate that.

"Mama?" she said. "You okay?"

Mama opened her eyes, startled. "I must have dozed off."

"I'm meeting Bertie," Rachel said, "for a little shopping downtown. She needs some shoes." The lie came easily. Protecting Mama was one of her new jobs.

Mama stood up. "Have a good time, honey. You'll be home for dinner, I hope." This sounded like a plea.

Rachel nodded and kissed Mama goodbye. Walking towards Broadway, she thought about how much smaller Mama's life had become without Jesse at home, studying and eating his weight in leftovers. Papa and Rachel had their jobs to occupy their time and focus. Mama only had her kitchen and maintaining their home. When I have kids, Rachel vowed, I'll keep working, even if it's part-time. Being a housewife seemed stifling. She wanted more.

What would Noah have to say? Not that she was ready to marry him, although so far, he'd ticked off all the boxes. Even Bertie approved, and the fact that he was Jewish won him bonus points from Mama and Papa. If they did end up together, their son could be bar mitzvahed at Temple Sinai, like his papa. Whoa, girl, slow down, she thought, laughing to herself. She was not in any rush.

Bertie met her at the corner as planned. She wore her usual work attire, a dark wool skirt and matching cardigan, her camel hair jacket unbuttoned. Inspecting Rachel's outfit, she shook her head. "Is that how you're supposed to dress for a protest?"

Rachel smiled. Her black pants and ivory wool sweater had been chosen for comfort, not style. "Yes, there are fashion rules in the fine print of the flier." She grabbed Bertie's elbow. "Listen. Noah said some protests get out of hand. If that happens, promise me you'll get to a safe spot. I'll try to make sure you're okay."

"You're scaring me, Rach," Bertie said.

"Let's just keep our eyes open for any trouble, okay?" She hugged Bertie and they walked down the block, hearing shouts as they got closer. Bertie grabbed her hand.

The gathered crowd overflowed the sidewalks into the street. The entire block was closed to traffic. Several workers in stained coveralls and hard hats must have come right from work. She recognized a few faces, white and Negro, as clinic patients. Families who might have been related to the sailors walked quietly, their expressions grim.

People carried handwritten signs tacked to wooden posts—"OVERTURN THE VERDICT!"—and "FREE THE PORT CHICAGO FIFTY!" The protesters marched slowly back and forth in front of the *Tribune* tower. Some called out encouragement to passers-by, "Join us! We're fighting for justice!"

"Were we supposed to bring a sign?" Bertie asked. "I can't believe there are so many people here." She scanned the crowd. "Everyone looks pretty normal."

"Let's face it, Bertie," Rachel said, "you and I have led pretty sheltered lives."

She stepped into the line of demonstrators, pulling Bertie next to her. At the end of the block she spotted Elena, carrying a spiral notebook. Of course she'd want to cover this story. Rachel was happy to see another familiar face. Elena waved and hurried over.

"Hi," Elena said, matching steps with Rachel. "I'm going to write this up for Margaret's Richmond paper. I didn't make a great impression on the bosses at the *Tribune*."

Rachel laughed. "Their loss."

More people joined the protest. Rachel liked feeling she was part of something important. She glimpsed Noah behind a small stage that had been set up on the sidewalk, a microphone stand in front. He wore his UC Berkeley sweatshirt and khaki pants, and carried boxes to the side of the stage. Her heart raced for a few beats; she loved his commitment to this work.

"Looks like they're ready for the speakers," Bertie said. "I see Noah over there, but I bet you already sensed him with your love detector." She always knew exactly what Rachel was feeling. Years of confiding their crushes to each other had made them both good detectives and loyal advisors.

The first person to grab the microphone was none other than Margaret from Tappers' Inn.

The crowd moved closer.

"That's Margaret Starks," Rachel said. "She manages Tappers' Inn, *and* puts out a small newspaper, *and* runs the Richmond branch of the NAACP. Noah's in awe of her. Me, too."

Margaret looked completely at ease in front of the crowd. She wore a long black wool coat over black slacks and black turtleneck, dark red lipstick accenting her oval face.

"Welcome, all of you," she began. "Great to see you here joining our fight! Yes, it's our fight now. Those sailors need our voices more than ever." Margaret stepped back and motioned to a young white woman dressed in coveralls, a red bandana tied at her throat. "Now I'm thrilled to present our first speaker. Mary Lindsay. Listen up, people."

Some cheers and whistles broke out. Elena moved through the crowd, talking to one person after another, scribbling in her notebook.

"Hello," the speaker began. "I'm a reporter for the *People's World*. For those of you who haven't heard of that, it's a progressive newspaper."

"Can't hear you," yelled a man. "Louder."

Rachel looked around and noticed Ruby Mae at the back of the throng, next to Peggy and her friend Marcy. Rachel caught Ruby Mae's eye and waved. The crowd had grown to at least a hundred, including some young kids clinging to their parents' legs or chasing each other.

"I was asked to write something by my friend," Lindsay said. "Thurgood Marshall. You probably know he plans to appeal the verdict."

Someone called out, "Tell it, sister!"

She pulled the microphone closer. "Do you remember Port Chicago? You should. Over 320 American sailors were blown to tiny fragments there, in less time than it takes to say 'Jim Crow.'"

Someone yelled, "That's right! Go on," which seemed to encourage her.

Out of the corner of her eye, Rachel noticed a small group of white men in Army fatigues had strolled over. They were unarmed, but she felt a ripple of unease.

Lindsay glanced at the soldiers, too. "In some ways," she said, "they were luckier than the eight or nine hundred sailors who didn't die—who were left to pick up the bits of charred flesh and put them into baskets. Those baskets contained all that was left of their friends." She looked out at the crowd.

"That's right!" someone shouted. "Worse than any battlefield!"

Bertie's eyes widened. "Is that what you saw, Rach?" Her voice shook. Rachel hadn't been nearly so graphic.

Elena appeared then at Rachel's side. "What do you think about those Army men?" Rachel asked. Elena had more experience with protests.

"I don't like it," Elena said. "Back home they always brought problemas."

Bertie heard her and turned around. "Those guys?" Bertie said. "No. I've seen them where I work, at the "Y." They're probably killing time until dinner. I wouldn't worry about them."

"The policy of the Navy is to segregate Negroes," Lindsay continued. "And give them every kind of dirty, heart-breaking shore duty." She paused and drank some water.

Rachel's shoulders had knotted. She took a breath and glanced at the back of the crowd.

"She's good, Rach," Bertie said. "And who are you glaring at?"

The soldiers had stepped back and were talking together, too loud, giving off the energy of playground bullies. They meant trouble, no matter what Bertie thought. Rachel considered pointing them out to Noah, but he was busy talking to an older man, who carried a framed photo in his arms. The young sailor in the photo had to be the man's son.

Lindsay stepped back to the microphone. "The Navy has denied them their rights as Americans to serve in active sea duty."

"You don't know what you're talking about, lady," one of the soldiers yelled. "If they were any good, they'd a been shipped out like all the other sailors."

Murmurs of concern swept through the group. Those around Rachel looked annoyed, but a few folks stiffened up and scanned the crowd.

"Sir." Lindsay lowered her notes and stared at the soldier. "You may believe that, but you're dead wrong." She moved closer to the microphone. "Those of us who are white are ignorant when it comes to racial prejudice in our society. Especially in the military. I suggest you educate yourself before you make such uninformed comments."

"Don't you call me ignorant, you stupid bitch," he said, making a fist and jabbing the air, his face beet red. His buddies seemed startled by their friend, but stayed close to him. Bertie grabbed Rachel's arm.

"I don't like this, Rach," she said, "It's getting ugly."

More people had joined the crowd, including some Negro men in Navy uniforms. Word had spread about the protest. A group of police officers loitered down the block, hands gripping their holstered batons.

"Those fifty men were not cowards," Lindsay said, running a hand through her hair. "The Navy failed to train them properly! Now the Navy wants to send them to a federal penitentiary for years."

"They didn't want to die for no reason!" a voice shouted.

"The Navy's doing a great job fighting fascists off foreign shores," she said, raising her voice. "But it's time it found out that democracy means equality for *all* the people."

Rachel joined the cheering crowd. Her heart pounded.

Lindsay grabbed the microphone. "The Navy has a slo-gan—'Remember Pearl Harbor!'—a reminder of foreign treachery against a democracy. There's another slogan the Navy should adopt. What treachery to our own ideals does to that democracy. The meaningless deaths of over 320 Americans must be given a meaning. So, *Remember Port Chicago*!"

The crowd erupted in loud cheers, some with raised fists, others applauding and whistling. Rachel clapped hard, swept up in the energy of those words. This was nothing like any talk she'd ever heard.

"We remember Port Chicago!" yelled a man close to Rachel. She jumped back, startled. He had a healed two-inch scar on his left cheek that extended to his ear. A face she recognized. She nodded at him and he stared back, then he smiled.

"Hey, you're that nurse, right?" he said. "Didn't recognize you without your uniform."

Rachel leaned closer. The crowd was loud around them, chanting and calling out.

"Floyd, right? Where are you stationed?"

"I'm at Treasure Island now," Floyd said. "I refused to load ammo, too. But when they threatened us with a firing squad, I went back to work." He pressed his lips together. "Got court-martialed, but no prison time. Now they got me training for sea duty. Finally. I ship out in two weeks."

"Well, good luck to you," she said, amazed that he still wanted to serve his country.

Up on the stage, the older man with the photo walked to the microphone. He raised the frame over his head so the crowd could see the young sailor's face.

"Hello," his voice boomed into the mic and everyone jumped. "Sorry," he said, stepping back. "My name is William Dunn, and this," he thrust the photo higher, "is my son, John H. Dunn. If you think he looks like a kid, well, that's 'cause he is. John is seventeen. He weighs 104 pounds. He was a second-class seaman at Port Chicago. Because he's so little, they said he was too light to work the dock. So they made him a mess cook." He took a deep breath and lowered his arms. Noah stepped onto the stage and held the photo up.

"My son," Mr. Dunn said, "had never loaded ammunition. So when they asked him to do that, weeks after the explosion where his friends had been torn to pieces, he said he was too scared." Tears rolled down his cheeks. Rachel looked back at the group of soldiers. They were quiet. "So what happened? They sentenced my boy to eight long years of hard labor."

Rachel's eyes burned. She thought about Jesse, how Papa loved him so fiercely.

Dunn wiped his cheeks with the back of his hand. "All he ever wanted was to get on a liberty ship and go fight for his country." He pointed at the soldier in the back. "So don't you dare tell me about my son and what he's worth." His voice cracked. "You ain't never lived in his skin. I'm gonna pray for you, son, that you live long enough to understand what I'm saying. That's right, and I hope the rest of you pray for my boy. Keep him safe 'til he's free."

He took the photo back from Noah, who put an arm around the man as they walked off the stage. The crowd stayed hushed for a moment, then clapped and whistled.

A moment later Rachel heard loud voices, an argument. Next to her, Floyd swore under his breath and moved through the crowd towards the back. Rachel looked past him and saw the group of soldiers now bunched in a menacing semi-circle. Facing them stood Ruby Mae, Peggy, and Marcy.

"Oh no, no," she said, her heart racing. "Bertie, stay here. I've got to make sure Ruby Mae doesn't get hurt."

Bertie grabbed Rachel's hand, her fingers damp. "No way. I've got your back."

Rachel followed Floyd, with Bertie behind her. Elena approached the group from the other side. On the stage, Margaret Starks was speaking to the crowd.

"Listen people," she said. "We need to focus on our mission. Get the Navy to overturn the verdict!" Her words echoed over the crowd. "We can't be distracted by those who don't understand what our people have suffered. Those sailors deserve justice!"

The crowd yelled their approval and "Amens" rang out. By the time Rachel and Bertie got to Ruby Mae, Peggy had her hand on her sister's shoulder, her eyes shooting sparks. Marcy looked ready to fight, her hands fisted. Ruby Mae scowled at one soldier.

"You need to shut up," Ruby Mae said, her voice harsh. "I been listening to you say things that ain't true, talking about these sailors like you know them. Mister, you don't know nothin'. I bet they never made *you* load bombs onto any ship. Or said *you* were too dumb to work up on deck, next to the white men. So quit spreading lies about our boys."

The soldier crossed his arms over his chest. "Who the hell are you, lady? You can't talk to me like that." His buddies looked behind them. One of them whispered to another and they laughed. Rachel walked up just behind Ruby Mae with Floyd and Bertie next to her.

The air crackled with energy. Rachel's body tensed. These soldiers were bullies, plain and simple. She grabbed Floyd's arm and pulled Bertie close. The three of them stepped next to Ruby Mae and Rachel linked arms with her. Ruby Mae looked surprised but held on.

"You are not welcome here," Rachel said to the soldier. "If you've come looking for a fight, you're in the wrong place." Her heart thudded in her chest. "We're here fighting for justice. These women, by the way, are building the ships our sailors rely on." She knew the soldier would react to her differently. A white woman. But he wouldn't like being told off by *any* woman.

The soldier shook his head. "Why are you defending these *niggers*?" He spit on the ground. The word vibrated around them. Ruby Mae didn't flinch. But Floyd let go of Rachel and rushed the soldier. He drew his arm back, clenched his fingers and smashed his fist into the soldier's face, knocking him off his feet. The punch ignited a powder keg. Men in the crowd jumped in. The other soldiers threw punches and wrestled their attackers. Rachel froze when one of the soldiers pulled a knife.

She grabbed Ruby Mae and yanked her out of the way toward the stage, pulling Bertie with her other hand. Peggy and Marcy hurried to catch up. Elena stayed back, taking notes, but away from the fighting.

Panting, Rachel and the others watched from a safer distance close to the stage.

"Everyone okay?" she said, inspecting her friends. No signs of any wounds, but all of them looked rattled. Reporters materialized. Photos were snapped. Police whistles sounded. Within minutes, there were several policemen yelling, pulling men off each other. One soldier sat on the ground, clutching his arm, a bit of blood trickling between his fingers. Rachel didn't go check on him. She was too angry. Besides, it didn't look serious.

Noah hurried over to where Rachel and the others stood, his face twisted with worry.

"What the hell happened? Are you all okay?" he said, wrapping his arm around Rachel and checking the others' faces. He groaned. "I can't believe this. We weren't looking for trouble."

"Maybe so," Ruby Mae said. She wiped her damp face with a bandana. "But don't be surprised. We deal with this all the time, right?" Peggy nodded, scanning the crowd. Marcy looked like she was ready to bolt.

"It don't always end up in a fist fight," Peggy said. "But yeah, it's always there. We always gotta watch our step."

Rachel looked around. The scuffle had ended. A policeman helped the wounded soldier to his feet before the soldiers all walked away. Another cop stepped over to a Negro man with a knife still in his hand. He grabbed the man and shoved him onto to the sidewalk where he handcuffed him. No one else was arrested. White cops and white soldiers versus Negro sailors and their supporters. A stacked deck. The crowd fractured into two's and three's and scattered down the block. Noah pulled Rachel aside.

"Look, I need to pack things up and load my car," he said. He tilted her chin up. "Are you okay?"

She nodded. "Just shaken. All that hatred." The ugliness she'd witnessed lingered. Riding the bus now felt too exposed. "Can you give me and Bertie a ride home?"

He kissed her cheek. "Of course. Give me about fifteen minutes to load up." He headed to the stage.

Rachel turned back to the group of women she'd stood up with. She smoothed Bertie's mussed hair. "You okay?"

Bertie nodded. "I'm fine. And so proud of you." She hugged Rachel.

"I sure was happy to have you by my side," Ruby Mae said. "I kept waiting for the police to come after us."

Rachel's body vibrated with energy. She'd acted on instinct. To protect someone she cared about. Not like her mute self on the bus ride. This time she'd found her voice.

CHAPTER 36

ELENA

November 17, 1944

"Elena, are you awake?" Mrs. Murphy's voice. "You have a phone call."

Elena sat up in bed, groggy, and looked at the clock on her nightstand. 6:15 a.m. Who would be calling so early? Her brain was still digesting the violent ending of yesterday's protest.

"Okay." She slipped into her bathrobe, tying it tight and opened the door. Her landlady stepped back. "Do you know who's calling?"

"Well, she was speaking Spanish," Mrs. Murphy said, her forehead creased, "and there was a lot of static. I think she said, "su madre."

Mamá? They had only spoken once since Elena had left home, the call when Elena had sung to her sister Lupita on her twelfth birthday. This couldn't be good news. She hurried down the stairs and picked up the phone's receiver from the side table in the hall. The wood floor chilled her bare feet.

"Hola, quién habla?" Force of habit, as if she didn't know who was on the other end.

"Hija," Mamá said, just the one word, followed by a sob. Daughter. That was all Elena needed to understand what was unsaid. Papá was dead.

Elena's body buckled against the wall. She slid down onto the floor. Her tears burst loose and she gasped for breath, sobbing. This was the call she'd dreaded ever since she'd left, and yet it seemed impossible. Papá was such a fighter, stubborn, unafraid. Now the policía had done the dirty work for the generals in charge.

Mamá described how she'd finally gotten a big enough bribe to get the local police jefe to admit what happened to Papá. Elena cringed, her heart breaking.

"Lo siento, mija," Mamá said. Papá had refused, for weeks, to give them the names of his sources. Eventually they shot him. Elena cried as she listened. Talking to her mami, the Spanish words flowed over her like a soft caress of comfort.

Mrs. Murphy came down the stairs and disappeared into the kitchen. She returned to where Elena sat, offering a cup of coffee and some tissues. She leaned down and hugged Elena, mouthing, "I'm so sorry," and stepped out the front door, headed to school, no doubt. Today was Tuesday, a regular workday for most, now carved on her heart as the day she learned the truth.

"How are Lupita and Memo?" Elena wiped her nose and sipped the hot coffee. Her sister and brother idolized Papá. Memo had been named for him: Guillermo Gonzales Guzmán, Junior. At only ten years old, he would have to step up now as man of the house, watching over his older sister and their mami.

"They're struggling to be brave. First they lost you, and now . . ." Mamá's voice faltered. "I don't know if I can do this anymore," she added, whispering. "It's not safe here. The whole country is crumbling."

"Did the jefe mention that policeman?" Elena kept her voice low, as if someone listened in. She shuddered, remembering again.

"Yes, he is finally back at work," Mamá said, "grácias a Diós."

What? She pressed her hand to her chest. She hadn't killed him. In fact, he was well enough to return to his job. Impossible. All these months she'd carried the certainty of what she'd done. Killing him had forced her to leave her life behind. But he was alive. Her heart thudded against her fingers.

"Where are you calling from, mami?" She knew the phone in Tía's apartment could not make international calls.

"I'm at the post office, mija," Mamá said. "They'll tell me what I owe when we're done. I couldn't give you this news in a letter."

Elena pushed herself up off the floor and stretched the phone cord into the living room. She sank onto the couch, morning sunlight warm through the window. Her body felt numb, but her mind scurried from one thought to the next. How could she help when her family was so far away? Grief settled deep in her chest. The phone line went quiet as she closed her eyes and slowed her breathing.

"Mami," she said. The solution was obvious. "Maybe you should think about coming here." That had never been an option while Papá was alive. But now . . . "Listen, you and the kids, Tía and the cousins, all of you." She put down the coffee cup. "You're a skilled seamstress. Or if you wanted, the shipyard would train you to weld, like me. Tía could find a job, too, for when the kids are in school. We could find a place to rent for all of us." The more she spoke, the better her idea seemed. She missed her family terribly. She stood up and paced in front of the couch. "Qúe piensas?"

There was silence on the other end, just the hissing static of a bad connection. Then Mamá spoke, her words barely audible.

"Ay, Diós, hija. You want me to move up there? I couldn't. It's too far." Elena imagined her clutching the phone receiver.

"Listen, mami," Elena said. "I would tell you exactly how to get here, which train to take, how to transfer in Mexico City. The kids would need passports, too." This conversation came too soon. Mamá wasn't ready. She should stop talking, but her heart ached for her family. She needed them, their hugs, their reassuring solid presence.

"But I speak no English, mija. How would I ask directions once we cross the border? What if we got lost? Or worse?"

Elena nodded, as if Mamá could see her. "I know this sounds scary, mami. But I can send a detailed letter, write down every step. You can show the letter to the ticket office at the train station. I'll write the important words in English, too. Mami, the police here aren't so dangerous. In fact, my landlady's husband is a policeman. He's very nice to me." She hardly ever saw Mr. Murphy, but he had been polite and seemed like a decent man.

"Well, mija," Mamá said, "I'll think about it. Later. It would be very nice to all be together again. I know you can't return here. The jefe said it was best that you'd left."

The jefe said that? Elena swallowed. "I have extra money saved," she said. "Please, mami," she said, wiping her eyes. "Talk to Tía about coming. I'll find out about renting a big home. Te quiero, mami."

They said goodbye and Elena put down the phone. In her mind's eye, she was already in the new sunny apartment with her family together again. Everyone except Papá. But he would be there, too, in spirit, watching over them.

She must have drifted off to sleep on the couch. When she woke up, the sun had shifted and her body felt cold and stiff. After a hot shower and a small breakfast, she climbed the stairs and pulled out a shoebox from under her bed. Her treasure box. Photos of her family, letters from home, the rosary Tía had given her for confirmation, and a few of her favorite articles that she and Papá had written for the paper.

The melted remains of the last votive candle she'd burned had hardened in its base. After digging out the wax, she placed a fresh candle and lit the wick. The small blue and yellow flame flickered. Next she arranged the photos, propped up by her hairbrush and a few books. Lupita and Memo seemed to frown their disapproval in the photo of the three of them, arms draped over each other's shoulders.

She wrapped Tía's rosary around the candle's base. "Sorry, Papi," she said, a slight smile on her lips. She'd taken his photo at the newspaper, proudly holding up the front page. He was not a believer, but the part of her that still believed in God reasoned that the rosary couldn't hurt. She so wanted to believe that his soul had found peace, and that his suffering was over. The small altar helped, her family watching her, sharing her grief. She closed her eyes and said a prayer for her father.

* * *

Elena considered calling in sick that afternoon, but it would be worse to stay home alone, weeping when she caught sight of the photos of Papá staring back at her. She didn't want to imagine his final weeks. Her dearest papi. If she stayed home, she'd have time to work on her story about the protest. But she couldn't concentrate on that. Not yet. At least at work she'd have a job to distract her.

When she got off the bus at the shipyard, she promised herself she'd be extra careful with the heated welding stick, no distractions. The last thing she needed was another bad burn. Maybe she'd stop by the clinic, and if Rachel was working, they could meet for coffee later during her break.

"Elena, is that you?"

She turned around and saw Ana, whose hand hooded her eyes against the bright sun. Ana stood in one of the long lines of workers waiting to catch the bus. Months had passed since they had last met. Elena had worried about running into Ana or Marisol, recalling their last awkward conversation and hurt feelings. Today was not a good day for another rough confrontation. She was already too raw.

"Ana," she said, "it's good to see you." Her stomach clenched at the lie. Crowds of workers shuffled past them, their voices loud and jarring. The change of shift always felt chaotic, with hundreds of men and women pushing their way in or out of the yard.

Ana put her hand on Elena's arm. "You look so sad. Are you okay, chica?"

The question cut through Elena's pretense. "No, not okay," she said, tears wetting her eyelashes. "It's my papi. Mamá called today with the news." The words blurted out on their own. "Está muerto."

"Oh, Elena, I'm so sorry." Ana hesitated a moment but opened her arms and pulled Elena into a hug. Elena's tears poured down, like a rushing stream after a winter storm. The comforting embrace of a friend, despite the unfinished business between them.

"I've missed you, Ana," she said, hiccupping between sobs. "You and Marisol were my best friends here. I'm so sorry I made you feel unwelcome in our home."

She took a deep breath and wiped her cheeks, then blew her nose. The sobs subsided. "If you love each other, then I'm happy for you. I don't really care about the rest."

"Oh, querida, the truth is we've missed you, too," Ana said, her gaze soft. "Are you still at Mrs. Murphy's? And is she still baking snicker doodles?"

Elena laughed, the knot in her stomach loosening. "Yes, still there. But I'm hoping to move eventually. I've asked Mamá to come up, bring the whole family. We'll have to find a place that fits all of us."

"Really?" Ana said. "Oh, that sounds great. Look, I have to catch my bus, but you should check out the area where we live. We found an apartment in West Oakland. It's like a little slice of Spanish-speaking heaven. People from all over, mostly Mexico, but a few from Guatemala and El Salvador. The clubs and restaurants feel like home. The bus to work only takes forty minutes." She smiled at Elena. "Maybe you can come visit; we'll show you around."

Elena nodded. "I'd like that." She hugged Ana again. "Call me and we'll make a date."

CHAPTER 37

November 16, 1944

Ruby Mae grabbed Peggy's elbow as they walked down the dirt road toward their trailer.

"Remember, sis," she said. "Don't be telling Momma and Daddy about the protest. Say we had a good time shopping. Leave it at that. Okay?" Ugly images from the street brawl raced through her mind, but she stuffed them down and closed the lid.

The sun had already set and the air felt chilly. Noah had given them a ride to the bus stop after the protest, six of them crammed in his car—Rachel, Bertie, Peggy, her, and Marcy. Elena had stayed behind to talk to the men involved in the scuffle. Ruby Mae admired Elena. People needed to know the truth. Except certain people, who were better off not knowing everything about everything.

"You think I'm gonna *tell*?" Peggy shrugged off her hand. "You crazy? Momma would strap our behinds onto the bus headed to Louisiana. I ain't gonna say nothing."

"Well, try to keep the truth off your face," Ruby Mae said. "Maybe look down at your feet or over Momma's head when you talk."

"Fine. *You* tell them the lie. I'll be the one laughing when you mess up."

"We should have bought something, a scarf," Ruby Mae said. A shopping bag from Capwell's would have been convincing.

By the time they got close to their trailer, Ruby Mae made out the dark silhouettes of Momma and Daddy, bent over the open trunk of a car parked in front. The lamp inside the trailer lit up the scene. Who'd come to visit, and what was in that trunk?

"What's going on?" Peggy said, grabbing her hand. They approached the car, Ruby Mae uneasy.

"Surprise!!" The twins, Aaron and Samuel, popped up from inside the trunk, waving and laughing. "We got us a car!" The boys hugged each other and then reached out their arms to Ruby Mae and Peggy. "Come see! We gonna drive all the way home."

A car? This black sedan belonged to her family? The unexpected news pushed aside any worry about reporting to Momma. Ruby Mae let out her breath.

"Daddy, is that right?" she said. She stepped close and hugged him. When she looked up, she saw the familiar spark back in his eyes. "You gonna tell me and Peggy or let these wild boys tell it their way?"

"That's right," Daddy said. The twins hopped out of the trunk and rushed around the side of the car into the front seat. One of them blasted the horn until Momma hurried over to hush them.

Daddy closed the trunk with both hands.

"I figured if we're going home," he said, "we might as well go by car." He chuckled, a sound Ruby Mae hadn't heard in a long time. And how did they have enough money to buy such a nice car? Their old truck back home barely made it to church and back.

"Seems like the good Lord's trying to help me out," Daddy said. "A guy I know from the yard put the word out that he needed to sell this here car, and the word came out to meet me." He shook his head. "Said he needed the cash. Even threw in the gas ration coupons he'd been saving. Engine's in pretty good shape, just a whole lot of miles on it. The body's kind of beat up, but that's okay. It'll get us home. So," he paused and held up the key, "I bought it 'fore he changed his mind."

"Oh, Daddy," Ruby Mae said, and hugged him again. Her tears fell, wetting his shirt. Buying this car worked like the blood transfusion he got in the hospital. "I'm so happy for you."

He pulled away. "Well, it's for all of us, Ruby Mae. Now that I got us this car, we can all head back together." She tried not to flinch. "Momma and me are gonna talk to folks at church about trading some food rations for more gas coupons. I figure we'll be ready to leave in a week or two. Leaves you all time to give notice at work."

"But Daddy," Peggy said, "me and Ruby Mae got plans." She put her hand on Ruby Mae's shoulder and squeezed, like she might fall over otherwise.

Ruby Mae could have pinched her. Not that Peggy was wrong, just that she'd wanted to keep Daddy's good mood going a while longer. Too late. Momma shooed the boys into the trailer so they could listen to the radio show they liked. She walked back to Ruby Mae and Peggy with her don't-mess-with-me expression glued on. Daddy stepped back like he knew what was coming.

"So, girls, how did your shopping trip go?" Momma leaned against the car. "Buy anything nice?"

The evening air's temperature dropped a few degrees. Ruby Mae moved closer to Peggy. What did Momma know? No one had phones out there in North Richmond, though they'd been promised months ago. It was too soon for the newspaper to be out. The evening edition of the *Tribune* might be printed by now, but not in the hands of their neighbors yet. Maybe Momma didn't know a thing.

Peggy spoke up, her voice strained. "We had a good time, Momma, didn't we, Ruby Mae? We went to some nice shops, tried on shoes and pretty dresses, ones we could wear to church." Her head bobbed up and down as she described their imaginary adventure, as if someone had wound her up like a kewpie doll whose head had loosened. "And then we stopped for lunch, and met up with Marcy. Didn't we, Ruby Mae?"

Ruby Mae pinched Peggy's arm, but she kept talking. "Yeah, and the reason we didn't buy anything is that there were too many nice choices. We couldn't decide. So I guess we'll have to go back another time and hope they're still there."

Ruby Mae's heart sank. No way would Momma hear all that and not know it was a pack of lies. But at least Peggy had tried, and she hadn't busted out crying or spilled the beans. Momma stood unmoving, her expression unreadable for a moment, then her eyes sparked and her mouth pinched.

"Peggy Alice Taylor, shame on you," she said, pointing a finger at her. "You about the worst liar I ever met." She shot Ruby Mae a glance. "The two of you trying to act all normal, like you didn't almost get your sorry selves killed. Standing up to those white soldiers. What were you thinking?" Her mouth loosened and suddenly Momma was sobbing, bent over, her hands on her knees, her breathing ragged.

"What you talking about, honey?" Daddy stared at Peggy, then at Ruby Mae, his arm tight around Momma's shoulders. "I don't know nothin' about this. You better tell me what happened. Right now."

Somehow Momma already knew. She'd kept quiet, waiting like an alley cat to pounce. Except now they'd made Momma bust out in tears. She hardly ever cried. Ruby Mae knew how to deal with Momma's anger, but not this. Her eyes burned.

"Who told you, Momma?"

"Never mind who," Momma said. She dried her cheeks with her hanky. "You ain't the only ones out looking for trouble. I ain't gonna rat them out."

"Oh, Momma, Daddy, we're sorry," Ruby Mae said, sniffling. "We didn't want to worry you." She wiped some tears. Her chest felt tight. Peggy looked miserable. "Let's go sit in the car. I don't want to scare the boys."

They walked around the car. Daddy took the driver's seat, Momma next to him. Peggy and Ruby Mae climbed into the back. The car smelled like hundreds of cigarettes had been smoked inside. The burgundy seat leather was worn, a small tear in one corner. But it was a wide enough space that both the boys could fit in next to her and Peggy. They wouldn't take up much room, though their energy could fill a few cars. Momma stared straight ahead, quiet in a way that was worse than her yelling.

Ruby Mae and Peggy took turns describing the rally, hearing Margaret Starks as she spoke to the crowd supporting the convicted sailors. How Mary Lindsay's passionate speech stirred things up.

"That white soldier started yelling insults, called the sailors cowards," Ruby Mae said, leaning forward in the seat. "I had to speak up. Those are Freddy's buddies, men he worked next to on the docks. They're survivors. Not cowards." Her body trembled. "That soldier was just ignorant and hateful."

Daddy turned around, his arm draped across the back of his seat. He looked Ruby Mae in the eye. "I know why you spoke up. I do. But sometimes you got to hold your tongue. If you speak your mind against a white man, he always gonna win, one way or the other. That's the sad truth of it. You of all people know that, Ruby Mae. Look what happened at the yard."

Momma started crying again. What had happened to their mother?

Peggy put her hand on Momma's shoulder. "We're sorry, Momma," she said. "Don't cry, please. I can't take it."

"Tell him," Momma said, her voice harsh, "what happened after that. How you could have been killed." She bent her head forward and sobbed.

Ruby Mae felt sick. Seeing Momma fall apart, the four of them taking up all the air in the smelly car, she remembered how angry she'd felt. Scared, too. What if one of the soldiers had pulled a gun? Her throat tightened and she tasted bile.

"I got to step out," she said, and opened the car door. Couldn't hear the details of the fight again. "You tell them, Peggy."

She slid out of the back seat, closed the door behind her, and leaned up against the trunk, gulping the night air. A quarter moon lit the sky and she caught sight of a few stars. Now that the truth was out, she'd have to convince Momma and Daddy it was okay for her and Peggy to stay in Richmond. They couldn't force their daughters to leave. After all, they were both adults. But right now she felt like crawling into Daddy's lap and letting him sing her to sleep. Momma was right. She could have been killed. Whatever happened from now on, she'd only have Peggy to catch her if she fell.

CHAPTER 38

RACHEL

November 16, 1944

Rachel walked with Noah into The Alley, a piano bar on Grand Avenue near her house. Bertie had declined to join them, claiming the protest had exhausted her. Brown leather booths lined one side of the narrow space, and a polished wood bar led back to the piano, where several customers crowded around, singing an off-key "Don't Fence Me In."

They sat at the bar and Noah said, "Definitely time for some whiskey." He ordered two. Rachel rarely went to bars, and usually ordered a glass of white wine. But today was different.

"You know I promised Mama I'd be home for Shabbat dinner." She propped her elbows on the bar, and shifted her weight on the stool.

"Well, better drink fast," he said, glancing at his watch. "Here's to fighting the good fight." He downed his drink, slapping the glass on the bar.

"You actually feel good about what happened, don't you?" She shook her head and sipped the whiskey, the heat of it burning her throat. "It could have been much worse, you know." Images of the fight flashed across her mind. Not a bloodbath like she'd seen at the base, but all that hate up close felt worse in a way.

Noah clinked his shot glass against hers. "I know. But honestly, everything that happened today, plus the press coverage, will bring more attention to the sailors. You should feel good about that."

She checked her watch. "Hey, let's stay here instead and get drunk." The whiskey had loosened the knot of tension in her shoulders.

Noah took her hand. "Do you want me to come home with you?"

She liked the idea of Noah sharing Shabbat with her family. This would be a first, bringing a guy—a boyfriend?—to join them. Maybe he'd distract everyone from missing Jesse.

"Besides," he said, "I know how to handle Gordon." He mimicked strangling her cousin with his bare hands. He knew Gordon from shared classes back in high school, but they'd never been friends.

She had to laugh. "Thanks, but I can handle him." She met his eyes. "Mama said you have a standing invitation to Shabbat. So, okay." She picked up her glass and swallowed the rest of the whiskey. "Whoa." She leaned forward and kissed him on the lips, her mouth tingling. "She likes you. And so do I."

By the time she and Noah walked in her front door, Gordon already sat between his parents on the couch talking to Papa. Gordon's wine glass was almost empty. Mama could be heard clanging pots in the kitchen. Smelled like pot roast.

"Hello, you two," Papa said, standing up to hug Rachel and shake hands with Noah. "We've been banned from the kitchen. As usual. Noah, I hope you're staying for dinner."

Noah glanced at Rachel and nodded. "Thanks, Dr. Stern. Who can resist your wife's cooking?" Rachel did a quiet eye roll.

"Please, call me Richard," Papa said. "Can I get you some wine? I want to hear about the protest." He poured two full glasses of red wine, handing them over with an expectant look on his face.

Rachel sat down in the easy chair and patted the ottoman for Noah to join her. She wasn't ready to rehash the day. "Let's save that for the dinner table, Papa. You know Mama will need to hear about it, too." She looked at her aunt and uncle. "You've all met Noah, right? His family belongs to Temple Sinai, too." She smiled. "What's new with you, Aunt Pearl? Seen any good movies?"

Out of the corner of her eye, she noticed Gordon studying her. What a putz. She sipped her wine, remembering Noah's feigned strangling, and hid her smile.

The conversation remained chatty and light, and then Mama appeared in the doorway, hair wispy around her face. "Noah, so glad you're joining us," she said.

Candles were lit, prayers were spoken, the challah was passed around from hand to hand. Mama carried in platters of meat, roasted potatoes and carrots. Noah sat in Jesse's old spot. Rachel was sure her parents had noticed, too. Having Noah at the table next to her felt like a soothing balm. Mama nodded her approval when he loaded his plate.

"This all looks delicious," he said, smiling at Mama. "Thanks for including me."

"It's good to have another young man at the table," Mama said. "Papa said you'd been to a protest about those sailors." She glared at Rachel. "Not shopping."

Noah hesitated. "Uh, yes, we had a good crowd. Have you heard of Mary Lindsay? She's written about the sailors' trial. She got everyone fired up."

Gordon snorted and put down his wine glass. "Mary Lindsay, who writes for that commie newspaper, was your speaker? What a joke."

"Gordon," Rachel said, poking her fork towards her cousin's face, "I can't believe how closed-minded your are. Don't you understand anything about what happened at the base?" She shook her head. "You're hopeless."

Noah put his hand on her shoulder but she twisted away.

"Don't worry, Noah," she said. The alcohol in her veins lit her up. "He's just scared someone might take away his comfortable life and make him work for a living."

"Rachel!" Uncle Max looked shocked. "Gordy has a good job. He knows he's lucky. But communism and fascism have no place in our country. Look what's happened in Europe."

Rachel looked at her parents. Mama was pretending to eat, moving the food around on her plate, her eyes down. Papa leaned back in his chair, watching the others. Next to her, Noah cleared his throat.

"If I can put in my two cents here," he said, squeezing her hand under the table, "let's focus on what's at stake. Fifty Negro sailors have been sentenced to years of hard labor by a so-called jury of all white Navy officers, for refusing to load live ammunition. After witnessing their friends be blown to pieces doing that same job. Would any of us go back to work under those conditions?"

Gordon gulped the last of his wine and wiped his mouth. "Listen, you two act like defending Negroes is some kind of holy calling. I know some Pullman porters who worked in the fields before the railroad hired them. They're grateful to have those jobs. When a passenger asks them for something, anything, they do it with a smile on their face and a 'Yes, sir.' They'd never refuse an order."

"Stop it!" Rachel's voice echoed in her ears. She slammed her hand on the tablecloth, causing red wine to splash onto the delicate lace. Gordon pushed back from the table.

"My God, Gordon," she said, her voice thick. "You can't equate those porters' work with the sailors' situation. Their lives were in danger." She blotted a patch of the wine-stained lace with her napkin. "Today, I watched three Negro women from the shipyard get bullied by a few white soldiers, just for being at the protest. When one of them called the women n—," she shuddered, unwilling to repeat the expletive, "tempers flared. A fight broke out. One guy pulled out a knife. If the police hadn't shown up, who knows what might have happened."

Mama stared at her. "Dear God, Rachel." She looked at her husband. "Did you know about this?"

Papa shook his head. "Of course not. I would have told you." He looked around the table, his eyes resting on Rachel. "What about Bertie? Didn't she go, too? Tell us the rest."

Rachel sighed, her anger at her cousin subsiding, embarrassed at her outburst. Everyone looked at her, waiting. Noah took this as a good moment to eat the food on his plate, while she described what happened.

"Lucky you had Noah there to protect you," Gordon said.

God, he was impossible. A wave of exhaustion swept over her. "I've lost my appetite, Mama. Save me a plate, okay?" She stood.

"Wait, honey," Mama said, reaching for her arm.

Papa spoke up. "Let her go. It's okay."

Rachel grabbed Noah's hand, which held a chunk of challah. "C'mon. I'll walk you to your car. Then I'm gonna sack out."

Outside on the front porch, she leaned against his shoulder, her head throbbing.

"Poor Rach," he said, putting his arm around her. "Your family's Shabbat dinners are sure lively. I expected you and Gordon to lunge across the table and duke it out."

"Yeah," she said, "tonight was worse than usual. I hoped we'd be on good behavior with you there, but obviously not." She looked up at him. "That's my family."

He pulled her close. "I'm glad I got to be part of it. More interesting than my family. Good manners get old."

"Really?" she said. "Well, I'm glad I went to the protest. Even when things got scary, it felt important to be there." She hugged him. "I'm glad you were there, too."

Upstairs, after Noah had gone, she sat on the side of her bed, slipped out of her clothes, and climbed under the covers. Something had shifted inside her, a tectonic plate had inched forward. Standing among the protesters, she'd glimpsed another world, unfamiliar but compelling. Something bigger than her. And she wanted to be part of it.

CHAPTER 39

ELENA

November 20, 1944

The air smelled earthy and sweet, and light rain was falling when Elena stepped out of the house.

Ana and Marisol had agreed to see her at their apartment. Elena needed to talk. Since telling Ana about Papá, she realized how deeply she'd missed her friends. She owed them an honest apology and hoped they'd accept it. But she doubted Marisol was ready.

She got off the bus at 7th Street in downtown Oakland. The street scene looked familiar, with families and couples walking down the block speaking Spanish. Like the countless walks she'd taken with her family in the zócalo, the whole neighborhood joining in after church, followed by a hearty lunch and siesta. She half expected Mamá to step up and throw her arms around her. But no. Instead there was Ana, alone, dressed in olive-green canvas pants and a thick gray poncho, a red bandana tied over her hair. She took Elena's hand.

"Bienvenida," Ana said, "welcome to our neighborhood. It's good to see you, away from work." She locked eyes with Elena. "We're glad you called."

"That's good to hear," Elena said, suddenly anxious. What if Ana was just being polite? "Where's Marisol?"

Ana linked arms with her and led her down the street. She frowned. "She's at home. We thought we could have coffee at our apartment. Then maybe go for a walk."

"Sounds good," Elena said, aware her breathing had quickened.

Ana stopped in front of a two-story apartment building. The windows on the bottom held clay pots with pink and red geraniums perched on the sills. "Here we are. Nuestro querido hogar." She smiled and climbed the front steps.

Elena followed her inside to a living room painted a rich gold. Colorful red, indigo and green Mexican weavings hung on the walls. The couch sagged slightly, its brown cloth worn.

"Oh, it's so pretty, Ana," she said. "I love the colors." Someday she'd have a place where she could decorate however she wanted.

"The apartment manager is mexicano. Jorge. He bought us the paint and seems happy with what we've done. We found the furniture at a second-hand store." Ana turned as Marisol walked into the room.

"Hola, Elena," Marisol said, nodding. She didn't step forward to embrace her old friend.

"Please, can we sit down," Elena said. She felt like she was interviewing for a job. If she said the wrong thing, or didn't say what Ana and Marisol needed to hear, she'd make things worse and lose their friendship forever. She sat in an uncushioned oak rocking chair, her spine scraping against the frame.

"I'll bring us some café, chicas," Ana said, heading towards what Elena guessed was their kitchen. Marisol sat on the couch, crossing her long legs and then folding her arms across her chest. Ana must have begged her to agree to this.

"Your apartment is really nice," Elena said, stalling. Maybe she should have invited them out for a drink instead. A shot of tequila might help.

"Sí, we're happy here." Marisol looked around the room. "Just the two of us. No one else around to bother us."

This was off to a bad start. Marisol obviously expected Elena to do the hard work. Fine. After all, Elena had been the one to ruin their friendship. She pressed her feet against the floor, rocking slightly, the wood floor creaking.

Ana came back, carrying a tray with three ceramic mugs and a plate filled with cookies. Elena smelled cinnamon, and recalled their first visit to Mrs. Murphy's house.

"Snicker doodles," Elena said, her back muscles knotted against the rocking chair. "Mrs. Murphy's recipe?"

Ana put the tray down on a black luggage trunk used as a coffee table. "Yes, we stopped by one day to visit her, and she wrote it down for us."

A twinge of sadness fluttered through Elena; she hadn't known they'd been at the house while she was out. Ana handed her a mug along with a cookie on a blue cloth napkin. "Black, the way you like it."

Why was Ana being so sweet? Probably to make up for the frosty glances Marisol kept shooting her way. Ana sat down next to Marisol on the couch, holding her coffee mug in both hands.

Elena sipped the coffee, strong and slightly bitter. "Look, I know I said some hurtful things. I'm very sorry." She took a deep breath and let it out slowly. Marisol watched her with narrowed eyes. Ana put her hand on Marisol's knee.

"I overreacted," Elena said. "I felt hurt that you didn't trust me. That you'd kept your secret from me. So I lashed out and said things that hurt you." She frowned. "You know, the way

I was raised, the priests taught us that homosexuals were bad. Dangerous. They drummed that into our heads at church, just like they did to you, right?"

She looked at Ana, who nodded. Marisol bit her lip and frowned. Better to keep talking.

"I've thought a lot about how I reacted," Elena said. She took another sip of coffee and put her mug down. "Before you, I'd never met any lesbians. But I know you. You were good friends to me when I needed that. You're good people. You're not dangerous. Thinking like that only leads to hate." A few tears squeezed out of her eyes. "That's why I reacted so badly. I hope you'll let me try again. I promise I'll do better." Ana's eyes were wet, too. But Marisol stood up, her hands on her hips.

"Look, Elena," she said, first glancing at Ana. "I'm here because Ana insisted we hear you out. But honestly, I don't trust you." She crossed her arms. "I feel like I can't be myself with you. I'm tired of people judging us." She stepped towards the hall. "You think we should have told you the truth earlier, but look what happened when we did. If they found out at the shipyard, we'd be in real danger. So, sorry, but I don't really want your friendship anymore." She turned and walked out of the room, her footsteps echoing down the hall.

Elena felt her words like a slap.

"Marisol," she said, her voice pleading, "wait, please. Can't we get past this?" There was no reply.

Ana stood up, her eyebrows raised. "Sorry. I hoped she was ready." She stepped away from the couch. "Stay here. Let me talk to her, okay?"

Elena nodded and picked up her mug. This had been a mistake, thinking they could just resume their friendship. She rocked the chair with more force. When the three of them had first met, each of them carried the pain of what they'd escaped from. Those wounds did not heal quickly.

No matter how much she wanted to forget what happened to her that night back home, it clung to her like a zippered jacket she couldn't rip off. Ana and Marisol had been shunned by their families, kicked out of their homes for loving each other. Their histories clung to them, too. And she had added to their pain.

She got up and looked out the front window, where a young girl holding her mother's hand skipped down the sidewalk. Still so innocent to the world around her.

"Hey," Ana said, coming back. Elena jumped at her voice. "Look, why don't we go for a walk? I'd like you to see what's happening at Sweet's. It's a ballroom where musical groups perform. On Sunday afternoons they hold a tardeada just like back in México. A big party with music and dancing. Sometimes famous musicians from home come and perform. And today it's Pedro Infante!"

"Who?"

Ana rolled her eyes. "He's only the best ranchera singer you'll ever hear. Makes me cry to hear him. I get very homesick. Anyway, I've got tickets and now Marisol is refusing to go. I was going to buy a ticket for you. Will you come?"

Elena hadn't planned on spending the entire afternoon with them, but how could she refuse? Lately she spent all her time either working at the yard or writing up a story. Her social life needed a boost, and being with her old friend felt good. At least Ana was willing to reconnect.

"Okay, thanks," she said. "I need some fun. But I'm not dressed for dancing." Her black pants and boots were still damp and a bit mud-spattered.

"Oh, don't worry," Ana said, "there's no dress code. You'll see."

Elena called out goodbye to Marisol, but got no response. She and Ana headed out and joined the other pedestrians ambling up the street, the sky overhead filled with fat gray clouds. Elena felt the tension fade from her shoulders and she linked arms with Ana, who smiled back. By the time they reached the block where Sweet's Ballroom stood, a long line had formed outside on the sidewalk, Spanish peppering the air as people chatted, laughed and called out to friends. She felt right at home.

"Feels like we're joining a family fiesta," she said. Several of the men in line wore zoot suits, their wide-legged pants cinched snug at the ankles, long jackets with padded shoulders. A few sported fedoras and porkpie hats. They looked young and full of themselves. Not her type at all. The men who caught her eye dressed like serious college students, like Rachel's Noah.

"Yeah, check out those pachucos," Ana said. "They like to get noticed, but there's been pressure on them to quit wearing those suits. Too much fabric wasted during the war."

Elena had read about the riots in Los Angeles a year ago, when Mexican-American men in zoot suits fought in the street against sailors and soldiers angry at their appearance, or just looking for a fight. Even Oakland had experienced its own smaller riot.

"This must be one of the places they feel safe," Elena said. Safety in numbers and broad daylight. She thought about the Port Chicago protest, how quickly things got out of hand. The protesters she interviewed had feared for their lives once the fight broke out.

"We all make choices, Elena," Ana said. "Sometimes we take risks that might put us in danger." She narrowed her eyes. "But you know that. Working with your papi on his newspaper took a lot of courage. He taught you how to be brave."

Elena nodded. She pulled a handkerchief from her pocket and wiped her eyes. "Sorry. I do miss him. I miss my family."

"Yeah," Ana said, "sometimes I miss mine, too. Who knows? Maybe one day they'll accept me and Marisol. Maybe not. I don't know if I'll ever go home." She squeezed Elena's arm. "But I'm glad you called. I've missed you."

By the time they reached the entrance to the dance hall, the music was loud enough that conversation was difficult. Mariachi! Elena looked inside at the polished wood dance floor filling up with couples, some kids darting in and out. The crowd was almost entirely dark haired, faces with indio features, skin shades of brown. Familiar. Even the smoky air reminded her of the cigars Papá occasionally smoked, the bitter scent of burnt leaves.

Up on the stage, the mariachi band that had been playing—two guitars, violin, and trumpet—were joined by a man dressed in a plain black suit. White shirt with a skinny tie and a large black sombrero embroidered in silver. His thin moustache arched as he sang and strummed his guitar. The audience went wild. He crooned of being a gray cloud in her way, and how he'd love her forever, even if she forgot about him.

"See?" Ana leaned close to Elena. "That's Pedro Infante. He sings from the heart."

Elena nodded, but she thought the words were too melodramatic. Everyone around them swayed to the music, some with eyes closed, others embracing their partners, slow dancing. Even Ana looked smitten by the slow confessional ballad.

Elena hoped the mood would switch up soon. She was ready for some upbeat mariachi songs and let-loose dancing. She'd had enough drama lately to last for days. If only Marisol had agreed to join them, that ballroom scene would have been perfect. As it was, she felt lucky to be there with Ana. Being alone hurt too much.

CHAPTER 40

RACHEL

November 21, 1944

"Ready to go, Rachel?"

Papa's impatient call echoed up the stairs to her bedroom, where she hurried to put on her black slacks and yellow sweater set. He'd invited her to join him for Grand Rounds at Merritt Hospital, and he'd expect her to be properly dressed. Thank God it was her day off, and she was liberated from the white stockings and stiff uniform of her job. Not to mention the required nurse's cap, that served no purpose other than keeping the makers of bobby pins in business. It certainly didn't make her a better nurse.

Papa would have asked Jesse to come instead, had he lived. Rachel was a poor substitute. Just Dr. Stern's daughter, the nurse who worked at the shipyard. Jesse would have been known as Dr. Stern, the Younger.

Was this invitation an attempt to convince her that medical school was still an option for her? He'd refused to tell her the topic of the morning's lecture, and she'd imagined it would be something like "How to Upgrade from RN to MD After the War." Ever since they'd worked together the night of the explosion, he'd been more interested in her work and the injuries she treated.

Maybe he felt she could fill Jesse's shoes. Even if she didn't want that.

Down in the kitchen, the smell of fresh coffee and toast countered the gray drizzle out the window. Mama stood at the kitchen table, her hands full.

"Here," she said. "Papa's already in the car. I've packed you a thermos and a snack. Grab your raincoat. But hurry; you know he hates being late." She handed the food to Rachel. God forbid anyone leave the house unfed.

Papa started the car as soon as Rachel walked out the front door. The air smelled musty, the fallen leaves of the Japanese maple in the front yard crumbling under her feet. Jesse had always done the leaf raking. Now the job was hers. One she enjoyed, remembering the two of them constructing leaf mountains to tumble through.

"Sorry," she said, sliding into the passenger seat. Papa put the car in gear and headed down to Grand Avenue, then over towards the hospital, driving like an emergency burst appendix awaited his arrival. Rachel didn't dare risk sipping hot coffee as he accelerated through turns.

Merritt Hospital, a brick three-story building with a grand columned entrance, sat on a spacious green lawn. Her alma mater, whose nursing school alumnae staffed most of the local hospitals. She wondered if she'd see some of her old faculty. They didn't usually attend Grand Rounds, too busy with their own patients and student nurses.

Papa pulled into the parking lot reserved for "Doctors Only" and found one of the last spaces.

"See? We almost lost my spot. Hurry up now," he said, grabbing his briefcase and black medical bag.

"Papa, it's not an emergency." She gathered her belongings and stepped out of the car.

"No, but we have rules here," he said, glaring at her. "We teach the med students and residents to never be late for Grand Rounds. I've got to set a good example."

"Fine," she said. Better be worth the rush.

She followed him into the lobby and down the hall to the auditorium. The room had been designed to mimic a theater, with graduated rows of plush fabric seating. The front rows were reserved for the attending physicians like Papa, but there were no two seats available together, so they sat in the back.

Unlike the usual bedside rounds, when the nervous doctors-in-training presented a verbal case summary and were then questioned by the senior physicians, the monthly Grand Rounds consisted of a lecture by an expert doctor in the field, who took questions from their colleagues. Papa expected his surgical residents to pay close attention, Rachel knew, so he could quiz them later. He'd probably expect the same from her, and she hoped the topic was interesting, like wound care advances, and not some kind of obscure hematology research.

She sipped her coffee and looked around. Among the crowd gathered for the lecture, mostly male physicians in white lab coats, stethoscopes draped around their necks an identifying status symbol, were several women in nurse's uniforms. A couple of them were familiar; they had trained Rachel during her in-patient rotations. She wondered why they had come.

The speaker was introduced. A woman—dressed in a navy blue skirted suit and a pearl necklace, no lab coat—walked to the podium. Her graying hair was short and fell in soft waves around her face. Rachel wondered what her specialty was; she had a kind face.

"Hello all," she began, her voice strong and energetic. "I'm delighted to be invited this morning, to let you know about the exciting work we're doing on the East Coast. My name is Catherine Dempsey. I'm a registered nurse, all the way from

Boston, and the first president of the American Association of Industrial Nurses."

She looked around the room and smiled. "That's right. We've finally organized the nurses who do the hard work of caring for the men and women whose jobs put them at risk for injury. Our job is to educate our workforce so they can safely do their jobs in our factories and shipyards."

Rachel clutched her thermos and stared at Papa. He grinned, the Cheshire Cat himself. No wonder he hadn't told her the subject matter. Catherine Dempsey had her full attention. Nurses had organized a union? Focused on worker safety?

"We know it's the worker's health that determines his efficiency," Dempsey said. "But an industrial nurse must educate, too. Many times, a little advice to a worker is taken home to their family."

She paused to drink some water and look out at the audience. Rachel felt sure the woman had spotted her in the crowd. "The urgency of the war program has focused attention on the need to keep its workers safe. We nurses make great teachers for our patients."

Yes, that's what she most enjoyed about her job—teaching her patients how to protect themselves and what they could do to stay healthy. But she could do this on a larger scale. Teach a class or visit work sites and evaluate their safety. Reach more people with the knowledge they needed to stay safe. Her pulse quickened.

Nurse Dempsey described the safety program at a munitions factory outside Boston, where the nurses had implemented training sessions. The subsequent reduction of injuries was dramatic, and the morale of workers had markedly improved. She showed slides documenting her research.

"In conclusion, I appeal to every nurse to consider this challenging field. Occupational health and safety. And," she looked at the doctors seated in front of her, "I hope all the physicians here will support our efforts to provide this level of preventive care. Thank you. I'll take questions now." She stepped back and sipped from her glass of water. "I hope my first question comes from a nurse."

Rachel's hand shot up. Papa smiled again.

"Yes, the young lady in the back?" Catherine Dempsey raised her eyebrows. "Are you an RN?"

Rachel smiled. "Yes. I work at the clinic in the Kaiser shipyard near here in Richmond. We see so many on-the-job injuries every day. Safety measures aren't always followed." She took a deep breath. "I also triaged patients after the explosion at the Navy's Port Chicago base. So many sailors died or were wounded due to unsafe working conditions. I'm wondering how you get the training to become an expert in this field?" She felt the eyes of many MDs on her, but she didn't care.

"That's a great question," Nurse Dempsey said. "I'm sure you've seen plenty of injuries at the yard. The war has only added to unsafe work environments. Port Chicago is a horrific example. There's too much pressure to get those ships built and loaded quickly." She bit her lip. "We have established several training programs, mostly back east, to teach those skills. Come talk to me when this is over."

When there were no more questions, most of the doctors in the room rose and headed for the exit. A couple of nurses walked up to the speaker, but the rounds were over. Papa stood up and adjusted the stethoscope around his neck.

"So, I gather this talk inspired you, Rachel," he said.

She got up and hugged him. "Thanks for inviting me, Papa. Yes, I'm very interested in learning more." She paused. "I know you and Mama hoped I'd go on to med school after the war, but . . ."

"What are you talking about?" He frowned. "Where did you get that idea?"

"Well, I guess I assumed that's what you'd want," she said, sighing. "You know, since Jesse's gone. That it was up to me now." Her eyes burned. Until she'd spoken those words, she hadn't realized how much pressure she'd felt to live up to Papa's expectations. She looked down, trying not to cry.

"Honey," Papa said, grasping her shoulder. "Listen to me. First of all, I don't expect you to replace your brother. Really. I asked you to come today because I'm so proud of you and the work you do. Ever since we helped out at the base, caring for those injured sailors, I realized you'd found a passion. Work that has meaning for you."

She looked up at him. Who was this man, speaking to her now? He had never said anything like this before.

"You don't need a medical degree to find that," he said. "I know you'll figure out a way to increase your skills, through a training program or whatever it takes." His gaze softened. "It sounds corny, but I believe in you."

Oh, those words reached right into her heart. A tear trickled down her cheek, and when she looked up at Papa, he handed her his handkerchief. The muscles in her neck and shoulder relaxed as something released, some psychic weight she'd carried for months.

"Thanks, Papa," she said, her voice shaky.

"You better go talk to Nurse Dempsey before she leaves." Papa picked up his belongings. "I'll see you at home tonight. Are you catching the bus?"

She tucked the handkerchief into the pocket of her sweater and straightened her shoulders. "Actually, Noah's coming here to pick me up. He wants to show me some of the work he's been doing."

Papa raised his eyebrows. "Seeing more of him lately, eh? Well, I approve." He laughed. "Not that you asked."

She reached up and patted his cheek. "Thanks for this, Papa. Really."

He squeezed her hand and walked away towards the exit. She took a deep breath and refocused, then grabbed her things and walked down the aisle to where Nurse Dempsey stood talking to another nurse. She had so many questions.

CHAPTER 41

ELENA

November 22, 1944

Elena walked to the corner of 8th and Madison in downtown Oakland. When Ana had invited her to lunch in Chinatown, she'd accepted right away, wondering if Marisol would be there. She hadn't wanted to ask over the phone. To be honest, she'd rather just see Ana. The last encounter at their apartment had been painful.

Ana greeted her with a big hug and a kiss on the cheek. No sign of Marisol, which felt like a soft blow to an already tender bruise.

"I'm glad you could come," Ana said. "I found this little place that makes fresh noodles, like spaghetti, but with Chinese spices. You choose the meat and they add vegetables." She brushed some hair off her face. "Sound good?"

"Yes, and then let's walk around, okay? I love seeing all the different shops."

Ana laughed. "I knew you'd like coming here. I've missed your curiosity. By the way, I did invite Marisol to join us, but she said she was busy." She shrugged. "I'm tired of waiting for her to move past her hurt feelings. You were our first friend here, and I didn't want to lose you again. I think she'll come around soon."

Elena nodded, hoping Ana was right. She wished the whole thing didn't feel so complicated, that she could undo what had happened.

They headed down the block, past a produce market with mounds of oranges and broccoli and unfamiliar root vegetables on display, then past a case filled with dried herbs and orange and brown mystery powders in small metal bowls. The air in the doorway smelled earthy and exotic. Almost all the customers were Asian.

"I read a little about this area," she said, following Ana into a dimly lit restaurant, dark wood tables pressed along the walls. The waitress gestured them to an empty table and brought them menus. "Did you know the Chinese were not allowed to come to this country for years? Except for the men who came to build the railroads and dams. The law didn't change until after Pearl Harbor."

Ana nodded. "I forgot how much you like history. But this country only wants immigrants when they need our labor." She studied the menu. "I do love the food variety."

"The only reason you and I are still here," Elena said, "is because the shipyards need us. Once the war is over, who knows how we'll be treated." She thought about the recent zoot suit riots. And the sailors' verdict. "This country pretends to be fair, but it has different rules based on what you look like."

"Yeah," Ana said. "We're always being judged."

The waitress came and took their orders, leaving them a pot of aromatic jasmine tea. The restaurant filled with shoppers stepping in for a quick meal, their bags of produce tucked under their chairs. Several spoke what she guessed was Chinese, their voices loud. She wished she understood their language, could speak to them and ask about their lives.

"Would you ever consider going back home?" Ana asked.

Elena shook her head. Maybe it was time to confide. "I can't imagine feeling safe there. Besides, there's so much I like about living here, in spite of what's wrong."

When her order of chicken chow mein arrived, Elena picked up the set of chopsticks and held them between her fingers, studying the technique of a man at the next table, who nimbly grabbed a heap of his noodles and slurped them into his mouth.

Ana sighed. "I need a fork. Last time the waitress felt sorry for me after I dropped some noodles in my lap. I should have been practicing."

"No fork for me," Elena said, trying to keep the pointed ends of her chopsticks firmly around the slippery noodles. "It smells so good, like it's teasing me to see how long it will take to get into my mouth. They must use a lot of garlic."

"And jengibre. How do you say in English?" Ana stabbed a piece of chicken with her fork.

"Ginger. Yes that's what I smell, too." Elena got close enough to the chopsticks to land some food in her mouth before the noodles slid back onto the plate. The flavors danced on her tongue. "We would lose weight if we used these all the time." She grinned at Ana and sipped some tea from the small porcelain cup. A slightly bitter, flowery taste.

"So tell me what's new," Ana said, "besides your writing. Have you met any handsome men? Honestly, those guys at the shipyard are old enough to be my father. I'm glad I'm not looking."

Elena froze. In the months she'd shared a room with Ana and Marisol, there had been several chances for her to confide in them. Instead, she'd only described Papá's arrest and her role as witness. But after she'd told Rachel, the burden of hiding the truth had lifted. What happened was not her fault. She'd only tried to protect herself.

"To be honest, I haven't been very interested in dating," she said. "I had a terrible experience back home." She put down her chopsticks.

Ana took her hand across the table. "Ay, pobrecita. Do you want to tell me? I've known something happened, but you never spoke of it."

So she did. Ana's face contorted as Elena described the attack and how she'd fought back. By the time she was done, they both had tears in their eyes. The waitress came and asked if there was something wrong with the food.

Ana dabbed her eyes. "No, it's delicious. Thank you." The waitress hurried off to another table. "I'm glad you told me. But I'm so sorry. No wonder you've been avoiding men."

"It's been easier to focus on my job and the writing," Elena said. "I'm not sure how I'd react if I met a guy. He'd have to be very understanding." She thought about Rachel and Noah. He seemed like a kind man, so sweet to Rachel. Part of her was jealous, but maybe she'd find someone like that, too. When she was ready.

"I think it's really important to trust the person first, get to know them," Ana said. "You know, Marisol and I were good friends first." She raised her eyebrows. "So when she kissed me after spending so much time together, it felt pretty natural, even though it surprised me. I thought I was the only one who felt that way." She looked Elena in the eye. "Are you okay hearing about this?"

"Yes. I've had a lot of time to adjust." Elena smiled. "I'm really glad you found each other. You're very important to me. I missed being part of your lives. I hope Marisol will forgive me."

"I know she misses you. But life hasn't been easy for us." Ana sipped her tea. "Ella es terca como una mula." Stubborn as a mule. "Give her time. She'll come around."

A warm rush filled Elena's chest. Much as she prayed that Mamá and the children would eventually come, she needed her friends, too, for support and companionship. Even if she never met a man she loved enough to marry, one who'd understand her history, she'd still have her work and her writing and her circle of friends. That would be enough.

CHAPTER 42

November 23, 1944

Ruby Mae wiped down the steel counters in the kitchen at Tapper's, her fingers like prunes from all the scrubbing and washing produce. Her legs ached from being on her feet all day with hardly any breaks. Chopping vegetables for the cooks had left her arm muscles throbbing.

The dinner crowd had gone home, so only a few of the kitchen staff remained, cooking for the customers over in the nightclub. Someone had turned on the kitchen's battered radio. She listened to the slow jazz saxophone and thought about Freddy, how she'd felt when she'd danced with him, his body against hers, the heat in her own skin.

"Ruby Mae." Was she dreaming?

And there he stood, in his dress blues, cap in hand, smack dab in the middle of Tappers' kitchen, grinning. The scar on his neck had flattened, now a pale caterpillar.

"Freddy Parker, you 'bout scared me to death. What're you doing here?" She smoothed her apron.

"I just got my orders," he said. "I'm shipping out in the morning." He took her hand. "I had to see you before I leave."

Tomorrow? Oh, Lord. "I'm gonna take a quick break," she told Chickie, who nodded and turned to Freddy.

"God bless you, son," the cook said. "And come back safe for your gal here."

Ruby Mae led Freddy out the back door of the steamy kitchen, into the alley. Her eyes burned. "I ain't ready for you to go, Freddy. Feels like we just getting started." A tear spilled onto her cheek.

Freddy put his arm around her. "You been a bright light for me since we met, Ruby Mae. And I'm gonna keep you as my guiding star on the ship. I'll follow that star home. I promise."

"I love you, Freddy," she whispered.

"I love you, too."

He leaned in and kissed her for a long time, like he wanted to save that kiss forever. Then he turned and walked down the alley, his cap on his head. She watched him until he disappeared around the corner, wiping her cheeks before she stepped inside and picked up a dishtowel.

"Ruby Mae." Margaret's voice startled her. When did she walk in? "I need to see you in my office." The swinging doors to the dining room flapped behind her.

Uh-oh. What had she done wrong? The last time she got called into her boss's office, it had been Mr. Graham and he'd had Jack there telling lies. Was Margaret going to scold her for eating too much on her break? Or had Chickie complained about her? She thought she'd been doing well. Her throat tightened. She'd just lost Freddy. She couldn't lose her job, too.

By the time she got to Margaret's office, she was close to tears.

"I'm sorry," she said, wringing the bandana in her hands. "I've been working real hard. Sorry if I been eating too much. Please, give me another chance."

"What are you talking about, Ruby Mae?" Margaret leaned back in her chair. "Sit down, okay?" She picked up a pack of cigarettes and lit up, exhaling a puff of smoke that hung over the desk.

"I love working here, Miz Margaret," Ruby Mae said, her voice wobbly. She sat in the straight-back chair and wiped the sweat off her forehead. Maybe one of the cooks had told Margaret about how she'd left a dish towel too close to the stove and it caught fire. Luckily no one got burned and none of the food was ruined.

"Ruby Mae," Margaret said, "I hear you've been doing real good in the kitchen. In fact, that's why I wanted to talk to you." She took another drag on the cigarette.

Oh. She let out the breath she'd been holding since she walked in the office. This was not the same as that awful day at the yard. She shifted her weight on the chair.

"Louise told me this morning that she's gonna be leaving," Margaret said. Louise had been cooking at Tappers' for years. "Her grandbabies down in LA need looking after. She and Chickie agreed that you're about good enough to take her spot. What do you think? Are you ready for more responsibility?"

Ruby Mae jumped up from the chair. "You want me to cook? Really?" She rushed over to Margaret and hugged her before she had time to protest. "Oh, this makes me so happy!" Tears spilled over and she practically danced back to her seat.

Margaret smiled. "You still have a lot to learn, girl. But Chickie said he's willing to teach you. By the time he's done, you'll know all his secrets for making a fine pot of gumbo and the best fried chicken west of the Mississippi."

Ruby Mae's whole body vibrated. She couldn't wait to tell Peggy. And Momma and Daddy. They'd be so proud. She'd write Freddy the good news as soon as she heard from him.

* * *

That first week as a full-fledged cook, Ruby Mae had a rough start. She was so nervous that she might mess up, she did exactly that, once spilling so much black pepper into the bubbling pot of gumbo she had to toss it out and start over. Another day she burnt her fingers trying to get the slippery pieces of battered chicken into the cast iron pan filled with hot oil. Not long after that she lost control of her chopping knife and almost sliced off the tip of her finger as the knife spun off the counter and clattered onto the cement floor.

"Ruby Mae," Chickie said, picking up the knife and placing it in the dirty dishes sink, "what is wrong with you? You acting like you *trying* to get fired." He shook his head. "It ain't gonna work. Slow down, okay? Pay attention to what you're doing."

She nodded, tears stinging her eyes. She so wanted to do a good job, prove to him and Margaret that they made the right choice. "I'm sorry, Chickie. I'll be more careful." And that seemed to help calm her down. By the end of the week, her confidence was back, and she held her breath when he tasted the gumbo she'd made all on her own, using the lessons he'd taught her. Lord, she prayed, let him approve.

"Well, Miz Ruby Mae Taylor," he said, licking his lips, "I believe I done my job with you. This here pot of gumbo's almost as good as mine. Almost." He threw back his head and laughed, giving her a pat on the back.

"I did it!" She waved the wooden spoon in her hand overhead and twirled around in a circle. Getting his approval meant everything.

This deserved a celebration. She had an idea. Wouldn't it be great to send off Momma and Daddy and the boys with a delicious meal, cooked with her own two hands? A going away party. She'd make a big pot of that gumbo and some rice, maybe a tray of cornbread, too. And she'd invite her friends, like Marcy and Elena, and even Rachel and Noah and Bertie.

Ever since the protest, when they'd all stood shoulder to shoulder, a small army of brave souls, she'd longed to bring everyone together, thank them for their friendship. A luncheon, with all the people she cared about in one room. Except Freddy, of course, but he'd be there in spirit. Tappers' was the perfect location. All she needed now was Margaret's blessing.

"'Course you can cook up some gumbo for your family," Margaret told her when she cornered her outside the dining room. Margaret stood at least half a foot taller than Ruby Mae, but it wasn't her height that made people look up to her. It was the way she treated everyone. Ruby Mae had never had a boss like that, where the respect went both ways.

"I'm planning on inviting a few friends, too, the ones who came to the protest," she said. "Maybe ten people if they all can make it. Okay? I'll do it around 2:00 when things quiet down a little."

"Sounds like a party. I hope you plan on inviting me," Margaret said.

"You want to come?" Ruby Mae beamed. "Of course you're invited. Without you, I'd be out on the street hunting down a job, cleaning houses, or worse. You're practically my guardian angel." She looked down, smoothing her apron and then glanced up at Margaret. "Seriously, I owe you a lot. You trusted me to work in your kitchen and keep your customers happy. Ever since I met you, my life's moved in a direction I never expected."

Margaret tilted her head. "I'm glad I could help. That's what folks got to do, help each other when they're down. Otherwise, what's the point of hard work if you can't lift up your sister or brother along the way?" She pulled out a cigarette and lit it. "If you're interested, maybe you can help me with this NAACP office. I'm swamped."

Ruby Mae nodded. "Yes ma'am, I'd like that."

She walked back toward the kitchen, thinking about Margaret's words. Helping others, especially those who were struggling, that notion came right from the Bible. But she'd never been in a position to do that, outside of her family. Learning more about the work of the NAACP, what Thurgood Marshall was doing back in Washington for the sailors' case, would mean so much to her, more than what she got from a church service. Doing God's work, as Momma would say, like the Good Samaritan. And even though Freddy was off at sea, she hoped that in some way her volunteering with Margaret would help keep him safe.

CHAPTER 43

GUMBO

November 25, 1944

RUBY MAE

Ruby Mae had run out of patience with her sister. They stood in the cosmetics aisle at Woolworth's, and Peggy was taking forever to decide on a new lipstick. Passion Peach or Victory Red.

"If you don't make up your mind soon," Ruby Mae said, wagging her finger, "I'm gonna jump out of my skin."

Peggy scowled. "Don't pressure me. Decisions are hard. You know that 'bout me. What if I make the wrong choice?" She held a lipstick in each hand.

"Listen, Peggy, Chickie said his aunt owns a home on MacDonald Avenue. She rents out a bedroom, with use of the kitchen. Walking distance to Tappers'."

She grabbed the tube of Passion Peach from Peggy's fingers. "Get this one. It looks good with your skin. Besides, everyone wears red these days. Try something new. If you don't like it, no one's gonna make you keep wearing it." She put her hand on Peggy's arm. "Like staying here. If you decide later it's a mistake, you can always go home."

Peggy cocked her head. "You promise you won't be mad if I decide to leave after a while? I hate thinking the twins will grow up without me around. And who's gonna take care of Daddy? Momma's gonna drive him crazy."

Those were the same worries Ruby Mae struggled with, especially at night when she couldn't sleep. Staying here felt right, but that didn't mean it'd be easy. To be honest, Ruby Mae worried about living on her own if Peggy did leave.

Ever since the protest, she'd felt sure she belonged here. Between her job and helping Margaret with the NAACP work, Tappers' had become her home base. She'd made friends with some of the staff. But it would be a big change living so far from her family. She'd miss them all, even Momma. Once Freddy came back from the front—and he had to return—she could be alone with him without Momma's constant spying. Now that made her heart race.

Peggy brought the peach lipstick to the cashier and paid for that plus a Hershey bar to share on the way home. They'd shared so many things. She considered Peggy a lifelong friend, not just a blood relation. They'd always have each other's back.

"Here's what I been thinking," Ruby Mae said as they walked to the bus stop. "Now that I've been promoted," pausing to let that phrase sink in, "I want to invite folks to Tappers' for a little lunch celebration. Nothing fancy. Margaret said it'd be fine with her."

Peggy raised her eyebrows. "She did? That's awful nice of her."

"We'd have our family all together before they leave," Ruby Mae went on, "kind of a goodbye party. I'll invite my friends, too. Chickie's taught me his secrets for gumbo. It's so good." She grinned. "I even got a little taste for okra."

The bus to North Richmond arrived and they climbed on and paid their fares. Almost everyone on the bus was dressed in denim and coveralls. She recognized a few faces from the yard. Peggy handed her half of the Hershey bar once they sat down.

"Sounds like an awful lot of work. Who's gonna pay for it?"

Ruby Mae stuck out her chest. "I am. Margaret's giving me a discount on the food. I already promised her I'd do all the cooking and stay to clean up after. It'll be on my day off."

She bit into the chocolate and stared out the window. The bus rumbled past blocks of shops followed by squat homes with little yards. It turned finally onto the unpaved road that led to the trailer encampment.

Ruby Mae got up. "Ain't nothing wrong with wanting to share food with folks who care for me. Like saying thank you for being part of my life."

ELENA

Elena had stored her lunch box in her shipyard locker when Peggy approached, a folded piece of paper twisted in her hands.

"Um . . . hi," Peggy said. She cleared her throat. "My sister asked me to give you this."

Elena froze. Something bad must have happened. Was Ruby Mae in trouble? Or was it about Freddy? Had he been injured? She took the paper and opened it, reading Ruby Mae's scrawl. "Oh. It's an invitation to lunch with your family." She let out her breath. "Why are you acting so nervous? I thought you were bringing bad news."

"I feel kind of foolish being her messenger," Peggy said. "Besides, you and Marcy are the only ones from the yard she's inviting. Oh, Rachel, too, and her boyfriend. Momma and Daddy are moving back to Baton Rouge. Taking the twins. Maybe me, too."

"Really? Ruby Mae told me you'd decided to stay."

"Well, yeah, I did," Peggy said. "And then the next day I changed my mind. Back and forth ever since. I'm driving everyone crazy."

"What are you afraid of?" Elena asked. Maybe that was too nosy; she didn't know Peggy very well.

Peggy pressed her lips tight. "I'm scared that no matter what I decide, I'll disappoint my family. Either Momma and Daddy or Ruby Mae."

Elena put her hand on Peggy's shoulder. "My advice? Choose what will make *you* happy. Don't try to please everyone else." Not that she'd ever made those choices. But now she wanted that for herself, too.

Peggy looked at her. "Yeah, I'm not very good at that."

Elena closed her locker, tucking the invitation in her pocket. "Me, neither. But I'm trying." She turned to leave. "Thanks for bringing the invitation. Ruby Mae has a big heart."

"And big ideas." Peggy grinned in a way that reminded Elena of Lupe. "See you later."

In Lupe's last letter she had begged Elena to come home. Mamá was smothering her ever since Papi died. Now twelve, Lupe sounded like she was locking horns with her mother the way Elena had at that age. And according to Mamá, Memo had slipped into his role as man of the house like a worn pair of slippers, bossing his sister and fussing over his mother. If only they could all live together here. Elena would happily step in and help raise Lupe and Memo. Sometimes their absence felt like a phantom limb, the ache so real yet beyond her grasp.

RACHEL

Noah had offered to drive them—first pick up her and Bertie and then swing by to get Elena en route to Ruby Mae's luncheon. He'd been very attentive lately, and in her mind he had earned official boyfriend status. Bertie had teased her, sitting in Rachel's room waiting for their ride.

"I'm a tiny bit jealous, Rach," she'd said. "Actually more like deep green with envy. How'd you find the one available, handsome, smart and young guy left? I've met a few cute soldiers passing through the Y, but after what happened at the protest, I'm steering clear. You can't always tell who's gonna turn out to be a jerk."

Now Bertie sat in the back seat of Noah's car, Rachel in front, headed to Richmond. It was almost noon, and the thick blanket of fog had started to roll back from the hills.

Rachel directed Noah to the house where Elena rented a room. They found her waiting at the curb, a sweater wrapped around her. She climbed in the back seat, pushing her hair off her face.

"Hi Bertie," Elena said. "I wasn't sure who else was coming."

Bertie smiled. "I think Ruby Mae is grateful we were there when things got ugly."

Rachel turned around and faced them. "I think it's great that she wants to show off her cooking. Besides, I've never tried gumbo."

"Ruby Mae told me it's all about the peppers," Noah said. "Sometimes they're so hot they'll make you cry. Chickie laughed at me when I tasted his recipe last week. I guzzled a lot of water after the first bite. It didn't help. He just spooned more rice onto my plate, looking amused." He glanced in the rear view mirror. "Elena, back home did you eat much spicy food? I've tried pupusas but not much else."

"Not really," she said. "Most dishes aren't spicy, but you can always add hot sauce if you like. My papi liked things hot."

Rachel listened to the conversation as they drove north. She had changed this past year, ever since she started at the clinic. The workers came from lives so different from her own. She'd had to learn about cultural differences and language subtleties. How they viewed healthcare, sometimes with mistrust, or expecting unrealistic treatment and quick fixes. She'd learned ways to prevent and treat serious injuries she'd never seen before. The job had forced her out of her comfort zone, and ignited her curiosity.

"I have so much to learn," she said aloud. "Once the war is over, I really want to see more of the world, beyond the Bay Area." She looked at Noah. He smiled as he pulled the car into Tappers' parking lot. She imagined the two of them one day, traveling far from home. "Okay, let's go help Ruby Mae celebrate. I bet she's in the kitchen seasoning her gumbo."

RUBY MAE

Ruby Mae paced back and forth inside Tappers' kitchen, peeking into the restaurant every few minutes. Momma and Daddy and the boys were already seated at the large round table, Aaron and Samuel spinning the lazy Susan in the center, trying to knock off the silverware as it gathered speed. Momma scolded them and sent them out to let off steam in the hallway.

Margaret Starks, who'd stopped by the kitchen first to hug Ruby Mae, sat next to Daddy.

He'd been excited all week as he and Momma packed up for the long drive home. Momma had given notice at the shipyard. The boys' teacher had prepared a homework package to take with them, like writing down the names of states and their capitols they'd pass along the way. The one thing no one in the family had talked about was how much they'd miss each other. The feeling just hung in the air, like Spanish moss dangling from the branch of a cypress tree.

Rachel stepped into the dining room, followed by Bertie, Elena and Noah. Ruby Mae came out of the kitchen and waved them over, past other tables to where her family sat. Marcy appeared next, handing Ruby Mae a bouquet of daisies wrapped in newspaper.

"Congratulations on your promotion," Marcy said, plopping down in the chair next to Margaret. "Is that your gumbo I'm smelling? Girl, I hope you didn't chicken out, kept it spicy."

"Spicy enough," Ruby Mae said. Yes, inviting her friends was a great idea. Helped distract her from dwelling on the move, and from missing Freddy. She'd yet to receive a letter from him. There'd be no time for moping with all this company.

"C'mon, y'all," she said, wiping her forehead. "Have a seat, wherever you like." She watched Rachel walk over to Daddy and put her hand on his shoulder.

"Nice to see you again, Mr. Taylor," Rachel said. "I hear you're heading home soon. How's your leg?"

He pushed himself up from the table, grunting with the effort. "Well, Miz Rachel, I expect my leg will be reminding me of this place long after I'm gone." He grimaced. "But it'll be good to get home. I don't really belong here." He sat down and looked at her. "I appreciate all you did for me. Now I gotta ask you to keep an eye on Ruby Mae. Peggy, too, if she's staying. That girl can't make up her mind."

"Daddy, quit talking 'bout us," Ruby Mae said. "I'm right here. And I can take care of myself." But fussing over his children was part of his loving them.

Once everyone was seated, she slipped back through the swinging door into the kitchen. Peggy stood next to the double ovens, pulling two large baking pans out. Chickie glanced over at her from his corner where he juggled battered pieces of chicken into the bubbling fryer. God, she loved how it smelled, the spices and peppers and hot oil.

"They're here," Ruby Mae said, helping her sister settle the pans on the steel counter. The cornbread's crust was slightly burned at the edges. Oh well. She'd leave those pieces for last.

"Sorry," Peggy said. "This oven is hotter than what we had back home. Don't fuss; I'll eat the edges."

Ruby Mae laughed. "Sis, I appreciate you helping me. Don't punish yourself if you fixin' to leave. It'll be fine either way, okay?" She'd made her peace with whatever Peggy decided.

She walked to the stove, where the pot of gumbo simmered next to another pot filled with white rice. Stirring the gumbo, she couldn't resist tasting it one more time. "I think it's as good as yours, Chickie," she said, licking her lips. She had gone easy on the spiciness, figuring not everyone wanted to burn their mouths.

He came over and tasted a spoonful. "Yes, ma'am," he said, nodding. "Now go serve your family 'fore they come in here and steal my chicken. I did promise your brothers I'd sneak them a piece."

She picked up the pot of gumbo with two dishtowels and carried it out of the kitchen, hoping it wouldn't slosh over the edge, and placed it on a cart next to the table. She'd ladle it out right there, a one-woman machine—hostess, cook, waitress and dishwasher. That was the deal, yet somehow she felt like a movie star greeting her fans.

"Here it is," she said, picking up the first soup bowl. "The best gumbo you'll ever taste."

"Wait, Ruby Mae, don't forget the rice." Peggy rushed up behind her and put the pot of rice down. "I don't know what you'd do without me. I'll get the cornbread."

Well, that sounded like she'd made up her mind to stay. Knowing Peggy, she'd wait until the last minute. Ruby Mae spooned rice into the bowl and ladled the gumbo on top.

"Here, pass it around the table," she said to Momma. "And that's homemade hot sauce in those bottles, in case you need it extra spicy." She looked at Rachel and Noah. "I'd taste it first."

"We need to go get the boys," Momma said, looking towards the lobby. "I know they're hungry."

Elena stood up. "I'll get them. We saw them on our way in. They were watching the barbers."

Ruby Mae ladled gumbo until everyone had some. Peggy returned with a platter piled high with cornbread. Elena came in, holding hands with the twins, whose lips were stained with chocolate. Elena smiled.

"I found part of a candy bar in my purse," she said. "Chocolate is always magic." She held onto the boys' hands until they pulled away and slid into their seats. Chickie had given each boy a drumstick and some mashed potatoes. Peggy and Ruby Mae sat down.

Daddy stood up, wincing. He looked around the table. "It makes me happy to see you all here," he said. "Me and Momma are proud of Ruby Mae. That goes for all our kids." He sat down and nudged Momma, who got up.

"Well, the good Lord has called us home to Baton Rouge," she said, eyeing her daughters. Ruby Mae felt Peggy pinch her leg under the table. "I hope He'll watch over us. I pray He keeps you all safe, too. Me and Earl done our best with our children." She folded her hands in prayer. "May the Lord keep the Devil away from my girls. Help them resist temptation and find their way back to the church." She paused before sitting down. "And, God bless this meal made by Ruby Mae."

Several "Amens" were said. Everyone picked up their forks and started eating. Ruby Mae watched her friends' faces, searching for any sign of distaste, but found none. Even Momma nodded.

"This is delicious," Bertie said. "Spicy and full of flavor."

"Ruby Mae, my compliments," Margaret said, wiping sauce off her mouth. "I want to say how impressed I've been with you young people." She looked across the table at Ruby Mae's guests. "Not that I'm old, but at your age I hadn't seen much beyond home. Having you all at the protest made me feel like our sailors won't be forgotten. We'll keep fighting until the Navy lets them go. Once the war is over, they'll have to come around." She nodded. "Now I'll be quiet and get back to my gumbo."

Ruby Mae stood up and raised her glass of iced tea. "Thank you for coming." Her hand trembled. She'd never made a toast before. "Here's to my friends. I've learned so much knowing you and fighting injustice together. You helped me believe in myself." She smiled at Marcy.

"And here's to my family for being there, even when I messed up. I'll miss you every day. I promise to make you proud." She started to sit, then paused. "Oh, and here's to Freddy, and all the men out there fighting in this war. May the Lord bring them back soon."

Peggy put her hand on Ruby Mae's arm. "I second what my sister said. She needs me here. I'm staying. For sure." She squeezed Ruby Mae's arm and leaned over and hugged her. "Burnt cornbread ain't the worst thing, right?"

Ruby Mae kissed her sister's cheek. She'd talk to Chickie's aunt tomorrow about renting that room. When Elena lifted her glass, Ruby Mae understood that each of them needed to be heard.

"I miss my family so much," Elena said, "but I'm grateful to know you." She smiled at the twins. "You boys are lucky to be part of this family." The twins looked down at their plates, as if embarrassed by the attention. She knew Ruby Mae would miss them so. She'd have to put money aside for phone calls.

Rachel spoke next, holding up her glass of lemonade. "I agree, Elena. Thanks for being my friends. This has been a hard year. Losing Jesse last summer was horrible. But what helped me was having you to lean on." Her cheeks flushed a deep pink.

People clinked their glasses and returned to their gumbo. The flavors of the chicken, the sausage, the peppers, and sauce thickened with just the right amount of okra, blended together into a flavor far richer than the sum of its humble ingredients.

Ruby Mae lifted a big spoonful of rice and gumbo to her mouth and bit in.

~THE END~

Author's note

Several of the characters in the novel are real people who dedicated themselves to change and social justice. These include Thurgood Marshall, Margaret Starks, Catherine Dempsey and Mary Lindsay. Tapper's Inn was one of the most popular blues clubs in North Richmond.

The chapters describing the trial of the Port Chicago 50 are based on the actual trial transcript. The Port Chicago Disaster is considered one of the worst incidents in US Navy history, and triggered desegregation of the Navy after the war. In July 2024, the US Navy finally exonerated the Port Chicago sailors, eighty years later.

Photo credit: Marie Pierre Arendt

ABOUT THE AUTHOR

VALERIE STOLLER grew up in New Jersey, went to college in Ohio, and kept heading west until she landed in the San Francisco Bay Area, where she worked as a nurse practitioner. *Shipyard Gals* is her first novel. She lives in Oakland with her husband and their two disobedient (yet adorable) cats.

ACKNOWLEDGMENTS

I am deeply grateful to so many people whose support and caring allowed me to finish this book. My husband, David Boitano, cooked many delicious dinners and kept the household running, while cheering me on and showing off how much history he knows.

To my local writing group, who have read these chapters countless times: I finally have a book in hand! Thank you to Janet Schneider, Susan Segal, and Ramsey Hootman.

To my writing instructors and mentors over the years: Clive Matson, Charlotte Cook, Sid Farrar and especially Lori Ostlund; thanks for believing in my writing and in me.

To my beta readers, Jane Dwinell, Kimberly Green, Andy Jefferson, Jim Davis, and Christine Pride: I so appreciate your thoughtful feedback.

To my online writing community, Pitch to Published, especially the Historical Fiction group: thanks for always rooting for me to get this book out there.

To my friends and family, who've supported me and this book: Janie Fox, Wendy Farrar, Matt Boitano, Sarah Boitano, Susan Light, Lynanne Jacob, Elizabeth Hedelman, Adriana Schoenberg, Ann Christiansen, Earl Whitfield, Jodi Demuth, Karen Bovarnick, Cheryl Choy, Tamara Lett, Laurie Slama, and Dee Stump—thanks for your loving care.

To my grandchildren, Lincoln and Vera, for bringing so much joy and laughter and love.

And to the wonderful women at Sibylline Press, for making my dream come true.

READER'S GUIDE QUESTIONS

1. Rachel and Ruby Mae both live at home with their parents. How do you think this affects their daily lives? What was your experience as a young woman or man leaving home for the first time?

2. Elena and Ruby Mae left their familiar cities searching for better opportunities and safer surroundings. Were they successful? Do immigrants today face similar challenges?

3. The WWII shipyard work environment required these young and inexperienced women to work closely with men who often resented their presence or harassed them. Elena and Ruby Mae each handled this differently. What would you have done?

4. Rachel isn't prepared for the antisemitism she faces on the bus. Do you think she should have confronted Chrissy? What would you have said?

5. As problems arise, in what ways do the three young women support one another? Think of a time when a friend supported you, or when you supported a friend through a hard time. What words or actions were most helpful?

6. Choosing a shipyard job was seen as patriotic during wartime. What jobs have that same appeal today? What influences have helped you choose a job?

7. At one point, Elena must confront her own homophobia. Discuss how you might have handled the situation back in 1944 versus today. How did you feel about Marisol's eventual

response? And Ana's? Have you been in a similar situation, and how did you handle it?

8. The Port Chicago trial and verdict were considered the US Navy's dirty secret, but eventually contributed to desegregation in the military. Do you feel the sailors' actions were justified? Would you have refused to load the live ammunition? How did the verdict make you feel?

9. Ruby Mae, Elena and Rachel decide to attend a street protest of the Port Chicago verdict. Have you ever been part of a street protest? If so, what was that experience like? If not, what kept you from participating, if it was for a cause you believed in? Do you think protests make a difference?

10. By the end of the book, Ruby Mae has left the shipyard and taken a job at Tappers' Inn. Although the book doesn't continue until the end of the war, we know that when the war ended, so did most of the non-traditional jobs for women. How do you imagine Elena reacting to the loss of her job? What sort of work do you think she would find? Rachel, as a nurse, was working a traditional woman's job at the shipyard. Do you think she would continue her interest in occupational health hazards in another setting?

11. Did you know about the Port Chicago explosion and its aftermath before reading this book? Did you learn about it in your American History classes? Why do you think it was or was not covered in your classes?

Sibylline Press is proud to publish the brilliant work of women authors over 50. We are a woman-owned publishing company and, like our authors, represent women of a certain age.